TURKEY SHOOT

BY

JAN DESPOSITO

PublishAmerica
Baltimore

F
De

First printing

At the specific preference of the author, PublishAmerica allowed this work to remain exactly as the author intended, verbatim, without editorial input.

ISBN: 1-4137-9609-5
PUBLISHED BY PUBLISHAMERICA, LLLP
www.publishamerica.com
Baltimore

Printed in the United States of America

TURKEY SHOOT

DEDICATION

Recently I suffered the loss of my brother. I have never met anyone that loved life and fishing more than he did. His fought a courageous fight of more than twenty years against diabetes. On September 23, 2005 my brother gave up the fight. This book is lovingly dedicated to my brother,

Robert (Rabbit) Anderson.

I love you.

ACKNOWLEDGMENTS

I would like to thank two of the most talented and professional ladies that I have been lucky enough to have in my life and to call them friends.

Lora Moore Web Designer www.writerinthewoods.com

Jillanne Kimble Editor www.Kimblemckay.netfirms.com

Prologue

THE SUN HINTED AN INDIAN summer day for this late November Saturday. The clouds that had hung heavily over the village through the night had disappeared, and a clear baby blue sky greeted the populace of Farmingdale. The morning dew gently dropped from the leaves in a rhythmical pattern like a forest concerto. The air felt alive, the fragrance of pine, and the smell of burning wood combined to intoxicate the senses. Rich, fall colors of brown, gold, green and blue touched the countryside like a patchwork quilt, and standing majestically in the background like a sentinel guarding the kingdom was *the* mountain, providing homes to the forest creatures, life to Farmingdale and beauty to all that came to gaze at its majesty.

A population of 1500, Farmingdale was like a picturesque Norman Rockwell painting or a Currier and Ives Christmas card. The star of the business community was Mel's Mercantile, with its sign advertising everything from penny candy and groceries to clothing and hardware. Mel was considered a newcomer to the area, in business for only 30 years. A short way down from Mel's was Belles Rooming House (her mother had opened the family home to boarders after the death of her husband), boasting the cleanest rooms and the best food this side of the International Dateline. Across the street was the Farmingdale Drug Store, complete with the original working soda fountain.

Ol' Doc Amos' office was located above the drug store. He had moved to the village in the late 1940s after finishing his internship at a large hospital. The funny thing was that he had always been referred to as Ol' Doc Amos from the day he opened his practice as a young man. The villagers never addressed him by his last name because they couldn't recall what it was.

Down the street was Cora's Café. Cora had retired, and her daughter was now in charge of the café. Although retired, Cora still came in early each morning to brew her special coffee and supervise the making of her cinnamon rolls. Cora's Café was the local hang out, and the place to get the best coffee and read the Gazette, the city newspaper, delivered daily from 50 miles away. Farmingdale was too small to have its own daily paper, so Cora's was the place to read all the big city news and catch up on the latest gossip.

Mel's, Kelly's Drug Store, Cora's and Belle's were the heart of Farmingdale, but the last few years several types of specialty shops had opened on Main Street, geared for the tourist. The locals viewed these newbies as necessary to the local economy, but did not consider them part of Farmingdale proper.

The newest building, erected twenty years earlier, housed the Sheriff's office and the volunteer fire department, and served as the village courthouse. A small office with an adjoining room, in the back of the building, was reserved for legal business and city council meetings.

Seth Peters was Farmingdale's judge, justice of the peace, and notary public. Seth moved to Farmingdale after World War II. No one knew if he had a family, and no one had ever asked. Seth was a loner, and the village respected his wishes for privacy.

Farmingdale residents felt they had taken a major leap when they elected Samantha Forbes as the first woman Sheriff. The Forbes family was one of the founding families, and had always been involved with the legal end of things. Samantha's great grandfather was the first lawyer in the village. Her grandfather was also a lawyer, serving as judge for several years. Norm Forbes, Samantha's father, had chosen law enforcement and was acting Sheriff for 35 years, until poor health forced him to retire.

Cora's day began around 5:00 a.m. Her special coffee had to be brewed, and the dough for her cinnamon rolls had to be made. Her regular customers would begin to arrive around 6:00 a.m., always welcoming the fragrant aroma that greeted them each morning.

However, as always on the Saturday before Thanksgiving, Cora's Café jammed with hunters in for the annual Turkey Shoot. All who participated called the century-old tradition "The Shoot." Farmingdale residents welcomed the shoot as the start of the holiday season, with all its hustle and bustle. Registration for the contest was held at Cora's. The bell above the door would jangle as more and more hunters arrived, the fall air combining with the warm sweet aroma of Cora's greeting each hunter on arrival, invoking memories of past hunts. The shoot was a family tradition among these men, since most had participated since an early age.

As in the past, the feeling of male camaraderie filled Cora's this particular Saturday morning. Familiar faces were greeted with a slap on the back, a firm handshake, and playful jabs. It was a time to renew old acquaintances and welcome new ones.

Amid this menagerie of male bonding, two more hunters were yet to arrive, Bentley Rogers and Bruce Williams. Their friendship could not be described as conventional. In fact, they were the most unlikely of friends. The shoot had been the core of their friendship, which had started their sophomore year in college, and had continued through the years.

1

BENTLEY ROGERS FELT POWERFULLY ADEPT this particular Saturday before Thanksgiving. He awoke with a heartfelt vigor before the alarm went off, sat for a moment looking at the figure of his sleeping wife and pretty much realized that life had turned out the way he had planned. Indeed, what else was there to covet? Everything was almost perfect. He had wealth, power, and a beautiful submissive wife.

At times, he wondered how his parents would react if they could see how much he had obtained of life's luxuries. Not that he ever wanted them to see or even remotely have an idea. Childhood thoughts had been nagging him lately. He did not welcome these thoughts, and he fought hard to suppress them to the darkest part of his mind. Thoughts that he had buried many years ago were now surfacing, bringing with them the anger and frustration that he had felt as a boy. He loathed people who could not control their emotions. Rubbing his temples, he tried to focus on the shoot, but the black images remained. "Why do these old feelings have to surface now," he thought aloud. "A long shower is what I need."

He turned to look at his sleeping wife. Amanda had been

challenging him on certain rules that governed their home. "I am losing control of her, and because of her I am having these thoughts of the past. I think Ms. Amanda needs to be taught another lesson. I will deal with her when I get back from the shoot today." Turning on the shower, Bentley let his mind drift back to the past.

Education was not a focal point in the Rogers' family. Consumed with the drudgery of making a living, Bentley's father worked in the local mill, where his great-grandfather and grandfather had labored until retirement. Working in the mill was a right of passage, starting when a young man turned sixteen. Higher education, frowned upon as a waste of time, would only encourage the young to rebel against their lot in life, the Rogers' family had accepted this philosophy for three generations.

Bentley felt that life had more to offer than this meager existence. He knew that he would never be happy living in this rundown part of town, where black soot covered everything including the people's souls. Riding the bus to school, Bentley noticed the wealthier neighborhoods. All the houses had manicured lawns and bright shiny cars in the driveway. This section of town was alive with colors, like the windows of the Main Street department stores. Everywhere you looked; there were flowers and huge trees that shaded the streets in the summer. The air felt cleaner, and there was a promise of a bright future. Bentley watched as the men left for work. They were dressed in suits, shined shoes and a brief case under one arm. The women waited patiently for their husband to give them a kiss goodbye, all the while smiling adoringly at the master of the house. Bentley knew that if he lived in one of these houses he would be able to feel the power that these men exuberated. Bentley longed to be a part of this community. He knew, deep in his heart, that fate had cheated him. Fate had mistakenly placed him on the wrong side of the tracks and with the wrong parents. Bentley felt that if there was a class below blue collar that is the class that his parent and his community would belong. Here the men left for work in worn clothes, dirty shoes and a metal lunch pail under their arm. The women stood at the door, glum look on their faces and several squawking kids pulling at their dirty house coats. Poverty, ignorance, and despair were the future that Bentley's parents offered him.

This made him a very angry young man. Bentley's anger was directed toward his parents, whom he blamed for his present situation. They had accepted what life had handed them and never thought to fight back. What was worse, they expected him to embrace their way of life. At an early age, Bentley expressed the disdain he felt for his parents and for the life that they offered him.

His actions and disrespect would result in beatings from his father. Bentley's mother tried to intercede in these battles to no avail. She would beg them to talk and to listen to one another. The beatings only made her son more determined and her husband more infuriated. Finally, in desperation, Bentley's parents conceded that their son was not like them and never would be. They couldn't understand why their son hated them. To have questioned their parents' wishes was unheard of, and the show of disrespect was unfounded. They had raised Bentley as they had been raised, but he did not accept their values or their way of life. Bentley challenged every rule they tried to set, and he openly scoffed at their dreams for him. It was finally agreed that Bentley must choose his own way. The struggle within the Rogers' family had ceased and an uneasy peace was now observed.

The struggle at home was put aside and Bentley began his quest for the good life. He knew what he wanted his future to be, and now he must formulate his plan to achieve that goal. Aware that a good education was his way out of poverty, he would settle for nothing but the best marks in school. Long hours were spent at the library reading articles and looking at pictures of successful men, committing the way they talked and dressed to memory for use in his new life. If Bentley had the ability to erase his parents from the face of the earth he would do it. As he scanned the pages he toyed with the thought of genocide of the masses. The answer to all his prayers would be the deliberate and systematic destruction of this community, the people living here and his parents.

The time spent away from home was a concern to his parents. Few words were spoken, and Bentley refused to let them know what he was doing. They rarely spent time in the same room, and family dinners were a thing of the past.

Confident that scholastically he was at the top of his class; his only worry was how to pay for this new life and college. The school advisor helped him fill out scholarship applications then made the suggestion of government grants. Bentley's excitement grew when he was told that this money didn't have to be paid back. The draw back came when the advisor said that Bentley's parent's income had to be listed. There was no way that he would ask his parents for this information then to have the advisor privy to the level of poverty that he came from was unthinkable. Bentley cussed his parents for the situation he found himself.

The rift between Bentley and his parents was growing. He never shared his plans with them or even asked their advice. They were not aware of his plans after graduation, but they knew that he would be leaving. In a sense, they would feel relief when he was gone. It broke their hearts knowing that their son felt such hatred for them. It would be hard for them to let go, but it was impossible for them to hold him.

Bentley's plan for after graduation was to leave his parents' home and never look back. He kept his plans secret from everyone. He would sever all ties with his family. As senior year was ending, Bentley's parents held out hope that they would be asked to his commencement. Other families in the neighborhood had children in Bentley's class and were excited about the coming event. Celebration parties were being planned—except at the Rogers' house. Questioning him brought a tirade accusing them of prying into his business.

By chance, the neighbor's son was graduating too and they were sent an announcement. Commencement was to be held June 6, 7:00 p.m. at the high school gym. Bentley had been named valedictorian of his class. This they read in the local newspaper.

The day before graduation, his parents waited to be informed of the good news and an invitation to attend. No news was given, and an invitation was never extended.

The following day, Bentley was busy in his room until around 5:30 p.m. At that time, he came out dressed in his best suit. His mother clapped her hands when she saw him and said, "Bentley you look so handsome in that suit. Where are you off to?" Bentley turned and with contempt in his voice said, "I don't think that is any of your business." Bentley's father dropped the paper he was reading and said, "Boy, I think you owe your mother an apology. Are you forgetting that you still live under our roof and eat our food? Until you move out your business is our business." Bentley smiled contemptuously as he said "not for long." His mother fought back the tears; his father drew the newspaper higher to cover his face. As the door closed behind him, it was clear that they had lost their son forever. Bentley's mother entered his room to find his belongings packed, nothing remained on the walls, and everything that made this Bentley's room was gone for good.

His parents were asleep when he returned and he planned to make his departure before they awoke. He gathered his things quickly, taking a moment for a last look and spotted a present on his desk. The gift tag read, "Congratulation on your graduation, Love Mom and Dad." Bentley pushed the unopened box to the floor. A feeling of elation descended on him, as he scanned his room for the last time. A slight smile touched his lips as he closed the door—for good. Taking in a deep breath of the cool night air Bentley knew that his new life would start when he reached college. He released any sentimental ties he might have had for these people he called his parents. Sentimentality was for the poor and weak. These people were dead to him and Bentley was now free to invent his past, create the present and envision his future.

Down the hill from Bentley Rogers' estate was the home of Bruce Williams. Bruce dreaded these shoots and was finding it harder to forgive Bentley for his cruel behavior. Reaching over to the nightstand, he turned off the alarm then lay back on his pillow. He tried to think of something pleasant but was unable to do so.

Dragging his large frame from the bed, he reached over and gave his sleeping wife a light kiss. He loved his family, his wife and two small children, and thanked God each day for his life. Stretching his arms, he tried to recall his childhood and how his friendship with Bentley had evolved, and why he had subjected himself to such continuing cruelty. Answers were not easily forthcoming…

Bruce Williams came from a large, loving family. His father was an investment banker, his mother volunteering for every committee available. Bruce was the baby of the family and the only boy. He was the apple of his family's eye, and could do no wrong. Bruce's childhood was filled with little league and other organized sports. He was doted on by his parents and catered to by his sisters. His high school class nicknamed him Teddy Bear, because his size intimidated everyone, but he had a big heart and loved to laugh.

At the start of Bruce's junior year, college took on the favorite topic of discussion at the dinner table. His grades were average, and his SAT scores were what could be loosely termed okay. "College will be the ultimate party with no supervision," thought Bruce.

He met with the high school advisor and found his troubles were not major. With a little effort and some studying, he would be able to attend State University. This worry behind him, he sailed through the rest of his high school years.

Graduation was a day of celebration for the Williams' family. A large party was thrown in Bruce's honor and was attended by the Williams family's closest friends. A new car was waiting in the driveway after the ceremony, as was a check, so Bruce could enjoy his summer. Teddy Bear was leaving for college in a few months and, as always, was the apple of his family's eye.

Bentley, on the other hand, spent his summer after graduation working at a burger place a few blocks from the university campus. He was anxious to begin his new life, and being close to the campus made him feel confident his dreams were coming true. Bentley's free time was spent on campus exploring the library and becoming familiar with the grounds. When fall semester started, Bentley knew the names of the buildings, and knew his way around. He didn't want to look like the typical freshman lost and bewildered on registration day.

Arriving at his dorm room early, Bentley started to unpack. He didn't have many belongings, so the process didn't take long. Once everything was put away, he decided to visit the bookstore to see about supplies for class.

While he was gone, Bruce arrived, Bentley's roommate. Seeing that one of the beds was made it was obvious that the roommate had already arrived.

Bruce unloaded his car, pushed his boxes around the room, and then began to hook up his stereo system. Putting on some music, Bruce left the room in search of his roommate. Everyone on the floor was very friendly and was free with information about the other neighbors in their dorm. Bruce was acquainted with many of the guys through school, but no information was available about his roommate, Bentley Rogers. All that was known was he had come on an academic scholarship, so he must be a genius, a real asset come finals.

Approaching his room, Bentley heard loud music coming through the walls. A sense of dread pulled on him. As he slowly opened the door, Bentley was shocked by the sight that greeted him. Boxes and clothes were scattered everywhere. The music was so loud he couldn't think. Rage was beginning to build as Bentley pulled the plug from the wall.

"Why, oh, why didn't my scholarship entitle me to a private room?" he spoke aloud. He sat at his desk and tried to calm his anger. Just then, the door swung open and in walked Bruce.

"Hey, bro', what happened to my music? You must be the roommate. My name is Bruce. What's yours?"

Bentley rose slowly, his anger still apparent and with a low clear voice said, "My name is Bentley Rogers, and we are going to have a long talk." Bentley closed the door, and then turned to look at Bruce.

"This isn't the way I thought college would be," Bruce said to himself.

Bentley quickly took charge of the room, posting rules, and setting visitation schedules. Drop by visits were unacceptable, and if help with classes was needed, they could sign for a time and there was a charge. While visiting their room, no one was to sit on Bentley's bed or touch any of his things. All of his things were labeled, so a mistake could not be made.

Bruce was also given rules, about his side of the room. The bed was to be made immediately after rising, clothes picked up, the desk kept tidy and garbage emptied daily.

At first, Bruce fought against the rules then found it easier just to comply. "I came to college for some fun. I never dreamed I was joining the Army," Bruce thought. "The guy is a freak!"

As with all things good and bad, time passes and heals.

To their surprise and everyone else's, the first semester rapidly drew to a close. The first couple of weeks had been chaotic to say the least, with Bentley organizing everything and Bruce learning to pick up after himself, trying to remember the rules. The main rule was Bentley did not loan, nor did he borrow. He was quiet and unsociable, expecting the same from Bruce. Bentley demanded excellence of his own person and couldn't understand anyone else's lackadaisical attitude toward academics or life in general. Bentley's summer job had afforded him the luxury of buying new clothes. For the first time he had money in his pocket and he spent everything he had on the latest fashions he had seen in GQ. Walking into a room Bentley felt everyone's attention turn to him. The feeling of power and elation washed over him and he knew that everything that he had ever dreamed about would be his. Bentley's determination to dominate and dictate was focused on Bruce.

Bruce was having a hard time trying to adapt to this military life style. He was quite content with average grades, and seemed more concerned with "Where's the party?" than what he would be doing with the rest of his life. Bentley was constantly preaching about the future, wealth and power. Coming from an upper middle class family Bruce had never thought about money and had never given the future much thought. Bruce lived for the moment and the future would take care of itself.

The holidays were extremely stressful for such opposite roommates, diametrically opposed in every way. Bruce was filled with holiday cheer, and wanted to talk about home, family, and his family's holiday traditions. Bentley was content staying in the dorm during the semester break. Solitude was what he wanted most for the holidays, and Bruce was more than happy to oblige his roommate. For Bruce, the holidays were a time to relax and forget about the rules. The Williams family celebrated the holidays in traditional style. Bringing home the Yule log, decorating the tree, and welcoming friends were all part of the unending tradition.

Bruce appreciated his home and his family more this year, because of his first semester at college. It took him several days to relax and be himself. His mother had commented that he was too quiet and reserved, and something must be wrong. Bruce would give her a big hug and tried to calm her concerns. A pall would descend on the celebrations when Bruce's thoughts were about returning to school.

As the break was nearing an end, Bruce's father took him to one side and inquired about school. "Son, are you having problems with your classes?"

Bruce began to laugh. "For once, Dad, classes are not a problem. There is a situation that I have to deal with on my own." Bruce decided on the drive back that he was not going to give up on Bentley. "No one is a loner by choice. I can be as stubborn as he is, at least for one more semester."

Bentley spent a quiet holiday season. That was just what he needed after a semester with Bruce. The dorm was completely deserted, which gave Bentley the solitude that he craved. Being an only child did have its advantages. Time passed too quickly, and the residents began to return. Bentley could only hope that Bruce would ask for a new roommate, or not return to school at all. The day before classes were to start, Bruce arrived back with a big smile.

Spring was in the air. The snow began to ebb, and patches of green grass were becoming visible. Bright colors emerged from the drab brown earth. The campus was in celebration of this rebirth, and Bruce was filled with elation. Entering his room Bruce roared and banged his chest. Bentley looked up from the book that he was reading and gave Bruce a cold stare. The look did not dissuade Bruce. "Come on Bentley; loosen up just a little bit. How about we get some beers and chase some ladies?" Bentley refused to answer and continued to read his book. Bruce got the message and silently closed the door behind him. Silence was the golden rule, and life at the monastery resumed until the semester ended and freshman year was history.

Bentley spent the summer learning about what made him tick. Taking a job at a posh resort was one way to keep his future in focus. The job didn't entail manual labor, and there was a lot of off time, so he could mingle with the rich. His biggest discovery was that he had a winning smile that brought out his charming nature, and most of the guests were quite generous with both money and advice when he displayed either. Feelings could be hidden beneath a smile, and this gave Bentley a sense of power. Power was exhilarating and was so easy to obtain. He had spent years butting his head against a wall, when all he had to do was smile and display a little charm. This was too easy. The entire summer was an experiment in the extent of this new power.

As he interacted with the guests on a daily basis, he realized that physical fitness was an important part of the agenda of these rich and powerful men. Trainers were on staff to provide assistance with exercise programs, and sports pros were available for help with golf, tennis, swimming and archery. Sports had never been an interest to Bentley, but the guests were very competitive, and took these games seriously.

Bentley knew of the great interest in golf, tennis, and swimming, but archery seemed so antiquated. An archery tournament was slated for the end of the month, and to Bentley's surprise, all the slots were taken. The day of the competition was exciting, with each archer displaying his equipment and his skill with the bow.

Mingling with the crowd, Bentley overheard several conversations about the Turkey Shoot in Farmingdale. This contest was spoken of with great respect, and was a tradition among many of the guests. Bentley could almost smell the fragrant aroma of the damp earth from these conversations.

Several more archery tournaments were held that summer, and at each contest, the Turkey Shoot was mentioned. Bentley's curiosity had been piqued, and he knew he must attend this Turkey Shoot. It was a tradition he wished to make his own. He was sure of it.

Bruce spent his summer in total relaxation, his family catering to his every wish. Life was good. The family had a summerhouse near the beach, so his days were filled with swimming and eating, and his nights were filled with partying. Too quickly, it was August, and thoughts of college were thrust upon him once again.

The vision of Bentley, on that last day of school, had haunted Bruce throughout the summer. The question that kept recurring was would he be able to endure another semester with Bentley. The guy was so self-righteous, and he made Bruce's life unbearable, but still Bruce felt sorry for this very lonely man. The whole summer he had wrestled with the notion of keeping Bentley or finding a new roommate.

One redeeming quality of Bentley's was the strict regimen that had enabled Bruce to bring home the best grades he ever received. Bruce knew his parents loved him, but their admiration was new, and he savored the feeling. Maybe the discipline wasn't that bad. Maybe

Bentley wasn't that bad. Maybe Bentley deserved a second chance. Bruce knew that Bentley needed a friend, and he had decided that he would be that friend.

Bruce arrived at school first, and immediately proceeded to the registration desk. Students were milling in the lobby area, renewing acquaintances, catching up on the latest news, and waiting in line for room assignments.

Bentley arrived later that day, registered and picked up his room assignment. Rubbing the envelope between his fingers, he paused before opening it. He knew that he had been hard on Bruce last year. "I bet the big slob asked for another roommate. I was the best thing that could have happened to him. With my help, he probably pulled down the best grade point average of his wasted rich life. I have had to break my butt for everything I ever got, and that rich kid got it all handed to him. I really wanted to try my new power out on him. If I can fool him after last year, I can fool anyone." With great care, Bentley extracted the slip from the envelope and was surprised to see Bruce Williams was again his roommate. A slight smile crossed his face before he proceeded to his room. Bentley was preparing himself for the chaos that was sure to greet him. Slowly opening the door, he was amazed to find the room in order, but Bruce was not present.

He started the task of putting his things away, when the familiar sound of Bruce's voice was heard. When Bruce entered a room, it felt like all the oxygen was sucked out. He had an easy way about him that Bentley sometimes envied.

"Welcome back, Bent. How was your summer?" was the greeting as the door was flung open.

Bentley resumed what he was doing, and then turned slowly to address Bruce. "The name, as I have told you on several occasions, is Bentley. Thank you for the greeting. My summer was fine."

Bruce ignored the crispness in Bentley's voice, and continued. "Same old Bentley, never a hair out of place, never a wrinkle to be found on his clothes, and never a smile. I thought a summer without me would loosen you up a bit. Guess I'll have to room with you another semester, and see if a little bit of me might rub off on you. Some of you rubbed off on me, as you can see by my side of the room. Nearly scared my mom to death, when she went into my room to clean it. All summer she kept feeling my head and looking into my eyes saying, "This is not the son I sent away to school."

With this statement, Bruce made a grand gesture toward his side of the room. Bentley stopped what he was doing. A slight smile appeared on his face, and then quickly vanished.

.

Bentley was at his best when he was winning. He would be verbally abusive while playing any game, and then flash a big smile after his win. At first, Bruce tried to dismiss Bentley's actions. When the abuse continued, Bruce refused to play. Bentley learned that he couldn't push so hard. Even Big Dumb Bruce had his limits. Bentley had to learn how far his smile could take him. Besides, the Williams family was rich, and he might need to use them sometime in the future. Bentley decided to share his new passion of archery with Bruce.

To his surprise, he learned that Bruce and his father had participated in the shoot. He didn't care if Bruce never wanted to do it again. He would use some of his charm, and talk him into being his partner. That would accomplish one of the goals that he had set for himself. He could use the Williams family connections to enter the first shoot, and then he would discard Bruce at a later time. "The end justifies the means," smiled Bentley.

This new interest of Bentley's had opened the door for the friendship Bruce wanted to give. Even though he didn't want to participate in the barbaric contest, he would do so for his new friend.

As fate would have it, by the beginning of November, it was decided they would attend their first shoot as a team. Bruce was beginning to enjoy this new Bentley, and he was determined to hold onto anything that would make his friend happy. Thus the Turkey Shoot became their personal tradition.

****

Turning onto the gravel in front of Cora's Café, Bentley began to reminisce about their first Turkey Shoot. "We were just boys," recalled Bentley. "It's hard to believe that it has been so many years." The first two years of college were confusing because Bentley flipped flopped between majors. Could he achieve his ultimate goal of wealth and power by majoring in business or was there an easier way? Sitting in his psychology class the decision became clear. A doctor was a respected member of society. A psychiatrist dealt with mental, emotional, or behavioral disorders. He could sit back and listen to the troubles of the fat cats of society. Information was power. He shifted his car into neutral, and sat back for a moment to take in all that was his. He had everything that he had envisioned in his youth. He was a respected psychiatrist, a member of the country club, a pillar of society and wealthy.

All of this was just dressing; the real accomplishment was the power he now possessed. Power was his ultimate rush. The practice of psychiatry was his means to power. With just a nod of his head, Bentley could elate or depress another human. He was invited into people's minds, and they would willingly reveal their weaknesses to him. He could either validate or invalidate that person's life. Total control was what made life good, and life was good this Saturday morning before Thanksgiving.

The sound of a car pulling in brought Bentley back to the present. He glanced over to see Bruce sitting in the car next to him. Bentley no longer found Bruce amusing. He was becoming a nuisance. Their friendship had lost its usefulness, and Bentley felt it was time to rectify the situation. Use and discard was the norm, for Bentley, but Bruce was the exception. While they were in college Bruce was a dummy that Bentley used to practice how far he could push someone before they retaliated. Bentley also needed the William's family influential connections while starting his medical practice. Most of all Bruce was the one person that Bentley didn't have to charm. He could be himself, show the black side of his personality, vent is anger and Bruce kept coming back. Bentley enjoyed verbally abusing him but the enjoyment was ebbing. It had taken many years, but Bruce was now expendable.

Getting out of their cars, the men exchanged cool greetings, retrieved their equipment, and then entered the commotion of Cora's Café. The café was packed with hunters, so it took some maneuvering to reach the sign in desk. The contest consisted of teams of two hunters each with one arrow that was furnished to them. There wasn't a time frame for the contest. The first team to register two kills won. In the case of a tie, the size of the bird was the determining factor. The winners' names were engraved on a trophy, which was displayed at the village courthouse. The first few years Bentley and Bruce participated, they were the ones to beat. These last years they had slowed, and only won the contest a few times. Bentley wondered why Bruce even bothered to show up. Their team had become a joke. Bruce was out of shape and his heavy breathing scared the game away. Bentley had grown tired of being the butt of the other hunter's jokes. He would inform Bruce when the shoot was over.

The contest began at 7:00 a.m. As that time grew near, the excitement built. Each hunter began to ready himself mentally, as he made his way to the door.

Bruce motioned for Bentley to wait for him to catch up. "I forgot something in my car. I'll meet you at the starting gate."

Bentley didn't speak. He just started for the gate. As he walked, anger began to build, "Just like Bruce to forget something. Thank God that he remembered before the shoot started. This is going to be a long day, but then I will be through with Bruce forever."

As the last hunter exited the café, Cora and her staff let out a sigh of relief. Another Thanksgiving shoot successfully accomplished.

At the starting gate, each hunter checked his equipment, strung his bow, and checked the slant of the arrow. Bentley and Bruce still had not exchanged more than a few words. Most of the teams had been attending this contest for years, and the coolness between these two men was apparent to all. The starter raised his arm; slowly the red towel dropped on what was to be the last Turkey Shoot for the team of Rogers and Williams.

Bentley and Bruce wove their way through the thick foliage. The years had made them adept at reading each other's signs, and allowed them to communicate without words. The path they choose was familiar. They would traverse to the south, and then wind their way up the steepest side of the mountain, to a glen. This trek was challenging for the fittest of men, but to Bentley it was just another way to show his prowess.

Bruce made a mental note that he would not return next year. Bentley might need to prove something to the world, but Bruce was content with his life. Besides, he had never wanted to participate in this contest, and only agreed because Bentley needed a friend. "Friendship," thought Bruce, "can only go so far, and after so many years, this is far enough." Bruce was aware that the friendship was one sided. He had endured years of Bentley's verbal abuse and condescending looks, not only at this contest, but also at the country club and around town. He felt used, and it was time to dissolve this friendship, if friendship was what it ever was.

Bentley stopped several times to check on Bruce's location. He silently cursed his partner for his weakness, and for letting age take its toll. "Weak people are a curse to all," thought Bentley. "Age is used as a crutch to let your body and your mind start to sag." Bentley refused to let his age deter him from the life that he had laid out for himself. Bruce was now viewed as a hindrance, a person who would slow him down no more.

Reaching the glen, Bentley took a moment for Bruce to catch his breath. Bruce looked pale, and was winded from the energy spent climbing the mountain. They stood side by side surveying their surroundings. The clouds were beginning to disperse, and the sun felt warm and welcoming on their shoulders.

A rustling broke the silence in the brush. Words were not needed. With a nod, each man removed his arrow and placed it on his bow. Now they were ready for the hunt. They could hear a tom just to the right of them. Each took a different route to surround their prey. The top of Bruce's hat was visible from where Bentley stood.

"Bruce is so slow that the bird will die of old age before he gets into position. No matter, this is our last hunt together. He can grow old at home. I don't have to watch. I wouldn't watch even if he asked me.

I'm not going to get upset. I'm in control of my destiny. Life is good, yeah, yeah..."

Bentley began to chant to himself, "Life is good," over and over. Chanting was a way to control his anger. While Bentley was chanting, thoughts of his past came floating through his mind. Today had been a day of reflection, something that was not normal for Bentley.

Bentley had achieved everything that he had dreamed. He had a successful practice, a beautiful home and a beautiful young wife, Amanda. His life appeared perfect, and Bentley worked hard to preserve that image. Bentley's earlier life was concealed from everyone including Amanda. It was believed that his parents had died when he was young. Bentley would become very agitated when questioned about his childhood, so the subject was rarely brought up. He was on the board of several charities and donated office time to abused children. Bentley was the pillar of his community, and was honored with the key to the city by the mayor. He demanded excellence from himself and those around him. He was a hard taskmaster, but the results were always above expectations. Again, the thought of his parents was present, and he wondered what they would think of his accomplishments. He had no regrets about the choices he had made. The results were all that mattered; the means to the result didn't matter. Bentley's life was good, and he had achieved it all. Nothing had been handed to him.

Bruce began to wave his arms to signal Bentley that he was in position. Bentley slowly raised his bow, and brought the prey into sight. Beads of sweat appeared on his brow, as he pulled back in readiness. The kill was in sight. This was his. He felt a rush of adrenaline, which always occurred when he found himself in control. This was the ultimate feeling, the ultimate high. He held life and death at his fingertips. At this moment, he felt like a god. There was a movement in the trees across from him.

In a split second, before he released his arrow, he saw a face. Anger and hatred had distorted the features, but he knew the person's identity. He hesitated for a moment, and then felt a terrible burning in his chest. Everything was in slow motion as he fell to the ground. In the distance, he could hear Bruce's frantic cries for help. He felt warm blood oozing from his chest. The burning had subsided, and was replaced with a tingling in his fingers and toes. The sun felt warm on his face. The scent of wet leaves and pine needles were strong.

His mind was clouded with images of the past, including his parents, his old house, and the department store windows. This couldn't be happening. He had it all, and life was good. Suddenly the face appeared above him. Hatred was visible in the eyes, and it was directed at him. The face stood over him, staring into his eyes, burning into his soul. No words were spoken. Bentley turned away, and then turned back. He tried to speak, but his throat was too dry.

Above the face, the sky was the bluest blue he had ever seen; the leaves were golden, red, and brown. Bentley had never noticed or appreciated the beauty of this glen.

Coldness was beginning to seep through his body. Bentley could feel his life draining away. He slowly raised his hand, to the face, but it was brushed away. Darkness began to descend, and Bentley was shrouded in fear. The face began to smile. It was a sinister smile that watched Bentley take his last breath.

2

BRUCE MOVED SLOWLY INTO POSITION, taking pleasure in watching Bentley trying to hide his exasperation. The last hunt was finally underway and, for once, Bruce was in control. It was like a huge weight had been lifted off his shoulders when he had made the decision. A reversal of fortune for Bruce, Bentley had things his way for too long with Bruce always subservient to his every whim.

Moving with a practiced care through the thick foliage, Bruce saw the partial clearing ahead where he would take his stand. From this vantage point, Bentley would be in plain sight.

Finally, all was ready, and Bruce waved his arm to Bentley that he was ready. As expected, Bentley raised his bow and, with calm precision, took aim, as a sinister smile played at the corners of his mouth, the sun peeking out from behind the clouds sending a cascade of sunbeams all around.

Time was suspended in Bentley's unexplained motionless.

Confused by Bentley's inaction at such a crucial time, Bruce didn't know what to make of things. *Could be the sun hindering his vision. Something's wrong though, an easy shot to be sure for even a lesser bowman. Bentley was hesitating. Why?*

Just then Bruce heard a hissing sound by his right ear and turned in that direction. The forest yielded no secrets as he strained to see beyond his human capabilities.

Checking his ear, he dismissed the sound as a passing insect.

He turned back to see an arrow in Bentley's chest. Bentley began to sway, and then collapsed to the ground. Bruce turned toward the forest, expecting a hunter to emerge. No one did. Bruce rubbed his eyes to clear this picture from his mind, but Bentley remained on the ground with the arrow protruding from his chest. Bruce's mind began to whirl, and he felt himself losing consciousness. Darkness began to envelop him, and a feeling of lethargy was upon him. Bruce tried to rouse himself. His body felt weighed down, and movement was restricted.

In the distance, Bruce heard a voice. "The hunter," thought Bruce "must be looking for his arrow." The voice was near, but it didn't sound human. There was an animalistic quality to the tone. Bruce scanned the area, but there was no movement. They were alone.

Taking a deep breath, Bruce began to run; unaware that the animalistic scream he heard was coming from deep within him. Picking the easiest trail, he made his way down the mountain. Running at full speed, he could feel the sting of pine branches brushing his face. The starting gate and the officials were now in sight.

As Bruce reached their arms, he collapsed from exhaustion. Everyone crowded around to get a glimpse, and to find out what had happened. As he tried to catch his breath, Bruce was offered a drink of water. A feeling of nausea swept over him, and his mind was clouded as he remembered his friend. Bruce took a deep breath "I need a doctor, my friend has been shot." Sheriff Forbes, who was among the officials at the starting gate, quickly cleared the crowd away, so that Bruce could get some air. "Mr. Williams did you say that your friend has been shot?" Bruce nodded his head unable to speak. "Mr. Williams you need to calm down. Take a deep breath then tell me exactly what happened," instructed the sheriff. Bruce closed his eyes trying to control his breathing. He slowly began to regain his composure. His breathing was becoming normal, and his color was beginning to return.

The Sheriff spoke, "What happened?"

Bruce shook his head and with a childlike voice, he said, "Bentley's been shot." His eyes were tearing, as he continued, "We have to get him a doctor. Bentley had a clear shot at the turkey but he was hesitating. I thought maybe the sun was in his eyes. Then I heard a buzz by my ear and thought it was an insect. When I looked back Bentley was falling. He needs a doctor right away. I'm not sure if Bentley is alive or dead," Bruce stuttered.

Sheriff Forbes stood, and then motioned for her deputy. They walked toward the patrol cars, but Bruce was unable to hear what was being said. The deputy left in great haste and the Sheriff retrieved a camera from her car. Returning to Bruce, she spoke with authority. "Mr. Williams, I have sent my deputy to bring Doc Amos. You and I are going to go to your friend and see if there is anything that we can do. Are you ready to show me where your friend is?" Bruce was reluctant to return, but the Sheriff didn't present him with a choice.

Sheriff Forbes left instructions with the officials, and then turned and motioned to Bruce. With great effort, Bruce rose and joined the Sheriff at the start of the trail. Bruce hesitated and then spoke, "Would it be possible to point out the location instead of going there? I really would rather not go back."

"Mr. Williams it is imperative that the accident scene is secured, so as not to be contaminated. We are looking at a vast area of the mountain, and I have questions that must be asked and answered. Your friend needs medical attention. You should be the first one up the mountain."

Her voice was harsh and impersonal; it scraped on Bruce's nerves. Seeing how Bruce recoiled from her, she cleared her throat and spoke in a softer tone. "I know this is hard, Mr. Williams, but the sooner we check on your friend the sooner he can get the help that he needs."

Bruce reluctantly began the trek up the mountain. The sheriff had to stop several times for Bruce to catch his breath. Noticing the difficulty that the climb was having on Bruce she laid a comforting hand on his arms saying, "It's okay; I know how hard this is on you."

The glen was now in sight. The sun was hiding behind the clouds, and a breeze had begun to blow. Bruce shivered, but it was not from the cold. There was a momentary pause as Bruce pointed to a clump of bushes, and the lifeless form of Bentley. Bruce's face was wan from the emotional and physical stress.

Sheriff Forbes pushed Bruce to one side, and made her way to Bentley. She was careful not to disturb the grass immediately around the body. Extending her arm, she made a quick check for a pulse. Bruce remained in place, as the Sheriff began to take pictures of the body and the scene around him. The crackle of her radio broke the spell that Bruce was under, and he moved closer to hear what was being said. The Sheriff was giving her deputy directions to their location, and inquiring if certain people had been contacted.

Communication was stopped, as she turned to face Bruce, "Mr. Williams, my deputy is bringing Doc Amos here to examine your friend. They will be here shortly."

Bruce interrupted to ask, "Is my friend dead?"

"Mr. Williams, I think we should wait for the doctor. Could you show me where you were standing when the accident occurred?" Bruce was relieved, and anxious to put some distance between him and Bentley.

"I was standing over here." He led the way to the other side of the clearing.

"I'm going to take notes. You tell me how all of this happened. I realize this is hard, and I admire how you are handling all of this. You have been partners for a long time, right?"

Bruce shook his head in agreement. "I was standing about here. You can see where the grass is still smashed down. I heard a sound by my ear, kind of like a zip or a buzz. I turned and looked over my shoulder. Seeing no one, I thought maybe it was an insect. I turned back and saw the arrow sticking out of Bentley's chest." Bruce closed his eyes and lowered his head; in the distance, voices could be heard.

"That must be my deputy with Doc Amos. I must show them the location of the body. Are you coming, Mr. Williams?"

Not waiting for a response, she left Bruce with his thoughts. The Sheriff joined Doc Amos, and they proceeded to check for any signs of life.

As Bruce approached, he could hear the Sheriff and Doc Amos whispering. "Excuse me," interrupted Bruce, "Could you let me know what is happening? I am his friend; I need to know if he is still alive."

"Mr. Williams, I'm sorry, but your friend is dead." The words hit him like a brick to his stomach, and he bent over with pain.

"Mr. Williams, are you alright? Maybe you should sit down." The Sheriff led him to a large rock where the sun was once again shining.

Bruce closed his eyes, and leaned his head back so that the sun was covering his face. The colored images danced before his closed eyes. Yellows, blues then bright red, like the color of blood. The Sheriff's voice seemed far away. Bruce tried to focus on what was being said, but it was like a cocoon was being spun around him. It was a silky cocoon, to protect him from what was to come.

The Sheriff's voice became louder, and Bruce was brought out of his dream state. "Mr. Williams, we have to wait here for the state police. Your friend's body cannot be moved until they arrive. I know that it is hard to see your friend there, but we don't want to disturb any evidence until the OMI boys get here."

"OMI, who are they?" questioned Bruce.

"OMI stand for Office of Medical Investigation," she chuckled, "Seems like everyone talks in codes now days. An autopsy will have to be performed, and our little village is not equipped for such a task."

"Excuse me, Sheriff. Why would an autopsy be needed? I think that it is apparent that he died because of his wounds," questioned Bruce.

"Anytime a person dies outside of a doctor's care or a hospital there must be an autopsy."

Bruce began to chuckle.

The Sheriff looked at him quizzically before asking, "Do you find this funny, Mr. Williams?"

Bruce regained his composure before he spoke, "I'm not laughing really. You would have to have known Bentley. The man was so concerned with his looks. Now he will have to be cut up, and he will take that destroyed body to hell with him. The thought of that just hit me as funny. Please go on with what you were telling me."

The Sheriff looked over at the body then back at Bruce. "As I was saying, the OMI boys will bag the body, and gather any information and evidence about the accident. You will have to wait here. My deputy called the state police when he went to get Doc Amos. It should only take them about an hour. It's good that the storm has held off. The roads up here can get pretty bad this time of year."

Bruce waited on the rock for what seemed to be an eternity. The

Sheriff and Doc Amos stood guard over the body. Bruce began to pace, and he noticed that the Sheriff kept looking in his direction. "Could she possible think that this was anything but an accident?" Leaving his perch, he started to approach the Sheriff, when voices could be heard in the distance. The deputy walked the trail, leading an army of men with equipment. They quickly took charge of the investigation, as the Sheriff conferred with one of the men. She referred to her notes, and pointing in the direction where Bruce stood.

Several minutes passed before the Sheriff approached Bruce. "Mr. Williams, would you mind taking me to where you were standing again? I would like to have another look around the area."

This was more of a statement than a request. The inactivity had left Bruce's body stiff, and his muscles were beginning to ache.

"Mr. Williams, I would like for you to stand as you were at the time of the accident, and I'm going in the woods behind you. Let me know when I seem to be in about the area where the arrow came from."

The Sheriff moved through the forest careful not to disturb any evidence. She questioned him as she moved, "Mr. Williams do you smoke?"

Bruce looked at her confused, "Occasionally. Why?"

The Sheriff did not respond until she had positioned herself directly behind him. "There I think that's about right."

The area showed signs of being disturbed, and it was littered with several cigarette butts. Pulling a plastic bag from her pocket, the Sheriff placed each butt in the bag. A red flag was placed on the bush. Then she rejoined Bruce.

"Did you find anything, Sheriff?" questioned Bruce.

"About how long were you standing in that position, Mr. Williams?"

"I'm not sure. It wasn't very long. I signaled to Bentley that I was in position. He always has to have the first shot. We always surround the prey, so in case one of us misses the shot the other one is ready. It also gives Bentley the chance to see if the bird is big enough. If he thinks the bird won't be the biggest, he lets me go first. Bentley always has to be the winner."

Bruce scratched his head before he continued, "Did you find something in the woods behind me?"

"Well there are some indentations in the grass, but they could have been made by one of the forest animals. I have marked the area, and the state police can check. They are more adept at finding clues. How long have you and Mr. Rogers been attending this event?"

"Since we were sophomores in college," responded Bruce. "That's a long time. Do you enter other archery events together?" the Sheriff asked.

"No, this is the only one. I really don't like to hunt. I feel it's kind of barbaric. I only attended because of Bentley." As the two had been casually walking and talking, Bruce had momentarily forgotten about the accident and the flurry of activity around Bentley.

The Sheriff stopped and looked directly at Bruce. "You guys must be great friends. I don't know of anyone who would attend an event that they disliked for so many years for the sake of a friend."

Bruce shook his head in agreement.

The sun felt warm on their faces as they looked up at the sky. On the horizon, dark clouds were approaching.

"Looks like we will have snow before late afternoon. The weather can change so quickly here," she commented.

Bruce paused for a moment, "Sheriff, you do believe that this was an accident. Don't you?"

They resumed walking before she spoke. "Mr. Williams it's not my place to comment. I see a lot of activity over there, so I better rejoin them and see how I can assist."

They quickened their pace until they neared the group. Bruce held back, not wanting to see Bentley. The Sheriff joined the group and quickly became involved in a deep discussion with one of the men. She pointed several times in the direction where Bruce had stood. Some of the men stretched a yellow police tape around the area, up into the trees where the Sheriff had walked. Doc Amos was accompanying two men with a stretcher. More pictures of the body were taken. "The glen is alive with activity except for poor Bentley," thought Bruce.

They were preparing to move the body. The shaft of the arrow was carefully cut and placed in a plastic bag. A black bag was then unfolded and laid beside Bentley. His body was placed in the bag along with the arrow. Bentley's face was then covered, and the body was placed on the stretcher.

The Sheriff motioned for Bruce to approach. "Mr. Williams, I would like to introduce you to Detective Malano. He is the head of OMI, and he will be conducting the investigation. Detective Malano this is Mr. Williams. He was the victim's partner in the hunt and was present at the accident."

The detective extended his hand and Bruce shook it weakly.

"Mr. Williams, these gentlemen will be moving the body. If you would like to accompany your friend, you may. We have some work to do up here, but I will need to speak to you, so please wait at the bottom. Maybe some coffee and something to eat will help you with the shock. I won't be long. Then we can talk."

Bruce nodded in agreement and started down the mountain once again following his friend.

People milled about waiting for the rescue party to descend the mountain. They pushed in on the party, trying to get a look at the body, seeking information on who it was and how it happened. Several people pulled on Bruce, as he tried to make his way to the ambulance where his friend was being loaded. The scene was bizarre. Bruce felt like he was going to laugh, cry, or maybe scream. Bruce could not wake up from this terrible nightmare. Everything seemed to be moving in slow motion, and at the same time moving to quickly. The doors closed on the ambulance, leaving Bruce alone.

A slight smile curved his lips as he thought, "Damn! Bentley still gets the last word! I didn't get to tell him that our partnership was over. Once again he got the last laugh, and I'm left to clean the slate with the cops."

A stiff wind blew over the land, the storm clouds gathering. As Bruce raised the collar of his jacket, he felt chilled to the bone. Maybe a hot cup of coffee would warm him while he waited for Detective Malano. One of the hunters had a thermos of coffee, and Bruce asked if he might have a cup. Not wanting to be questioned about the accident, Bruce poured himself a cup, and then moved away from the crowd, deep in thought, not aware the Sheriff and Detective Malano approached.

"Mr. Williams," called the detective.

Bruce jumped.

"I'm sorry; I didn't mean to startle you."

"That's okay," said Bruce, "I was just trying to think if I could remember something more about the accident. I can't— I told Sheriff Forbes everything."

"I'm sure you have, but I would like to talk to you. We are going to question everyone that was involved in this contest. We will be taking statements from everyone. It is getting cold, so the Sheriff suggested that we move the questioning to her office and I agreed. I don't think anyone would object to that. Would you Mr. Williams? Why don't we talk while I walk you to your car? You can fill me in on all the details as you remember."

"Sure," said Bruce as they started to the car.

Bruce felt numb and was having a hard time concentrating on much of anything. He explained the course that they took, and the events leading up to the accident. No other hunters had been seen or heard. This was their area. All the teams had their favorite areas to hunt; it was like squatter's rights.

"I don't know the exact spot the arrow came from. It was behind me. I can still remember the sound as it zipped by me. If I had been standing a little more to my right, it would be me in that ambulance and Bentley would be talking to you. I waited for the hunter in question to emerge, but no one ever came. I don't know how long I waited. After I saw Bentley go down, everything seemed to stop. I knew Bentley's injuries were serious, but I just couldn't move. Everything went black. I don't think I fainted. I don't know what happened."

They stopped and watched the crowd beginning to disperse. The cold wind grew stronger, and snowflakes began to fall. Detective Malano looked at the sky, tightened up his coat and said, "Looks like they are going to get hit hard by this storm. I'm glad I live in the city."

Bruce nodded in agreement. Bruce indicated to the detective that his car was in front of Cora's. As they started in that direction, they were both surprised to see the Sheriff waiting for them.

"The 4x4 is mine. The gold Mercedes is Bentley's."

"Beautiful car," said the detective.

"Yes, Bentley liked people to know that he had achieved everything that he ever wanted," the statement made matter-of-factly by Bruce.

"This car will have to be impounded, and a thorough search will be done. Sheriff, could you take care of having the officials notified that the car needs to be picked up and taken to the impound lot."

"I will be glad to. Now if you gentlemen would like to follow me to the station."

Bruce was surprised when the detective waited for him to unlock the car door. "Are you riding with me detective?"

"I thought I would if you don't mind."

"No, I just thought...Never mind what I thought. Right now, my thoughts are a mess anyway."

The Sheriff's station buzzed with activity as they entered. Several of the hunters were being questioned. As the warm air greeted Bruce, he began to feel lightheaded. The room was spinning, and Bruce knew that he needed to find a chair, or he would pass out where he stood. Detective Malano grabbed his arm, and guided him to a back office. Bruce took off his coat and gloves and leaned his head on the table in front of him.

"Mr. Williams are you feeling better? I brought you some coffee. Do you need anything else?" the Sheriff asked.

"Could I have a little cream and sugar? I guess everything that has happened just caught up with me. I've never fainted in my life. This is very embarrassing."

"Don't be embarrassed it can happen to the best of us." The Sheriff brought the cream and sugar, and smiled as she handed them to him.

"I want to thank you for being so nice to me," said Bruce. "I don't think reality has hit me yet that Bentley is dead."

The Sheriff sat in the metal chair next to him. "Mr. Williams were you and Mr. Rogers close friends?"

"Not close in the conventional way. The shoot was something that bound us together. We were just boys when we started this tradition. Did I tell you we were sophomores in college?" The Sheriff nodded, and Bruce continued, "Bentley had a summer job in some ritzy place and found that archery was an 'IN' thing with the rich people. That's all it took. Bentley always wanted to do what the rich people did. My father and I had attended this shoot once when I was a teenager, and I told Bentley. After that, he badgered me until I finally agreed to attend as his partner. I never meant for this to go on for as long it just did. The rest is history." Bruce became silent and stared straight ahead.

"Mr. Williams are you okay?"

The sound of the Sheriff's voice brought him back to the present. "Yeah, I'm okay. I was just reminiscing about the past. It has been a shock.

"We have been hosting this event for a very long time, and we have never had a major accident. Oh, we have had bumps, bruises, and cuts, but nothing like this. Poor Doc Amos, I was worried about him making that climb, but he's tougher than he looks," chuckled the Sheriff. "Well your color is starting to return, so I'm going to see if there is anything I can do to speed things up. If you need anything, call my deputy or me. Try to relax. Detective Malano will be in shortly." Sheriff Forbes rose and left the room.

Bruce was physically and emotionally drained. The folding chairs were hard and uncomfortable. Bruce kept shifting in his chair trying to find a comfortable spot, but it was hopeless. "I just want to go home," thought Bruce. "Home! I have to call Alice," he said out loud, "I should have been home by now, and she will start to worry."

After a long wait, the deputy poked his head around the corner and asked, "Do you need anything Mr. Williams."

"I need to call my wife. It's getting late and I don't want her to worry. Do you know how much longer I'll be here?"

The deputy gave a shrug and pointed to the phone down the hall.

"I guess that means you don't know?" Bruce stated, but the deputy was gone. Bruce sat for a moment longer wondering what to tell Alice about the accident. It would take a long time to explain everything, and right now, he didn't have the energy or the inclination to go over the accident again. "It would just cause her needless worry, so it's best I tell her that I will be late, because something important has come up and tell her I will explain later." Bruce punched in his home number and waited. "Please pick up, Please pick up," Bruce chanted into the phone. Bruce had to settle for Alice's voice on the answering machine. The message was short. He was detained, and would be home as soon as possible. The hardest part was to hang up the phone and disconnect with his wife. Alice was his security. He felt she would stop this nightmare and bring him home.

Bruce returned to the room and found the Sheriff waiting. "Mr. Williams were you able to talk with your wife?"

"I left a message on the machine," replied Bruce, "She is probably out buying the fixings for our Thanksgiving dinner."

The Sheriff stayed silent for a moment, "Thanksgiving is next week. I had forgotten all about it. I haven't even bought my bird yet. Mr. Williams do you have a family?"

"Two children," replied Bruce, "A boy and a girl. Are you married, Sheriff?"

Looking wistful, she spoke, "I'm not married. I think the holidays are the hardest. Most of the time I don't think about a family. It has always been my grandfather, father, and I and it seems to be enough until the holiday's roll around. Did Mr. Rogers have a family; I mean a wife and children?"

Bruce hesitated for a moment before he spoke. "Bentley was married, but had no children. I don't think that he wanted children. Bentley lives a very orderly life. He knew what he wanted and didn't care how he got it. Children would put a crimp in how he pictured his life."

"Mr. Williams are you saying that Mr. Rogers was a control freak?"

Bruce let out a loud laugh. "You should have seen him in college. The first year we roomed together, I thought we would kill each other. He posted rules everywhere. It was like being in the military."

"So how did you two become friends? I mean if he was that bad, it must have been hard on you."

Bruce smiled as he remembered, "I had my doubts if I could make it for four years with him as a roomy, but at the end of our first year there was a moment when I saw the real Bentley, or what I thought was the real Bentley. I saw a lonely man that needed a friend and I thought I could be that friend."

The Sheriff glanced at her watch then said, "Mr. Williams, I'm sorry that this is taking so long, but Detective Malano has been assisting with the other statements. He is in charge of the investigation, so we have to wait on him. I'm sure that it won't be much longer. Is there anything that I can get for you while you wait?"

"Would it be possible to get some more coffee and a sandwich? I haven't eaten since early this morning."

The Sheriff motioned to her deputy and told him to get Bruce a sandwich and some coffee. "A man of few words but lots of shrugs," chuckled Bruce.

She gave Bruce a slight smile then spoke softly, "Mr. Williams there is one thing that we have not been able to locate and that's your hunting equipment. Do you have any idea what you did with it? I realize there was a lot of confusion, but try to think about that for a while. Your food will be here shortly, and if there is anything else, you need just ask. I will check with the detective about how much longer he will be. I know that the location of your equipment will be something that he will want to know."

A large mug of steaming coffee and a sandwich was brought in for Bruce. The aroma alone made him dizzy. He quickly consumed the sandwich, and savored over the hot coffee. The refreshments helped clear Bruce's mind and renewed his energy. He beckoned the deputy, and asked if the detective was available. While waiting, he carefully went over the events of the day. First, there was the sound by his ear. It had to be the arrow. Then he turned and watched Bentley's body crumble to the ground. This image was still so vivid. Would he ever be able to shut his eyes and not relive that moment? Bruce knew that it would be a long time before anything about today would begin to fade. He remembered feeling ill and sinking to the ground. There was no recollection of what he did with his bow and the arrow. The only explanation was someone picked up his equipment and forgot to tell him or the Sheriff. Maybe he tossed it to the side as he ran for help. A logical explanation had to surface as to the whereabouts of his equipment.

The wait for the detective seemed forever. Bruce became edgy. He began twisting in his chair, crossing and uncrossing his legs. Drumming his fingers on the table, Bruce was ready to scream when finally the detective entered the room carrying a large stack of papers and a folder with Bentley's name written across it in red.

"I'm sorry this has taken so long, but we have been taking

statements from all the hunters involved in the shooting contest. Were you aware there were 76 hunters in today's contest, including you and Mr. Rogers? That's a big contest. How long have you and Mr. Rogers been involved in this shoot?"

Bruce sat up straight rubbing his chin. "I have told all of this to the Sheriff. Bentley and I have been a part of this tradition for many years. There are hunters from all over the state, and most of them have been attending since they were old enough to shoot a bow. I have made many great friends here."

Detective Malano moved his chair closer to Bruce. "I never liked to hunt poor animals. It sounds kind of funny being a cop and all, but I just don't like hunting down a poor animal that has never done anything to harm me."

Bruce chuckled and said, "I feel the same about hunting. I never enjoyed it, but Bentley wanted to be a part of this tradition so I have gone along."

The detective looked straight into Bruce's eyes when he spoke. "You mean you have participated all these years because of your friend. You guys must have been very close, or did he have something on you?"

"Not really," replied Bruce. "Other than the shoot, we didn't talk much at all or see each other socially. Of course we know some of the same people and we both belong to the country club, so occasionally we are forced to see each other at those functions." Bruce began to fidget and was feeling closed in with the nearness of the detective. He tried to move his chair but the wall impeded his movement. Detective Malano seemed not to notice that Bruce was uncomfortable, and continued talking,

"Talking with some of the other hunters, I get the impression that Mr. Rogers could be a difficult man. Was he a difficult man, Mr. Williams?"

Bruce shifted in his chair. "Detective, the Sheriff told me that you couldn't find my equipment. Is that right?"

"Mr. Williams, it's true that we haven't been able to locate your bow or the contest arrow but we are still looking. Do you have any recollection of what you might have done with it?"

Bruce's head began to throb and he rubbed his temples. "I have been sitting here trying to go over each event as it happened, but I don't remember what became of my equipment."

"Hopefully the weather will clear and we can resume the search of the area where the accident happened." The detective pulled a pack of cigarettes from his pocket and offered one to Bruce. Bruce gladly accepted. "Not too many smokers anymore," said Malano. "I was hoping that you were a smoker. I haven't been able to have a good smoke since I arrived."

Bruce took a long drag on the cigarette. "Yeah, I normally don't smoke. Alice won't allow it in the house or around the kids. I don't have many vices, but I do enjoy an occasional smoke."

"Okay, what I have written so far is that you and Mr. Rogers always hunt in that same area. Neither of you observed another hunter as you were getting in position. Mr. Williams, your back was to the trees when you heard a noise by your ear. You turned in that direction seeing nothing; you focused on your partner and saw your friend go down. Do you have any recollection of how long before you started down the mountain?"

Bruce pondered the question before answering. "It was like everything was in slow motion. I watched as Bentley fell."

"You never went near the body at any time?" Malano interjected.

"No, it was like I was paralyzed and couldn't move. I found myself yelling and running down the mountain for help. I have tried to remember where I left my bow. I don't know if I dropped it at the accident scene or when I was running down the mountain for help. I'm sorry I just can't recall."

"That's okay. I'm sure that when the weather permits we will be able to locate it. Did Mr. Rogers shoot first or did you take turns?"

Bruce sighed. "Bentley always had to be first in everything, not just the shoot. In school he had to be number one in the class, on the dean's honor roll or any other activity that he participated in."

"So you never got to shoot your arrow today?" questioned Malano.

Bruce shook his head. "I'm going to have your statement typed. Then I will bring it back for you to read over and sign. Would you like another cigarette before I leave?"

"No thanks," said Bruce. "I have a pack in my coat pocket. Before you leave detective, I do have one question. Have any of the other hunters said they saw anything?"

"No, sorry Mr. Williams. Now let me get this typed up, so you can sign it, and be on your way home. The roads are getting pretty dangerous. This won't take long."

"Before you go detective, I just wanted to know if you do believe that this was an accident."

The detective stood motionless. "I can't say. Do you know if anyone would have a reason to hurt Mr. Rogers?"

"Only our whole community, including his wife," chuckled Bruce.

"How about you, Mr. Williams? Did you want to hurt Mr. Rogers?" the detective questioned.

"I don't even like to kill animals. How could I hurt Bentley?"

"Well I can't answer that question, only you can Mr. Williams. Do you know of any other family besides his wife?"

"No, I think Bentley told me that his parents were dead and he was an only child. Bentley didn't like to talk about his past. He would get very angry and clam up. Maybe Amanda might know. Has anyone talked to her yet?"

Malano relaxed slightly. "When I get through here, I will go over and make the announcement. It's not a part of this job that I relish." The detective left the room.

Bruce reached into his coat pocket, retrieved his half-empty pack of cigarettes, and lit one.

It was not long before the detective returned with Bruce's statement in hand. "Mr. Williams you need to read over your statement carefully. If any part of the statement is incorrect, please scratch that part out and correct it with this black pen. Put your initials by the correction. When the statement meets with your approval sign it at the bottom." He waited while Bruce read the statement.

There were mistakes, and Bruce corrected them as he had been told. He signed the document and handed it back to the detective.

"What will happen next, detective? I mean, since it was an accident, will there be an investigation?"

Holding the signed statement, Malano scanned the corrections that were made. "This is just the first step. An autopsy will be performed on Mr. Rogers. Tests will be done on the arrow. We need to do another search of the area and find your equipment. In addition, I have all of these statements to go over. I'm sure there will be more questions for you. We have your phone number and address. Since we have taken over the investigation, someone from my office will be in contact with you. Do you have anymore questions right now?"

"Will you let me know when my equipment is found?"

"I will let you know of any developments. Here is my card; it has my office and home phone number. If you have any questions or if you remember something call me. If there are no other questions, you can leave now." Malano picked up the ashtray as he was leaving.

After all the hours of waiting, the abruptness of this statement took Bruce by surprise. "You mean I can go home?" asked Bruce.

The detective extended his hand, and Bruce shook it. "That's all I need to know right now. Drive carefully, Mr. Williams. I'll be talking to you soon."

Bruce put on his coat and gloves, and left the room. The Sheriff's station was calm compared with the earlier confusion. Bruce waved to the detective and Sheriff, as he neared the front door.

A cold blast of wind and snow greeted Bruce as he opened the door. The air was refreshing, but bitterly cold. His car was covered with snow, so he brushed off the windshield and around the driver's door.

His body ached, and he couldn't shake the cobwebs from his mind. So much had happened today. At times, he didn't feel like himself. It was as if he was standing outside of himself, watching this other Bruce react to the events that were happening. He remembered having a black feeling before, but never with the intensity of today. He needed to get home to Alice; she would make everything okay. Bruce started his car and turned on the heater full blast. Waiting for his car to warm, his thoughts were of home. He was sure Alice would have a nice fire going, and one of her great meals. He just wanted to be home. Bruce pulled away from the station and started for the main highway.

The sheriff watched until the tail lights of Bruce Williams' car disappeared then she turned to Detective Malano and said "Detective I have a couple of questions that I would like to ask you." Malano put down his coffee cup and said, "Shoot."

Sheriff Forbes paused before she spoke. "This is really none of my business but I was watching as you questioned Mr. Williams and I noticed the way you kept moving closer to him. He seemed uncomfortable and tried to move away but the wall stopped him. Was that move deliberate?"

Malano sat back in his chair and lit a cigarette. "The first lesson in interrogation 101 is to invade the suspect's space. Two things will happen; either the suspect will feel nervous and tell everything he knows to get you away from him or he will feel a sort of bonding and tell you everything you want to know. Either way you get the info that you want. Is there anything else?"

"There are two other things I noticed and was wondering about. When you were moving closer to Mr. Williams he was becoming very uncomfortable. At least that is the way it looked from where I was standing but you seemed to not notice. The second thing is you told Mr. Williams that you don't like to hunt. I was just wondering if that was true."

Malano chuckled, "Okay the first thing when you are interrogating a suspect is you listen and watch. I was well aware of the discomfort that I was causing Mr. Williams. I didn't bring it to his attention because that would have given him the opportunity to put up a barrier between us. If I act as if I didn't notice he lets his guard down a little because he thinks he has the upper hand. The thing about the hunting is he let you and then me know that he hated the shoot. I told him I hated to hunt and that created a bond between us. That made him feel more at ease with me and that also makes for buddy talk instead of an interrogation. Does that answer your questions?"

Sheriff Forbes blushed as she said, "I have a lot to learn."

"Well Sheriff that's the first lesson and the hardest to learn, to admit that you have a lot to learn. Every day on the job is a learning experience. Now if you don't have anymore questions for me I think I need to head to the city and break the news to Dr. Rogers's wife. I think we have something more than an accident here."

The sheriff watched as the detective loaded his thing in the car. The detective paused before getting in, looked toward the office, smiled and waved. The sheriff eagerly waved back.

3

AMANDA ROSE EARLY ON SATURDAY before Thanksgiving. Bentley would be attending his annual Turkey Shoot, and she had a million things to get done before he returned. Bentley always left his equipment by the front door so they could load it together before he left for the shoot. He had two bows and several quivers of arrows. Amanda had once asked, "Why do you bother to bring extra bows and arrows when they are furnished at the contest?" Bentley's answer was, "What if, by accident, my bow was broken, that would end the day for me. Do you want to ruin the shoot for me? You must think before you speak. Don't I always have a good reason for what I do? Think next time before you ask senseless questions that waste my time."

A long lecture ensued, the main point of which was to never question him about his activities. These lectures always made her feel ignorant. They reinforced the fact that Bentley was a genius, and she was so lucky that he took the time to try to teach her and take care of her. She had no one except Bentley to care for her, and she was not smart enough to survive without him.

This morning Bentley handed her the quiver of arrows. She started for the door, when her arm bumped a vase of flowers. The vase began to teeter. As she grabbed for the vase, the quivers tipped, and the arrows fell to the floor.

Bentley turned and looked at her with great disgust. Amanda knelt down and was gathering the arrows, when Bentley pushed her aside. "Let me do that before you bend one of the tips. Do you think you could manage to take these bows out to the car without breaking anything?"

Amanda was mute, but she shook her head in agreement. Taking the bows, she carefully walked to the back of his car waiting for him to unlock the trunk. Bentley placed the quiver of arrows in first, and then roughly grabbed the bows from Amanda. Her long hair tangled in the bowstring and a several strands of her hair were pulled.

In a small voice, Amanda yelped and said, "I'm sorry."

Bentley put the bows gently in the trunk then slammed the lid. "Make sure you are here when I get home tonight. I left a list of to-dos. Make sure they are accomplished," spoke Bentley in a controlled voice.

Amanda knew that he was angry. "I will. Have a great shoot," she replied.

No more was spoken as Bentley got in his car and sped away. Amanda waved, but he never looked back. As she walked to the door, she wondered why he wanted her to be home when he arrived. It was as if he barely tolerated her. After the commotion of this morning, she was sure that her list would be accomplished, and she would be waiting for him. Rubbing her head where the hair had been yanked, she thought, "I sure hope he wins this year." Amanda hated this Turkey Shoot tradition, but Bentley and Bruce had been attending since they were in college.

Before their marriage, Bentley had made it clear that she was not to interfere with any of his activities or question him about them. His friendship with Bruce was a true puzzlement to her, but she had learned the hard way not to question him about it. Bentley and Bruce were so different from each other. Bruce was very friendly and outgoing, whereas Bentley was quiet and controlling. Bruce had told her on several occasions that he found this contest barbaric. Still every year around the first of November, these two men would begin planning the next hunt. Except for the shoot, Bentley did not socialize with Bruce, and a friendship between Amanda and Bruce's wife was not encouraged. On the rare occasions that the couples met at a social function, Bentley would ignore the Williams or greet them casually and always with condescending behavior. Bruce and Alice were nice people; it was hard to understand why either of them put up with Bentley's behavior. Bruce was a successful engineer, had a beautiful home and family, and well respected by the community. He didn't need Bentley's friendship.

The other acquaintances in Bentley's life were there for a reason. Either Bentley needed their business connections or they were dependent on him for some reason. Bentley used people's weaknesses against them. He was a charmer, and he could make you believe that he was your best friend until you disclosed your weakness. With this ammunition, he would control you until you were of no more value to him. Then he would discard you like yesterday's garbage. Amanda had seen Bentley use this ploy on many people. They had no real friends, just opportunities. Bentley felt that he was respected and admired, but in reality, people feared him and what he could do to their lives.

Amanda was beginning to wonder why she married such a man. The simple reason was that she too was dependent on Bentley. Their marriage was unusual by conventional standards, but for the majority of Amanda's life she was totally devoted to Bentley. His affection gave her life meaning. Amanda would subject herself to any kind of humiliation at Bentley's hand, just to be with him. She knew that Bentley married her to adorn his life. Talk of love had always come from Amanda, and Bentley greedily accepted her adoration. Amanda was young, beautiful, and, most importantly, dependent on him. Bentley had molded Amanda to be the exact person that he wanted. He made her into the perfect wife, hostess, and lover. At times she felt like a Stepford wife, but she didn't know how to change her life or if she really wanted to change it.

Amanda met Bentley when she was young and impressionable, introduced to him by her caseworker because of her eating disorder. After the death of her parents she was placed in the foster care system, and her self-esteem became non-existent. In her first days in the system, she was told that she was too old to be adopted, and never to get attached to any of the foster parents. The situation was temporary, and she had nothing to say about where she was placed. Control was up to the state. Amanda's life was no longer her own. She felt lost, and her only means of control was what she ate. This one part of her life she had control of and it didn't matter that it was harmful to her. Amanda felt to give up this control would mean to give up her life. Doctors terrified her because of the harsh treatment she had received since being in the system. She was referred to as a "charity case," and bedside manner was reserved only for paying customers. Amanda was never given a gentle touch or a reassuring smile. Everything was always clinical and sterile, as if to touch her would contaminate the doctors.

Amanda was informed that she would be meeting with Dr. Rogers to talk about her problem. Mrs. Black, her caseworker, always referred to her eating disorder as her problem. Despite Amanda's protest and promises to control her problem, it was settled that a visit to Dr. Rogers was warranted.

Dr. Rogers' office was a large cavern with leather furniture and wood adorning most of the reception area. The receptionist was seated behind a huge desk that was covered with telephones, folders, and slips of paper. Amanda pulled back as they entered but Mrs. Black held her hand firmly. The receptionist's appearance sent a chill through Amanda. Her black hair was pulled straight back, her dress was plain black; a small broach her only jewelry. Amanda tried to hide behind Mrs. Black's skirt as they neared the desk. The severe looking woman didn't intimidate Mrs. Black, who cleared her throat, and then announced that they had a 10:00 o'clock appointment. The receptionist slowly raised her gaze from the appointment book, and asked, "Is this Amanda Walker?"

"Yes, it is, and I'm Mrs. Black, her case worker." Amanda wished that she didn't have to say that she was a caseworker. It made them aware that she was a charity case. She slipped farther behind Mrs. Black.

"Well, Miss Amanda Walker, you are a little early. The doctor is with a patient, but the session is almost over. If you would like to take Mrs. Black over to the couch both of you can make yourselves comfortable. I'll let the doctor know that you are waiting." The receptionist's voice had a lilt, which made it sound musical. When she smiled her whole, face lit up and her appearance softened.

Amanda was determined not to let her guard down. This was just a ploy to make her feel at ease, so they could hurt her. She puckered up her face in a grimace and lead Mrs. Black to the large leather couch. Curling up in a ball, she sat as close to Mrs. Black as possible. She rubbed her hand over the leather: it was smooth, but cold to the touch. Amanda had never been to a psychiatrist before, and not knowing what to expect made her shiver. She made an involuntary shudder, and Mrs. Black placed her arm around her.

Talking softly, so only Amanda could hear, Mrs. Black whispered, "Don't be afraid baby. It will be okay. You're a big girl and the doctor just wants to talk to you and make you better. Okay?" Amanda shook her head in agreement, but her fear remained.

The receptionist asked if they would like some refreshments or a magazine. Mrs. Black looked to Amanda for a response, but she quickly looked down at her dress. "I don't think we need anything right now but thank you for asking."

The receptionist walked in front of Amanda and knelt down, taking Amanda's hand in hers. In the sweetest voice she spoke, "Amanda, has the cat got your tongue?"

Amanda looked puzzled and shook her head.

"I haven't heard you speak yet. My name is Mrs. Miller, and if you have any questions, I would be glad to answer them. Dr. Rogers is a very nice man, and will be able to help you with any problems you have. You can talk to him about anything and he will help you. He is nice and loves children and they all love him. There is no need to be afraid." She gave Amanda a warm smile and patted her knee as she rose.

Amanda's fear began to ebb as she thought, "Maybe this doctor will be different."

Presently, the door to the inner office opened, and out walked a small boy and the most handsome man Amanda had ever seen. The little boy was wiping his face with his sleeve and the doctor bent down to whisper something to him. When the doctor was finished speaking, the little boy reached up, hugged the doctor, and then gave him a big smile.

"Now Matt, Mrs. Miller will make your next appointment, and I want you to think about all we talked about today."

"I will," responded Matt, "See you later Dr. Rogers."

The doctor gave a wave to the small boy, and then disappeared into his office. Moments later the intercom buzzed to signal Mrs. Miller that the doctor was ready for Amanda and Mrs. Black.

Fear began to grip Amanda's stomach, as they rose and started toward the huge wooden door. "Matt must have been a paying customer to receive that kind of treatment," thought Amanda, "It will be different with charity."

The inner office was furnished like the reception area, except there were bookcases that ran from floor to ceiling behind the doctor's desk. Two chairs were positioned in front of his desk. As they entered, the doctor motioned for them to take the seats. His chair was very large, and he rocked back and forth while holding a file in front of his face. Amanda fidgeted with her hands while she waited for the doctor to speak.

"Amanda, I'm Dr. Rogers, and I was told by Mrs. Black that you have a problem. Well I think I might be able to help you, and we will certainly give it the ole college try. I have a few questions for Mrs. Black. Then we will ask her to leave, so you and I can get acquainted. Does that sound like something that you want to do?" He looked straight into Amanda's eyes and gave a radiant smile.

Amanda couldn't find her voice to speak. She had never been asked that question before or seen such a beautiful smile. In a dazed state, she shook her head.

The doctor asked several questions about the foster care system that Amanda was living in. Amanda was surprised that he never questioned Mrs. Black about payment or mentioned charity.

He rose abruptly from his chair, and asked Mrs. Black to wait in the outer office. He walked Mrs. Black to the door, and then closed it gently behind her. Dr. Rogers casually walked back to his desk, but didn't return to his seat. Leaning against the desk, in front of Amanda, he crossed his arms and smiled down at her.

Amanda tried to avert her eyes and not look at the doctor. She raised her eyes slowly until she could see the doctor's face. She was surprised to see him smiling at her.

There was a slight pause before the doctor began to speak. His voice, like his face, was magical to Amanda. The tone of his voice and the way he looked at her gave her an uneasy feeling that he knew her deepest secrets. Amanda knew that in these first few minutes the wall, which she had constructed around her, was beginning to crumble. The doctor's voice was like a soothing balm on Amanda's wounded ego. She listened attentively, but was not hearing his words; she just wanted him to continue to talk and to smile at her. Amanda shuffled, in her chair, to try and clear her thought; she must not forget where she was and who she was.

The first lesson she learned when she came to the shelter, was to trust no one and to always remember no one is your friend. That lesson was learned the hard way, and the price was costly to Amanda emotionally. She learned quickly to disguise the hurt and repress her feelings.

This doctor was playing a part and didn't care about her. He just played the game better than anyone she had met before. This was a real change. This doctor was pretending to be nice, but she must remember that no one really cared about her. Amanda sat back in her chair and refused to look at the doctor. She was trying hard to guard her feelings and not to expose herself to possible hurt.

Dr. Rogers' voice and smile was weaving a cocoon around her. She was mesmerized by his presence, like she had been with her father. Amanda adored her father, but she must remember that Dr. Rogers was not her father. She tried to escape the web, which the doctor was spinning around her, but in just a few minutes Amanda knew that she would do anything that the doctor asked. She loved his smile and the sound of his voice. For the first time, in a long time, she felt safe and secure and she was welcoming this warm feeling.

"Amanda," called the doctor, "Did you hear my question or would you like for me to repeat it?"

Amanda had not been paying attention so in a small voice she asked him to repeat it.

Dr. Rogers cleared his throat and asked, "How do you feel about your current situation?"

She thought, "How can I explain that I have no choice in my present situation? I'm here because everyone thinks I'm too young. What would Dr. Rogers say if I told him how I really feel? I must remember to keep my guard up and not let anyone know how I feel.

Only good little girls get love, and I want to be loved by someone. It doesn't matter how I feel, anyway. Nothing can be changed. I think it is best if I don't express my feelings or maybe express the feelings that will please Dr. Rogers."

Dr. Rogers saw that Amanda was pondering his question and was having a hard time answering. "Amanda do you have an answer for me?"

The sound of Dr. Rogers' voice startled her. Amanda's response to the doctor's question was a shrug.

"Amanda, can you talk? Do you have a voice? Can you answer questions, or do you need that case worker to answer for you?" The doctor's voice had a slight edge as he asked her these questions.

Amanda was taken back, and stared at him with contempt.

"Answer me now, or you can just forget about getting better. They can come and put you in the hospital where they can force feed you. You will have no control over what they put into your body. I am giving you a chance to speak for yourself. Looking at you, I see a beautiful little girl that has not been given a chance to speak for herself. Here, in this office, you are safe and can tell me anything. I will never tell anyone your secrets. I want to be your friend. Now, let me ask you once again, what do you think of your situation?"

Amanda was taken back by the harshness of his tone and the fact that he knew about her wanting control. "How could he know? Lucky guess I bet," thought Amanda. It took a moment for her to regain her composure and voice. "I don't know how I feel about my situation." Her voice quivered with emotion but she was determined to nullify any observations that he thought he made about her. Taking a deep breath, she proceeded with a strong clear voice. "I have been placed in this situation because of the death of my parents, not by choice. Why do you act like you care? You don't know me; I'm just a charity case to you, something you do to make yourself look like a good person to the community. Don't pretend to care what happens to me." Amanda felt such anger spring up inside her that she lowered her gaze from the doctor's face to hide the feelings that he had stirred.

"Had she tipped her hand and made him aware how much she wanted to control her life? Will he use this information against her? She will not show her anger. She will not feel. She will not be controlled. She will not be hurt." These thoughts ran through

Amanda's mind, as she sat in the big chair, with her arms crossed and her chin buried deep into her chest.

Amanda was puzzled by Dr. Rogers' reaction. He continued to smile, and then sat in the chair next to her. In his most gentle voice Dr. Rogers began to speak while taking her hands in his. Normally Amanda would have pulled away but his hands felt so large and warm that she let them remain.

"You have a temper, Ms. Amanda. This is very good. I was afraid that the system had robbed you of that. Your anger means that deep down there is a beautiful young lady waiting to get out."

Amanda pulled away when Dr. Rogers tapped her chest.

He seemed unaware she had drawn back from his touch, and continued to speak to her in a soft voice. "You are a beautiful girl, Ms. Amanda. I'm sure you haven't been told that much lately, but I promise that I will tell you often. I want to be your friend and I'm willing to wait until you feel comfortable enough to give me your friendship. For one hour every week you will have my undivided attention. You can say and do whatever you feel. You are in control; there are a few rules that we will discuss. How do you feel about that?"

Amanda sat back, deep in her chair, and took a moment before she spoke. "Whatever you say, sir."

The doctor released her hands, stood and walked around his desk. He began shuffling papers and did not look at Amanda.

He was silent for a moment, but it was an eternity to Amanda. She held her breath hoping that she had not offended him by her answer, and wished she could take it back. She wanted to see his smile again and have him hold her hands. In a small weak voice Amanda said, "I would like that very much Dr. Rogers."

The doctor's eyes were like a knife as he glared at her. Amanda didn't know what to do but hold her breath and wait for him to speak. The corners of his mouth began to turn up until his smile had returned. A sigh of relief escaped her lips as she shifted in her chair.

"Ms. Amanda, I think we are going to be great friends. In order to continue our friendship, I must set some boundaries. These boundaries must never be crossed, or I will be forced to end our friendship. First, what we talk about or do in these sessions must never be discussed with anyone. Second, you must do as I say and never question me. If I tell you to stop something—anything—you will do as I say, with no questions asked. I don't feel that I'm asking a great deal, and it is for your own good. I promise I only have your best interest at heart. Do you believe what I have just told you?"

Amanda shook her head in agreement, and the doctor continued. "I will agree to see you once a week, Ms. Amanda, if you will agree to the boundaries that I have set. Well, do you agree?"

"Yes, Dr. Rogers I do agree," Amanda said breathlessly.

"Okay, since both of us are in agreement, Mrs. Miller will schedule your next appointment. How does all of this sound to you, Ms. Amanda?"

Amanda was relieved that the doctor was no longer angry with her. She began to smile, shook her head in agreement, and then took the doctor's outstretched hand. They both rose and started toward the door. Amanda felt elated. The way he said her name was like magic. She promised herself to never say or do anything that would upset Dr. Rogers.

That was the beginning of years of therapy under the great Dr. Rogers. The woman that Amanda would become was due to Dr. Rogers' work. He helped her overcome her eating disorder, and gave her a reason to live. She was now the perfect woman, according to Dr. Rogers. Dr. Rogers' therapy had molded her to think what he wanted, act as he wanted, dress as he wanted, and make love as he wanted. Amanda wasn't quite sure when she stopped existing and Dr. Rogers' creation began.

A continuance of the therapy was inevitable. Amanda remained the dutiful patient, never questioning, always seeking Bentley's approval. On some occasions, she would feel an awakening of old emotions that had long been dormant. The strain would, however, start to take its toll. Amanda was growing tired of the rules, and of Bentley being in control of every moment of her life.

When she questioned him on several occasions, Bentley was quick to remind her how cruel he could be. Bentley would withhold any affection, and his verbal abuse would bring her to tears. It would take several days of begging for forgiveness, and swearing to never question him, before he would again bestow his attention. He would dry her tears, and gently raise her off her knees. Holding her close to his chest he would whisper, "Ms. Amanda has been bad and has to be punished. Ms. Amanda must learn not to question. Does Ms. Amanda agree to be a good girl or must the punishment continue?" Amanda would shake her head and cry on Bentley's chest agreeing to never question again. Bentley would smooth back her hair, wipe her tears, and take her to bed.

Bentley's approval meant everything to Amanda. Her mere existence depended on his approval. The old Amanda had ceased to exist.

After the last holiday season, Amanda was feeling a stirring of new emotions, or maybe old emotions that she thought were dead. A voice deep inside her was screaming to be heard. She had been taught to never upset or question Bentley, but lately she had the need to feel an emotion. At times like these, she wanted a confrontation, and wanted to feel the anger burn deep inside. She wanted to scream and lose control. For many years, she had to repress her inner feelings, and could only feel what Bentley told her to feel. Now those feelings would no longer be denied. They would surface much to Bentley and Amanda's dismay. She was perplexed by this new emerging personality, because she had always longed for Bentley's approval. She had even groveled at his feet, just for one of his smiles or a pat on the head. "I feel like his damn lap dog instead of his wife," Amanda had inadvertently told one of the ladies at the country club. Realizing what she had done, she was remorseful and tried to pretend it was a joke. Airing her feelings and giving an outsider a glimpse into their lives was a major infraction of Bentley's rules.

Bentley's anger was apparent when he confronted Amanda with his discovery. "You broke a rule. What do you have to say for yourself?"

Amanda chewed her nails as she thought about her reply. "Don't chew your nails! That is a bad habit," reprimanded Bentley.

Amanda could no longer control her anger as she spoke, "Rules! Rules! Rules! Who elected you God? I don't remember being asked to vote. Bentley, your life is governed by rules, and mine is governed by your rules. When I started therapy, you promised that I would have control of my life, and I believed you. You have been in control ever since. You act like my father, not my husband."

As Amanda spoke these words, she could see Bentley's anger growing. She had never seen Bentley so angry, and she knew there was going to be hell to pay. She had broken too many rules to count. She had never before challenged Bentley's authority, not this far, and a cold chill gripped her stomach. Amanda's only hope, to appease Bentley, was to get down on her knees and beg for forgiveness. She did so immediately, but Bentley was unmoved. Coldness had descended on his face, and his emotions were veiled. Amanda remained on her knees with her head bent. Bentley cleared his throat, while Amanda waited for her punishment. With the quickness of a cat, Bentley delivered a stunning blow, which sent Amanda sprawling across the floor. Dazed, she lifted her hands to her face. The taste of blood was in her mouth.

Bentley reached down and grabbed a handful of hair, and pulled her to her feet. "Amanda," said Bentley in a controlled voice, "Look at me." Removing her hands from her face she looked into Bentley's eyes. They were cold, and he had a sinister smile. "You must learn to obey the rules."

An inner heat was welling up inside Amanda. She returned his stare with defiance. Amanda stood firm, as Bentley raised his hand to slap her again. The blows sent her to the floor. She bumped her head, and lost consciousness.

When she awoke, the room was dark and Bentley was gone. Amanda felt sore and her head ached. She slowly got to her feet. The house was quiet. She made her way upstairs. Her belongings were thrown outside the master suite. Remorse was replacing the anger felt earlier. "Why had she challenged him in that manner?" Amanda placed her belongings in a spare room, which she would have to occupy until Bentley said otherwise. During her banishment, Bentley refused to speak to her, touch her, or allow her to accompany him to any social function. Amanda was devastated by Bentley's actions. It was as if he had erased her from existence. She begged, cried, and degraded herself at Bentley's feet.

After a month Bentley decided that the punishment was over, and he bestowed his attention upon her. Amanda was so grateful that she took an oath to never break a rule. Bentley graciously accepted her apology. Life returned too normal.

Amanda checked her watch, and admonished herself for wasting time reminiscing. Bentley was constantly berating her for her lack of organization and her ill use of time. Her list of to-dos had been budgeted so that she would be home when he returned. With the holidays approaching, she wanted to make sure things were in order. Now was not the time to antagonize Bentley. He was already upset with her because of the incident this morning. She tried so hard to be the perfect wife, but something always went wrong. *Why was I so clumsy with his equipment this morning? Dropping his quiver of arrows was an accident.* She didn't have time to explore such feelings in depth. *I must make sure my list is completed and that I'll be waiting drink in hand for Bentley. After the holidays, I'll deal with these feelings and the anger that I've been feeling. Right now, I have to get to the caterers to check the menu for Thanksgiving dinner, the florist to check on the centerpieces, the linen shop to check on the Irish lace tablecloth, and the seamstress to check on my new gown. Everything must be perfect for Bentley. I'll show him I'm a capable adult and not one of his helpless little patients.*

Dinners at the Rogers house were always black tie affairs. The invitations were coveted, and only the elite of the city were deemed worthy for this honor. Amanda's to-do list was always arranged in order of importance, accomplished in that order.

First on the list was to pick up Bentley's tuxedo from the cleaners. Amanda felt rebellious feelings arise as she drove past the cleaners. "I will make the decision on how I will accomplish these errands. I'm an adult and it's my time, so I will do as I want." This act of defiance gave her a warm feeling deep inside. "Bentley doesn't have to know everything," she said to herself.

Glancing at her watch, she realized she had lost another ten minutes. This was costing her precious time, and she would have to hurry to get everything done.

Her stomach began to growl. "I have to stop for lunch. It wouldn't do to have my problem return. People might think that Dr. Rogers isn't all that great," chuckled Amanda. She pulled into a fast food joint and ordered a cheeseburger, large fries and a large coke. She could hear Bentley's voice, "You know that is not good for your body. There is not one ounce of nutritional value in that meal." Amanda consumed every morsel, and then discarded the garbage.

She took a moment to relish the feeling of this defiant act, before heading to the bathroom to purge. "Well, that will keep it from contaminating my system. Just what the good doctor would order." These acts alone brought great joy to her. She was in control. Returning to her car, Amanda made sure that all evidence was removed then sprayed the car with air freshener to remove any lingering odors. She then popped a breath mint and pulled out of the parking lot.

All that was left to be done was to pick up Bentley's tuxedo. The streets were crowded with holiday shoppers, so Amanda decided to take the frontage road. The exit was just ahead. Amanda began to slow her car when suddenly a sharp pain shot through her eyes. Almost blinded by the pain, Amanda was able to maneuver the car off the road and out of traffic. Her head was pounding, and the pressure in her eyes was unbearable. Leaning her head against the steering wheel, she tried to control her breathing. Could she have hurt herself when she purged or had she damaged her stomach? The funny thing was that her stomach didn't hurt. She rolled down the window, and welcomed the fresh air on her face.

The pain was beginning to subside when the rapping of the passenger window startled her. Amanda opened her eyes to see the face of a police officer. "Ma'am, are you okay?" he questioned.

Amanda was confused as she spoke, "Have I done anything wrong, Officer?"

"No, Ma'am," was his reply. "I was concerned when I saw you bent over the steering wheel. Are you okay? It's not safe to be sitting on the side of the road like this. Is there anything I can do for you?"

"No, officer. I had a bad headache so I pulled to the side of the road hoping it would pass. I'm feeling better now so I will be on my way home. Thank you for your concern."

Rubbing her temples, she leaned back in the seat. Looking over at the officer, she had the feeling she knew him. "Really, I'm feeling much better now. Do I know you from somewhere?"

The officer looked down at his shoes; "I was the officer that interviewed you after you were attacked. I was at the hospital."

Amanda's smile quickly vanished as she started her car, "Thank you again for stopping. I'm fine now, and must be going."

"Okay, if you are sure everything is fine. We have a storm headed this way so it might be best if you started home. Would you like for me to follow you?"

"No! That won't be necessary. I'm feeling better now," Amanda said abruptly. The officer returned to his car, and Amanda looked around. The area was unfamiliar to her and she had no recollection of driving to this remote spot.

"How did I get here? The last thing I remember was the pain in my eyes, and taking the off ramp to the frontage road. This road is the interstate to the mountains. I'm afraid to drive in the mountains. It has to be all the stress that I live with. That can be the only explanation. Bentley would kill me if he thought I had gone up to the Turkey Shoot. I just hope that officer doesn't tell him that he found me here. I have a terrible feeling that I'm in big trouble."

Amanda sat for a while. Fear gripped her heart. Confusion about finding herself in this situation was compounded with worry about the officer. She started her car, and pulled onto the interstate. "I'm going to make myself a promise that after the holidays I will get in touch with all the feelings and emotions I have repressed for so long."

Her exit was just ahead, so Amanda decreased her speed and glanced at the clock on the dash. The clock had to be wrong. She checked her watch. It was also wrong. "How long was I sitting on the roadside? Somehow, I lost several hours. How will I explain this to Bentley? I must have passed out from the pain. I don't even remember driving there. What is happening to me?" she cried aloud, knowing she would be hard pressed to come up with a good excuse.

"I have to get control of myself. Everything is fine." She pulled into her driveway and began to gather her parcels. Her list fell to the ground as she exited the car. Picking it up, she checked to assure herself that each errand had been accomplished. The first errand was still not checked.

"Bentley's tux, I forgot to pick it up. I have to pick it up right away. Bentley will be furious with me." Amanda quickly returned to the car, and proceeded to the cleaners. Having no time to waste, she had the claim check in hand, as she entered the cleaners. Careful not to crease the tuxedo, she laid it on the back seat, and then drove straight home. Anxious to beat Bentley home, she was oblivious to the traffic lights and the honking of an irate motorist that she cut off. Driving down her street, she said a prayer that Bentley was late. She sighed with relief when the garage opened and Bentley's car was not there.

She rushed to gather her packages and noticed her boots were muddy. She thought to herself, "When did this happen? I was never off the sidewalk or out of my car. She glanced at the interior of the car, and found the same mud on the carpet interior. "Bentley is going to kill me. I have to get this cleaned up before he gets home "

Careful not to make a mess that could be seen; she placed her boots by the door. "The gods are with me today. I will have to remember to thank them later," she said breathlessly.

Amanda busied herself attending to small details around the house, collect the mail and sorting into individual stacks, just the way Bentley liked it.

She glanced around the rooms. Everything was in order, and still Bentley had not returned. Looking out the window, she saw that a storm was approaching. Maybe the weather was what was detaining Bentley. Mixed feelings swept over her as she envisioned Bentley in a number of possible scenarios.

She tried to occupy her time. "I think I will make myself a cup of tea and try to read," she said aloud. The sounds of her own voice startled her. This house was too large for just the two of them. It was large, orderly, and much too quiet for her, but this was what Bentley wanted, and Bentley always got what he wanted. Amanda would have preferred a smaller home with a couple of children. That was not how Bentley envisioned his life, and children were not wanted. That was another dream that could be put in a box. Amanda brewed her tea, and then entered Bentley's study to select a good book. The wind was beginning to howl, and snow had started falling.

Taking a quick glance to see if Bentley was home, Amanda closed the drapes in the study. With great haste, she selected a book, and turned to leave the study. Amanda always felt a strange coldness in this room, and tonight it was particularly strong. As she left the room, she paused at the door to look back at Bentley's desk. For an instant, a vision of Bentley's ashen face appeared then was gone. Amanda gasped and felt as if the room was closing in on her. She had to get out of this room. Holding onto the doorknob for support, she turned off the light, and then closed the door soundly behind her.

Amanda made her way to the den, found her tea, and collapsed in a chair. This whole day had made her confused and uneasy. She sipped the tea. The warm brew was having a calming effect. Amanda was starting to relax, when she saw the headlights of a car pulling into the driveway. She waited for the sound of the garage door opening, but it didn't come. The sound of the doorbell startled her, and a cold feeling gripped her stomach.

Cautiously, Amanda made her way to the front door. Looking through the peephole, she saw a police officer buffeted by the cold wind and snow. Amanda opened the door slowly.

"Mrs. Rogers?" questioned the officer.

"Yes, I'm Mrs. Rogers," Amanda replied in a girlish tone.

"Mrs. Rogers, I'm Officer Reed. May I come in? I have some news to deliver."

"Of course, Officer. Where are my manners? Please come in," Amanda stepped back to let him enter.

The officer seemed nervous. It was apparent to Amanda that he was there to deliver bad news.

"Officer Reed, would you like some hot coffee or tea?"

"No, thank you, Mrs. Rogers. This is not a social call. I have some news about your husband. Your husband is Bentley Rogers, correct?"

Amanda hesitated before answering, *this was the same officer that had tapped on her window earlier in the day and had also been at the hospital after her attack. Why is he acting like he doesn't know who I am,* Amanda thought. "Yes, Bentley is my husband. What has happened? Has there been an accident? Is Bentley okay?"

"Mrs. Rogers, please calm down. Would you like to sit?" Officer Reed could see that Amanda was pale and had started to shake. "Mrs. Rogers, there isn't an easy way to tell you this. There was an accident this morning at the Turkey Shoot, and your husband was shot."

Amanda's voice quivered as she asked, "Was it bad? Is he in the hospital? I need to get to him. Do you know what hospital he is in?" Amanda began to play with her hands and her eyes darted from side to side. She wouldn't look directly at the officer.

"Mrs. Rogers, I have to tell you that your husband is..."

Amanda raised her hand to stop the officer from speaking. "I don't want you to say it. I will not listen. I think you need to leave now."

The officer was confused by her reaction. "Mrs. Rogers, I have to tell you that your husband is dead. I was sent to escort you to the hospital to identify the body."

Amanda placed her hands on her ears and started rocking back and forth. She was aware that he was speaking, but she refused to grasp what he was saying.

"Did they say Bentley was injured?"

"No, Mrs. Rogers, your husband is dead, and you have to identify his body. Is there someone that I can call for you?"

"No, I have no one. Are you sure they said that he was dead and not just injured? You and Bentley are playing a trick on me."

"Mrs. Rogers, I'm sure. Now can I get your coat for you?"

"No! It will take me only a minute. I have to check my appearance, get my coat and purse, and then we can leave." Amanda rose and left the room leaving a stunned officer in her wake. Shortly she returned, "Okay, I'm ready," Amanda spoke in a cheery voice. The officer stood and helped Amanda with her coat. They then made their way to the patrol car.

The ride to the city morgue was quiet. Amanda pressed her face against the cold window, and watched as the blizzard began to grip the city. The driving was slow, but finally the lights of the city hospital came into view. The policeman pulled the car as close to the entrance as he could. The wind made walking difficult. As Officer Reed walked around the car to open the door for Amanda, he slipped several times. They locked arms, and leaned on each other for support on the icy sidewalk. As the doors of the hospital opened, a blast of warm air greeted them. Amanda stood for a moment. She felt as if she was standing outside of herself. She could see the other Amanda being helped to the elevator, and then taking the ride to the bottom level. There she was lead to a small room with a large curtained window. The officer asked her to sit. They had to wait for a Detective Malano. Presently, the detective arrived and introduced himself to Amanda. He explained to her what was needed, but his voice seemed far away. Officer Reed helped her to her feet, and led her closer to the window. Detective Malano rapped on the window, and the curtain began to rise.

There lay Bentley on a metal table. His face was ashen. This was the vision that she had seen in Bentley's study. The room began to spin and the two men helped her to a chair. She was offered a glass of water and a few moments to herself. Deep in thought Amanda jumped as the detective placed his hand on her shoulder.

"Mrs. Rogers, I know this is hard. I just have to ask you if that is your husband, Bentley Rogers?" asked the detective in a hushed tone.

"Yes, that's Bentley. Can you tell me how it happened?"

The detective cleared his throat then spoke. "There was a hunting accident during the Turkey Shoot this morning. We are conducting an investigation. As soon as I have any news, you will be the first to know. Officer Reed will take you home now. Is there someone we should call? Someone needs to be with you tonight."

"Detective, was Bruce with Bentley? Bruce Williams, that is, Bentley's partner in the shoot."

"Yes, Mrs. Rogers, Mr. Williams was with your husband at the time of the accident." Amanda stared at the curtained window. "Mrs. Rogers, I'm going to have the officer drive you home now. I will be talking with you in a couple of days. If you have any questions, call me. Here is my card." The detective motioned for Officer Reed, and they both assisted Amanda to her feet.

Walking to the door Amanda paused, and then spoke, "You could call my housekeeper, Mrs. James. She will stay with me. The weather is so bad that I hate to have her drive."

"Mrs. Rogers, do you have her phone number and address? I will have someone call her, and then drive her to your home."

"Yes, I do have that information right here." Amanda looked through her purse, found the information, and gave it to the detective.

"Mrs. Rogers, she will be waiting for you when you get home. Try to get some rest. I know that this has been a terrible shock. I'll be talking to you. "

Amanda felt nothing, no grief, no sorrow. She knew that she should be upset. Her husband had been killed, but the feeling that was occurring was fear. Everything around her was spinning and unreal. The Officer was being so kind and thoughtful to her. Amanda felt that she should be displaying strong emotions for him to comfort but she was unable to react. Amanda thought, "I want to go home. I want to be by myself. I have to think." She could see her house just ahead. Mrs. James opened the door as she and Officer Reed approached. The officer spoke briefly to Mrs. James, and then once again said his condolences to Amanda.

Mrs. James was like a mother hen taking care of Amanda. Amanda was put to bed with a cup of hot tea. "Mrs. James, thank you for coming."

"Ms. Amanda, drink your tea, and try to rest. If you need anything else, I will be right here. You just have to call."

"Thank you, Mrs. James." The show of kindness brought tears to Amanda's eyes. Mrs. James took this for grief. She wiped Amanda's cheek, and then quickly left the room. As the door closed, Amanda could feel emotions beginning to surface. She started to cry. She cried for herself, for her parents who died so long ago. She cried for her lost innocence, and she cried for Bruce. It was a cleansing of her soul. Amanda lamented for everyone but Bentley. When she could cry no more, she waited. Deep down she thought this is a cruel joke, and Bentley will be coming to teach me another lesson.

4

DETECTIVE MALANO PULLED OUT OF the hospital parking lot, heading for home. It had been a long day, and the weather was the last straw. The streets were beginning to ice, and visibility extended to the front of his car. Taking his foot off the gas pedal, he reached for his cigarettes and lit up. "I should really quit this nasty habit," he spoke aloud. Taking a long drag on his cigarette, he replayed the events of the day.

At first glance it was a simple hunting accident, but there was only a victim and a partner who said he didn't do it and he didn't know where his equipment was. No one on the mountain saw or heard anything, but all agree that the victim deserved what he got. The victim's widow acts like a zombie afraid of her own shadow. The only good thing about the whole day was meeting Sheriff Forbes. He didn't know they grew women like that in the mountains. He chuckled as he slipped a CD in the player. The smooth voice of Frank Sinatra filled the car. *Bentley Rogers, you were a hated man,* he thought.

Now do I look deeper into your life, and find who did this to you, or do I take the easy way out and rule it an accident? Rubbing his head, he spoke aloud. "Malano, my boy you have never done anything the easy way, so I guess we find out what made this man so hated."

Stopping for a red light, he pulled his notepad from his pocket and wrote down Sheriff Forbes' name. He had to remember to ask the Captain if he could use her on this investigation. She lived in Farmingdale and knew well of the contest. If something were to be learned from the citizens of this village, he would need local cooperation. As he waited for the light to change his thoughts drifted back to earlier in the day.

"Detective, I think we should call it a night. I don't know about you but I'm bushed," smiled the Sheriff. Closing the file, with Bentley's name on it, she opened her desk drawer and drew out a pack of cigarettes. "Do you mind if I smoke, detective?"

Malano grinned widely, "Mind, never! I have wanted a cigarette for a couple of hours now. I really hate all of this political correctness and the talk of how bad secondhand smoke is on other people. Give me the good old days when we didn't know better."

"Thank goodness that I live in a little village that is kind of stuck in the '50s. We haven't caught up about non-smoking, yet," agreed the Sheriff.

"You know, Sheriff, I was surprised to see a woman Sheriff. I mean," Malano stammered, "I don't want to get myself in hot water here or sound like a chauvinist, but most of these little villages still believe in the good ol' boys network."

The Sheriff was enjoying the pickle the detective was in. "I'll help you out of this one, detective. I think one of the reasons I was elected was because my father had been Sheriff for the past 35 years. I think it had something to do with my last name. I have always loved law enforcement, so I was happy to take over."

"Is this the biggest case you ever handled?" questioned Malano.

"I can truthfully say that I have never been involved in this kind of investigation. I don't think my dad ever had one either. The whole village is in an uproar, and this will be a major topic of conversation for years to come. Detective, let me ask you how you feel about this case? I mean do you think it was just an accident?"

Malano pondered the question before answering. "Something isn't quite right. Mr. Williams let some information out that I need to check on. I also need to bag the cigarette butts from the ashtray that was in the interrogation room. You said earlier that cigarette butts were in the area from where Mr. Williams claims the arrow was shot. He told me that he was not a smoker, or at least not allowed to smoke around his kids. Then he tells me that he has a pack in his coat pocket. We need to see if they are the same brand, and if so we can test them for DNA. I will have a better picture when the autopsy comes back. Until then I will not form an opinion. What are your feelings, Sheriff Forbes?"

"Like I said before, I have never been involved in an investigation of a death, but I did have time to observe and talk with Mr. Williams before you and your team arrived. I don't know. Something didn't seem right. That team of Rogers and Williams has been participating in the shoot for years, and the feeling was that one day one of them would not walk down from that mountain. I never spoke with Mr. Williams before today, but I have exchanged a few words with Mr. Rogers. To me he was a man that was in love with himself. The one thing he did have was a beautiful smile when he wanted to share it. I was never that impressed with the man. Mr. Williams was always laughing with the other hunters, and they all seemed to like him. My gut tells me that he didn't do it, but, as I said before, I have never been involved with a case like this. If he did do it, why not just say it was an accident? Then there is the missing equipment which makes one believe that it wasn't an accident. Mr. Williams says that he can't recall what he did with his bow, and that he never got to shoot his arrow, but we have accounted for all 76 arrows that were handed out this morning."

Malano stood and looked out the window at the storm, "I was going to ask you about the arrows. How do you know that those arrows were the one's that were handed out this morning? Do you mark them or assign a certain arrow to each hunter?"

"Yes, "replied the Sheriff, "The contest furnishes one arrow to each hunter. The brand, tips, and the feathers are all the same. Each year we change the color of the shaft. This year is a red shaft. We have been hosting this shoot for so many years that we have a storage room full of the arrows," chuckled the Sheriff.

"Who decides what color the shaft will be each year, and who registers the hunters?" interjected Malano.

The Sheriff took a drag on her cigarette before she spoke, "That would be Seth Peters. He once participated himself, but I think that age has put a stop to that. He is acting judge of the village. He volunteered to register the hunters and we gladly accepted. He has been doing it for the last 10 years."

Standing and stretching, Malano turned to the Sheriff, "Did we get a statement from Mr. Peters?"

"No, he didn't show up at the starting gate after the registration. In fact, I haven't seen him all day. That is kind of strange. You would think with all the activity around here he would have stopped by to see what happened. I will have to check on him later."

"Well, I think we're done for today. I gave instructions to have Mrs. Rogers brought to the morgue around eight. If I leave now, I should be able to just make it. I really hate this part of the job. I want to commend you on your professionalism today. You handled yourself very well. Would you like to be involved with the investigation? I know this is not usual, but this being your territory I think you will be a great help."

"I would love to be involved," smiled the Sheriff, "I hated to be left out."

Malano returned her smile, "Let me clear it with my superiors, and I'll call you on Monday. This storm is really bad, so I'm going to take off."

Malano flipped the cigarette butt out the window, as he pulled into the driveway. Mulling over events of the day, he had to agree that Bruce Williams seemed to be a likely suspect if indeed this was a homicide. The missing equipment was the confusing part of the whole thing.

Dragging his tired body out of his car, he started for the front door. Waiting for him was Rex, his golden retriever, tail wagging and voicing his objections about being left alone so long.

"Okay, I'm sorry I was gone so long. Let me close the door and make us some dinner. But first I need a beer, and I'm sure you need to have a john break." He let his dog out the back door, and headed for the fridge and a cold beer.

Sheriff Forbes tidied up her desk, turned out the lights and walked out to her car. She smiled as she thought about the compliment that the detective had given her. Jumping into her car she thought, "I can't wait to tell Dad."

The snow fell heavily, the wind whipping down the mountain sending residents and visitors behind closed doors. There was an exodus of hunters determined to put distance between themselves and the hunting accident. As the hunters reached the interstate, their car taillights combined to resemble a long strand of Christmas lights, twinkling brightly in the distance and then disappearing from sight.

Samantha had not been this excited and happy since she had been appointed Sheriff. She had to pinch herself to be sure that she was not sleeping. She talked to herself as she drove, "I must control my excitement. The detective has to talk with his superiors to see if I can be a part of his team. Those city people will probably turn him down thinking I don't have enough experience coming from this little village. On the other hand I have to keep a positive attitude, and keep this information to myself, except Dad, of course."

As these thoughts drifted through her mind, she rubbed her hand together and grinned broadly. "Come on, Sam, you have to keep your cool. There are things to get done, and this storm is going to complicate everything. One very positive thing is this storm will help keep my mind off the detective's job proposal. I have to make sure that my village is locked up tight and that everyone will come through this storm okay."

Main Street was deserted, except for a few cars that were heading towards the interstate. Samantha waved as she passed, and prayed that they arrived at their destinations safely.

Just ahead, she could see the neon sign from the Farmingdale Drug Store flashing "COLD DRINKS." Samantha chuckled, "There won't be too many takers." The lights above the drug store were still burning, "Doc Amos must be catching up on paper work. I must check on him tomorrow," thought the Sheriff, as she made a mental note. "Today must have been physically draining for him. He's not a young man anymore."

The "No Vacancy" sign, in front of Belle's Boarding House was swinging wildly in the wind. All the windows were heavily draped, and only little glimpses of light could escape through the holes in the fabric. The porch light gave off an amber beam, welcoming her boarders. "Belle is probably smiling like the Cheshire cat right about now. Many of the hunters had opted to remain at Belle's, and start home in the morning," thought Samantha.

The summer shops were closed for the season, and most of their windows were boarded up. The locals refused to think of them as a part of the community. Still it was Sheriff Forbes' duty to make sure nothing happened to the shops during the winter months.

"No one in his right mind would be out on a night like tonight," thought Samantha, "and I don't think I'm going to get out and check the doors tonight."

Mel's Mercantile was ahead and Samantha decided that she would pick up a few things and head for home. Exhaustion was beginning to set in. A nice hot bath, a glass of wine, and a cigarette were just what Doc Amos would prescribe. Well, maybe not the cigarette, but it helped her relax.

Pulling into the parking lot, it looked as if most of the residents expected the storm to last for several days and they were obtaining provisions.

Finding a parking spot, Samantha pulled the collar of her jacket up and braced herself for the cold blast of wind that she knew would greet her upon opening the door.

The snow and wind stung her face as she made her way around snowdrifts to the entrance. One of the stock boys helped Samantha open the door. The warmth and noise of cash registers and shoppers greeted her. Mel was at one of the front registers. He waved and smiled broadly calling to her, "Not a fit night out for man or beast, right Sheriff." He chuckled loudly.

"You have that right, Mel. A little busy tonight I see," called Samantha.

"Just a little, I think the whole village decided to shop tonight," Mel smiled as he continued checking groceries, "Tell your dad and granddad hello and Happy Thanksgiving."

"I sure will, Mel, and Happy Thanksgiving to you and your family." Samantha grabbed a shopping cart, and started her shopping. The aisles were crowded, and the shelves were almost empty. Maneuvering down the lanes took time, as each person

Samantha passed wanted to exchange a greeting. Samantha knew most of these people all of her life. They all shared in her pride at being elected Sheriff. It would be considered disrespectful not to exchange greetings no matter how busy or tired a person might be. Samantha did her duty as Sheriff and respectful daughter, greeted people by name, and asked about their family. There were a few newbie's, whose family lived in the village less than 50 years. For a time the population had grown with the opening of the Anderson Lumber Mill. When the mill closed, the population declined.

Two of the newbie's were an older couple named Franklin and Laverne. They moved to the area shortly after the opening of the mill. Franklin worked at the mill until he retired a few years back. Not much was known of the couple. They rarely socialized and declined to participate in village activities. Both Franklin and Laverne were and could be considered friendly, until the subject of family or children was mentioned. These subjects would immediately cause the couple's discomfort. They would excuse themselves, and retreat to the safety of their home. This bewildered the town folk, and the couple was the subject of idol gossip for many years. It was rumored that the couple had a child but the neighbors never recalled seeing any visitors. After several years, the town dismissed the rumors and accepted that Franklin and Laverne had no family to speak of. Like Seth Peters, their past would always be a mystery. Curiosity began to wane, and subjects that were more interesting took the forefront.

Franklin and Laverne looked over the selection of frozen turkeys. Finding a turkey small enough for the two of them was difficult. Samantha shared the same problem, but this year she decided to buy a bigger turkey and invite Doc Amos and Seth Peters to join her. Both men, being bachelors, usually took their Thanksgiving Dinner at Cora's, but this year the Forbes' would extend an invitation. Samantha joined Franklin and Laverne, at the cooler, and warmly greeted both of them. Startled by Samantha's sudden appearance, Laverne dropped the turkey that she had been holding. Lowering her eyes she softly said, "Hello, Sheriff." Franklin wiped his hand on his pants, and then offered it to her. "I think we are in for a rough one tonight, Sheriff," he spoke warmly.

"Yes, we are," Samantha leaned over to look at the turkeys. There was an uneasy silence. Samantha spoke without thinking, "I hope you don't have family coming for the holiday. This storm is going to put a cramp on travel, at least for the time being." As she spoke, she wished she could erase her last comment. The couple glanced at each other then politely made their exit, wishing the Sheriff and her family a Happy Thanksgiving.

As they turned down the next aisle, Samantha cursed herself under her breath for the thoughtless comment about family. Offering the couple an apology would just make the situation more awkward. Hopefully, they wouldn't hold her foolish statement against her. It was a common statement for people to ask about the family during the holidays. She made herself a mental note not to repeat that mistake again.

Finding a turkey, Samantha decided that the rest of the groceries would have to wait. She was tired, and the detective's proposal came back to mind. She was anxious to share the news with her father.

She made her way to the checkout stand, paid for her groceries, and prepared herself for the storm raging outside. Mel's youngest son offered to help her, but she graciously refused. "There is no reason for the both of us to freeze," she laughed. Waving warmly and in a loud voice, Samantha wished everyone a good night and Happy Thanksgiving, and then out the door she went.

The wind had lessened in strength, but the temperature had dropped, and the heavy snowfall made visibility almost nil. The parking lot was icy, and walking was a challenge.

Eventually, she got to her car. She picked her steps carefully, juggled her sack of groceries, and searched her pocket for the keys. She had forgotten to put her gloves on before leaving the mercantile. Her fingers were numb from the cold and the weight of the groceries. She fidgeted with the key in the door lock, and finally heard the click. As the door opened, the dome light reflected on the cars around her. A couple of cars down, she could make out the silhouette of a man trying to hold the hood of his car up.

Samantha put her groceries in the car and pulled on her gloves making her way to the stranded motorist. Visibility was so poor that Samantha was almost upon the motorist before she recognized Franklin.

"Franklin, what seems to be the problem," she called out over the wind.

Startled by her approach, Franklin almost lost his grip on the hood. "Oh, Sheriff, I didn't hear you. Sorry. I think my battery is dead. Wouldn't you know that it would pick a night like tonight to die," he spoke between clinched teeth. The man's thin coat didn't offer much warmth against the bitter cold.

"I have jumper cables in the back of the patrol car. Let me bring the car around and I can give you a jump. Now you wait in your car until I get my car in position."

"Thank you, Sheriff. I think I will take you up on that proposition." Franklin seemed relieved to get back in the car. The dome light was dim as he opened the door, but Samantha could see that Laverne was huddled in the front seat. Samantha thought to herself, "Poor old couple; they could of froze to death. I'll get them started and follow them home just to make sure they make it safely. I think I will take one more look around town to make sure no one else is stranded."

Samantha got back to her car, turned the key, and breathed a sigh of relief when it roared to life. She turned the defroster on high, and waited for the car to warm before moving, not wanting to take too much time because Franklin and Laverne were waiting in very cold temperatures. She put the car in gear, and the tires began to moan as they broke the ice holding them in place.

She pulled in front of Franklin's car, and pulled the latch to release the hood. The jumper cables were on the back seat; she grabbed them and prepared to hook up both batteries. Franklin was getting out when Samantha motioned him to stay in.

"I know how to hook them up. You stay in the car and turn the key when I give you the signal." Franklin shook his head in agreement. It didn't take long before both cars were running. Samantha once again got out and removed the cables.

"Let the battery charge for a little while. Then I will follow you home." Franklin made an effort to protest, but Samantha waved his protest aside. Waiting for the couple's car to warm she thought about all that had happened today.

This was a red-letter day in her book. The first hunting accident resulting in death in the history of the Turkey Shoot, the chance to work with a big city detective on a case, and then this terrible storm.

"I'm going to have a lot to be thankful for on Thursday. Well everything but this storm," laughed Samantha.

The car was finally warm, and Franklin slowly pulled out of the parking lot and started up the street. Samantha followed close behind. Franklin and Laverne's house was very modest, and located on the outskirts of town. If Farmingdale had a poor section of town, this would be the heart of it. When the Anderson Mill opened, they had erected houses for the workers who would be moving in. The workers were charged outrageous rent for these houses, but they were all that was available. When the mill began its layoffs, most of these houses were left vacant, except for a few, which were offered to the renters to buy. Franklin and Laverne had saved most of their life for this opportunity, and jumped at the chance to finally own their own home. You could see their pride in ownership. Franklin waved to Samantha and called out, "Thank you, Sheriff. We are okay now. Have a Happy Thanksgiving." Franklin was smiling as he waved.

Samantha had never seen him smile before, and it warmed her heart to know that she was the reason. She called out, "Happy Thanksgiving to you and Laverne. If you need anything just let me know." Both Franklin and Laverne stood for a moment at the door waving to the Sheriff. Samantha felt elated by this gesture. She knew that she had made the right choice when she decided to become a cop. She slowly drove down Main Street looking for anyone else in need. A quick tour of Mel's parking lot found it almost empty, meaning most of the residents were on their way home.

Secure in the notion that the village was safe and all her residents safely tucked in their homes, she would check on her grandfather then head for home. Samantha could feel her excitement growing again in her stomach. "Dad will be so excited. Nothing like this ever happened when he was Sheriff. I just know he'll want to be part of everything." Samantha pulled into the drive, and took a moment to gather her wits. The house looked warm and inviting. Smoke from the chimney was curling around mingling with the snow and wind. Samantha could tell that her father had shoveled the walkways, even though the snow was still falling. There was a momentary flash of anger as she thought of her father shoveling the snow in the bitter temperatures. This was pointless labor, because the snow was still falling. It was blizzard conditions outside, and Samantha paid one of the neighbors to do any physical labor around the house and yard. He was aware that he didn't have to do this, but he still insisted on exerting himself physically over Samantha's strong protests. Taking a deep breath she told herself, "I don't want to fight with Dad tonight. So much has happened and the holidays are coming. I was in a good mood earlier, and dad is not going to ruin this for me."

As she neared the door, it swung open, and there stood Norm with a look of concern.

Samantha handed the groceries to him then spoke, "Hi, Dad, there is a terrible storm raging, and some crazy person shoveled the drive and walkways. You should have called to report that person because they need help and I don't mean with the sidewalks. I mean medical help," she pointed to her head. "A sane person would not shovel a walkway in the middle of a blizzard," Samantha chided.

Norm began to smile, and started toward the kitchen to put the groceries away. "Okay, Bear, I lost my head. I thought if I cleared the walks, then tomorrow there wouldn't be as much to shovel," Norm said, speaking apologetically. Norm had always called Samantha "Bear." He said that it was because a bear could be cute and cuddly but when angered it would eat you alive. It was true of his daughter.

"Dad, you know that I get upset with you because I love you. I hired the neighbor to take care of the snow removal and the yard work in the summer, because I want you to enjoy your retirement. There is no reason for you to exert yourself. We have been over this a hundred times," Samantha said in an exasperated tone.

Norm stopped Samantha and hugged her, "Baby girl, I won't do it again. I apologize for picking up a shovel, and I swear I will never do it again."

Samantha began to smile as Norm stood in front of her holding three fingers up in a salute. She grabbed his hand and gave him a big hug, "I don't believe a word you say, but I love you Dad," she whispered. "It has been a busy day and all I want is a hot bath and a glass of wine. I'll start dinner after that, unless you are starving right now"

Norm thought for a moment then spoke, "How about one of my world famous omelets with toast and jelly?"

"That sounds wonderful, and maybe you will make some coffee?" Samantha interjected.

"You got it Bear. Now go take your bubble bath or whatever you girls do. It will be ready when you come down." Samantha poured herself a glass of wine, and then started up the stairs to run her bath smiling all the way. She had so much to tell her dad, but right now, her muscles were crying out for a hot bath.

As Samantha ran the water, she thought about Franklin and Laverne. She didn't know them very well, but somehow she felt that they had a rough lonely life. They seemed so alone and isolated, and there had to be a reason for their self-imprisonment. "I'm going to invite them over for Thanksgiving Dinner. If they refuse dinner, then I will ask them for pie and coffee. I refuse to let them be alone for this holiday. That's the least I can do. They need to know that someone cares. After all, they have been a part of this community for a very long time. I'll go over tomorrow and invite them, and that will give me a chance to check on them." That settled she laid back for a long soak.

Samantha was startled out of her daydreaming by knocking on the bathroom door. "Bear, are you okay? I have everything ready, if you're ready to join me," Norm whispered through the door.

"I'll be right down, Dad. I have some exciting news to share with you. Give me just a minute," Samantha replied.

"Okay, I'll be waiting in the kitchen."

Samantha pulled herself up, grabbed the heavy towel, and started drying off. She pulled the clip holding her hair, and the golden curls fell down her back. Leaning her head back, she drew her fingers through her tresses and shook her head. Doing this, she remembered how as a child her Mom gave her a bath and washed her hair. After her bubble bath, her Mom would put her nightgown on, comb her hair, and tell her daughter all the dreams that she envisioned for all of them. Patting her on the butt, she would tell Samantha, "Go let Daddy see his beautiful little girl." Samantha would run down the stairs pull the paper out of Norm's hand and climb on his lap.

"Smell my hair, Daddy," Samantha would say. Norm would bury his face in her soft hair and say, "Gee, your hair smells terrific."

Samantha would hug his neck, jump down from his lap, and then blow him a kiss as she started to bed.

Just as she reached the first step Norm would call out to her, "Do Farrah Fawcett for me Bear."

She would throw her head back and shake it, and then start up the stairs. Norm's laughter could be heard throughout the house. This was a nightly tradition, which Samantha cherished and remembered especially after the death of her mother. Samantha's mother died of breast cancer when she was still in college. Now it was just Samantha and her dad.

Checking herself once more in the mirror, she did a little Farrah Fawcett and joined her dad for late supper.

On her way downstairs, Samantha decided that she would try to hold the really big news until after dinner. Keeping secrets was not her strong suit, but tonight she was trying to wait for the right moment. The table was set, the coffee poured, the aroma was intoxicating. Talk was casual as they ate, both father and daughter lingered over coffee.

Norm at last broached the subject of the accident. "The whole town is buzzing about this morning's hunting accident, Bear. What exactly happened?"

"Right now we think it was just a terrible accident. We thought that it was his partner, but he swears that the arrow came from behind him. We had to call the boys from OMI to take away the body. They want to do an autopsy and conduct an investigation. All the hunters had to make statements. I don't think I've ever seen the Sheriff's office so busy. Those boys know their stuff. Dad, it was so exciting." Samantha was breathless, as she tried to get everything out at once.

Norm chuckled and patted his daughter's hand, knowing that news more exciting was to follow, "Did they let you help, Bear? Sometimes those boys are so full of themselves, and they tend to talk down to small time officials. They better treat you with respect, or old dad will have a long talk with them."

"Now, Dad, just relax. Everything was great." Unable to keep the big news to herself any longer she took a deep breath and continued in an excited voice, "In fact, the detective in charge of the investigation has asked if I might be interested in helping. Don't get too excited. He has to check with his superior first. He said that he would call me with the news. Detective Malano actually told me that he liked the way I handled myself. He said I was, let's see, how did he put it, yes, very professional. Dad, I have been so pumped all day." Samantha danced around the kitchen while Norm smiled.

"I would have never guessed you were excited," laughed Norm. "That's great! Is there really going to be an investigation, or is it pretty cut and dried?"

Samantha rubbed her chin, "Well, dad it's kind of a mystery. From the statements taken, no one saw anything. The partner of the victim doesn't know what happened to his equipment. Mr. Williams claims he never got to shoot his arrow. The most puzzling thing is that all the arrows from the shoot have been accounted for, to the last arrow. When we find his equipment, if his arrow is there, that will put the count over by one. Hopefully this storm will move on by morning, and I can conduct a search for the missing equipment."

Norm poured himself another cup of coffee and gestured with the pot toward Samantha.

"Sure I'll take another cup. I know I won't be sleeping much tonight," Samantha chuckled.

The wind was beginning to howl. "This storm is going to make the investigation harder. Evidence will be scattered everywhere, or buried under a mountain of snow," Samantha stomped her foot.

"Bear, how many times have I told you, you can't fight Mother Nature," Norm laughed as he picked up the dishes. Samantha joined him at the sink, and together they rinsed the dishes and placed them in the dishwasher. There was a silence between the two, but it was an easy silence that was shattered by the ringing of the phone.

"I'll get it," Samantha said as she handed a glass to Norm.

"Anything to get out of doing dishes," Norm said, as Samantha grabbed for the phone. Norm was unable to identify the caller from the conversation on Samantha's end. The only information that was clear was that Samantha was trying to convince someone to come for Thanksgiving dinner.

Norm furrowed his brow at the thought of someone else intruding on their dinner, but Samantha was always bringing home strays. Norm wiped the counter, and started another pot of coffee, as he waited for his daughter to finish her conversation.

Samantha smiled as she told the caller, "We'll see you at one o'clock on Thursday. No, there is no need to bring anything, and if you are still having trouble with your car, I'll send Dad to pick you up."

Norm leaned closer hearing that he was being called to service. Samantha casually hung up the phone and started to pour herself another cup of coffee.

"Dad, let's go into the living room, and sit by the fire. I have something that I would like to discuss with you."

"I thought you did, Bear," said Norm in a serious voice. "I take it by your conversation that we are going to be having guests at Thanksgiving dinner."

"I know I should have talked it over with you first, but I didn't think that you would mind. It has always been you, granddad, and me, but this year I wanted to include other people in our celebration. We have so much to be thankful for, and we should share our happiness with less fortunate people," said Samantha in a childlike voice.

Norm put his hands to his face knowing that he didn't want to hear what she was going to say.

Samantha looked at him and ignored his gesture, "Come on Daddy, listen to me."

Norm removed his hands and waited for his daughter to speak.

"Father, you know that Thursday is Thanksgiving."

Norm shook his head, but didn't speak.

"Well there are some townspeople who are not as fortunate as we are, and we should share what we have. I bought a huge turkey that the three of us could not possible eat. I have also ordered six pies from Cora's, and that is way too much for us to eat. Besides, you really don't need to be eating so much." Samantha pointed to his potbelly.

Norm took a deep breath and held it.

"Sucking in your gut will not help, Dad. I was thinking that it would be nice to have someone else over for dinner and dessert. I knew that you wouldn't mind, so I already invited them—well, some of them, anyway. I just want to make sure that you will be your charming self. This will give you a couple of days to work on your charm," chuckled Samantha.

"Funny girl. Now tell me who will be messing up my Thanksgiving dinner."

Samantha took her time waiting for the right moment. "Dad, I invited Franklin and Laverne, and I also want to ask Doc Amos and Seth Peters to dine with us on Thursday."

As she spoke these names, she ducked her head in anticipation of an outburst, but there was just silence. "Daddy, did you hear me?"

Norm shook his head in agreement.

"Well are you going to say anything?"

"Not much to say, Bear. The invitation has already been extended, and being the charming person that I am, it would not be polite to rescind the invitation now. Besides, I know when you start with Daddy that I have already lost the fight."

Norm smiled and Samantha hugged his neck. "Daddy you're the greatest."

The morning brought bright sunshine, but the temperature was bitter cold. Samantha rose early, and started breakfast. Normally she didn't go to the office on Sunday, but she needed to check the stores for damage, and to make sure the residents had weathered the storm. Samantha also wanted to drive by the accident area to see if access to the accident scene was possible. Her first priority was to check the village and make sure that the residents were okay.

Samantha grabbed the shovel and prepared to tackle the snowdrift probably blocking her car. To her surprise, the drive and walkway had been cleared. She looked around to find her benefactor, and spotted Franklin turning the corner. "What a nice man," Samantha thought.

Driving through the village, the force of the storm was visible. Huge snowdrifts transformed Main Street into alien territory. Familiar landmarks were no longer visible with the walls of snow. Business signs had been tossed helter-skelter, and a couple of the summer businesses had windows shattered. Samantha would have to call the owners and see what they wanted done. In the interim, she would have a couple of men board up the windows so no more damage could be done. Cars were blanketed under mounds of snow with only radio antennas protruding to show their location. The village was stirring, and from all accounts, everyone was okay.

Samantha drove slowly down the streets waving her greetings as neighbor began to help neighbor. "This is a great place to live," thought Samantha as she pulled into the Sheriff's station.

She was surprised to see Doc Amos' car pull in behind her. "Doc, what are you doing out so early? No one sick, I hope?"

"Couldn't sleep, Samantha. Thought I would get out and make sure that everyone made it through the storm okay. Also, I was wondering if there was anymore information about the accident."

"Come on in. I'll make some coffee, and we can talk." Samantha motioned, as she unlocked the door. Samantha turned up the heat, and grabbed the coffeepot, as Doc removed his coat. Samantha spoke as she got the coffee started, "Well, the boys from OMI took the body for autopsy to the city hospital. All the hunters involved in the shoot made statements, and that's about it."

"How was the partner? I can't remember his name," questioned Doc.

"Oh, you mean Mr. Williams?"

"That's the guy. I was afraid that he was going to have a heart attack before the end of the day. He was really huffing and puffing," laughed Doc.

"Yeah, we were a little concerned about him too, but he came through the ordeal. I just hope everyone got home okay. They were leaving at the height of the storm," stated Samantha. She poured two cups of coffee and joined Doc at the desk.

"I don't think those city boys work on Sunday, so there won't be any news today. I was going to drive by and see if I might be able to make it up the mountain and have a look around. This is the most exciting thing to happen to our little village, right Doc?"

"Sure, Samantha," Doc spoke in a distracted manner.

"Doc, are you okay?"

"I was just thinking. Did you find that other fellow's equipment?"

"No Doc, we didn't, but there was so much excitement and so many people around that we figured that someone picked it up and neglected to inform us," stated Samantha taking a cigarette from her pocket.

"I was just privy to bits and pieces of information, but the whole thing was a little strange," uttered Doc.

"The missing equipment is very strange. Did you notice something more?" questioned Samantha.

"I heard that all the arrows were accounted for. Something doesn't seem right. It's just a feeling. It's nothing that you could actually put your finger on. Just mannerisms, the man seemed more nervous than upset. I mean they had been friends and partners for a very long time and his reaction to the accident just wasn't right. I'm an old man, so don't put any weight on my gut reaction." Doc rose to leave.

"Leaving so soon, Doc?"

"Yes, I didn't get much sleep with the wind howling all night. I was worried about the townsfolk, so I had to check on them. I was curious if you had any more information. Now, I'm satisfied so I think I will take a little nap. Keep me informed, will you Samantha?"

"I will give you any information I can. You be careful driving. The storm might have moved on, but we still have to deal with the aftermath. Have a good sleep. Oh, and by the way Doc, I was hoping that you would have Thanksgiving dinner with us."

Doc smiled as he answered, "I would be delighted to have dinner with you and your family. Cora's serves the best dinners, but it just doesn't feel really special. Old Seth Peters isn't much of a conversationalist."

As Doc closed the door, the phone rang. "Sheriff's office, Sheriff Forbes speaking," the sound of her title still made her smile. "Sheriff, this is Detective Malano."

Samantha took in a quick breath. "Yes detective, what can I do for you?" "I was just calling to see how everyone came through the blizzard. I'm surprised that the phone lines are still up. I was watching the weather report on TV, and they said you got hit pretty hard."

"Yeah, we got hit hard, but we come from strong stock," chuckled Samantha.

"You would have to, to live up there. Don't get me wrong. It's beautiful in the summer, but I wouldn't want to spend a winter up there."

"Well it's nice to know that you made it home safely."

Samantha sat back in her chair and took a deep drag on her cigarette. Her hands were shaking, as she spoke and tried hard to contain her excitement. "Was it hard to give the news to Mr. Rogers' widow? That was a stupid question. Of course it was hard," babbled Samantha taking another drag on her cigarette.

"Are you having a cigarette?"

Samantha was confused by his question, "Yes, why do you ask?"

"Well, right now I'm having a cup of coffee and a cigarette, and I just wanted to know if you were doing the same."

"Yes I am. I made my morning rounds to assess the damage. There is nothing life threatening. I thought I would stop by the office and," she paused to gather her thoughts, "I really don't know why I stopped by the office." Samantha could hear the chuckle from the other end of the line and questioned, "Are you laughing at me?"

Malano quickly regained his composure. "I would never laugh at you. I filled out the paper work requesting you be assigned to the case. I put it on the Captain's desk last night. Of course, he won't be in until Monday, but it will be the first piece of business."

Samantha tried to contain her excitement, "That's great! I was thinking of driving up to the accident scene and checking to see if I could locate Mr. Williams' equipment."

"Wait just a minute, Sheriff. I think it would be best if you just waited. I'll be coming up tomorrow afternoon, if there aren't any storms moving in. While we are waiting for the results of the autopsy, I thought we could search the area, and go over the statements. I have some things to check on in the morning, but I will be leaving after that. Do you know if there are any rooms available?"

"Are you going to be staying?" smiled Samantha.

"The thought had crossed my mind. It's a long drive, and my time could be better-used collecting evidence. You do have a motel there?"

Samantha pretended to be angry, "Yes, we do have a boarding house, which is better than a motel. You might be surprised to know that we have running water and indoor plumbing."

The detective quickly apologized, "I'm sorry I didn't mean that the way it sounded. It was just that I didn't notice any lodging when I drove through. I wasn't putting your town down, really."

Samantha enjoyed having the upper hand, and she decided to let the detective stew in his own juices for a while. "I can check with Belle, and see if she has any vacancies. How long do you plan on staying?"

Malano paused for a moment, "Tomorrow I'll have to drive up there, take a couple of days to go through the statements and compare notes. Then I want to go over the accident scene again, probably need a room until Friday or Saturday."

"Aren't you forgetting about Thanksgiving? I'm sure your wife and family would be upset if you missed dinner," Samantha questioned.

"Thanksgiving?" the detective yelled. "That is what is delaying this case? Wife and family? Who told you I was married?"

Samantha stuttered, "No one told me. I just assumed."

"Well, Sheriff, you know what happens when you assume," he snickered.

"Please forgive me for jumping to conclusions," Samantha said, fearing she had offended him.

"It's okay. Being single, I don't do the holiday thing. In fact, I usually work, so the married guys can spend time with their families. It really isn't a big deal. I wouldn't expect you to work on Thursday."

"How's that?" Samantha said, silent and formulating a plan.

"Did I shock you by saying what I did about the holidays, Sheriff?"

"No, I'm sorry, just thinking. Belle goes all out for the boarders on Thanksgiving, but I would like to extend an invitation to dine with my family and me. My dad would really enjoy meeting you, and we have plenty to eat. I don't want to intrude on how you spend your holidays, but since you are in the area, and you do have to eat."

"Well, if you are sure that your family wouldn't mind and that it won't be any inconvenience, I would be happy to accept. You don't have to feel responsible for me because I'll have lots of work to do."

"Detective, it won't be any bother, and I promise not to feel responsible for you. You have to eat. I bought a huge turkey. Besides, it will keep my dad from eating too much."

"Well thank you for the invitation. I will see you tomorrow afternoon," he laughed.

Samantha hated to hang up and break the connection, but suddenly there was a click and then nothing but static. She held the phone for a moment before returning it to its cradle. She could feel her face aglow at the thought of his coming for a whole week and spending Thanksgiving Day together. Samantha shook herself, "You have to get a grip, girl. He is doing a job and he is just a friendly guy. Oh, to hell with being cautious. All my life I have been cautious. Now I'm going to live for the moment. He's not married." Samantha kept saying. She was beaming as she left the office and started for home.

As she turned onto her street, she remembered that she hadn't checked with Belle about a room. Pulling into a neighbor's drive, she made a U-turn and started back. The sun was shining brightly, and the temperature had started to rise. Samantha hadn't even noticed the change because of the elation that she felt. *I must not let Belle see my emotions. Must be professional at all times,* she told herself. She found a place to park, and entered Belle's. The place was alive with activity, as guests were leaving, and morning dishes were being cleared away. Samantha found Belle saying goodbye to one of the families.

Belle turned around and was surprised to find the Sheriff standing there. "Anything I can do for you, Sheriff?"

"Belle, I need to reserve a room starting tomorrow. He will be staying until Friday or Saturday."

Belle smiled and checked her reservation book, "You did say HE. Right Sheriff?"

"Yes, Belle, I said he."

"Out of town visitor? Maybe a boyfriend?" Belle smiled and pointed her pen at the Sheriff.

"I'm sure you heard about the hunting accident yesterday. The gentleman that will be staying is a detective that is conducting the investigation. I'm doing this as a courtesy for a fellow officer." Samantha couldn't meet Belle's eyes.

"Oh, so this is just professional courtesy on your part." Belle grinned.

"Yes it is. Now do you have a room for the detective?"

"You are in luck. I do have one room left. Will he be eating Thanksgiving Dinner with us?" questioned Belle.

"No, he will be eating with me and my family," Samantha shifted as she spoke.

Grinning like a cat, Belle opened her book, "Is that professional courtesy too?" Samantha declined to answer. Belle looked at the Sheriff then asked, "Well, I need the man's name."

"I'm sorry Belle, Detective Malano is his name."

"What no first name, just detective?" questioned Belle.

Samantha looked sheepish and said, "This is a professional relationship, so I know him only as Detective Malano."

"Girl, you better get busy and find out his first name. You can't go around calling him detective all the time especially if he is coming to Thanksgiving dinner."

Samantha smiled, and gave a big wave to Belle. Thinking to herself she said, *"I have a thousand things to do before Thursday. The silver must be polished, and I need to get the recipes out for stuffing. I will make regular and cornmeal stuffing. I have to check if I have enough wine. Men like beer, so I better lay in a supply of beer. I will also pick up some scotch and a nice brandy for after dinner. I have to buy a bigger bird too. This is going to be our best Thanksgiving ever."*

Samantha beamed as she entered her house.

5

THE SUN LAY JUST OVER the mountaintop and brought bright light to the valley below. Sunbeams formed intricate patterns on the bedroom carpet to shake Bruce away from a restless night. Bruce didn't welcome the warm rays playing on his eyelids. Not wanting to wake himself from his fitful sleep just yet, he grabbed the comforter and pulled it over his head.

This tactic didn't work, so he lay on his stomach and placed a pillow over his head. Tossing and turning around the bed, he finally gave up the fight deciding to lay still and listen to the sounds of his home and family. Everything seemed normal, and maybe yesterday was just a bad dream. It seemed so real.

Downstairs, the sounds of his family getting ready to leave for church could be heard. His son Scott couldn't locate his coat, which was normal, and his small daughter Mindy had lost her mittens. They were both calling for Mom's assistance, while Mom was trying to quiet them.

"Your father is sleeping. He had a very rough day yesterday and he needs his rest." Her words struck Bruce with such force that his hands went to his face. The accident really had happened, and Bentley was dead.

He lay back on the pillows and closed his eyes tight. Colors danced on his eyelids. Cool pastels of baby blue, pink, and then red. The tighter he closed his eyes, the darker red the color. It was the color of the blood that ran from the wound in Bentley's chest.

Bruce's eyes opened, and he sat upright in bed. His head began to ache, and he held it with both hands. His only thought was of aspirin.

Throwing back the blankets, Bruce fumbled for his slippers. He found one shoe, but the other scooted under the bed. He realized at once that his head hurt too much to bend over and retrieve.

Giving up the search, he made his way to the bathroom. The tile felt cold on his feet, as he fumbled for the light switch. Pulling the medicine cabinet open without glancing in the mirror, he found the bottle and fought with the childproof cap. Cursing the manufacturer, he tried to focus his eyes so he could align the arrows on the bottle. His hands felt swollen, and wouldn't react to his brain's commands.

In exasperation he slammed the bottle on the counter causing the top to pop off. Bruce began to laugh. He shook his head in disbelief. Taking out a handful of pills, he replaced the lid and put the bottle back on the cabinet shelf.

Bruce closed the cabinet and stood watching the water run into the glass. He was mesmerized as the glass filled and the cold water began to run down on his hand. He remained like this for some time until the acid taste of the dissolving aspirins broke the spell. Bruce drank the water, and then gently placed the glass on the counter.

Slowly, he brought his head upright and looked into the mirror. The reflected image was distorted, so Bruce wiped the mirror with his hand.

Rubbing his eyes to clear his vision, he once again peered at the image. He ran cold water again, this time filling both hands and splashing the cold liquid on his face. The cold water was invigorating. He once again filled his hands with water and splashed his face.

Leaning on the basin, he slowly looked in the mirror. The image remained the same.

The man looking back at him was not he. The image looked old and tired. His eyes were red and dark circles out lined his eyes. Bruce closed his eyes for a moment, hoping that the man in the mirror would reflect the Bruce that he had always seen. That Bruce was light hearted, friendly, happy and young. What had happened to that

Bruce? The accident and Bentley's death is what happened to that Bruce.

Leaving the bathroom, Bruce stubbed his toe and began cursing every inanimate object in the room. He normally refrained from using profanity in his home, but after yesterday, nothing would ever be normal again.

His father always lectured him that an educated man had no need for profanity, and that using it only proved to the world his ignorance. Bruce had witnessed his father in very heated arguments where the other person used profanity, and his father always quickly demonstrated his point. The other person was usually degraded by a lack of education and limited vocabulary. Bruce admired his father, and had always followed his advice. Now Bruce neither felt educated nor a gentleman, so he vented his anger the only way he felt was appropriate.

He sat on the edge of the bed hanging his head and thinking, *"What's happening to me? I feel like my world is falling apart or, at best, my life is over. I have to get a grip for Alice and the kids, if for no one else."*

Bruce raised his aching body off the bed and headed for the closet to get his robe, "Maybe a cup of coffee will help. It can't hurt," Bruce chuckled. He scanned his closet for his robe, but he couldn't find it. "I know it's here, but where." His nerves were on fire, and just rubbing his chin was painful. "I can't deal with this," Bruce screamed. "Where's my robe?" Frustrated with the search Bruce turned to leave and there on the peg hung his robe. "Of course, I always hang it there. I always hang all my clothes, just like Bentley trained me all those years ago." The thought made Bruce clinch his fists. Anger started to burn in his stomach, and his vision blurred. Bruce was unaware of how long he remained in this catatonic state.

The closing of the front door, as his family left for church, brought him back to the world of the living. As the door shut, it resounded through Bruce's brain like a jackhammer, bringing tears to his eyes. "Why do the kids insist on slamming doors? I will have to have a long talk with both of them on the proper way to shut a door."

"I need coffee and I need to calm down. I don't know what's happening, but I better get myself together before Alice and the kids return from the service."

Wiping his eyes with the back of his hand he started down the stairs to get coffee and read the Sunday paper. "I know that Bentley's death must have made the front page. I just hope they spelled my name right."

Bruce welcomed the aroma of brewed coffee and cinnamon toast. Everything appeared to be normal for a Sunday. Outside, the snow had stopped falling. Jack Frost had left beautiful snowflake designs on the windows. The large tree branches, weighed down with snow, hung low as if trying to kiss the ground. The reflection of the sun's rays on the snow appeared to scatter millions of diamond chips across the landscape—a beautiful morning, indeed, not a trace of the winter storm to mar the horizon.

Bruce poured a large mug of coffee, grabbed a couple pieces of toast, and plopped himself down in the nearest chair. The Sunday newspaper was folded in half so Bruce pushed it to one side as he situated himself. Taking a drink of coffee and a bite of toast, he was ready to read the paper.

There on the front page was a large picture of Bentley with the caption "LOCAL DOCTOR KILLED IN HUNTING ACCIDENT!"

Bruce couldn't move. He just sat and stared at Bentley's picture. Everything seemed suspended in time. The one thought that kept floating through his mind was that everything wasn't normal this Sunday morning.

He stared at the photo of Bentley, unable to focus on the print beneath the headlines. He knew that the news would make front page, but not the top headline. "Bentley was an important man in this city. Of course his death would make the headlines. After all, Bentley always had to be in the limelight," Bruce hissed through clinched teeth. Rubbing his eyes to clear his vision, he began to read the article about his friend and partner. The reporter had written a glowing revue of Bentley the man, psychiatrist, and benefactor to the underprivileged.

Bruce crumpled the paper in anger, and threw it across the kitchen. "They make him sound like a damn saint. Anyone that really knew him would refute that," Bruce yelled thinking he was alone.

The sound of Alice's voice startled him.

Bruce quickly ran his fingers through his hair, put a smile on his face, and prepared to stand and greet his wife. The idea was there, but his body would not respond. Bruce's legs felt weak and shook with the effort; his body ached and total exhaustion overwhelmed him. He slumped back in his chair.

Alice called his name softly. Not getting a response, she climbed the stairs to check their bedroom. Not finding her husband in bed, she quickly ran down the stairs and made her way to the kitchen.

Slowly opening the kitchen door, she once again called out his name. There was still no response. She opened the door wider, and found Bruce sitting at the table with a blank stare on his face.

"Bruce, Honey, are you okay?"

He looked at his wife and tears began to well in his eyes. A hopeless feeling had engulfed Bruce, and Alice knew that he needed her as he had never needed her before. Alice placed her arms around his neck and tried to comfort him.

"What's wrong, Honey?" Alice cooed. The sweet sound of her voice made Bruce feel like a child. The lump in his throat kept him from speaking. He tried to get his emotions in check, but didn't trust himself to look into Alice's concerned face. He knew that his feeling of hopelessness was exaggerated by her nearness, but he couldn't wipe away the feeling.

Bentley's death was tragic, yes. They had been friends for their entire adult life, but there was never closeness or a bond between them. Bruce felt a depression descending on him that was black and cold: he knew he had to fight this feeling, or he would lose his sanity. He began to explain to Alice about the black feeling he had been experiencing for some time. It never lasted long, but each experience with the black feeling was getting more intense. He was not the Bruce Williams everyone knew and loved when this feeling was upon him. This feeling had occurred several times over the past year, but he had been able to rally himself and carry on as if nothing was wrong.

The first time he remembered the blackness, as he called it, was after last year's Turkey Shoot. They had failed to bag their game, and Bentley had been verbally abusive all day. Evil thoughts of doing harm to Bentley had swirled through his head. As they put their equipment away, Bentley continued his tirade.

Feeling as if his head would explode, Bruce slammed down the trunk lid and yelled, "Blow it out your ass, Bentley!" Bruce had casually got into his car and drove away, leaving a stunned Bentley in his wake.

Bentley shook his head in dismay and said to no one in particular, "I can't believe that was Bruce." The incident was never mentioned between the two men. Bruce remembered the outburst and relished the feeling that energized him for weeks. This was the background to the infamous New Year's Eve Party at the country club. There were other encounters between the two men, but nothing of the magnitude of New Year's Eve.

The intensity of the black feeling, as Bruce called it, seemed to ebb after this incident until the morning of the Turkey Shoot, truth be known. Bruce had been dreading the contest as much as spending the day with Bentley, knowing that Bentley really didn't want to be partnered with him anyway. As always, however, Bentley got a sadistic pleasure out of berating, belittling, and abusing him. Bruce had been a willing victim for all these years and Bentley would not easily give up such a prize.

Driving to Farmingdale for the shoot, Bruce fought to control the black feeling. He felt that he had a handle on his emotions until pulling in next to Bentley's car and seeing the sneer on asshole's face.

Bruce tried to explain all of this to Alice, the black feeling and the headaches, but she looked at him as if he were a stranger. Alice was at a loss for words, and could only nod in agreement.

Bruce finished his explanation and hung his head low, waiting for Alice to speak.

She only uttered one question— "Did you shoot Bentley?"

Bruce slowly lifted his head, tears streaming down his face. In a hushed tone he spoke, "I really don't know."

Alice quickly began clearing the table and formulating a plan as she worked. Turning, she lifted Bruce's eyes to her and spoke in a commanding voice, "Have you told anyone about this black feeling or what happened yesterday?"

Bruce shook his head, unable to speak.

Alice continued, "Good, you will tell no one about any of this. Do you remember what you told the Sheriff?"

"Yes," said Bruce softly, "I said that I heard an arrow zip by my ear, and then I saw Bentley fall."

"You will say nothing more to anyone. I think we need to get a lawyer, just in case, but you will not tell him anymore than you told the Sheriff. We have to treat this like a terrible accident and nothing more. First, I think you need to get upstairs, shower, shave and get control of your emotions. It's okay to be saddened by your friend's death, but not devastated. After all, the whole town knows about the episode at the country club and how Bentley abused you through the years. Appearance is everything." She thought a moment then said, "Bruce, Darling, I promise I won't let anything happen to you. I'll take care of everything. You just have to do as I say. Okay?"

Bruce shook his head in agreement.

"Now, you go take a shower. I'll think about what we should do next."

Bruce was glad that Alice was taking control because he didn't feel he could think clearly. Besides, he didn't care to make the effort.

Being careful not to glance in the mirror, Bruce turned the water on and waited for it to get hot. "That was not me this morning," Bruce said as he passed the mirror. "No, no— Not me."

The shower was hot, soothing his aching head and muscles. His energy level was rising, and he was beginning to feel like himself. The mirror was steamed, but Bruce refused to wipe it as he shaved.

Finished with grooming, Bruce leaned against the counter, "Okay, I'm going to look in the mirror and the real Bruce will be looking back. Please, dear God let it be me!" Bruce pleaded it be so.

Taking the towel he wiped the glass clean and there staring back at him was the real Bruce, at last. His eyes were a little swollen and red, but the image was his. Giving a sigh of relief, he quickly dressed and rejoined Alice downstairs. She was just hanging up the phone as he entered the kitchen.

"Who was that?" Bruce asked innocently.

"My sister, she is keeping the kids today. I explained about the accident, and she agreed it was best we spend the day together— alone," Alice smiled warmly as she spoke. "You look a hundred per cent better. How are you feeling now?"

"Much better, thank you. You always know how to take care of me," Bruce smiled, "I love you, Alice."

"I know you love me, baby. Now, I have thought about it, and I think that we have to make an appearance at Amanda's house."

The words hit like a lead balloon. Bruce started to protest, but Alice put her hand to his mouth, "I know it will be hard, but we have to make an appearance just out of common courtesy. How would it look for Bentley's oldest friend not to offer his widow condolences? Besides you did nothing wrong. You were not the one that shot Bentley."

"Of course you are right, Alice. I just don't know what to say to her. What if she asks me how it happened?"

Alice spoke in a strong voice, "You will tell her exactly what you told the Sheriff. You heard an arrow zip by your ear, and saw Bentley fall. After all, that's the truth, anyway. There was nothing you could do. Do not elaborate. You don't have to. Just ask if there is anything that she might need help with, if funeral services have been arranged and where and when they will be held. That's all you have to say."

Alice took Bruce's face in her hands and kissed him gently, "I don't mean to treat you like a baby. What I'm doing is for your own good, and for the good of our family. You do understand, don't you?"

He shook his head, and then hugged her tightly, "I know you are helping me. I don't know what I would do without you. You are my rock. Right now, I'm not thinking too clearly and I need you to hit me up side the head and get me to focus. Anything you say Boss, it will be done."

Bruce stood back and saluted her. They both laughed and hugged each other walked arm in arm to the front door.

"Do you want to drive, or do you want me to?" questioned Alice. Bruce had slowed at the front door, so Alice grabbed his hand, "Okay, I'll drive but I don't want you to be a back seat driver," she laughed.

Bruce sat like a robot, and spoke in one-syllable words.

Alice tried to keep the mood light and offered encouragement to her husband. "Come on Bruce, you have to remember what we talked about this morning. Keep it sweet and simple. Offer your condolences, and don't talk about the accident unless she presses you for details. If she does press you, tell her that it was just a terrible accident and that's it. Bruce, are you listening to me?"

Bruce looked straight ahead and answered, "Yes, dear."

As they turned into the Rogers' estate, Bruce grabbed Alice's hand and squeezed. Several cars were in the driveway. Alice was relieved that there would be other people present, and Amanda would not be able to focus on just Bruce. Alice found a parking spot, said a little prayer for her family, and then got out of the car. Bruce remained in place, as previously discussed. Alice walked around, opened the door and took Bruce's arm helping him out. "Everything will be okay, Baby. Just hang on to me, and we will get through this, I promise." Bruce clung to Alice's arm not just for support, but also for the security that she offered.

As they approached the front door, it opened, and there stood Amanda. Bruce hesitated for just a moment, and then continued inside with Alice's encouragement.

Amanda looked small and frail, eyes were swollen from crying, a pale complexion. "I glanced out the window when I heard your car approach," muttered Amanda.

Alice felt sympathy for this young woman. Bruce was shocked by Amanda's appearance. Bentley would be so upset with her because she was showing emotion. Bruce had heard Bentley berate Amanda on several occasions because she dared to drop the veil and let people see that she was a real human being. Bentley always lectured that to show emotions was to weaken oneself in the eyes of another. That is, once you showed weakness, it made you vulnerable to the control of another. Amanda looked like a lost soul in need of guidance. All of Bentley's lectures had been for not. Alice briefly embraced Amanda, offering her condolences. Amanda shook hands with Bruce, clasped them tightly in a gesture of condolence. She looked into his face, and a slight smile played at the corners of her mouth. Bruce felt that he must be imagining the smile, or maybe Amanda was just happy to see him because they had known each other for so long.

Bruce pulled her close and wrapped his arms around her, whispering how sorry he was about the accident. Amanda sobbed into his chest, and Bruce held her tenderly. Alice approached, and Amanda pulled away trying to regain some control of her emotions.

Amanda looked into Bruce's eyes and said, "Thank you for coming, Bruce, and you too Alice. I know this must be hard on you, too. I apologize for being such a mess. This whole thing has been such a nightmare. I don't know what I'm doing, and everyone keeps asking me questions that I don't know the answer to. Bentley didn't tell me anything about our finances, his practice, even about this house. He took care of everything, and now everyone wants me to have the answers," she said, burying her face in her hands.

Bruce rubbed her shoulders to try and comfort her. He spoke softly, "Amanda is there anything with which I can help? Have you arranged funeral services yet?"

Amanda shook her head and tried to speak between sobs, "I don't know when they will release his body. The detective said that they would let me know. Someone from the police called this morning, and they are coming by later today to talk with me. I don't know what I can tell them about the accident, since I wasn't there. I don't know anything about our finances or any of his business associates. My head hurts so badly. I just want everyone to go home, and leave me alone for a while."

Bruce and Alice quickly stood up. "Oh, I didn't mean you two. I meant the other people. I don't know why they have come. Maybe they didn't believe the newspaper article, so they came to check for themselves. I'm afraid I was lax in asking their names and what business they had here."

As Amanda spoke, the phone rang and the maid motioned for her to take the call. Amanda turned to Alice and looked so pitiful that Alice said, "I'll see if I can handle that for you." Amanda shook Alice's hand, and remained on the sofa next to Bruce. Alice returned shortly, and said that it was the mayor offering his condolences.

"I told him that you were being taken care of, and when the funeral arrangements are made, they will be announced in the paper. He also asked about sending flowers, or if you had set up a charity to accept donations in lieu of flowers. I told him that I would find out and the information would be included with the funeral information. I hope that was okay?"

"Thank you so much, Alice. I don't think I could talk to another person."

"Amanda dear," Alice spoke in a motherly voice, "You look so tired. Why not go upstairs and get some rest. I will take care of the visitors here and anyone that might be calling. I won't make any decisions. I will just take down the information, and I will make a list for you. I'm going to send Bruce home. He didn't sleep well last night, and he needs to rest, too. I can take a taxi home later after I have arranged everything for you. Does that sound like something you would like me to do? Now, don't be polite. If you would rather someone else take care of this, I will understand."

Amanda stood and hugged Alice; "You are a godsend to me today. I'm alone here and feel so lost. I know Bentley would be so ashamed of my behavior, but he always took care of everything, and I just don't know what to do. I just need to rest for a while. If you wouldn't mind I would really appreciate it."

Amanda looked down at Bruce, "Will you be okay if Alice stays with me for a couple of hours? I know this has been hard on you. You and Bentley were friends for so long even though you had your differences."

Bruce stood and hugged Amanda, "I think you need Alice more than I do right now. I'm holding up just fine. Bentley would want us to look after you. Don't worry about it. You go upstairs and rest. Alice will get these people out of here and organize everything."

"Thank you both so much. I think I will take your advice and rest for a while."

Bruce and Alice watched as Amanda slowly climbed the stairs. They then turned to each other as Alice spoke, "You go home now. I will take care of everything here. You did wonderful, my darling. I want to be here when the police question Amanda to see what information they are looking for, so when they question you, we will know what to expect. Make sure you don't talk to anyone, and let the answering machine take all the calls. After the police visit here, I will see if Amanda needs anything else. Then I will come home. Don't worry about the kids. My sister will keep them until everything settles down. You go home now, rest and leave the worrying to me, okay?" Alice kissed Bruce as she ushered him toward the door, handing him the car keys and whispering instructions as she closed the door.

Alice turned just as one of the gentlemen approaching the house asked, "Wasn't that Bruce Williams?"

Alice replied in a controlled tone, "Yes, and I'm Mrs. Williams. May I ask why you are asking about my husband?"

The gentleman extended his hand in greeting and introduced himself; "My name is Marc Carpenter."

Alice shook his hand, and then asked, "Are you an acquaintance of the Rogers family?"

"No, Mrs. Williams, I'm a reporter with..." Alice didn't give him the chance to finish his sentence before inviting him to leave.

"But, Mrs. Williams, you haven't given me a chance to get any information. Mrs. Rogers promised me an interview when she invited me earlier."

"Mr. Carpenter, was Mrs. Rogers aware that you were a reporter?"

"I introduced myself and gave her the name of my paper. She said that she would give me an interview later."

"Mrs. Rogers has suffered a terrible tragedy and is not in her right mind right now. You talked with her under false pretenses, waiting in the shadows to get a story. Well, you can just leave now, and wait like all the other reporters until Mrs. Rogers is up to giving a statement." Alice's voice was loud, and the other gentlemen listened as she dismissed the reporter.

"Mrs. Williams, I didn't mean any harm." This was all that he could say before Alice closed the door on his face. Alice walked to the desk took out a tablet and pen and approached the other gentlemen standing in the living room.

"Okay, gentlemen, Mrs. Rogers has retired for some well needed rest. I'll take down your names, numbers, and what you need and give that information to Mrs. Rogers when she gets up. Who's first?"

Alice was like a drill instructor and no one challenged her authority. Each man gave the information needed, gathered his coat, and then quietly left the house. As the last visitor left, the maid entered the room with a tray of sandwiches and hot coffee. She was stunned to find the room empty except for Alice. Alice smiled and gestured to the empty room, "All gone," she said.

The maid returned Alice's smile and set down the tray, "Did Mrs. Rogers go upstairs?"

"Yes, she did." Alice spoke while scanning the list.

"Poor little girl," the maid cried. "She has been walking around in a fog. I didn't know how to handle those men. Mr. Rogers always told me to mind my own business and never question his guests. I always did what Mr. Rogers said and now I don't know what is expected of me. Mrs. Rogers needs someone to help her. Is there anything else you want me to do?"

Alice paced as she thought, "Mrs. Rogers needs to get some rest so I will interview anyone coming to the house. If I feel that it is really important, I will make the decision to wake her or take a message. I will answer the door, so you don't have to bother. Has Mrs. Rogers eaten anything today?"

"No, Mrs. Williams, not that I have seen."

"Maybe you could warm up some soup so when she does wake you can take it up to her." The maid smiled as she was leaving the room. "Oh, and I will answer the phone so don't bother." The maid shook her head in agreement.

Alice went upstairs to check on Amanda. On her way up the stairs, she was made aware of how sterile everything was, to a fault. No fingerprints were visible, even on the banister. Each picture was hung at a precise angle. The hall tables were laden with expensive vases, and the dollies were made of imported lace.

Alice thought to herself as she made her way to the double doors at the end of the hall, "Bentley had expensive taste. This could have been my house."

Alice opened the door just enough to peek in and she saw the sleeping form of Amanda looking like a small child curled in her parent's bed. Entering the room on tiptoes, Alice pulled the comforter up. Amanda smiled and muttered something unintelligible.

Alice pulled the door closed behind her and started down the stairs. Just then, the front door bell rang.

"I'm Detective Roberts with OMI. I need to speak with Mrs. Rogers. I just have a few questions."

Alice invited him in before she answered, "I'm Mrs. Williams, a friend of Mrs. Rogers. She is resting right now, but maybe I could help you. Did you say you were from OMI?"

"Yes, Office of Medical Investigation. We are conducting the investigation into the accident."

"Would you like some coffee or something?" Alice offered.

"Coffee would be nice Mrs. Williams. It is very cold outside," the detective replied.

"Let's go into the living room. We have a nice fire going. I will get you some coffee. Sit anywhere. I'll be right back."

Alice quickly made her way to the kitchen and requested the refreshments. The maid seemed relieved to have something to do.

Alice returned to the living room and sat opposite the detective, "Now what can I do for you?"

"Well, I really need to talk with Mrs. Rogers. Do you know how much longer she will be resting?"

Alice waited to answer until the maid had sat down the tray with the coffee and sandwiches. The detective smiled as he took the cup of coffee and a sandwich.

"She had a very rough night, and today there has been a steady stream of reporters and well wishers. I just checked on her before you came, and she is sleeping soundly. I really hate to disturb her. Are you sure there is nothing I can help you with?"

The detective sat back and sipped his coffee; "This is great coffee, and thank you so much for the sandwich. I didn't get to eat lunch yet, and I hadn't realized how hungry I was."

Alice smiled and picked up her coffee, "The whole town is buzzing about the accident. It even made headlines on the front page. Most of the calls today have been about the funeral arrangements. Mrs. Rogers needs to know when her husband's body will be released for burial. Everyone is hounding her for information about these arrangements, and she doesn't have an answer. Could you tell me when the body might be released so that services can be arranged?"

The detective put down his coffee and glanced at his watch before he spoke, "The autopsy is scheduled for tomorrow morning. Mrs. Rogers will be notified some time tomorrow about the release of the body. She can then contact the funeral home and arrange to pick up the body and set the time for the services. I don't mean to be rude, Mrs. Williams, but do you think Mrs. Rogers will be getting up anytime soon? I have another appointment this afternoon."

Alice glanced at her watch; "She was really worn out. I could give her a message if you would like. I can also take down what information you need, and she can get back with you."

The detective cleared his throat before speaking; "I really need to talk to Mrs. Rogers in person about some of this. However, there is some background information that you might be able to help me with. How long have you known Mr. and Mrs. Rogers?"

Alice shifted in her chair; "My husband is Bruce Williams, Bentley's hunting partner. They went to college together. I was introduced to Bentley through my husband, and we were acquainted before he married Amanda."

The detective took a notebook from his jacket pocket and began to write, "So you have known the Rogers for a while? Can you tell me if they had a happy marriage? I mean, Mr. Rogers is quite a few years Mrs. Rogers senior."

Alice spoke in a clear voice, "Bentley was a lot older than she was. She was his patient for several years before they married."

The detective was writing rapidly in his book, "You say that she was one of his patients before they married? From your vantage point, as a close friend, are you aware of any marital problems?"

Alice pondered the question before answering. "Bentley was a very private man and he kept his marriage very private. All I can say is that they seemed happy?"

The detective sat back in his seat and looked Alice in the eye, "Mrs. Williams do you know of anyone that might want to hurt Mr. Rogers? He was a respected man in this community, not only as a doctor, but also as a humanitarian. This man is now in the morgue, and I need to know all there is to know about him. Was he a nice man, or was that all political dressing? Did any of his friends, or even his wife, hate this man enough to kill him? Were all of his business dealings above board, or was there something underhanded? Are you ready to answer these questions for me, Mrs. Williams?"

Alice was stunned to hear these questions; "I don't know exactly what you mean, detective? My husband and I knew them socially. Yes, my husband was his hunting partner for many years, but Bruce hated attending and was going to tell Bentley that this was the last shoot for him." Alice suddenly stopped, thinking she had said too much.

The detective waited for her to continue but Alice remained silent. "Mrs. Williams did your husband and Mr. Rogers have a close friendship? You stated that Mr. Williams was going to end the hunting partnership. Did they have some kind of argument?"

Alice remained silent, folding and unfolding her arms.

"Mrs. Williams, did you hear my question?"

"Yes, detective, I heard the question," stammered Alice. "Bruce just didn't like to kill anything. That's why he was dissolving the partnership. He wasn't angry or anything like that. They had been partners for a long time, and it was getting very old, socially worn out, if you will."

The detective continued to write in his book, "Do you know if your husband had discussed this with Mr. Rogers before the accident?"

Alice bit her lip, and then spoke in an uncertain tone, "Bruce was very upset when he arrived home last night. The most I could get out of him was that he was a witness to a terrible accident involving his friend. I gave him some food and a good stiff drink and put him to bed. This morning we took our children to my sister's, and came over here to see if we could help Amanda. I sent Bruce home a while ago to get some rest, and I stayed to see if I might be of help to her. I don't know what exactly you want me to say. First, you ask me about the Rogers' marriage, and who would want to hurt Bentley? Then you imply that my husband might have fought with him before the accident. Are you trying to get me to supply you information you can use against my husband?"

"Mrs. Williams, you offered to help. I'm not trying to get you to tell me anything but the truth. If it would make you feel any better, I will come back and talk to Mrs. Rogers later. As for your husband, I left a message on your answering machine about setting up an appointment. I didn't mean to make you feel uncomfortable. If I did, please accept my apology."

Alice looked the detective straight in the eye, "I guess I overreacted. This was a terrible accident, and everyone is a little on edge. I didn't mean to imply that you were putting words in my mouth or anything. Bruce and I belonged to the same country club as the Rogers, but we didn't move in the same social circles. The only time Bruce socialized with Bentley outside the club was the Turkey Shoot. If you knew my Bruce, you would understand how he hated that shoot, but went along with Bentley because it was a tradition they had started in college. Bruce is not in great physical shape, and the contest was just getting too much for him physically. That was the reason that he was going to tell Bentley that he couldn't do it anymore.

They were the best of friends. Bruce is a very warm and loving man, and may I add a loyal friend. He knew that it would break Bentley's heart to end this tradition, and that is why Bruce has tried to keep up. I don't know what more I can tell you. Bruce loved Bentley as a brother. This has been a terrible blow to him. I mean, seeing your friend accidentally shot in front of you, and then the shooter never came forward. It has been a terrible tragedy for all of us."

The detective closed his book and stood, "Mrs. Williams, as I said before, I have another appointment. Could you just leave Mrs. Rogers a message that I will call later and set up a time to talk with her? I guess I will be seeing you again. Thank you for the coffee and the sandwich." The detective extended his hand to Alice.

Looking confused, Alice shook his hand then asked, "Detective, you said you would be seeing me again. May I ask why?"

"Well, Mrs. Williams, I will have to interview Mr. Williams."

Alice stuttered, "I thought I had answered all your questions. Why would you need to talk to Bruce? My husband already gave a statement to another detective after the shoot."

The detective started for the door, and turned to answer her question, "You have been very helpful, but I still need to know exactly what Mr. Williams saw and did the day of the accident. I left my number on your answering machine. If you would just have your husband call me."

"I will," Alice said, "and I will leave a message for Amanda. Goodbye, detective." Alice shut the door, closed her eyes and prayed she hadn't said too much.

6

AMANDA WAS RELIEVED TO SEE Bruce and Alice coming to her door. Finally, someone she knew could help her sort out why all these people were coming to her house.

The house was filled with men and women in business suits. As each arrived, they would shake her hand, offer their condolences and hand her a business card. Bruce and Alice would know what to do with these people. She needed time alone to think about what was happening. Her world was spinning out of control and she didn't know how to stop it.

The question that was burning in her soul, "Is this a joke?" In her heart, she knew that Bruce and Alice would not go along with such a cruel joke, but Amanda also knew that her husband could make people do whatever he wanted. She was happy just to have them with her and taking control.

In the back of her mind, she could still hear the officer's words, "Mrs. Rogers we need you to identify your husband's body." He said it with little feeling, and she didn't know if he was serious or just playing a part. When they met the detective at the morgue, the policemen kept looking at her for some response.

Not knowing if this was one of Bentley's jokes, she concealed her feelings, and waited for the curtain to be lifted on the viewing window. But, no, there was Bentley, lying on the metal table. His face was ashen and lifeless. He looked as if he were sleeping. Pulling back in fear, she felt as if she might faint. The officer offered her a chair. The detective's voice was far away, as he asked her if this was her husband. All she could do was nod her head. Her mind raced for control. This had to be a very elaborate joke. When she looked back to the window she waited for Bentley to sit up and point that accusing finger at her and laugh, but there wasn't any movement.

The detective arranged for her housekeeper to be brought to her house. She was glad not to be alone in that big house. Mrs. James was waiting at the door as they arrived. Amanda embraced Mrs. James, and then made her way slowly up the stairs.

She felt she was out of her body, and she was afraid. A part of her wanted the news to be true, so she could be free. The other part feared that Bentley was alive and was angry about today. She was afraid to sleep lest Bentley sneak into the room to terrorize her. He loved to scare her, and took sadistic pleasure in reducing her to a quivering mass curled in the corner. Bentley had played these terrible jokes on her many times before—

One of the most terrorizing episodes was after last year's Turkey Shoot...Amanda had waited dutifully for Bentley's return. The hour was growing late, and still Bentley had not returned or called. Growing frustrated, she decided to call the Williams' home and see if Bruce had returned. Finding the number, she dialed and waited for the phone to be answered. On the forth ring Bruce picked up and said "Hello?" Amanda panicked, and didn't know if she should question Bruce on Bentley's whereabouts.

Bruce, not hearing anyone, once again spoke, "Hello is anyone there?"

In a shaky childlike voice, Amanda blurted out, "Bruce, this is Amanda Rogers."

The edge on Bruce's voice eased, "Amanda, nice to hear your voice. At first, I thought someone was playing a crazy joke on me. We've received several calls tonight. Once we answer, they hang up.

I must admit I was getting kind of angry. Enough about that; what can I do for you?"

Still undecided, Amanda took a moment before she spoke, "Bruce you were with Bentley today at the shoot, weren't you?"

There was no hesitation in the reply, "Yes, I was. We're still partners. Why do you ask?"

Amanda stammered and then continued, "Bentley hasn't returned, and I'm worried. Did everything go okay today?"

Bruce could hear the concern in her voice and tried to ease it, "Bentley was fine. We didn't bag our turkey, so he was out of sorts. Maybe he stopped at the market to pick up a frozen bird." Bruce chuckled, trying to lighten the mood. "Listen Amanda. Bentley was fine, just upset. You know how moody he can get. He paid particular attention to my physical attributes, or the lack of them." Bruce was hiding the anger but it was apparent to Amanda.

"Bruce, I'm sorry to have bothered you. You are probably right about Bentley going somewhere to blow off steam. Please let me apologize for the way Bentley treats you."

Bruce interrupted the apology, "Amanda you have nothing to apologize for. It's my own fault for not putting Bentley in his place a long time ago. I shouldn't have said anything to you. He will be home soon, so try not to worry. If he hasn't returned in a couple of hours, let me know and we can start looking for him."

Amanda agreed, and then replied, "Please Bruce, don't tell Bentley that I called. That would make him angry. Please just forget that I ever called."

Without giving Bruce a chance to reply, Amanda severed the connection. Slamming down the phone, Amanda began to pace. Fear gripped her stomach, and she berated herself for calling Bruce.

"If Bentley was upset about the shoot, calling Bruce will make him livid. I'm so dumb. Why do I give Bentley reason to punish me," Amanda was on the verge of tears. The nerves in her neck were on fire, and she rubbed them as she paced.

The phone rang, and Amanda leaped back. Startled by the sound, she cautiously picked up the phone, "Hello?" She could hear breathing but there was no response so she once again spoke, "Hello is anyone there?" The caller remained silent.

Amanda grew angry and said, "This is not funny. If someone is there you better answer or I will hang up and let the police know that someone is playing with the phone."

The caller remained silent. Amanda was in no mood to play games, "Okay, that's it. I will not play your games anymore." Amanda was about to hang up when she heard noise and put the receiver back to her ear. In the distance could be heard a low moaning, as if someone was hurt.

Once again, she said, "Is someone there? Are you hurt? Please tell me, so I can get help. Tell me your name."

There was no response, but the moaning became louder and there was an animalistic quality to it. Amanda was losing patience with the caller, "If you are hurt tell me where you are so I can send help. If you are playing a game, it's not funny, and I refuse to play your game."

Once again, she started to hang up, when an eerie voice was heard, "Amanda, help me."

A cold chill ran down her spine, "Bentley is that you?"

Once again the eerie voice called out, "Amanda, help me."

She was growing nervous and madder by the second and her voice shook as she spoke, "Bentley, please let me know if that is you. Are you hurt? Where are you? Please Bentley speak to me."

The voice became stronger and replied, "Amanda, are you in that big house all by yourself?" Amanda froze and every nerve tingled as she waited for the voice to continue.

"Have you checked all the doors to make sure they are locked?" The voice laughed, "It's too late now, because I'm already inside."

Amanda looked around, and couldn't remember if she had checked the locks. With her worry about Bentley, she never thought to check. There was a noise in the kitchen. Amanda tried to disconnect the caller, so she could call the police, but the connection remained. She could hear laughter coming from the receiver, and she slammed down the phone. The noise from the kitchen grew louder and Amanda slumped to the floor. Fear gripped her, and the room began to spin. Amanda pulled herself into a small ball, and prayed for Bentley to come home. The noise grew louder and louder, and Amanda closed her eyes tightly rocking back and forth trying to hold on to consciousness.

Just when Amanda felt the blackness start to envelop her Bentley called out, "You are such a baby, Amanda."

She could hear Bentley's voice in the distance but the blackness offered protection, so she continued to drift. Suddenly she felt a strong grip on her arms and her body was being shaken violently. "Amanda, your not going to faint, are you?"

It was Bentley's voice and she slowly opened her eyes. He smiled, one of his wonderful smiles, and caressed her face as he spoke softly, "Amanda, it was a joke." He threw his head back and laughed.

Amanda could feel the anger rise in her as the darkness waned. Her first instinct was to lash out and she hit Bentley's chest, "You scared me. That wasn't a joke. What if I had a heart attack?"

Bentley continued to laugh, "Well, the death certificate would have read SCARED TO DEATH." He drew her close, kissing her neck and caressing her breasts.

Amanda tried to pull away. "Do you expect me to make love to you after you scared me? I don't think so."

She struggled to free herself from his embrace but he was too strong. Bentley pushed her to the floor and groped at the buttons on her blouse. Growing frustrated, he ripped the blouse and took her roughly on the cold tile of the entryway.

Bentley finished and his craving satisfied—Amanda then curled into a fetal position. She felt like her husband had violated her. Amanda was unaware of how long she remained in this position, but the cold from the tile had seeped into her bones and they ached.

She stood slowly, gathered the shreds of her clothing, and started up the stairs. It was not clear to her what hurt more, her body or her wounded ego. As she slowly opened the bedroom door, Bentley's sleeping form could be seen by the moonlight. Everything he did to her this evening seemed forgotten by him. She could still hear the eerie voice, and feel the terror. Amanda made her way to the bathroom. She was careful to close the door, so the light would not disturb Bentley's slumber.

Looking into the mirror, Amanda was shocked by her appearance. Her eyes had a wild look to them, lips swollen from the rough way Bentley had kissed her. Her blouse and bra had been ripped beyond repair and large bruises formed on her upper arms where Bentley had shaken her.

She turned on the shower, and waited for the water to warm. She brushed the tangles from her hair, and found the back of her head was sore. It must have happened when Bentley threw me down on the tiles, she thought. It occurred to her that lately the only time Bentley became aroused was after he had frightened her. Their lovemaking was becoming more infrequent and bizarre. After one of these encounters, Amanda was always left bruised and confused by Bentley's aggression.

Another such time...The holidays were here and Bentley was preoccupied with his young patients, and the many social gatherings being held in his honor. Amanda had questioned him about why she was not allowed to accompany him. Bentley busied himself with his papers and said, "You weren't invited." Amanda refused to leave stating that she wanted more of an explanation. Maddened by this interruption, Bentley threw down his papers and glared at her.

Amanda tried to smile to lighten the moment, "Are any of the other wives invited to these gatherings?"

Bentley didn't like to be questioned, and he let his exasperation show, "What concern is that of yours? I told you that you weren't invited. That should be enough for you. Do you really think that these educated people want to be around a moron like you? Do you dare to question me?"

Amanda did not dare antagonize Bentley further, "I didn't mean to question you, Bentley. It's just that I was always invited to awards banquets before, and I was wondering if maybe I had done something to upset them."

Bentley came around his desk like a wild animal and Amanda cringed in her chair. "Yes, you have offended all of them. These are people of breeding, and they are able to spot someone from the gutter a mile away. You don't know how to carry yourself, and you are constantly questioning, which is very irritating. Haven't you heard the gossip and laughing behind your back? These people think you're a clown, the way you dress and put on your make-up. You only need a big red nose, and they could introduce you center ring at the circus."

Amanda began to weep and tried to cover her ears, but Bentley was enjoying himself.

"Amanda, I have been hoping to spare you this humiliation, but you insist on questioning me."

Amanda looked at Bentley's face, and saw a sadistic smile peering down at her. She made her way from the study to the sanctuary of her greenhouse. Closing the door behind her, she collapsed to the floor in tears. The words that Bentley spoke stung her ego.

"Are people really making fun of me?" she wondered. "Have I been such a dope to think that these people have accepted me? I will never show my face at another social function without wondering what is really being said," she cried.

Christmas day was spent alone. Bentley had given the staff the day off since he was spending the day elsewhere. When Amanda woke, the house was quiet. She made her way down the stairs, hoping that Bentley would be in a good mood. To her surprise, no one was there to greet her. The tree was lit, but the only presents to adorn it were the ones she had wrapped for Bentley. Entering the kitchen, she noticed a note pinned to the coffeepot. It read: "Amanda, I am giving you this day to think about your life. Bentley."

She laughed as she threw the note in the garbage. At least today she wouldn't worry about saying or doing the wrong things. She decided to do as Bentley had suggested and use the day to dream and relax.

Amanda was sleeping lightly when Bentley returned home around midnight. He must have had a good time Christmas Day, she told herself in a whisper, because he smelled of booze. After tossing and turning for five minutes, Bentley quickly fell into a deep sleep.

The next morning, she opened her eyes and felt the pressure begin to build behind her eyes, praying he would remain asleep as she made her way off the bed. Standing next to the bed and gathering the nerve to open her eyes, she peered over and noticed the bed was empty.

Grabbing her robe she went downstairs. Mrs. James was busy making breakfast and became startled as Amanda burst through the door. "I'm sorry, I didn't mean to alarm you, Mrs. James. Good morning." She scanned the room for any sign of Bentley.

Mrs. James smiled broadly as she spoke, "Good morning, Ms. Amanda. Did you have a nice Christmas?"

Amanda was distracted and muttered, "Yes. And you?"

Mrs. James started to describe her day when Amanda butted in, "Mrs. James, have you seen Mr. Rogers this morning?"

Mrs. James was pouring a cup of coffee and stopped to answer. "Mr. Rogers was getting ready to leave as I arrived. I offered to get breakfast for him, but he declined. He did leave this envelope for you." Taking the envelope from her apron pocket, she handed it to Amanda.

Amanda took the note and started to leave when Mrs. James spoke, "Ms. Amanda, will you be wanting a big breakfast or the usual coffee and dry toast?"

Amanda stopped at the door, and turned with a smile, "Mrs. James, I think I want a big breakfast this morning. I'm going up to shower. Then I'll be ready to eat."

Climbing the stairs two at a time, Amanda felt elated that she wouldn't have to face Bentley. She waited until after eating her breakfast to read Bentley's note. Amanda's hands shook as she extracted the note from the envelope. Taking a deep breath she began to read.

The note read, "Amanda, I'm going hunting for a couple of days. I have left a list of to-dos. Make sure everything has been accomplished before my return. We are hosting several couples for New Year's Eve at the country club. Find a proper gown, so you won't cause me any embarrassment. Use your time wisely. Bentley."

The second page was the to-do list. Amanda dropped both pages on her plate, and ran up stairs to purge. She wiped her lips with the back of her hand, and smiled at her image. This is one part of me that Bentley will never control," she said smiling.

Amanda hired a make-up artist and a beautician to come to her house and help her dress for the New Year's gala. Her self-confidence was zero, and she didn't trust herself not to be an embarrassment to Bentley. Amanda had kept her gown and this regiment of beauty artists a secret, hoping to make a grand entrance. She hoped that the look in Bentley's eyes would convey that he had been wrong to call her a clown.

Early on New Year's Eve, Amanda locked herself in a spare room with her beauty entourage. She wanted to wait until the last moment to make her entrance. Bentley had a rule about not being late. He called to her several times. Amanda knew that she had to leave immediately, or Bentley would be angry. The evening would be ruined if this were to happen. Several of their guests had already arrived and had been served drinks. Since they were to take a limo to the club, Bentley had been drinking heavily since early afternoon. Amanda had begged him to go lightly on the liquor, because it was going to be a long evening. Bentley had pushed her aside and warned her to mind her own business.

"Amanda are you coming down or are we going to leave without you?" bellowed Bentley. Amanda took a deep breath, and started for the staircase. She paused at the top stair, and smiled radiantly as all eyes were focused on her. Slowly and with grace she descended the stairs as Audrey Hepburn had done in "My Fair Lady." She felt beautiful, since she held the attention of all, that is, all except Bentley. He was busy fixing another drink, and didn't acknowledge her presence. At first, she felt dejected by Bentley's action, but she was determined that tonight would be hers.

Bentley felt all eyes on him and knew he would lose respect of his friends if he didn't offer some kind of compliment to his wife. Putting down his drink, he embraced her, and then muttered a compliment. Amanda knew that he was doing this for the benefit of their guests, but she took the compliment with grace, and accepted Bentley's outstretched arm. They led the procession of partygoers to the waiting limo, and started for the club.

The country club was decorated with lights and flowers. A live band played as the guests arrived. A large table in the center of the dining area had been reserved for Bentley and his guests. Conversation stopped as Bentley and Amanda made their entrance. Amanda could hear the glowing compliments that were being made about her appearance and what a lucky man Bentley was for having such a beautiful wife. She could feel Bentley began to strut as they walked to their table. In Amanda's heart, she knew that these people were not laughing behind her back. She could feel the women's envy as she passed them. Her gown was silver lame and clung to her every curve. Amanda had to stifle a laugh, as a couple of the wives elbowed their husbands in the ribs. She wanted this feeling to go on forever. Amanda now knew how Bentley felt to be the center of attention, intoxicating like liquor that became addictive.

Dinner was announced. The lines were forming for the buffet, and Bentley rose and pulled Amanda's chair. The other gentlemen at the table did the same, and they made their way to the tables that were laden with lobster and crab and shrimp. As they neared Bruce and his wife, Alice stepped into line. Bentley rubbed his hands together and smiled at the other couples. Amanda knew that he was going to make a scene, and Bruce and Alice would be the victims.

Bentley responded as predicted and began making rude comments about there not being enough food after Bruce and Alice went through the line. Amanda could see how these sarcastic remarks were hurting Alice's feelings, yet Bruce seemed immune. Alice quickly filled her plate and left for their table. Amanda felt ashamed of her husband, and she gently touched Bruce's arm to offer an apology for Bentley's behavior. Bruce gave her a friendly smile of acknowledgment then joined his wife.

The food looked and tasted delicious, but Amanda was unable to eat, as were most of the people at their table. Bentley was becoming loud, obnoxious, and an embarrassment to everyone. Amanda was relieved when coffee and dessert were announced, and Bentley offered to get her a cup. He made his way to the coffee urn and started to speak with the mayor and several city officials.

Amanda caught her breath as she saw Bruce also rise and start for the coffee table. Bentley seemed unaware of Bruce's approach, and Amanda prayed that there wouldn't be a scene.

Bruce lingered at the table and inched his way closer to Bentley. Amanda looked at Alice and found that she too had an expectant look on her face. Something was going to happen, and neither wife could stop it.

A line was forming around the table which held the coffee urn and desserts. Bentley was engrossed in his conversation and becoming quite animated. Bruce saw his chance and stepped forward and, with a slight push, sent Bentley into the pool, taking the mayor with him.

Amanda was shocked at first. Then she started to laugh uncontrollably. Trying to regain her composure, she watched as Bruce casually walked back to his table, took his wife by the hand and started for the door. Taking a backward glance, Bruce gave Amanda a radiant smile. Unable to control her laughter, she gave Bruce a thumb's up and turned away.

Several waiters assisted Bentley and the mayor out of the pool as Amanda walked closer. Bentley raged at everyone near him then turned and saw Amanda smiling. The look that he gave her was full of hatred, and it sent a shiver down her spine. She tried to take his arm to assist him, but he refused, and slapped her hand away.

Amanda stood alone, as Bentley made his way to the door. She didn't know what to do, go after him or remain seated? Everyone was looking at her and laughing. Mustering all her dignity, she held her head high, and walked slowly to the exit. Bentley had taken the limo, so Amanda had to ask the doorman to call her a cab. She waited just inside the entrance until it arrived.

Sitting in the back of the cab, she began chewing her nails and fretting about her next encounter with Bentley. He had let her know her behavior had been unacceptable, and she would have to be punished. She fought with the idea of going to a hotel until Bentley had time to cool off. As angry as he was, it might take weeks for Bentley to forget, and she knew that he would never forgive Bruce or her.

The front door to their estate was open, but all the lights had been extinguished. The driver asked if she wanted him to wait or to check out the house before he left, but she declined. Bentley would go into such a rage if a stranger were allowed to enter the house. This was probably one of his little games and meant for her alone.

"Thank you for the offer, but I will be okay. Maybe if you just wait until I turn on some lights?" The driver was agreeable and waited until she had turned on the entry light and waved that everything was okay.

The house felt cold as she walked to each room turning on the lights and calling out Bentley's name. Their bedroom dresser drawers had been pulled out and clothes scattered everywhere.

Amanda began to tidy up the room when she heard a noise coming from one of the guestrooms. Terror gripped her stomach as she walked down the hall.

Opening the door, she turned on the lights, relieved to see the window open and the drapes whipping against the nightstand. Amanda gave a sigh of relief and quickly closed the window. Her nerves were on edge, and she decided that a glass of wine and a hot shower would relax the tension.

She poured a large glass, taking a deep drink and waited for the numbness to set in. Closing her eyes, she took another drink.

Then an upstairs noise startled her. Cautiously, she climbed the stairs and listened. There it was again. The sound was coming from the guestroom, the room that she had just checked. Amanda reached for the doorknob, and then hesitated, pulling back as if it were hot. Her hand hovered just inches from the knob. She didn't want to enter the room, but she knew that she had to for her own peace of mind.

She quickly pushed open the door, reached around for the light switch, flipped it on and stepped back to the safety of the hall. Waiting several seconds, she summoned her courage and peeked through the door.

The window was once again open, and the drapes had knocked over the vase of flowers. She scanned the room for some sign of Bentley, but the room appeared to be empty. Taking a deep breath, she walked directly to the window, closed it, and this time checked the lock. She would alert Mrs. James of the damage in the morning.

She took one more look, bent over, and peeked under the bed. This was a favorite hiding place for Bentley to jump out at her.

She scanned the corners, and decided the wind must have forced open the window. Amanda admonished herself for not paying attention to details. "The first time I must not have secured the lock. I have to learn to be more careful."

The doors could be locked from the outside, so Amanda left the room, locked the door, and put the key in her pocket. Smiling to herself, she thought, *"If Bentley is hiding in that room, he won't be able to get out until morning."*

Feeling better, she entered their bedroom with the idea of taking a hot shower and retiring to bed. There was no telling where Bentley had gone or when he would return. He was very angry about the incident, and probably went off somewhere to lick his wounded ego.

Grabbing her robe, she adjourned to the bathroom for a hot shower. As she closed the door she thought, "I have grown tired of Bentley's games. I won't give him the pleasure of seeing me scared."

Amanda loved hot showers. Nothing could be more relaxing than the feel of the hot water pulsating on her soft skin, massaging her tight muscles. Tonight she lingered under the water, washing her hair. The steam from the water, combined with the smell of the herbal shampoo and conditioner, eased her tension. The water began to cool. With reluctance, she turned off the shower, grabbed a heavy towel, and leisurely dried off. Putting on her terrycloth robe, she wrapped her hair turban style, and walked to the mirror, wiping the glass with the sleeve of her robe.

Out of the corner of her eye, she noticed that something had been written on the glass. Standing back to read the message Amanda gasped as she read the words. Written on the steamed glass were the words, "Amanda! Have you ever watched PSYCHO?"

She grabbed for the hand towel on the counter to wipe away the message, but something fell to the floor with a clatter. She looked down to see a glistening butcher knife.

Amanda began to shake all over. She was having trouble breathing. She closed her eyes, and began to take deep breaths. Hoping to calm herself, she began to chant, "I will be okay. I will be okay. It's only Bentley trying to scare me."

Taking deep breaths, Amanda began to calm down. Sitting on the bathroom floor, she thought about what was happening, and concluded that this had to be one of Bentley's jokes. "Of course he is up to one of his tricks. He wants to see me as a quivering mass of jelly. What better way to restore his self-image than to have me babbling? What a lunatic. He wants to see me scared," she thought. Her anger was growing stronger, as she planned her next move.

Amanda decided that the best revenge she could take on Bentley was to humiliate him as he had always done to her. She slowly opened the bathroom door and scanned the room. Satisfied the bedroom was safe she sat on the bed and dialed the police. There was a crackle on the line, and then a voice, "911! May I help you?"

Amanda was about to speak, when a hand clamped over her mouth. A struggled ensued and the phone was knocked from her hand, the connection to 911 broken. The assailant was masked, and spoke in a husky voice that she didn't recognize. Fighting with all her strength, Amanda was no match for the man.

He began to slap her across the face with one hand, while holding her hair in the other. Repeatedly he said, "You rich bitches need to learn some respect." Amanda could taste her blood, and it enraged her. A quick knee to the groin and her assailant rolled off her, screaming in pain. This provided a momentarily distraction to free herself from his grasp and make a dash for the door.

She cleared the bedroom and was almost at the top of the stairs when she heard the heavy footsteps just behind her. A powerful hand grabbed her by the hair, causing her to lose her balance and fall crashing to the floor.

Momentarily stunned, she fought for consciousness. She knew that this was a life and death struggle, and her only chance for survival was to reach the house alarm. All she had to do was push the button and the siren would sound throughout the house and alert the police. Amanda hoped the gardener was home. Since it was New Year's Eve, Bentley had given all the staff the evening off to celebrate. She wasn't aware of what time it was. Using her feet, she was able to push him away just long enough to reach the alarm.

She pushed it, and waited to hear the sound. Nothing happened.

There was a deadly silence, and then the sound of a deep throaty laugh. Amanda turned to see him standing, just inches from her. "Bitch, do you think I would leave the alarm connected?" he yelled and then laughed.

She stood silent, not realizing he expected an answer. Once again he spoke, "Bitch, did you hear me?"

She remained silent, staring into cold blue eyes. There was such anger in those eyes. The man grabbed her arm and led her back to the bedroom.

Slamming the door behind him, he threw her on the bed and began tearing at her robe. Amanda was in shock and could only make whimpering sounds. He tore her robe in shreds and began tying her hands and feet to the bedposts. She closed her eyes and began to pray. The man slapped her and angrily said, "Keep your eyes open, bitch. I want you to see exactly what is going to happen to you."

In a weak voice Amanda cried, "Why are you doing this to me? If you want money, I can give you money."

He slapped her hard across the face snarling out, "You rich bitches always think that everything is about money. I don't want your money. You look down your nose at me and think that I'm scum. You wouldn't dirty your hands on someone like me much less let me touch you. Well I'm in control now, and you will beg me to touch you."

Amanda's head was reeling from the last blow and the taste of blood had returned. She prayed that she lived through this ordeal. "Bentley," she thought. Hopefully he would return and save her. "Please!" she prayed, "Let Bentley return and save me."

The man turned on the lamps beside the bed. The light shone brightly in her eyes, and she squinted because of the pain in her head. He used the butcher knife to remove her panties and ran the blade up and down her body. She shivered as the cold steel touched her inner thigh. He began to disrobe, and she closed her eyes, which made him laugh.

"Do I make you sick? Does my touch revolt you?" he sneered. Amanda looked away. Grabbing her chin, he brought his face close to her and squeezed until she felt her jaw would break.

Bringing the blade of the knife to her face, he outlined her features. She pulled back.

Grabbing her hair in one hand and putting his full weight on her, he stared into her eyes. "Poor little rich bitch. I think I have you at a disadvantage," he laughed. Laying the knife on her chest, he reached his hand between her legs and started to massage. "You like that, don't you bitch. I bet your rich hubby doesn't excite you like I do. Does he?"

Amanda remained silent.

He slapped her so hard that she saw stars. "When I talk to you I expect an answer. Where are your manners? Were you raised in a barn?"

Amanda shook her head.

"That's much better. You know that you and I will have a lot of fun tonight. We are going to have our own New Year's celebration. We'll start the New Year out with a big bang," he snickered. "We don't need those uppity rich people at the country club now, do we Ms. Amanda?"

When he called her Ms. Amanda, there was a moment of recognition, a time of crossing the threshold between fantasy and a known reality. Could he have gone too far? Bentley always called her Ms. Amanda when he was punishing her. "Could this be Bentley?" thought Amanda. *Bentley could be very sadistic when doling out punishment. Had the accident at the Club earlier this evening unhinged him even more? If indeed this was Bentley, just how far is he going to take this prank?*

Amanda decided to engage the man in conversation. This would take his mind off the physical punishment that was surely coming. She had to be careful not to let him know of her suspicions. The man lay to her one side, naked except for his mask and careful not to show his body to her face. He ran the blade along her body, and lingered just above her mound. Amanda held her breath, as he placed the point of the knife on her abdomen, and balanced it with one finger.

Softly, he spoke, "I have always wondered how it felt to stab someone. I also want to know how it feels to be stabbed. I wonder if I will feel the knife piercing your organs from the front side on its way to your spine. Do you think there will be a lot of blood oozing through the hole, or will the blood stay inside your body cavity?"

Amanda couldn't speak, but shook her head.

"I also wondered if the blade will feel hot as it goes through the body. Right now, the blade is cold. I wonder when it turns hot. Have you ever thought about things like this?"

Amanda's throat was dry, but she managed to say, "No, I have never thought about things like that."

This angered him, "Are you saying that I'm sick because I have thought about this?"

"No! No!" she cried. "I don't mean that at all. I guess I have just been more concerned with other things." She hoped he didn't take that to mean an intended sarcasm.

He sneered at her, but the anger passed. "Do you love your husband, Ms. Amanda?" Again, he used Bentley's phrase.

"Yes! I love him very much."

"Liar!" he snapped.

"No! No! No!" she cried. "I love him very much. He is my life."

This seemed to calm him, and he smiled as he started to move the blade again. He pinched her nipples until she cried out in pain.

"Does your husband satisfy you? Do you cry out with pleasure when he takes you?"

Amanda felt embarrassed to answer, but she nodded in agreement. She felt her face swell from the beating and the dried blood on her nostrils and around her mouth. Amanda asked in a small voice, "Do you think I could have a drink of water?"

"Sure!" he said as he got off the bed and started out the door, "Now, don't go away," he laughed.

Bentley was the only one that knew that she had an aversion to bathroom water! She now knew that her assailant was no one else but her husband, Bentley. Presently, he returned with the glass of water and lifted her head so that she could drink.

Amanda smiled and thanked him for his kindness.

He didn't return her smile. In fact, it infuriated him. "Bitch, how many men have you been with since you got married?"

Amanda stuttered, "I have never cheated on my husband. I love him with all my heart."

"Likely story!" the masked man said, but it seemed to sooth him for the time being.

Amanda's wrists and ankles throbbed and began to swell from the restraints. She tried to shift her position to ease the pressure on her limbs.

He laughed saying, "Getting a little uncomfortable? Well, baby, you haven't known what it is like to be uncomfortable. You should try living in a shack on the wrong side of the tracks—

"My Father beat my mother and made me stand and watch. If I looked away or tried to stop him, I would be beaten. I remember when I was very young my mother was fixing dinner, peeling potatoes when my father came home drunk. You could smell the alcohol on his breath. It smelt sour, and I gagged when he leaned in close to talk to me. This made him angry, so he slapped me so hard it knocked me off my feet. My Mother stepped between us and took the beating meant for me.

"He always told me it was my fault that my mother was bleeding. If I hadn't been born, their lives would be so much better. It was because of me that he drank and then had to hit my Mother. I heard this shit everyday until I was old enough to tell him to shut the hell up. I hated him for making me feel that I had caused my mother so much pain. As time went on, I learned to hate my Mother for giving me life.

"So you see, you don't know what uncomfortable is bitch. Uncomfortable is when you haven't any power or control over your own life. You are forced to stand by and watch as someone you love takes abuse because of you. You are forced to see the rich kids enjoy life while you stand outside and watch. I swore to myself that one day I would have the power to control and I do."

Amanda wanted to reach out and comfort the man, but her restraints kept her at bay, so she spoke to him in a motherly tone; "I'm so sorry that happened to you. No child should have to be abused like that."

The intruder began to laugh, "Did you really believe all that shit I just told you! You are so stupid! None of it is true, none! My Father never beat my Mother. Their only fault was that they were poor and wanted me to follow in their footsteps. I fooled them! Left and never looked back."

Amanda stopped speaking sensing his anger growing. Terror gripped her as he raised the knife over her. She pleaded knowing that he was going to kill her, "Please, Bentley don't do this."

The saying of his name stopped him and he looked into her eyes, "So, Ms. Amanda, you know who I am."

She cried as she said, "Yes, I know it's you. I don't understand why you are doing this to me. I love you and you hurt me. Why?"

Bentley ripped the mask from his head, and revealed a distorted angry face. "I do this to you because you love me. I do this to you because you let me. You make me want to puke because you are always talking about love and children. Do you think I want you to have my children when you can't even protect yourself? You let me degrade you and hurt you and you don't have the power to stop me. What would you do if you had a child? How would you protect that child if I hit him, when you don't have the power to stop me from hitting you? You make me sick."

Amanda heard a voice in the distance calling her name. She tried to speak, but her throat was too dry. She touched her face, and felt bandages and tubes coming from her nose. Her body ached. Again, she heard the voice speaking softly calling her name. Comforting hands caressed her face, she opened her eyes, swollen from the beating, and her vision was blurred. Slowly, the image was becoming clear. Someone dressed in white. Could it be an angel? *"Why are angels always in white?"* she thought. *"Why can't they be in black...?"*

"Amanda, please wake up," the voice cooed. "You are safe now! You are in the hospital and going to be alright."

She was confused, and tried to speak, but there were tubes down her throat that made it difficult. "Don't try and speak, dear. You are safe."

Amanda managed to say, "Bentley."

The voice spoke louder. "Your husband is fine. He is the one that found you. Thank God that he came home before that maniac could do any more harm to you."

Still confused, Amanda questioned, "Harm to me? What happened?"

The voice continued, "There was an intruder in your house. You were beaten badly and stabbed. You had to have surgery to repair the damage, but you are going to be just fine. The doctors here did an excellent job and you will be okay."

Amanda struggled to speak, "Surgery, why?"

There was a moment of hesitation, "The intruder had a knife and cut you. The doctor had to perform surgery to repair the damage the intruder did to your body."

Amanda began to cry.

The voice was comforting; "You are going to be fine. You are a strong young woman. The scars will heal and won't be noticeable. You will be able to lead a normal life. You just won't be able to have children."

The last statement was like a slap in her face and she cried out in pain, "No children, why?"

The nurse tried to restrain her, "Please, Mrs. Rogers you have to lay still. The doctor saved your life with the surgery. It had to be done. The intruder sliced your ovaries and you were bleeding. If your husband hadn't returned home, you would have bled to death. You are very lucky to have such a wonderful husband."

"Did he catch the intruder?" Amanda said, barely managing the words. "Did he catch…"

"Be still now. You're lucky…"

Amanda closed her eyes and cried, "Yes, I'm very lucky."

7

DETECTIVE MALANO ROSE EARLY ON Monday with the idea that there were several things he needed to check before heading out to Farmingdale. He had requested Detective Roberts talk to Mrs. Rogers and set up an appointment with Mr. Williams. So far, he had not received information from the detective about the results of those interviews, and that disappointed him. The autopsy was scheduled for seven this morning, and he needed to check who was assigned to witness. There was also not the small matter of the Sheriff being assigned to his team.

The intercom buzzed to let him know the Captain was ready to see him.

Rubbing his sweaty hands on his pants, he prepared to do battle with the Captain, "Be professional, Sheriff Forbes knows everything about the contest and the area where it's held. She will be beneficial to this case," he said to himself. Taking a deep breath before entering, he was prepared for any objections that the Captain might present.

The Captain raised his head, smiled and motioned for the detective to sit down. Sitting back in his chair the Captain held the request in front of him. The detective felt uneasy but didn't want to be the first to speak. Several minutes passed before the Captain spoke,

"Detective, I've been looking over your request to use the Sheriff of Farmingdale as part of your investigative team. Do you really think the investigation is going to go that far? From some reports, it appears nothing more than a hunting accident. I'm not sure that it is necessary to pull the Sheriff off her community duties."

Malano took a moment before he spoke, composed his thoughts and said, "Captain, at first glance this appears to be an accident, but, and, that's a big 'but.' Something just isn't right. For instance, Mr. Rogers, the victim, was not a well-liked man. Several of the hunters, including Mr. Williams, the victim's partner, have stated this. The most puzzling part of the accident is that it appears that all the arrows used in the hunt have been accounted for, to the last arrow.

"Mr. Williams insists that he never shot his arrow, but Mr. Williams' equipment is, shall I say, missing. We questioned everyone at the accident scene about the equipment, and no one is aware what happened to his bow and the arrow that was assigned to him. When the Sheriff arrived at the accident scene, there were two sets of footprints near the body. One set of footprints appears to be that of a man, and one a smaller set that could belong to a woman, smaller shoe, lighter indentation in the soil, that kind of thing.

"When questioned, Mr. Williams swears he never went near Mr. Rogers' body until he returned with the Sheriff. We have taken molds of both sets of footprints. There are a lot of loose ends to this alleged accident.

"If in fact this wasn't an accident, I think Mr. Williams is involved in some way. The saying, 'He doth protest too much,' fits Mr. Williams and this accident."

"Detective, have you received the autopsy report yet?"

Sitting back in his chair he said, "No, the autopsy is to be performed this morning. The medical examiner doesn't work on weekends. I also need to check Mr. Rogers' records in his office to see if there is anything out of the ordinary. He was a psychiatrist, and maybe one of his patients had a grudge against him, if not Williams. Can't hurt to check."

The Captain tapped his fingers together. "There was quite a write up in the Sunday paper about the doctor. That was a pretty good picture of him and the mayor that was on the front page. I'm waiting for the mayor's office to call and inquire about the investigation. I really hate when one of these country club types gets killed. I not only have pressure from the public, but the mayor's office thinks they should be informed constantly, and then we will have the DA breathing down our necks. I don't want this to be a dragged out investigation. I'm not concerned about whose toes you have to step on, but please make sure that our respective butts are covered. It has been my experience that these rich people usually have a lot to hide, and they will flex their political muscle at every turn when it might look that their shit stinks.

"I just want you to tread softly, but don't be afraid to use the big stick."

"Do you have an agenda for the next few days? Thanksgiving Day will slow everything down this week."

The detective took out his book and began, "I have to go over the hunters' statements, and I want to check the accident scene again. Mr. Williams' equipment has to be somewhere on that mountain. The Sheriff also told me that the arrows used in the contests have different colored shafts each year, and this year is red. She said that the arrows are kept in a storage shed. The contest has been held for several years, so they have several different colors stored. I need to find out how many of the red arrows were stored, and who besides Seth Peters had access to that shed.

"I also want to get the arrow that was in Mr. Rogers from the medical examiner, and check if it is one that was used for this shoot. It is my understanding that they buy all of their arrows for the shoot from the same manufacturer, and we need to know if it is from the same dye cast. Until I get some answers to these questions, I have no comment on whether it was an accident or murder.

"As for the medical examiner saying the prints on the death arrow were too blurred for examination, I'm going to recheck that as well. Probably the ME's right."

The Captain began to write in a notebook, and then looked up, "How did the widow take the news?"

The detective scratched his head, "Kind of hard to explain. Something didn't feel right about her reaction. I have been dealing with bereavement for years, and I know that no two people react the same way. But Mrs. Rogers' reaction was a first. She was scared, I mean real scared. I don't mean that she was afraid to see her husband, but she was afraid of her husband. It was as if she was expecting him to rise up and jump at her. I know I have never seen anyone react like that."

"Expectant," chuckled the Captain, "I don't think I ever got that reaction either. Do you think she really expected him to get up?"

Thinking to himself a moment, "Yes, I think she really did, sir. How can I say it? Mrs. Rogers was almost relieved that he didn't get up. That got me thinking about their marriage and such.

"Another thing, I sent one of the detectives to the house on Sunday to interview her. I haven't spoken with Detective Roberts today to see how that went. He was also supposed to set up a time to speak with Mr. Williams. I will get with him before I leave for Farmingdale."

"Okay, detective, I've heard enough. I'll sign the request."

The Captain put his John Hancock on the request, and handed it back to Malano. Coming around the desk, the Captain extended his hand and slapped the detective on the back. "Well, if I don't see you before Thanksgiving, have a happy one, Bill."

"You, too, Captain, and wish your good family a Happy Thanksgiving for me, sir."

Malano smiled as he left the Captain's office. On the way down the hallway, he met Detective Roberts.

"I was on my way to your office, Bill. I tried to speak with Mrs. Rogers on Sunday but she was resting and Mrs. Williams refused to wake her up. I did have a chat with Mrs. Williams and she let some information out. Did you know that Mrs. Rogers was a patient of the Doctor before they got married? I also got the impression that the Williams's didn't care for the Doctor.

"As Mrs. Williams said they only socialized at public events, not as friends. I left a message, on their answering machine to set up an appointment. I also told Mrs. Williams but so far haven't heard anything. I'm going to give both Mrs. Rogers and Mr. Williams another call and set up an interview for today. I'll let you know the outcome later."

"I'm going to visit Doctor Rogers' office this morning then up to Farmingdale for the rest of the week. After the interviews, give me a call on my cell. Remember, I need you to write up what was said and don't forget to get a copy to me," ordered Malano.

"No problem, Bill."

"Thanks. By the way, did you get any vibes when talking with Mrs. Williams," Malano asked.

"She didn't want me to talk with her husband. She got upset and told me it was not necessary to speak with him, that she had given me all the information that he would and he told you and the Sheriff everything on Saturday. That kind of stuff.

"I told her I would be speaking to both Mrs. Rogers and her husband come hell or high water. We left it at that. She didn't seem too happy, if you know what I mean," said Detective Roberts.

"Let me know what develops there and if they give you any trouble about the interview. I'm going to head out now. Keep in touch. You have my cell number," Malano said as he headed down the corridor.

"Hey, Bill, what are you hoping to find at the doctor's office? I thought this was just a hunting accident?"

Malano stopped, turned to face the Detective and said, "The big picture shows a simple hunting accident. If you look beneath the picture, it's a messy puzzle. Do something for me, could you? Check if there ever was any kind of complaint of domestic abuse tied to Dr. Rogers. Mrs. Rogers gave me the impression she was scared of her husband. It might just be nothing but it can't hurt to look. I was under the impression that Dr. Rogers was a child psychiatrist, so I'm wondering how long ago Mrs. Rogers was his patient?"

Malano rubbed his chin and said, "I think this calls for a little detective work. Think I'll call Dr. Rogers' office and see if his secretary can give me some background information on the good Doctor. Maybe I can find something in his records—"

Malano gave the high sign to Roberts and returned to his office to look up the phone number to Dr. Rogers' office. The ad in the Yellow Pages said he was a psychiatrist and specialized in the treatment of children with eating disorders.

Malano dialed the number and waited for someone to pick up. On the third ring a lady's voice came on, "Good Morning, Dr. Rogers' office. How may I help you?"

"This is Detective Malano. I'm heading the investigation into the recent hunting accident."

"Good morning, Detective. I'm Mrs. Miller, Dr. Rogers' office manager. What can I do for you?"

"Mrs. Miller, I need to speak with you about the doctor. Will you be at the office the rest of the morning?"

She took a moment to gather her emotions. It was clear she had been crying. "Detective I will be here all day taking care of closing the office. I don't know what I would be able to tell you about the Doctor except about our professional relationship."

"I understand. I just need some background info. I know this is under difficult circumstances but it won't take long. I'll be right over."

Malano hung up before Mrs. Miller could voice any objections.

Mrs. Miller was on the phone when Malano arrived. He entered the office and waited until she had finished her conversation. Extending his hand, he introduced himself. She seemed uneasy with his presence but he got right to it.

"Mrs. Miller, how long have you worked for Dr. Rogers?"

Putting her hands in her lap, she slowly lifted her eyes to Malano, "About twelve years."

Malano took out his book and started writing, "I know this is hard, bringing up past memories and all. I just have a few questions and I would like to look around the Doctor's office and his files."

Mrs. Miller stood up quickly and said, "I'm afraid you will not be allowed to go into the Doctor's office and his patient files are private."

"Mrs. Miller, I don't think you understand. The Doctor is dead and I'm leading the investigation into his death. His private office will be searched and you will answer any questions I have. We can do it here or downtown. The first question I have is what are you doing in the office this morning?"

She was clearly taken aback and said, "I'm here calling other psychiatrists to take over Dr. Rogers' current patients. I was going to take their files and turn them over to the psychiatrist and then inform the patients' parents of the name and location of the new Doctor."

Malano leaned on the desk and looked straight into Mrs. Miller's eyes, "I'm afraid that is going to have to wait. You can call the patients and cancel any sessions but I have to see their files. Nothing will be leaving this office until I give the okay. Do you understand?"

"Yes," she answered in a small voice.

"I would like for you to get me a list of all the Doctor's patients and their parents' names with phone numbers. Where do you keep old records?"

Mrs. Miller gave him a questioning look and said, "Do you want all records? I mean, I know where we stored the patient's records since I have been here but before that I haven't any idea."

"The last twelve years will do for now. If you can get those for me I'm going to have a look around the office."

Mrs. Miller hesitated then asked, "I don't know if I should ask for a search warrant or if I should call Mrs. Rogers before I let you have those records or to let you into his office."

"Mrs. Miller, this is a police investigation and I have every right to seize these records and to check out his office—with or without your presence. If it would make you feel better, call Mrs. Rogers and I will make an inventory of whatever I take from the office. Now I'm going to go about my job—"

She picked up the phone and started dialing the Doctor's home number.

Malano entered the office and began browsing around the room. From the doorway, she peeked in and Malano said, "Is there a problem, Mrs. Miller."

"No, not really, it's just that the doctor was a very private man and didn't like anyone looking through his things."

In his city-best effort, Malano walked to the door and slightly eased Mrs. Miller from the office, telling her as politely as possible, "Mrs. Miller, I'm sure Dr. Rogers wouldn't mind."

He felt he needed to close the door on a reluctant Mrs. Miller who didn't voice an objection. He rubbed his hands together and started for the desk.

Didn't like anyone looking through his desk, huh, thought Malano. *Well, does that mean he had something to hide?*

He began pulling out desk drawers and scanning the contents. The bottom drawer contained some patient files with the names scratched out. He carefully placed those in a box. He pulled out the top drawer. At first, it glided gently then became stuck. Looking into the drawer, he found a pencil had lodged itself in the corner of the drawer. He tugged on the pencil but it was jammed. Moving the drawer backward he was able to fit his hand in and work loose the pencil. As the pencil dislodged so did a shelf containing a small wooden box.

Placing the box atop the desk, he tried to open it but it was locked. "Mrs. Miller, could you come in here, please?"

"Yes, Detective?" she said in a not very well hidden, indignant voice.

"Have you ever seen this box before?" he asked straightforward.

She crossed to the desk, picked it up carefully and examined the box. Gently putting it back down, she said, "No, I have not. Is there anything else?"

Malano knew he had upset her and knew too that she was not going to be free with any information or help. "Did the Doctor leave a set of keys, to the office here, I mean?"

With a crisp voice, she said, "There are two sets of keys to the office. Dr. Rogers has one and I have the other. You can see my keys if you wish. I have them in my purse. I will get them if you wish."

"Is there a key that might fit this lock?" Mrs. Miller left the room without speaking returning with her keys. "Here's the keys," she said, dropping them on top of the box."

Malano examined the ring and found that none was small enough to fit the lock. "Thank you for your help. You may return to what you were doing."

She was almost out the door when Malano said, "I need to use the phone. Do I need to Dial 9, or is it a direct line?" She left without speaking. "Snippy, snippy," Malano chuckled out loud.

Malano called the police station and asked to be connected to the Property Room. The phone rang several times before a familiar voice answered, "Properties, Sgt. Pepper."

"Sarge, Malano here."

"Hey, Detective, how the hell's it hangin'?" the Sarge said with merriment in his voice. "You married yet?"

"Peppy! Peppy! You know you married the only girl for me."

The Sarge gave a hearty laugh and said, "What can I do for you?"

"I'm heading up the investigation on the hunting accident that happened on Saturday. I'm hoping you have the contents of the victim's pockets in property. Please tell me that they have been sent over from the hospital."

"Sorry, Bill, Mrs. Rogers picked up her husband's personal belongings just a little while ago. Let me get my log and I can tell you the exact time. Rogers, Rogers, here it is, yes, she was here at 9:00 sharp. I was surprised because she looked like one of those people from the hill. You know the type not up 'til noon, a real looker," he said.

Malano tried to hide his disgust. "I would like for you to explain to me why that evidence was released before the case is closed?"

There was silence as Sgt. Pepper checked his paper work. "I guess I made a mistake, Detective. I do apologize for my error. Nothing was noted on the properties bag that the case was pending."

Malano huffed, showing his displeasure. "I guess I'll have to make a trip to the Rogers house to pick up the evidence."

"I'm sorry Detective. Didn't think much about it. My mistake. I'll note the mistake on our log to make sure this kind of error isn't repeated."

"Okay, Peppy sounds good. Tell Martha hello for me. Oh, and have a Happy Thanksgiving."

"Thanks. You, too, Bill. You know you can come and eat with us. The whole family will be there and everyone would love to see you, especially Martha."

"Thanks anyway, Peppy but I'll be out of town until Saturday. With all your family there, I'm sure you won't miss me."

"Bill, you're like one of the kids. If you find yourself free, drop by. Martha is making your favorite. Pecan Pie."

"Save a piece for me, Peppy, and I'll try and drop by when I get back."

Malano smiled as he hung up. That Peppy and Martha are great people, he told himself. Peppy will be retiring soon. I must get by and visit, real soon.

Gathering the files, he placed them in a cardboard box and scratched the words DOCTOR'S OFFICE on a label. He carefully placed the wooden box on top of the files. Mrs. Miller entered the office as he prepared to leave.

"Detective will you be removing those things from the office?" Mrs. Miller said.

Malano placed the box down and said, "Yes, Mrs. Miller, I am removing these files from the office. Do you have a problem with that?"

Mrs. Miller walked to the desk and placed her hand on the cardboard box, "I don't think you have the right to remove these things without a search warrant."

Malano had tired of the interference and said, "Mrs. Miller I have every right to remove these files."

She kept her hand on the box as if her life depended on it and said, "I will need you to sign a paper stating what files you have taken. Have you done that? I will need it for my files."

"Ask and you shall receive, Mrs. Miller. Ask and you shall receive—" From the top of the box Malano pulled a paper with all the files carefully listed.

"Does that meet with your approval?"

Removing her hand from the pile, she said with some trepidation, "Yes."

Malano leaned against her desk, "Mrs. Miller, I want you to box up all of the files that we talked about earlier. I will have someone come and get them. I also want his active files included. Do you understand?"

Resigned that she had no choice, she shook her head in agreement and said, "What do I do about the Doctor's appointments."

"You can call and cancel them but none of the files are to leave this office unless it is by an official with this investigation. Thank you for your help."

Malano smiled and left Mrs. Miller with a puzzled look on her face.

Malano placed the box in his car trunk then checked his notepad for the address to the Rogers house. Taking the interstate would be the fastest route to the High Hills Estates area. Pulling out of the parking lot Malano smiled, "Finding that hidden compartment was a real coup. The contents of that box could shed new light on the case.

Excitement began to build as he pulled off the interstate and entered the Estates area. The homes in this area could comfortably house five families instead of one. As he drove past the fenced and gated mausoleums he thought, *Is all this security to keep them safe or to keep the public safe from them? These people are so afraid of the common man that they jail themselves behind these huge walls.*

Pulling to the front gate of the Rogers estate, he announced himself at the intercom.

There was a moment of hesitation then, "I'm sorry, Mrs. Rogers is indisposed at the present time. Please call next time to arrange an appointment."

Angrily, Malano pushed the button on the intercom, "Listen, I'm the Detective investigating Dr. Rogers' death and I will talk with Mrs. Rogers now. I don't care if she is indisposed! So un-indispose her! She was perfectly fine this morning when she went to the police station. If she had the strength to do that then she has the strength to talk to me now."

The gate began to open slowly and Malano drove down the entry road to the huge curved driveway of granite marble and as close to the front door as he could get. He got out of his car and admired the expensive, imported Italian stonework, gathered his thoughts and made his way to the front steps just as the door opened and the housekeeper gave a greeting. From the scowl on her face, it was obvious she was upset. "Ms. Amanda is in bed and I'm not supposed to disturb her the rest of the day. Is there something else I can help you with, Detective?"

"No, I need to speak with Mrs. Rogers," Malano said, speaking through clinched teeth. The housekeeper started to close the door but Malano placed a hard hand against the door to stop it and said, "I realize this is a trying time for Mrs. Rogers but I'm sure she would want to talk to the police."

Mrs. James looked down at her feet then looked at the Detective; "Mrs. Williams instructions were that Ms Amanda was not to be disturbed by anyone."

Malano lost his cool. "Listen, Ma'am, I either disturb her now, here in her own home or I will have some officers take her to the police station to be disturbed, so that I may question her there. Which do you think Mrs. Williams would want you to choose?"

Mrs. James didn't speak, just started for the stairs, muttering as she climbed each step.

A voice from the top of the stairs drew the Detective's attention.

Standing on the landing was Mrs. Amanda Rogers. With a soft voice, she assured Mrs. James that it was okay.

The Detective watched as Amanda descended the stairs. She walked directly to him and extended her hand as she spoke, "Hello, Detective Malano." Her voice was enchanting and the detective was caught off guard.

Stammering but in control, he cleared his throat and said, "Mrs. Rogers, I didn't think you would remember me?" She spoke as she led him into the living room, "of course I remember you. You and the other Officer were very kind to me the night I had to identify Bentley. I meant to thank you and I apologize for that oversight."

Malano gauged Amanda's pale face and felt a tinge of sympathy for this young woman, "You've obviously been through a terrible shock. Please, there is no need for an apology. It's all part of my job." After saying this, he realized how cold it sounded and covered with, "Mrs. Rogers, I understand you made a trip to the police station to retrieve your husband's personal belongings."

Amanda motioned for him to be seated and took the chair opposite him. Biting her nails, she said, "Yes, Alice told me that I should get them as soon as possible because they might get lost. I called the hospital and they told me that his things had been sent to the Property Room at the police station. Did I do anything wrong?"

Taking the notebook from his pocket, he began to write words only he understood, "No, you didn't do anything wrong. The hospital and the Property Room were in violation. We need those things, just until the investigation is finished. I will write you a receipt for the contents of the bag. As soon as the case is closed, and I mean just as soon, your husband's belongings will be returned to you. If you could just give me the bag."

Amanda was reluctant, and Malano picked up on that right away. Waiting several moments without any words said between the two, the Detective said, "Mrs. Rogers, nothing will happen to your husband's belongings. You must return the evidence immediately."

Amanda remained in her chair, did not move, and said nothing.

Malano spoke with more authority, "Mrs. Rogers I must insist that you return those things. I would hate to have to charge you with obstruction." He often used this method to persuade reluctant witnesses. Hearing the tone of his voice, Amanda rose slowly and left the room, returning straightway with the bag.

She unexpectedly said, "I opened the bag. I just wanted to see what he had in his pockets. That was all. I put everything back."

Taking the bag, Malano turned it upside down, emptied the contents on the coffee table, and began to list each item. Counting the money in Bentley's wallet, he listed the amount. After everything was returned to the bag, he signed the list, dated it and passed it to Amanda. "A receipt for everything. I have put a case number on the list and the same number is on this bag." He showed her the number.

Slapping his knees and looking forward to leaving, he said, "I'll be going now. Is there anything you would like to ask me?"

Amanda stammered, cleared her throat then spoke with a strong voice, "When will Bentley's body be released?"

Amanda's hands trembled and he reached over to comfort her and said, "An Officer will be in touch with you some time today."

He said nothing else and rose to leave.

Amanda walked him to the door and lingered as he drove away.

One question kept repeating in his mind, "Why was she so reluctant to turn over her husband's belongings. Is she really this innocent and sweet or is this an act? I've dealt with these 'High Society' types before and something doesn't feel quite right about her."

Once at the station, Malano made his way to the Property Room. Sergeant Pepper was out to lunch so he left instructions that nothing pertaining to the Rogers case was to be released to anyone. Taking care of that problem, he returned to his office and emptied the contents on his desk. This time he would be able to inspect the evidence without the wife looking on.

Sorting through the things, he found two key rings. There were several pictures of children. He removed them from the protective plastic. The name of the child and a year was written on the back of each picture. The last picture was of a beautiful young girl, on the back the words, Amanda Walker. Taking a closer look, he spotted the resemblance to the young wife. Both pictures showed the same blank eyes, the smile at least rehearsed. Strange the doctor kept the child's picture but none of the wife, he told himself.

He carefully replaced all the pictures then recounted the money. As he replaced the money, a small tip of paper could be seen under the leather flap. Lifting the flap, he pulled the paper free. On it was scribbled a series of numbers. The numbers didn't make any sense so he replaced it in the bag. He extracted the keys to Bentley's car, from the key ring and placed them on a second key ring with the case number on it.

Sitting back in his chair, he took out a cigarette and lit it quickly. Smoking always helped him think. "Mrs. Rogers and the secretary are hiding something," he said out loud. "It's as if they are trying to protect the damned Doctor. Protect him from what? Or are they trying to protect themselves? Was the doctor having an affair with the secretary? No way! His wife's too beautiful. Mrs. Rogers was scared to death when she was viewing her husband's body."

The phone rang and Malano picked it up. "Bill, this is Brian. I'm glad I caught you before you left town. I have some news on the Rogers case. I didn't find any record of abuse but the Rogers house was broken into on New Year's and Mrs. Rogers was stabbed. The report on file is not real clear but apparently, the husband reported the break in and drove his wife to the hospital. That was it for the report."

"Who took the report?" Malano said. "Ah, Officer Reed," was the reply.

"Can you bring that to my office?" Malano said.

"Be right there."

Detective Roberts dropped the file on Malano's desk then flopped in the side chair. Malano slowly opened the file to find pictures of Amanda's battered body. It was hard to see the face with all the swelling and the blood. From the looks of the wounds, she was lucky to be alive.

"Where was her husband while all this was happening?"

Reaching over and pulling out the report, Brian read, "Dr. Rogers called at 5:45AM to report that his wife had confronted an intruder and was injured in the process.

"Injured, bullshit! She was beaten and stabbed! I think that's a little more than injured. Glancing back at the first page he asked, "Was 911 called?"

"Supposedly, Dr. Rogers called the station directly then informed the Officer that he would call the hospital himself because he was a doctor," Brian said, pausing to think a moment. "But that doesn't make sense. First, he is a psychiatrist not a medical doctor. Second, you find your wife beaten, bloody, and possibly raped and you take the time to look up the number to the police station and inform them that you will call the hospital and take her yourself. Why then did he even bother to call the police? The doctor was questioned and stated that they had attended a New Year's Eve Party at the Country Club, earlier in the evening but he knew nothing of the attack. He was with the Mayor at the time this incident occurred. Mrs. Rogers states that the intruder was masked so she couldn't identify him. The report ends there."

Brian waited to gauge Malano's reaction. Malano sat up straight and said, almost gagging, "That's it!"

"That's it, Bill," Brian said.

"Were any statements taken? When did the couple leave the party? Was the house checked for prints? Where is the emergency medical report? A first year rookie would have done a better job filling out this report. Major evidence is missing or never taken."

Malano angrily threw the report back down on his desk. Walking around the desk he stopped and checked the report again, "Reed is not a rookie. How could he botch this report? He is a good officer. We need to talk to him and find out what happened."

"I'm a step ahead of you, Bill. When I read this report, I wanted to talk to him. He's on vacation 'til next Monday."

"I want to talk to him the minute he gets back," Malano said. "You got it, Boss!" Brian waved as he left the office.

Malano grabbed his Rolodex and began thumbing his way through, looking for the number to the hospital. Thinking out loud, "Mrs. Rogers had to be taken to St. Francis Hospital because that was the closest to their home."

He punched in the number then waited to be connected. "St. Francis Hospital, how may I direct your call?"

"This is Detective Malano with the Metro Police. I need to speak to your Records Department."

"Just one moment, sir, while I connect your call."

"Medical Records, this is Julie. How may I help you?" The voice sounded jovial.

"This is Detective Malano, Metro Police—"

"Yes, Detective, how may I help you this morning?"

"Well, Julie, I need to know if you have medical records on Amanda Rogers. She was taken to emergency on the morning of January 1. According to our police report she was beaten and stabbed, possibly raped, but I don't know if surgery was required."

"Can you hold for just a moment, Detective, while I look up those records?"

"Sure thing."

The line went silent. Tapping his fingers on the desk, he took out a cigarette as Julie returned to the line.

"Detective Malano, I'm sorry, sir, but there isn't any records on Amanda Rogers. You do spell the last name ROGERS, correct?"

"Yes, that is the correct spelling. Are you sure, no one was admitted to emergency on January 1 with that name? Try Bentley Rogers."

"One moment please—"

He lit his cigarette and waited.

"Detective, I also tried Bentley Rogers and there isn't a file. Is there anything else I can do for you?"

"You gotta be kiddin' me!" he told himself. The detective was silent while he looked for the number of Memorial Hospital.

"Detective, is there anything else?"

"I'm sorry, Julie. No there is nothing else. Thank you for your time."

"I can't believe that the doctor would have taken her to Memorial that's across town—" he said out loud.

Malano punched in the number and waited for the mechanical voice.

"Good morning, Memorial Hospital. How may I direct your call?"

He once again gave his information and waited for Records to pick up. This voice was not as jovial as Julie's. "Records, this is Jane. How may I help you?"

Malano gave her the information and waited for the records to be called up. Jane returned to the line, "Detective Malano, I have the records for Amanda Rogers." He slammed his fist against the desk for being wrong.

"I need a copy of those records." There was hesitation then the words, "I'm sorry, Detective, but those records have been sealed."

Malano was infuriated as he inquired, "What do you mean the records are sealed?"

"Sir, that means we are not allowed to give out information on this patient."

"Jane, I'm not just anyone. I'm a Detective with the Metro Police. I need that report for a case under investigation."

"Sir, when a report is sealed that means no one is allowed to view the record, not even the medical staff. I could loose my job if I turned this report over to you," her voice had a slight edge.

"We'll just see if a court order will free up those records."

"That would be the only way for this office to officially release these records to you."

"I will get that court order and be right over to pick up the records."

"Fine, sir."

He called the Captain and explained the situation.

"I'll call the judge right now and you can pick it up."

"Thanks, Captain."

Malano gathered Officer Reed's accident report and placed it in an envelope. Placing the personal effects back in the bag, he took the keys to Bentley's car and placed them in plain view with a note to Detective Roberts. Checking his notebook one more time to make sure he hadn't forgotten anything, he picked up the evidence and started for the door. The courthouse and judge's chambers were in the building next door. Stopping by his car on the walk to the courthouse, he placed the evidence in the trunk then made his way to the third floor.

The judge's personal secretary was placing files in a cabinet when Malano called her name and she turned and greeted him with a large smile.

"Hello, Bill, how are you today?"

"I'm fine, Beverly, how are you and your little boy?"

"Fine, growing way too fast for me. I would love to keep him a baby but he has a mind of his own," she said, laughing and starting for her desk. Beverly's husband had been a police officer, killed in the line of duty. After her husband's death, she began working for the judge and started taking classes to become a lawyer.

"How are the classes going?" he said.

"Fine, I suppose. Trying to study for finals. I will be graduating in May and taking the bar next August."

"Wow! That's fantastic! Then you will become a rich lawyer and forget all your old cop buddies," he said smiling.

"I would never forget my cop buddies. I do think I could get used to the good life though. Well enough of this, what can I do for you, Bill?"

"The Captain called the judge about getting a court order to release some medical records."

Beverly walked to her organized desk and picked up an envelope then handed it to Malano.

"I think this is what you came for."

"Thanks. I've really got to run."

"You always seem to be running somewhere," she chuckled. At the door, he stopped and said, "Beverly, Happy Thanksgiving."

"Happy Thanksgiving to you too, Bill," she said, and out the door, he went.

He drove directly to Memorial Hospital and took the elevator to the basement. "Why do they always put Records and the morgue in the basement," he thought to himself. Just ahead was the office clearly marked MEDICAL RECORDS. Entering, he found it empty. He called out in the hope someone, anyone, was there in some distant aisle, perhaps even in the restroom.

In the distance came Jane's voice, "Just a minute—"

Malano took the chair nearest the desk and waited for Jane to return. While waiting he tried to picture what she looked like, "Probably in her late thirties, hair pulled straight back, overweight and doesn't wear make-up." What a surprise. The door to the storage room opened and out stepped a lady in her late twenties, jet-black hair, professionally dressed and in great physical shape.

Malano stood up as she entered, extended his hand and introduced himself.

"Nice to meet you, Detective. I'm Jane. We spoke earlier about the Amanda Rogers medical records."

Malano was taken completely off guard, "Yes, we did." Jane daintily stepped behind her desk, sat down and waited for the Detective to continue.

"I have a court order."

She took the paper from him and carefully examined the document.

"Now may I have the medical records?"

"Yes, Detective. It will take a few minutes to make a copy for you," she said, her smile radiant but with a voice that didn't fit her body.

Malano took his chair and said, "I don't mind waiting."

Jane got up and made her way to the back room. He couldn't believe that he had misjudged her voice so completely.

A long fifteen minutes went by, and upon her return, she handed Malano a large envelope. On the front was written Amanda Rogers.

Taking the envelope, he started to leave.

"Just a minute, Detective. I need you to sign the log that says you received the records."

He signed off in a genuine way and, a pleasant smile on his face, said, "Thanks for your help, Jane."

"Anytime, Detective."

He glanced at his watch. Already past 2:00 O'clock. Everything was taking so long. He pulled out his cell phone and dialed the Sheriff.

"Sheriff Forbes here."

"Sheriff—"

"Detective, did you get lost? I've been waiting for you." The way she said, "waiting for you," was like music to his ears.

"Gathering all this information has taken longer than I expected. I do have some good news. Do you want to hear it now or wait 'til I get there?"

"Did the Captain approve your request?"

"Just a minute, Sheriff, should I take your question to mean you want the news now?"

"Please— I'm all ears. I've been on pins and needles all day wondering."

"You know, I'm a little hurt that all you're interested in is if the Captain approved my request! I think I'll let you wait," he said, teasing a bit.

"No! I am very interested in everything about the case and can't wait to see you but please tell me your good news."

Laughing, his point made, Malano said, "Okay, my request was approved."

The phone dropped and Malano could hear her screaming,"Yes! Yes!"

Retrieving the phone, she picked up the handset and said, "Detective, are you still there? Sorry about that. Did I break your eardrum?

Malano remained silent.

"Detective, are you there?" she said.

"Yes—I'm here. My hearing will never be the same, though. But, yeah, I'm here."

"I'm so sorry. I promise by the time you get here I'll have my excitement under control and all you will see is a real professional."

"Just kidding, Sheriff. You have every right to be excited. This could be a big boost to your career.

"I have also uncovered some evidence that I'm excited about. That's what's taken so long.

"I'll tell you all about it when I get there. Be ready to work. I'm leaving soon. Just have to gas up my car. I should be there in about an hour."

"Drive careful. I'll put on a pot of coffee and I'm ready to work."

Malano smiled as he hung up the phone.

8

LATER THAT AFTERNOON AND STILL in a fog as to how things fit together, Malano pulled into the Sheriff's station. The long trip to Farmingdale had given him time to think about the new information gathered that day. All incidents had to be explained to get to the bottom of what really happened, events tied to the accident, and it was his job to find answers to the puzzle.

Malano popped the trunk. Looking up, he saw the Sheriff coming out of the station, a smile on her face. At first sight, his breath caught in his chest. He thought to himself, "Get a grip old man. You have a murder to prove." Putting on his professional face, he forced himself to turn away and started to retrieve some items.

Malano was in control of his emotions when the Sheriff reached the car and he gruffly said, "Sheriff, good to see you again. Grab some stuff and let's get this inside and organized."

The Sheriff's smile faded, "Well, good to see you, too, I guess—" She grabbed a box and followed Malano into the station.

Malano looked around for a suitable place to set up. Turning about, he asked, "We need to set up some tables, so that we can sort out everything. Any suggestions?"

The Sheriff set her box down and motioned to the deputy, "Go into the back room and bring out four of the folding tables. Set them up along the wall."

The deputy retreated to the back room and she turned to Malano, "We can set up the tables along this back wall. Will that be suitable to you?"

Malano set down his box on the nearest desk, "That will do for now. Let's get the rest of the stuff out of my car."

The Sheriff followed him and said nothing. They emptied the trunk in silence.

Malano grabbed a box and put it on the first table. The Sheriff stood back, and waited for him to give her instructions.

He stopped unpacking the statements, and turned to her, "I'm sorry I've been so abrupt. The information I found out this morning has been nagging at me all the way up here. Let's have a cup of coffee and a cigarette, and I can fill you in on what I have discovered."

The Sheriff nodded and headed for the coffee. Malano sat at a desk near the Sheriff's desk and pulled out his cigarettes. She returned handing him a cup of hot coffee and sat down.

"Do you have any cream?" smiled Malano.

The Sheriff refused to return his smile, and motioned toward the coffee urn, "There's cream and sugar by the coffee pot. Feel free to get what you need."

Malano took a couple packets of cream and began emptying them in his cup. With a sly smile he said, "I don't need any sugar. I'm sweet enough."

The Sheriff smiled and relaxed a little as she took out her cigarettes.

Malano rubbed his hands together, "Now I want to fill you in on the information that I received this morning. I went to Dr. Rogers' office this morning, and I got my first glimpse of the real man. The secretary was not very helpful, kept insisting that the doctor was a very private man, and wouldn't like me going through his things. I had to keep telling her that the doctor was dead and at this point wouldn't care who touched his things. I was looking in his desk when I came across a secret compartment that contained this box."

Malano went to one of the big boxes, and brought out the small wooden box. Pulling keys from his pocket, he began searching for the key to open the box. None of the keys on the ring fit.

He turned to the Sheriff, "Can you bring me that box that is labeled Doctor's Office?"

"Sure," she eagerly retrieved the box and set it down on the desk where he was seated. Returning to her desk, she waited for him to continue.

Malano sat motionless, staring into space. Not wanting to interrupt his thinking, she just sat waiting and watching the detective.

Several moments passed before he spoke, "I was just thinking about Dr. Rogers. This is just a feeling, but his secretary and his wife are hiding something. When Mrs. Rogers was called to identify her husband's body, she was afraid. I don't think the reason was the finality of his death. It was as if she expected him to jump up and scare her. This morning, I found out that she had been attacked in her home on New Year's Eve. Her husband called the station to report the attack, refusing to have an ambulance called and took her to a hospital across town. The funny part of all that is they have a hospital maybe only ten minutes from their home. He took her across town to Memorial, which is maybe a thirty-minute drive—and that's if you hit all the lights right and do sixty in the 45 mph zones. That's not all."

Malano walked over to the table, brought back Amanda Rogers' hospital records, and placed them on the desk. "I picked up these records this morning, but first I had to get a court order, because they had been sealed. I haven't looked at these records yet, but I have looked at the police report that was filed. Take a look at Amanda Rogers after the attack."

He handed the Sheriff the pictures from the report. She gasped as she looked at the ravaged body of the victim.

Malano held up a finger before she could speak, "The police report that was filed was not complete. An investigation was never conducted into the attack. The whole thing has the smell of a cover up. The officer that conducted the so-called investigation is a good cop." He stopped speaking and appeared to be deep in thought.

Taking this time, she looked over the police report and scanned the pictures once again. Feeling the detective's gaze, she looked up to catch him smiling at her.

"What's wrong? Am I doing something funny?"

"No, you are not doing anything wrong. You just had such an intent look upon your face. Did you know that?" chuckled Malano.

He stopped himself, "Never mind. Let's see what these medical records have to say about this attack." The Sheriff moved her chair closer to his desk. They looked at the medical records, and were puzzled by some of the notations. It stated that Amanda Rogers was treated for minor cuts and bruises. Looking at the police pictures, these cuts were not minor. There was not a record of the rape. The last page had them do a double take. There in bold letters was stated that a complete hysterectomy was done on Amanda Rogers. The doctor of record was Dr. Powell.

Malano and the Sheriff said nothing both trying to digest what they had just read.

The Sheriff was the first to speak. "Do you know the name of Mrs. Rogers's primary doctor? It would be interesting to know if she was having medical problems before the attack. The name, Powell, rings a bell, but I can't recall why."

Malano picked up the phone and dialed Detective Roberts. "Detective Roberts here, how may I help you?"

"Brian, Bill here. I have a couple of things that I need for you to check for me and I need it immediately."

"Sure Bill, what's up?"

"I just went over the medical record on Amanda Rogers. It states that she was treated for minor cuts and bruises. The big thing is that a complete hysterectomy was performed on her, even though she had just been a victim of a brutal attack. The police report stated that she had been stabbed several times. The medical record makes no mention of the stab wounds being treated, or if this is the reason that a hysterectomy had to be performed. I need you to find out who is Amanda Rogers' primary doctor, and if she was scheduled for a hysterectomy around the date of the attack. I also want you to talk with Officer Reed's superior and see what has been happening with him since the first of the year. I smell a pay off. Try and find out if Reed has had money problems in the past and if anything has happened to change that situation."

"I'll get right on that. Are you in Farmingdale?" questioned Roberts.

"Yes, I'm in Farmingdale, and I will be here until after

Thanksgiving. If anything important comes up, get me on my cell phone. I also left the keys to Dr. Rogers' car on my desk with your name on it. I want you to be present when they start going through the car; let me know what you find. If you can't get a hold of me, leave a message with Sheriff Forbes. She is a primary on this investigation. Any information can go through her," Malano looked at the Sheriff. She was smiling.

Slapping his thighs, he stood and began going through the box labeled Doctor's Office. "I found these files in the bottom drawer of the doctor's desk. There are three of them. The first one is not labeled, so let's see what it holds."

The first ten pages were pictures preserved in plastic of children. The children were different ages, boys and girls all smiling. Under each picture was a series of numbers.

Looking at the Sheriff, Malano said, "Maybe he kept pictures of all the children that he had treated. For a man that didn't like children, he was in the wrong business."

The Sheriff added, "Maybe the reason he didn't like children was, because he saw them all day and didn't want to put up with them at home."

Malano pondered the idea, and then nodded in agreement.

"Wonder what the numbers under the pictures mean. At first glance, I thought maybe that was the times that they had seen the doctor, but the numbers are not months and years," interjected the Sheriff.

"There must be at least 100 kids here," stated Malano.

Following the pictures were pages of numbers. The numbers were not in a specific order and there was not a key page to explain what the numbers meant. The Sheriff turned back to the pictures, and then to the numbers. The numbers under the pictures were the same in length, but didn't match numerically. She pointed this out to Malano and he saw the similarity.

"Matching the numbers to the pictures is going to take some time, and even when we match the numbers we still don't know what they mean," pointed out Malano.

Setting the file aside, they looked to the next file. The file was labeled Matt Smith. The child was ten and suffering from depression.

The last page took both of them by surprise. In bold letters was written DECEASED. Under the captions was a brief description that stated that young Matt had hung himself.

Malano spoke first, "Who would think that a child that young could get so depressed to hang himself."

The Sheriff continued to read, "It doesn't say if it was an accident or suicide. Wonder when this happened?"

Malano had a questioned look on his face as he closed the file. The last file was of a teenage girl named Alice Morgan. The girl was suffering from low self-esteem. Looking through the file there was nothing of real importance. It appeared that he treated the girl for about two years and suddenly the sessions stopped.

Malano sat back in his chair and looked directly at the Sheriff, "Well, what do you think, Sheriff?"

The Sheriff filled her cup with coffee, and then spoke, "The first file I think is a collection of all the children that he has treated through the years. The numbers could be numbers on their files. The second file could be the one child that he was not able to help, and I have absolutely no clue why he would have the girl's file on hand. There wasn't anything in the file to indicate why she quit going to him."

Malano stood and stretched, "We have to find out what those numbers mean. I also want to show you what the doctor had in his wallet at the time of the accident.

Malano retrieved Bentley's wallet handing it to the Sheriff. "Look at the pictures that are there. The picture of the young girl is labeled Amanda Walker. That is a picture of his wife. I'm guessing that is what she looked like when she started taking sessions with him."

The Sheriff looked at all the pictures. "There isn't a recent picture of his wife. Wonder why?"

Malano shook his head.

Both Malano and the Sheriff were taking a cigarette break when Doc Amos entered the station.

"Hey Doc," greeted the Sheriff. "This is Detective Malano," she reintroduced both men.

Standing, Malano extended his hand, "Good to see you again, Doc."

"You too, detective. Saturday was a very hectic day. I didn't think you would remember me," chuckled Doc.

"That's my job, Doc. Remember names, faces and events," smiled Malano.

"What brings you here today, Doc?" questioned the Sheriff.

"I was driving by and saw the lights still on and a strange car in the parking lot, so I thought I would make sure everything was okay."

The Sheriff glanced at her watch. "I didn't realize that it is already seven. I need to call dad and let him know that I'm still at the office. Detective, we need to get you registered at Belle's, so she doesn't give away your room."

Malano walked around the desk, "You know, I'm starving. I haven't eaten today. Do you think after I register we could have dinner?" he looked at the Sheriff.

The Sheriff blushed a little, "Sure. That would be nice. Let me call dad. We can go to Belle's and get you registered."

"Is there somewhere that we could get a nice steak and a drink?"

The Sheriff thought for a moment, "There is a new place out near the interstate. I haven't been there yet, but it's a steak house."

"Let's give it a try," smiled Malano.

The Sheriff dialed her home number. While she was talking to her dad, Doc began looking at some of the boxes of evidence.

Malano joined him, "Doc, how long have you lived here?"

The doctor continued to scan the boxes as he spoke, "I have been here longer than I can count. I moved here after my internship in Chicago. I wanted a small little town to make my home and here I am. I have delivered most of the residents here. I delivered Samantha."

Malano had a puzzled look on his face, so the doctor explained, "Samantha is Sheriff Forbes."

Malano looked sheepish. "I didn't know her first name. In my business, we go by our last names or titles. I guess that is very impersonal," laughed Malano.

The Sheriff heard the laughter and joined the men. "I let dad know that I wouldn't be home for dinner, and that everything is fine with me. He worries. Are you ready to go to Belle's? Detective, do you want to follow me to Belle's? Then we can decide what car to take to dinner?"

Malano stood at his car door, "Why don't we just take my car to

Belle's, and then go to dinner. I can drop you off here when we are finished with dinner."

The Sheriff started towards his car, "That will work."

Doc Amos called from his car, "You kids have fun and be careful. Talk to you both tomorrow."

They both waved to the doctor and wished him a good evening. Getting in the car, the Sheriff gave Malano directions to Belle's. It was a short drive. Malano grabbed his bag from the trunk, and they entered the warm cozy inn. The smell of dinner was delightful as they entered. The Sheriff tapped the bell and waited for Belle to come.

Belle greeted the Sheriff warmly and turned to Malano. "You must be the detective that Samantha made the reservation for. My name is Belle, and you can sign the register please." She smiled at the Sheriff as Malano signed in. "Let me get my son to show you to your room."

Malano felt uncomfortable as the two women watched him.

Belle's son appeared, she gave him the room number, and Malano followed him up the stairs.

When he was out of earshot, Belle grabbed Samantha's hand. "He is gorgeous."

Looking at the register, Belle whispered, "His first name's Bill."

Samantha blushed, "I already know his first name."

Malano descended the stairs and started for the front door. "Are you coming Sheriff?"

Samantha smiled at Belle and joined Malano at the door.

Belle called out, "You know your room includes meals, detective."

"Thank you, but we have other plans," Malano replied. Out the door they went.

Walking to the driver side, he looked up to see Belle peering through the curtains. "Looks like we have an audience." Then he motioned towards the house.

The Sheriff stammered, "I have to apologize for Belle, but she gets so excited when there is someone new in town. I hope she doesn't hound you with questions. It's not meant in a mean way."

Malano interrupted, "Meant in a nosy way." He smiled at her and she returned his smile. "I'll try and be cooperative and give her some spicy information."

"Don't make it too spicy, remember I have to live here after you leave," she laughed. They drove to the restaurant in an easy silence.

They were shown to their seats and the waitress appeared quickly to take the drink order. Malano looked to the Sheriff. "I'll take a glass of red wine," she ordered.

Malano rubbed his chin, and then spoke, "I want a double scotch on the rocks." The waitress smiled at both of them before disappearing to the bar. Malano took out his cigarettes, and offered one to the Sheriff. They both leaned back and Malano rubbed his temples.

"Do you have a headache?" asked the Sheriff.

Before he could answer, the waitress returned with their drinks. Malano took a sip, and then answered, "Not really a headache, just a nagging pain."

The Sheriff smiled, "I think that pain in your temples is called a headache."

Malano grinned in agreement. "Have you always lived here?"

The Sheriff played with the stem of her glass, "Yes, I have always lived here except for the four years that I was away at college. How about you? Have you always lived in the city?"

Malano cleared his throat, "No, I moved here about five years ago. I'm originally from California, but I decided that I needed a change, so here I am."

The Sheriff laughed, "That could explain your reaction to our little snowstorm on Saturday. What brought you to this area? I mean you could have gone to Florida for a change, and you wouldn't have to put up with snow."

"I didn't want just a change in locations. I wanted to experience the seasons. My parents were from New York, and would always talk about the changing seasons. My dad was transferred to California. They love it there, but they fondly recall white Christmases," Malano replied. He smiled to himself at the thought of his parents.

The dinner arrived, and the evening passed quickly, to the delight of both Bill and Samantha. They still had a million things to talk about and much to learn about each other. Unfortunately, the restaurant wanted to close.

Samantha was having pleasant dreams of the past night when the phone beside her bed brought her to attention. The clock read 7:20, as she reached for the phone, "Hello?" she said in a puzzled voice.

"Sheriff, is that you?"

The voice was familiar to her. "Yes, this is Sheriff Forbes."

"I thought you country girls got up early," chuckled Malano.

Coming completely awake, "Good morning detective," she said groggily.

"I have been up for hours, and right now I'm waiting for you at Cora's. Do you plan on working today or sleeping?"

Trying to get her bearings, "Let me get dressed and I will be there in 30 minutes."

Malano laughed again, "Okay, I'll have some more coffee a couple of cigarettes, and then if you are not here I'm going to eat some breakfast. Shake a leg, Samantha." He hung up before she could make a comment.

Sitting up in bed she smiled, "He called me Samantha. How cute." She jumped out of bed, and made her way to the bathroom.

As she entered Cora's, she greeted some of the regulars, and spotted Malano sitting in a back booth. Making her way through the tables, Cora called out a greeting to her and said that she would get a waitress over to take her order.

Samantha plopped down on the seat opposite him with the waitress right behind her. "I'll have some coffee and a cinnamon bun." She looked to Malano, "I have already ordered."

Malano continued to look at a file without acknowledging her presence.

"Excuse me," she interrupted, "I'm sorry that I'm late. I don't remember us setting a time to meet this morning."

He looked up for a minute, and returned to his reading. The Sheriff sat with her hands on her lap. His breakfast arrived, so he closed the file and made room for his plate. Presently, the Sheriff's cinnamon bun was placed before her. Finishing his meal, he pushed his plate aside and motioned the waitress for more coffee. When the table had been cleared, Malano put his hands on the table and stared at Samantha.

"Sheriff, I was just going over the file that was found in the doctor's desk. I was up all night trying to figure out what the numbers mean. There has to be a key to those numbers. I have already put in a call to Detective Roberts, and he will be sending up the arrow. I haven't heard from him yet."

Malano glanced at the pad that he had been writing on, "I also want to look at the storage shed where the arrows for the contest are kept, but first I wanted to know if you are up for a hike?"

Caught off guard she stammered, "A hike?"

"Yes Sheriff, I thought we could walk off this breakfast with a little hike up to the scene of the accident. Maybe some of the snow has melted, and we can locate Mr. Williams' missing equipment. If you have had enough coffee, let's get started."

Not waiting for her answer, he made his way to the register to pay the bill. She gulped down her coffee and ran to catch up with him.

Outside the Sheriff called out, "Let's take my car."

Malano reluctantly walked to her car.

"This is my county, detective, so I will handle the driving. Okay?" Not waiting for his answer, she started the motor and waited for him to buckle up. Gravel sprayed from the back tires as she left the parking lot.

The Sheriff pointed to the large clearing where the starting gate for the contest was held. "There is a back way to the glen where the accident occurred.

Taking a back road, they made their way up the hill. The snow covered the trail, so she put the car in park and pointed to a clearing in the distance. "That's where it happened. Dr. Rogers was standing on this side and Mr. Williams was on the other side. I thought that we could look through the brush on this side, and then make our way to the other."

"Just a minute, Sheriff. I'm head of this investigation, and I will make the decision how it will be conducted," Malano said in a stern voice.

The Sheriff stopped and looked at him and waited. "Okay, I think we can look through the brush on this side, and then make our way to the other side," he laughed as he said it.

They made a thorough search of the area and came up with nothing. "We did get a cast of the two sets of footprints that were found around the body, right?"

The Sheriff nodded in agreement.

"I need to tell Detective Roberts to get the boots that Williams was wearing the day of the shoot. We can compare them to the prints that we found."

The Sheriff stopped, "We don't need Mr. Williams' boots. I took a mold of them the day of the accident. While we were waiting for you and your boys to arrive, Mr. Williams was resting on a rock. I took pictures of the bottoms of each shoe, which also show the size, and I made a mold when he went down the hill with the body."

Malano looked at her with surprise, "How did you know that we would need that evidence?"

The Sheriff smiled and started walking, "I guess you could say that I was born for this kind of work. We also have the prints that could belong to a woman, and the cigarette butts that were found in the area directly behind Mr. Williams."

The detective shook his head and caught up with her, "I'm very impressed. Good job."

They both searched the areas where the victim lay and Bruce's position, but found nothing. Gazing around, Malano asked, "Which direction did Mr. Williams take down?"

The Sheriff pointed, "Right through that opening. The trail is pretty defined."

"I think I will walk down that way, you can get the car and meet me at the starting gate."

"You got it, Boss," the Sheriff gave a salute. Her parting words, "Don't get lost, city boy."

She was out of sight before he could answer. He smiled to himself, as he headed for the trail.

The Sheriff smoked a cigarette while waiting. The sky was an unforgettable blue and the sun felt warm and inviting, but the temperature still had a bit of a bite.

Pulling out her notepad, she made herself a list of what had to be done before Thanksgiving. "I still have to invite Seth Peters. He should be in the office today I'll do it then."

She put her notepad away when she saw the detective coming. "Find anything?" she asked.

"Nothing," he stated, "You told me before that you have the

arrows stored in a shed. Do you have the key to the shed?"

"Sure, I'm the Sheriff of these here parts, and I have a key to everything." She thumbed her nose as she said it.

"Get in the car, Sheriff Dillon, and take me there."

"I don't mean to correct you, but Dillon was a marshal, not a Sheriff."

"I stand corrected, Sheriff," Malano smiled.

"Do you want to pick up your car before we go to the station?" she asked.

"No, I kind of like having a driver. Makes me feel important. Will my car be in the way at Cora's?"

"Well, if Cora decides that she wants it towed she will call me and I will explain that you are a very important man and we have to be nice to you."

"Drive on, Sheriff," Malano directed.

Pulling up in front of the Sheriff station, Samantha indicated that the shed was located behind the building. After opening the door, she searched for the light switch. From the door, racks and racks of bins could be seen. As they walked down the middle aisle, they passed each bin. The bins were labeled with content and amount contained. When they reached the area where the arrows were stored, Malano stopped. He looked at the tag that was attached to the bin. Each tag listed the number of arrows contained, the color of the shaft, and the years that this color was used.

Malano turned to the Sheriff, "The arrows that were used on Saturday have not been returned to this bin. Have they?"

The Sheriff indicated no and said, "The arrows that were used Saturday have been placed in one of the back rooms at the station. That room is locked."

"I'm glad that they have been secured. Who else has a key to that room?" "I have one key and Seth Peters has one," she said.

"Why does Seth Peters have a key to an evidence room?" questioned Malano.

"Seth has an office in our station. He is also the village judge, and sometimes needs the room to hold town meetings."

Malano continued to check the labels on the bins. "This tag says that there are 125 red shaft arrows in this bin. There were 76 arrows handed out on Saturday and we have accounted for all 76, but Williams states that he didn't shoot his arrow. That means that this bin should hold 49 arrows, right?"

The Sheriff looked at the tag, "These are not the arrows that were used in this year's shoot. The label says retired. That means that Seth bought new arrows for the shoot. There should be 125 arrows in this bin."

She unlocked the bin and they began to count. The count was 124. The Sheriff looked again at the tag on the bin. The number clearly stated 125.

"There has to be a mistake," stated the Sheriff. She began to count them again with the same result. "Seth must have made a mistake when he put these away after the last shoot. The last time these were used was four years ago. The man is meticulous about everything. He couldn't make a mistake like this. I'm sure that he just forgot to log an arrow that was damaged in a prior shoot"

"Where is the bin for the arrows that were used this year?" questioned Malano.

"Since a new order was used this year, he might not have made up a bin yet. When a new shipment is bought in, Seth always goes through the color being retired, and then gives the usable arrows to a charitable organization, like the Girl or Boy Scouts. They use the arrows to earn merit badges."

"Well Sheriff, I think we need to talk with Mr. Peters."

The Sheriff put the arrows back, locked the bin and left the storage shed.

The Sheriff led the way to the station, and then to the evidence room. She took her key out, and opened the door for the detective.

There, on two tables, lay the arrows. The Sheriff took the table nearest the door, and began to count the arrows. When she had finished, she turned to Malano, "I have 43 arrows here. What is your count?"

"My count is 32. Together that makes 75, and we have the arrow that was in the doctor, so the count is 76. I think we need to talk to Mr. Peters, and find out how many arrows were bought for this years shoot."

The Sheriff nodded in agreement and walked to Seth's office. She knocked. Not waiting for him to answer, she opened the door.

"Seth, may we talk to you?"

Seth closed the book that he had been writing in, "Good Morning, Samantha. Sure, come in and have a seat." He motioned for both to enter.

"Seth, this is Detective Malano. He is leading the investigation into the accident that happened at the shoot on Saturday." Both men shook hands.

Seth spoke first, "Nice to meet you, detective. What can I do for you?"

Taking the seat across from Seth, Malano spoke first, "Mr. Peters, I understand that you are in charge of registering the hunters and handing out the arrows that are used."

"Yes, I am. Is there a problem?" Seth looked from one face to the other.

"We need to know how many arrows were bought for this year's shoot. The tag in the storage shed states that the red arrows were retired. The count on the tag states that there should be 125 arrows in the bin, but we counted only 124. Did you have to substitute and old arrow?"

"No, I did not," said Seth.

"Did you purchase new arrows this year?" questioned the detective.

"The red shaft was retired, and I did purchase new arrows this year," Seth said with a huff. "When the arrows are used for two shoots, we retire any that remain. If some have been destroyed, I log the incident in my journal and the count is changed on the bin tag. You must have counted wrong."

Malano looked at the Sheriff. "There isn't a bin for the arrows that were used this year. Do you make up new bins or do you recycle the old ones."

Seth was upset and felt that he was being challenged. Rubbing his hands together, he said, "I have not had time to go through the old arrows yet. As soon as I have the time, I will donate the old arrows and record the new arrows and the year that they were purchased. I have not been in the storage shed since the shoot. The new bin has not been made, because the arrows are in the evidence room."

Malano could see that the old man was upset and tried to sooth him, "I'm not challenging you, sir. What I'm telling you is that we counted the arrows in the retired bin, and it is off by one arrow. I want to know if you have an explanation. The Sheriff and I counted twice and there is not 125 arrows in that bin there is only 124. We just need to know who might have had access to that shed and a key to the bin."

Seth cleared his throat, and spoke in a strong voice, "The Sheriff and I are the only one with keys to the shed and to the bins. I don't think I like what you are implying, detective."

Malano took a moment, "Sir, I'm not implying anything. I just need to know why there is a missing arrow, and who had access to that shed."

Standing abruptly, Seth placed his hands on his desk and spoke calmly, "I have answered your questions. If there is nothing else, I'm a busy man, and I would like for you to leave my office."

Malano could feel his anger rising as the Sheriff took his arm and led him from the office. She closed the door, and put her finger to her lips in a motion to silence him.

Malano pulled his arm away and stopped. He turned to the Sheriff, "What just happened in there?"

"I'm not quite sure. I don't think I have ever seen Seth get that angry before, and I can't explain his actions," she said.

"Why did you push me out of there? Is he hiding something? I can't believe that he just dismissed me like that," Malano stormed. "Who does he think he is?"

The Sheriff got him a cup of coffee and suggested that he take a seat. "Calm down; will you? You are going to blow a gasket," she said with a concerned voice.

"Blow a gasket? What is that supposed to mean?" he laughed.

The Sheriff laughed and took a deep breath, relieved that Malano's tirade seemed to have passed. "I have no explanation for Seth's behavior. We need to speak to Doug about the count, since he was the other one that initialed the tag. Where is he, anyway?" She looked around the station.

She then noticed that the message light was blinking on her phone. "Maybe he left me a message."

Hanging up the phone, she turned to Malano, "That was Doug and he says that he is too sick to come to work today. I guess we will have to wait until tomorrow to talk with him."

Taking out his cell phone, he waited for the party to pick up. "Brian, this is Bill. How come I haven't heard from you? I told you to keep me up to date with everything that is happening. Did you go to the impound lot? Have you gotten an interview with Williams?"

Brian waited until Malano was done with his questions. "I was just getting ready to call you. First, I was present at the autopsy. The ruling was he died from the arrow in his chest. Big surprise!" he chuckled.

"The arrow nipped the edge of his heart, so death wasn't immediate. Whoever shot that arrow was a hell of a shot. Second, I went to the impound lot to witness the sweep. There was nothing unusual in the car. The trunk held a couple of quivers of arrows and another bow. There were some long strands of red hair found tangled around the drawstring. The strands were bagged for evidence. They could belong to Mrs. Rogers. We did find a safe hidden under the carpet in the trunk."

"Did you open the safe," Malano asked gruffly.

"Bill, I said that it's a safe, and we didn't find the combination."

"Just a minute. Samantha, get me the doctor's wallet out of that box."

She retrieved the wallet, and he rummaged through it until he found the small slip of paper.

"Brian are you still there?"

"Sure."

"Write down these numbers, and see if they open the safe." Giving the numbers, Malano gave final instructions, "Write this down, and I want you to call me the minute you get them done. First, try those numbers on the safe. If any of them work, call me immediately. Second, I want you to go to the Williams' house and get the interview. I also want you to pick up the boots he was wearing at the shoot. I want you to send those to me overnight. Have you spoke to Mrs. Rogers to find out who her primary doctor is? If you haven't got that information for me yet, GET IT. Last and this is really important, get the arrow to me immediately."

"Got you, Boss. I will go down to the property room, and get the arrow boxed to be mailed. By the way, what is the address up there?" Malano turned to the Sheriff, and relayed the address to Brian.

"Now when you get any information, you call me," ordered Malano. He hung up before the detective could say anything else.

Malano shook his head as he disconnected the call. "I really hate to have to be on these guys all the time. If I wasn't constantly on their asses, nothing would ever get done."

Samantha questioned him, "Why did you want him to get Mr. Williams' boots. I told you I got a cast of them and pictures?"

Malano grinned at her. "If Mr. Williams is hiding something, taking those boots is going to make him nervous. He is going to wonder why we want them. When a person gets nervous, they do dumb things. That, Sheriff, is a first lesson of a good detective."

The Sheriff listened, and committed the information to memory.

Malano slapped his thighs. He then rose and walked back to the evidence table, "Let's get started on the statements. I don't think we are going to find anything, but it's worth a try. You take a stack, and I'll take a stack. Call out if you find anything."

The Sheriff grabbed a stack and started for her desk.

After several hours of tedious reading, Malano stood and stretched his arms. He walked to the window and peered out, and was surprised to see that darkness had settled on the village of Farmingdale. He turned to watch Samantha at work. She was deep in thought and absently twisted a strand of hair that had come loose from the tie.

"Sheriff," he called.

Startled, she jumped and looked up in surprise, "Yes?"

"It's hard to believe, but it's already dark outside," he glanced at his watch, "In fact it is after seven. I think we need to quit for the night. Do you want to grab something to eat?" Samantha didn't answer, but continued to flip pages of a statement.

Thinking that she hadn't heard him, he once again asked, "Do you want to grab something to eat?"

"I think I have something," she motioned him to her desk."

"What is it?" he asked anxiously. "Wasn't the doctor that performed the hysterectomy on Mrs. Rogers a Dr. Powell?"

Malano pulled the medical report from one of the boxes. "Yes, the doctor of record is Dr. Powell. What did you find?"

"I knew that name sounded familiar, and now I know why." She handed the statement to Malano.

There the name was written Thomas Powell, MD. He was one of the hunters at the shoot.

"This could be our first break. Do you know Dr. Powell?" he asked. "I can't recall who he is right now, but give me time. Seth has the records of how long each hunter has participated in the shoot. I can ask him to get us that information."

She knocked on the door, but there was not response. She tried the doorknob. The door was locked. They had both been so involved, with the statements that they hadn't been aware that Seth had left for the day.

"What time is it anyway?" she glanced at her watch. "Bill, did you know that it is already after seven? I have to call dad, and let him know that I'm okay and will be late." She was so excited about finding a link to the accident.

Malano asked her again, "Do you want to grab some dinner before you go home?"

"Sounds great. Let me call dad first, then we can grab something to eat at Cora's and you can pick up your car."

"Sounds good to me."

9

BRUCE SAT AT THE BREAKFAST table drinking his second cup of coffee and reading the newspaper. "Alice," he called out.

She came running in from the living room and said as she turned into the kitchen, "What's wrong?"

"Look here," he pointed to an article about Bentley Rogers, "It says his funeral is on Wednesday. That's tomorrow, right?"

"Yes, dear, tomorrow is Wednesday. Does it list the place and time for the funeral?"

"Memorial Hills at 10:00 AM."

"I guess we should send some flowers out of respect for Amanda," Alice said.

"No, it says instead of flowers make a donation to a charity in remembrance of Bentley…"

Alice turned around and slapped her hands on the table, "I refuse to make any donation to a charity in Bentley's name. Why should I do anything to make that creep look good?"

Bruce was surprised by the vehemence in her voice. Putting down the paper, he stood to hug her, but she pushed him away. "Honey, what's wrong?" Bruce said.

Alice began to weep, "I guess everything is just getting to me. I'm so worried about you, and that Detective Roberts is relentless about an interview with you. It's like they don't believe it was an accident, and since you were there they are going to blame it on you."

Bruce hugged her, wiping away her tears. "Don't think like that. They're just trying to find my equipment and arrow, and that will clear everything up—hopefully."

The doorbell rang, and Bruce left her to answer the door.

"Good Morning, Mr. Williams. I'm Detective Roberts. I have left several messages on your machine asking for a call back, but there seems to be a lack of communication here. I took it upon myself to come here and talk with you."

Alice joined Bruce at the door.

"Good morning, Mrs. Williams. I've come for the interview. May I come in?"

Bruce turned to Alice as if asking for permission. Alice was the first to speak, "Sure, detective. Sorry about the delay. Please come in."

Alice led the way to the living room, and motioned for the detective to take the wing chair, as she and Bruce sat next to each other on the sofa. Taking out his notepad, the detective settled back in the chair. Bruce was nervous, and began to wring his hands. Alice took one of his hands and held it in her lap.

Alice began, "Detective, what can we do for you?"

"Well, Mrs. Williams, like I told your husband, I have left several messages and my calls have never been returned." He waited for a response, but the couple remained silent.

"Mr. Williams, I need you to give me the shoes that you were wearing the day of the accident," the detective stated.

Alice spoke up, "Why would you need my husband's shoes?"

"Footprints were found around the body, and we are checking to see exactly who was there. It is all part of the investigation."

Alice spoke again, "Has my husband's equipment been located?"

"As far as I know, Mr. Williams' equipment has not been found. Now would you like to get me those shoes?"

Once again Alice spoke, "Has the hunter that shot the arrow come forward? Why hasn't this whole thing been ruled an accident?"

"Ma'am, I am not in charge of the investigation, so I can't tell you when a ruling will be made. Mr. Williams, have you remembered anything more than what you told Detective Malano?" Bruce began to speak, but Alice butted in, "He told both the detective and the Sheriff all that he could remember."

"Well, Mr. Williams, if you don't have anything further to say, I would like your shoes."

Bruce looked to Alice before he stood, "My hunting clothes are in the garage," Bruce led the way.

The inside of the garage was neat and tidy. Tools hung along the wall, kids bikes in stands at the end of the garage.

Opening a door to a small room, Bruce brought out his hunting shoes.

"Do you have a bag that I can place them in? There's some dried mud on the soles."

"Sure we have some bags in the kitchen. Just let me get it. I'll be right back," Bruce hurried off.

This gave the detective time to look around the garage. A dark colored car was parked inside. The snow on it had melted and left a mess of damp mud all over the floor.

Bruce returned with the bag and saw the detective looking at the car. "That car belongs to my wife, Alice. She uses it to drive the kids around and do errands. I don't think it has been out of the garage since Saturday. I have a 4X4 that she likes to drive when it snows."

"I don't blame her. I hate small cars in the snow. It's not so much the small car, but the crazy drivers that don't seem to see small cars," chuckled the detective.

He placed the boots in the bag and gave Bruce a receipt for them.

"Mr. Williams, you and Dr. Rogers knew each other for some time. Do you know of anybody that would have a grudge against him?" questioned the detective.

Bruce chuckled, "You are fortunate if you didn't know him. Bentley was a selfish arrogant individual, who enjoyed putting people down. He liked to see people in pain."

"I'm not sure I follow you, Mr. Williams. He was a doctor and has been recognized by the city for all of his charity work."

Bruce rubbed his chin, "I don't know if you are aware of the fact that Bentley was going to be investigated in a wrongful death of one of his patients. The case was a long time ago, but the parents finally decided that the truth needed to be told. Their son committed suicide by hanging himself."

"It sounds to me like the kid was just depressed. How could the doctor be held responsible for his death?"

Rubbing his hands together Bruce continued, "The kid was under his care. Something happened during his treatments that made him depressed. His parents told me everything was going well, but after one session, the boy came home crying, and later that night he hung himself. Of course the parents were grief stricken at the time, but now they feel that the doctor did something wrong and they want it investigated. An acquaintance of mine told me that Bentley was so angry that they thought he was going to have a heart attack. To bad about the accident, because now we will never know if Bentley did something wrong."

The detective placed the shoes in the bag and started for the door. "Mr. Williams you said that the car is your wife's?"

"Yes, she likes the small car to do errands and to run the kids around. It's very good on gas."

The detective smiled, "They are really good on gas. From all that mud it looks like she either got stuck or went four wheeling."

Bruce opened the garage door without a comment.

Alice was deep in thought when the detective and Bruce entered the living room. "Mrs. Williams, I'll be going now."

Alice turned with a start, "Happy Thanksgiving, detective."

"Happy Thanksgiving to both of you and your family," he said as he left the house.

When the door was shut, Alice turned to Bruce, "I hope you didn't say anything to the detective in the garage."

"No, I just showed him where my boots were and we talked about your car and Bentley," he responded.

"What did he want to know about my car? Did he look inside?" Alice asked angrily.

"Alice, calm down. We were just making small talk. It wasn't anything to do with the accident. Why are you so upset?" Bruce was bewildered by his wife's behavior.

"I'm just afraid that they will try and turn this whole thing into a murder and blame it on you. I love you so much, Bruce, and no one would ever hold it against you for killing that monster. What was he asking you about Bentley?"

Bruce grabbed her by the arms and spoke softly to her. "It was just general questions. I don't have anything to hide. I just know that I didn't harm Bentley. I never even got to shoot my arrow. When they find my equipment, it will prove that there was another hunter that killed Bentley."

Alice remained in his arms weeping.

Detective Roberts drove to the Rogers' home, and was reluctantly allowed to enter the estate.

As he got out of his car, the housekeeper met him at the door. "Mrs. Rogers is waiting for you in the living room."

"Thank you."

Mrs. James showed him to the room where Amanda was curled up at one corner of the sofa gazing into the fire. "Ms. Amanda, Detective Roberts is here."

Amanda rose slowly and extended her hand.

Detective Roberts shook her hand, and was amazed how cold her fingers were. Mrs. James turned to leave, but Amanda asked her to stay.

"Mrs. Rogers, I hate to disturb you, but I have just a few questions. I know that your husband's body has been released to you."

"Yes," said Amanda in a small voice, "his service will be tomorrow at ten."

"Are you doing okay?" he asked in a concerned voice. She looked so pale and weak. "Mrs. Rogers, it has come to our attention that you were the victim of a brutal attack on New Year's morning. From the police report, it shows that you required hospitalization for your wounds. Your medical records show that a hysterectomy was performed on you while you were hospitalized. Was this procedure a planned surgery or a result of the attack?"

Amanda looked at him with a puzzled stare, "My attacker stabbed me, and they had to do the surgery to save my life. I was never told that they performed a hysterectomy. I was told that I would never be able to have children because of the attack. What does any of this have to do with Bentley's accident?"

"In an investigation we have to look at everything concerning the victim. Could you tell me who your primary doctor is?"

Amanda thought for a moment, "I don't have a primary doctor. I have never been sick, and Bentley says that to go would be a waste of money."

"So you never went for a physical or a Pap smear. Maybe you had a bad cold and had to see a doctor?"

Amanda looked puzzled, "No, Bentley was a doctor and he took care of me when I was sick."

"Mrs. Rogers," interrupted the detective, "your husband was a child psychiatrist, not a medical doctor."

Amanda stood and began to pace, "I have never been seriously ill. Bentley always told me that he was all that I needed."

"Mrs. Rogers, were you Dr. Rogers patient before you married him?" the detective questioned.

"Yes, of course. Bentley groomed me to be a perfect wife."

The detective was taken back by her comment. "You were just a child when you started seeing him. Right?"

"I was 12 when I started taking sessions with Bentley. I was an orphan and a ward of the state. I had an eating problem and the social worker knew that Bentley could help me. He was so nice and had the most beautiful smile. I would do anything for him to smile at me and hold me close."

Amanda was lost in thought, and the detective didn't want to interrupt her, so he took out his recorder, placed it on the table, and let her continue to talk.

"I could tell him anything and he always kept my secrets. When I was good, he would hold me close and tell me that I was beautiful and if I was good one day I could be his wife. Sometimes I was bad and had to be punished. I tried really hard to be a good girl all the time, but sometimes I would forget what he told me."

Softly the detective asked, "How were you punished when you were bad?"

Amanda continued to speak as if he wasn't present, "When I was little he would not speak to me and would not let me see his smile. When I got older, I was put into a dark room to think about what rule of Bentley's I had broken. I'm scared of the dark."

She whimpered and curled in a ball, "When I couldn't control my eating problem, Bentley threatened to make Alice his wife. I wanted to be Bentley's wife, and make him smile that special way he did when I touched him. Alice was older than I was and she was fat.

Bentley told me he didn't like fat people, but if I wasn't good and didn't obey his rules, then he would give his smiles to Alice."

The detective was shocked by what Amanda was saying, and tried to steer her revelations to the attack. "Amanda, what happened New Year's night?"

Amanda closed her eyes, and for the moment seemed that she was finished talking. "I was very bad on New Year's Eve. Bruce pushed Bentley in the pool, and I laughed at Bentley. I made him lose respect with all of his important friends. He had to punish me for laughing at him."

"How did Bentley punish you?" he said softly.

"He left me at the country club. I didn't have a way home, so I took a cab. The house was open when I got home and all the lights were off. I was scared to go inside, but I couldn't let the cabdriver into our house without Bentley's approval. Bentley always said that our life is private, and to never let anyone see us. When you show weakness, you give control of your life to another person. We could never tell anyone about our lives." Amanda recited this as a lesson with no emotion.

"I should have never laughed at him. I knew when I did it that I would be punished, but I never thought he would hurt me like he did. I begged him not to hurt me, but he was crazy. I tried to pull the alarm, but he had cut the wires for the alarm. My hands and feet hurt so badly and he wouldn't turn me loose. The knife blade felt so cold. He wouldn't stop hurting me. He thought I didn't know that it was him under the mask.

He kept telling me "Ms. Amanda has to be punished."

I kept telling him that I loved him, but he kept hurting me. Why did he have to hurt me?" Amanda began to weep. "He told me not to tell anyone that it was him. He said that no one would ever believe me, not even the police that came to the hospital. Bentley is friends with the police, and they would never do anything that would hurt him. They would not break his rules like I did. The nurse at the hospital was like an angel, and she told me that I had to be punished, but it wouldn't hurt. The doctor would take away my pain. The doctor took away my babies."

Amanda began to weep loudly, so the detective tried to comfort her by touching her arm. As he rubbed her arm, she came out of her trance and stared at him with wild eyes. She moved from his touch and tried to regain her composure, "Detective, I apologize for my behavior. This whole thing has left me a little crazy. Please don't take anything I said to heart."

Mrs. James was weeping and reached out to comfort Amanda. Taking Mrs. James' hand, she smiled and continued, "I was just rambling, and probably not making much sense. Please forgive my outburst."

Trying to put her at ease the detective spoke softly, "Mrs. Rogers I realize that this has been a hard time for you. If there is anything I can do for you let me know. Here is my card and I will write my home number on the back. Please call me if you just need to talk." The detective rose and gathered his recorder and notepad.

"Are you going to come to Bentley's memorial?" she asked.

"I didn't know your husband, but if you want me to attend, I will," he replied.

Walking the detective to the door, she paused before she spoke, "I guess I broke another one of Bentley's rules. He would be so angry with me."

She hung her head, and the detective rubbed her arm, "its okay, Mrs. Rogers, your husband would understand what stress you have been under. It's okay. No one is going to hurt you."

Amanda gave a half smile as he left the house.

Detective Roberts let out a huge breath as he reached his car. This revelation was going to put a new slant on the accident. "I have to let Bill know what I have just learned," he said to himself. As he looked back at the house, he could see Amanda peeking out of the window. He punched in Bill's cell number, started the car and drove away.

"Malano."

"Bill, this is Brian. I just had an interview with Amanda Rogers, and you will never believe what she told me?" he said breathlessly.

"Okay, well spill it," said Malano.

"Okay, we were talking about the attack and if she had a primary doctor. She said that her husband took care of her there was no need for a doctor. I asked her if she had been Dr. Rogers' patient before they were married, and she went into some kind of trance and started reliving her past. I think that he sexually molested her. She was only 12 when she started seeing him. It gets even better. She said that he was the one that attacked her, and that she didn't tell the police, because her husband had friends on the police force."

Malano interrupted, "Did you get a statement from her?"

"No, but I did get it on tape. I put the recorder on the table in front of her, and she just kept talking."

Excitedly Malano asked, "So you got everything on tape?"

"Yes! This guy was a real creep. She said that everything that he did to her on New Year's Eve was a punishment because she laughed at him when Bruce Williams pushed him in the pool."

"Okay, this is what I want you to do. Did you get the shoes from Williams? Also, did you try the numbers I gave you on the safe in Rogers' trunk?"

"I was waiting until I got everything done before I called you. This is what I have done. Those numbers did open the safe in the trunk. Inside was another set of keys and a black address book that I have with me right now. I have the boots from Williams and I also have the arrow from the autopsy. I was going to FedEx everything to you."

"Where are you at right now?" questioned Malano.

"I'm on the interstate. Why?"

"You can be here in about 45 minutes which will be faster than FedEx. The Sheriff's station is at the far end of Main Street. Call me when you get into town," Malano hung up before he could respond.

Malano turned to the Sheriff who had been listening to his conversation. "I think we have a major break. Roberts just had a conversation with Mrs. Rogers that puts a new slant on our accident. From what he told me the gist of their conversation implied that the great doctor had sexually molested Amanda Rogers since the age of 12. There's more. She said that her husband was her attacker on New Year's Eve. Roberts got it all on tape, and is on his way here as we speak."

Malano grabbed the file that contained the pictures of the children. "These numbers have to mean something. We have to break this code. Roberts is bringing the arrow, and he also found another set of keys and an address book in the safe. That book could hold the key to these numbers."

"If the doctor was molesting Mrs. Rogers as a child, maybe he was doing it to all of his patients," the Sheriff added. She took the other two folders and reread Matt Smith's file, "Wonder if there was a write up in the paper about the boy's death? The library has old newspapers on file. Maybe I can find something about the accident. There is a date in the file, so I can start from there." The Sheriff jumped up, and out the door, she went.

Malano stretched and got himself another cup of coffee. Looking out the window, the scene was peaceful. Malano thought, "It is so beautiful here. How could something so terrible be happening just 50 miles away?"

He returned to the desk and began to play with the numbers again. There were six numbers under each picture, and some of the pictures had a letter after the numbers. The numbers weren't in chronological order. The only similarity was the first two numbers. They were all the number 19. In frustration, he busted out, "God, I hope that address book holds the key." He leaned back in his chair and said a silent prayer.

Malano was deep in thought when he heard the gravel crunch in front of the Sheriff's office. Jumping up, he peeked out the window and saw Detective Roberts getting out of his car. He hurried to the door. "Hey Brian, you made good time."

The detective was taken aback by Malano's presence. "Hey, Bill. There wasn't that much traffic. It sure is beautiful here, but colder than shit."

Malano chuckled, "Yeah, but the Sheriff assures me that since I've slept in the shadow of the mountain, I will have the desire to return."

The detective had a puzzled look.

Malano continued, "It's a legend in these parts. Never mind, where is the stuff that you brought?"

The detective motioned to the trunk and slapped his chest indicating the recorder was in his pocket. They both walked to the trunk and took out the shoes and the arrow. Malano took the arrow and shoes and put them on the back evidence table.

"The Sheriff should be back soon. She wanted to check the old newspaper records on the death of one of the children that was under

Dr. Rogers' care. You want some coffee while we wait?"

The detective nodded his consent, and joined Malano at the coffee table. "I also learned something today from Mr. Williams. He told me that the doctor was going to be investigated in a wrongful death suit. Something about one of the kids he was seeing who hung himself."

Just then, the door opened and in walked Seth Peters. He had a sour look on his face, and barely acknowledged both detectives. Malano was going to introduce Seth to Detective Roberts, but he hurried along to his office and shut the door soundly behind him.

Detective Roberts looked at Malano, "Who was that?"

Malano smiled, "That is Seth Peters. He's the judge, justice of the peace and man of many talents here in the village of Farmingdale."

"He doesn't seem to care for you, Detective Malano," said Roberts.

"I think I hurt his feelings. I was questioning him about his count of arrows. He thought I was implying something, and now he refuses to talk to me."

"With your winning charm, Bill, you will have that little man eating out of you hand in no time," Roberts laughed, and gave Bill a playful punch.

They were drinking their coffee and looking over the evidence table when Sheriff Forbes entered the station. Malano turned and smiled as she approached.

"Brian, I mean Detective Roberts; I would like to introduce you to Sheriff Forbes." They exchanged handshakes.

"Nice to meet you, Sheriff Forbes," smiled Roberts. "Nice to meet you too, Detective Roberts," she smiled and went to her desk.

While her back was turned, Brian nudged Malano and indicated that she was sexy. Malano pushed him aside and followed her to the desk.

Brian pulled up a chair and pulled the recorder from his pocket sitting it on the desk. Both Malano and the Sheriff looked at each other and sat down. The Sheriff pulled a note pad from her desk, and began to take notes as Amanda went through her story. When the tape had finished, the three of them sat in silence.

Sheriff Forbes was the first to break the silence. "I was able to find the newspaper report on Matt Smith's death. It was a small article about him being treated for depression by Dr. Rogers. His death was ruled a suicide; then there was the normal stuff about being the only child of City Council Member Darren Smith and his wife, Judy. That was about it."

Malano turned to the detective. "Do you have the keys that you found in the safe?"

The detective handed Malano the set of keys, as he returned with the box. One of the keys fit, and Malano slowly opened the box as Detective Roberts and the Sheriff looked on.

Malano reached in the box, and brought out a small address book. He scanned through the book at the various names and addresses including e-mail addresses. He read out loud some of the names, "We have Mayor Johnson, City Councilman Smith; there are also some state representatives here and other high officials."

He closed the book and reached in the box again. This time he brought out several sheets of picture negatives enclosed in plastic.

He set these to the side and brought out a ledger book. The last entry was for November, a deposit for the amount of $100,000 dollars with the initials MJ after. Glancing through the ledger, there was a deposit for each month, all of which equaled or exceeded $100,000. The initials were different each month. Malano stopped and looked at them, "If this ledger is correct and these amounts were deposited in the doctor's bank account it's over a million dollars. Since this ledger was hidden away, my guess is that the money is dirty and probably not in a U.S. bank. We need to find out where this money is hidden."

The last item in the box was a tape. Malano turned to the Sheriff. "Do you have a TV and VCR here in the station?"

"Yes, we do. It's in the evidence room, in the back." She led the way.

The two detectives took seats, while the Sheriff turned on the equipment and put in the tape. They all waited as the grainy pictures began to flash across the screen. At first, the pictures were not clear.

Then there was an image of a young girl. The girl was sitting on a sofa in just her underwear. She was crying and a male voice was berating her for being fat. The voice was telling her that as long as she continued to overeat she would not be allowed to sit on his lap. The voice told her what a beautiful young woman she would be if she would just stop eating. The girl continued to cry and she promised in between sobs that she would not eat cake or candy. She promised that she would lose weight, because she wanted to be close to him. Finally, the voice became soft and told the girl to quit crying and that she could now sit on his lap. The girl stood and went off camera.

A second child was lying on a couch, and the same male voice was giving her instructions on how to touch herself. When the child didn't perform the act as the voice wanted, a tirade of vulgarities would ensue, and the child would cry and beg for forgiveness. The instructions continued until finally the voice said that the session was over. The voice was warm and loving as he told the child to get dressed. The tape became snowy, and the three waited saying nothing.

The image of a boy was then visible, with the same voice giving instructions in how to undress and how to lie. The boy began to cry, and refused to continue. The voice became irate, and began to degrade the small boy. The child cried more. The voice yelled, "Matthew, don't make me punish you. You know that you belong to me. Your father gave you to me, because he is a bad person. You are mine. No one will ever believe you if you tell them about this. You are mine!" The voice laughed, and the film ended.

It was several minutes before anyone spoke. Malano straightened in his chair, and then cleared his throat. "Well, that was an eye opener."

The Sheriff ejected the tape and handed it to Malano. "Do you think that the voice on that tape was Dr. Rogers? That voice called the boy Matthew. Do you think that the boy could be the Matt Smith who committed suicide?"

Malano scratched his head, "At this point, I feel like we have stepped into a snake pit. With what we have learned about Dr. Rogers, he deserved to die, and I don't know why he wasn't murder sooner."

They all agreed as they left the back office. "The first girl on the tape looks familiar, but that girl is probably an adult now and might look totally different. I know I have seen her somewhere. On the tape, Mrs. Rogers refers to a girl named Alice who was fat. I wonder if this is the same Alice that she was talking about. If that is the case, we need to see the doctor's files from the time that he was treating his child bride. I'm wondering if Alice was the first child that he had been grooming for his wife until he started treating Amanda. This is all very sick. If the doctor was a molester, there could be hundreds of children that were involved. From the amount of money that looks to be involved, I don't think that he was doing this alone. There could be some kind of organization of these child molesters. These sick bastards like to share their filth. We need to break the code under these pictures, and find out who exactly is involved. Sick bastards," Malano yelled as he threw the tape back in the box.

Malano lit a cigarette and sat down. He rubbed his head to free the tension. The Sheriff paced, and Detective Roberts looked out the window. The silence was becoming unbearable, and Malano stated, "People! What we have here is a murder! Someone knew how sick the doctor was and decided to take things into his own hands. We needed to look at who hated him the most. I vote for the wife. He molested her from the time she was a young girl and continued to torture her as an adult. Brian, did you talk with the doctor that performed the hysterectomy?"

The detective turned from the window. "No, sir. When I got that tape, I thought that you needed to hear it. Give me a list of what you need, and I will get it accomplished. Oh, by the way, I was asked to attend the doctor's memorial service tomorrow."

"Who asked you to attend the service?" Malano questioned.

"The doctor's wife. It might be a good thing. I can see who shows up. On this murder thing, Boss, I don't think it was the wife. It's just a feeling. She is so young and weak."

Malano interrupted, "Don't let appearances deceive you. This woman has been a prisoner of the doctor's for many years. Can you imagine what he has done to her mind? Be careful, Brian. Don't let that woman get under your skin."

Brian smiled as he left telling Malano, "You might want to take your own advice."

After Detective Roberts had left the station, Malano sat down, took out a cigarette, and turned to the Sheriff. "You have been very quiet today. What did you think about the tape?"

The Sheriff looked at him and thought a moment before she spoke, "I think that we are dealing with a very bad man. I feel that the deeper we dig, the more filth we are going to bring to light. I don't think that Mrs. Rogers is the only one that had a reason to put an end to this man.

I think that a former patient or their parent could have wanted to hurt him for what he did to them as children. Right now, I'm trying to put everything that we have learned into perspective. Did Detective Roberts bring Mr. Williams hunting boots and the arrow?"

Malano rose and went to the evidence table, "Yes, he brought the arrow and the shoes." He carefully removed the arrow from the plastic bag.

Placing it on the table, he turned to the Sheriff, "We need the other arrows that were used for the shoot."

The Sheriff pulled her keys and started for the back room. Both the Sheriff and Malano were surprised when they saw that the door was slightly ajar. The Sheriff pushed the door open slowly, and was startled to see Seth Peters standing over the arrows.

Malano pushed past her and confronted Seth, "Excuse me, Mr. Peters, may I ask what are you doing in here?"

Seth jumped and stammered, "I was just looking at the arrows. I really came in to file these papers and just happened to see the arrows."

Malano spoke gruffly, "Well, I think until we remove the evidence for this investigation from this room that you should hold off on your filing."

Seth became angry, "I didn't touch anything, and besides I have always used this room for some of my files and it has never been a problem."

"I'm sure that it won't be a problem when we have removed the evidence. I'm just saying that for the time being I don't want you in this room."

Seth turned to the Sheriff, "Samantha, do you feel the same way?"

Samantha stood tall and replied, "Seth it's nothing against you, but Detective Malano is leading this investigation and what he says goes."

Seth slammed the cabinet drawer and left the room in a huff.

Malano chuckled as Seth left, "What is his problem. You know, if I was a suspicious man, I would think that he is covering up something."

The Sheriff nodded and grabbed a stack of arrows and returned to the main room.

The Sheriff placed the arrows on the second table, and Malano placed his next to hers. He picked up the first arrow, and examined the evidence tag placed on the shaft. The medical examiner had placed Bentley's name and case number and his initials on the tag. He walked over to the second table and started picking up arrows and comparing the color of the shaft on each arrow. The colors were slightly off.

He motioned for the Sheriff to join him, "Look at these arrows and tell me what you see?"

She also compared the shaft colors. "The color doesn't match. It's not noticeable until you hold them next to each other."

They continued the comparison until all the arrows had been looked at. The shaft didn't match any of the arrows that were used in the shoot.

Malano started for Seth Peter's office. He opened the door without knocking.

Seth Peters looked up from his paper work. "May I help you, detective?"

Malano took the seat across from Seth, "Mr. Peters, I need to know if you have a record of when you bought the arrows that were used in this year's shoot."

Seth opened a bottom drawer and pulled out a file. The top paper listed the names of the hunters in this year's contest and the amount they paid. The next sheet was a purchase order for 80 arrows with red shafts.

"This was the first year for those arrows to be used. We have to buy in increments of 10 arrows and a minimum order is 50. Every two to three years we place an order, because the hunters don't take great care of the arrows. Sometimes the tips get bent, and the majority of the time the shafts get bent. When a shaft is bent, it has to be replaced; it cannot be fixed. The hunters that participate respect our shoot, and because most of the hunters are experienced marksman, we want to ensure that the arrows that they use are the best. I placed the order for the 80 arrows on July 1st."

Malano sat back in his chair and crossed his legs, "Why did you order 80 arrows?"

Seth didn't hesitate in his reply. "The last 10 years, there have been 70 to 80 participants. I wanted to make sure that we had enough arrows for all the hunters."

Malano continued, "Where did you put the other four new arrows that were not used this year?"

In a shaky voice Seth spoke, "I placed them in the storage shed with the old arrows."

"Did you mix them with the other arrows or were they held in a separate area? If the new arrows are separate, that means the count is off on the tag. Right, Mr. Peters?" Malano questioned.

Seth drew a deep breath. "They were placed separate in the box that they were delivered in. The box is in the back of the shed. We never mix a new purchase with arrows that are going to be retired."

Malano stood, "Thank you for your time, Mr. Peters." Seth stood, "Do you want me to show you where the new arrows are stored?"

"No, thank you. The Sheriff and I will check it out." Malano left the office without looking back.

The Sheriff was at her desk going over the pictures of the children.

Malano approached, "Sheriff, we need to look in the storage shed."

She jumped up, "What happened with Seth?"

"He says that 80 news arrows were purchased this year and that the four that were not used are in a box in the back of the shed."

They opened the shed. There in the back sat the box with the four new arrows.

"I want to take these old arrows and compare the colors."

They each grabbed the old arrows, and returned to the office. They placed them on the third table, and Malano brought over the first arrow. He picked up an arrow from the table and the color matched. He handed the arrow to the Sheriff, and she repeated the comparison test with a second arrow and it matched.

Malano spoke first, "It looks like we have found the missing arrow from the shed."

The Sheriff nodded, "It also proves that the arrow that was issued to Mr. Williams was not the one that killed Dr. Rogers."

Malano slammed his hands on the table, "Where could his equipment and the arrow be? Someone picked it up, but who could it be, and what did they do with it?"

The Sheriff started towards Seth's office. He was leaving as she approached, "Seth, I have to speak to you."

Seth turned, "I was just leaving Samantha. Can't it wait until tomorrow?"

"No, Seth. We either talk in your office or in mine."

He unlocked his door and they both entered. Malano joined them.

The Sheriff started, "Seth, we compared the arrow that killed Dr. Rogers and the old arrows and they match. The arrow was not from the new batch. We need to know who had access to the shed besides you."

The old man was visibly upset, "You and I are the only one with keys. The deputy and I took the arrows out at six the morning of the shoot. I always lock the door after the arrows are removed."

He looked at the Sheriff, "Samantha, you know how I follow the rules. You know how I check and double check everything that I do." Seth began to cry, "I always lock the door when I leave."

He looked at Malano, "After the accident, I came back to the office to put the ledgers away. When I left, I went out the back door, because there were so many people in the station. The wind was really blowing and I heard the shed door banging. I went and closed it and locked it. I always lock the shed when I leave."

The Sheriff reached out for his hand, "Seth, why didn't you tell us this before?"

He hung his head, "Because people would think that I'm getting too old to do the job anymore. This job is all that I have. I don't have any family."

Malano spoke, "Did anyone have access to your keys?"

Seth rubbed his hands together, "After the deputy and I had taken the arrows to Cora's, I remembered that I had forgot to bring the ledger to sign in the hunters. I came back for it, and I guess I forgot my keys in my office door. After the accident, I found them hanging there."

He rubbed his head, and wouldn't look at either the Sheriff or the detective. Malano left the office. The Sheriff rubbed Seth shoulders and gave him words of encouragement before she left.

Malano was at the evidence table when the Sheriff entered the office. "What are you thinking, detective?"

Malano was angry, and there was an edge in his voice, "Why didn't he just tell us that before instead of giving us the run around."

The Sheriff came to Seth's defense. "He was worried about what everyone would think. He is old and all alone. Can't you understand that? Have you ever been afraid of being alone?"

Malano gave her a stern look. "This is an investigation. The information that he withheld is very important. For one thing, this could prove that this was indeed a homicide, and for another it proves that someone had access to the arrows. The killer wanted this to appear to be an accident, but didn't know that new arrows had been purchased for this shoot. When we find Williams' equipment, we might just find our killer."

10

THE SOUND OF BENTLEY'S LAUGHTER startled Amanda out of an uneasy sleep, the deriding syllables still permeating the walls like a smell that couldn't be expunged. Sitting up in bed, she looked around the room clutching the covers close to her, hoping against hope that he was gone, dead, for good, never to be again. "It was a dream," she told herself, "just a bad dream. He can't be alive. He has to be dead. It has to be. Bentley's dead and can't hurt me anymore."

The reality of the coming day's events meant something, gave her comfort. She lay back on the pillow and tried to think pleasant thoughts. She would have to pick up Bentley's ashes, attend the memorial service, then, maybe, then; she might finally be rid of the man.

She felt a mixture of emotions. One part ached for his touch, for his not unattractive smile. The other part was relieved and happy beyond belief, that she would no longer have to follow his rules and could discover herself, finally, the real Amanda. The scary part was that she would be all alone in the big house.

Bentley had always been the focus in her life. He told her when to get up, what to eat and what to wear. She never had to think for herself. Right now, all she wanted was to pull the covers over her head and sleep, but she had one last responsibility to Bentley.

Throwing the covers back, she lifted her nightgown and looked at the scars from the attack on New Year's Eve. She closed her eyes and ran her hand over her abdomen.

Tears began to flow as she thought of all that she had lost. She could never have children. This was Bentley's legacy to her.

Slowly, she pulled herself together and made her way to the bathroom. As she turned on the shower, the steam from the water fogged the mirror, and she thought back to the attack, including the message that Bentley had left and the night of torture she had endured. Clearing her thoughts, she jumped into the shower.

The day was cold and heavy clouds hung low on the mountain. Amanda's head ached and she longed for the end of this day. She took her time to apply her make-up. "I have to look good for you, Bentley," she said to her reflection. She picked a black wool dress for the occasion and a large hat with a black veil. Holding the hat, she looked at her image in the mirror and gave a small smile. She thought to herself, "I can't wait until I can smile again."

Picking up a small black purse, she left the room and made her way to the kitchen. Mrs. James was busy preparing finger sandwiches for the wake after the memorial.

"Good morning, Ms. Amanda."

"Good morning, Mrs. James. May I have some coffee and toast?"

"Yes, ma'am. You sit and I will bring it to you."

Amanda took the seat nearest the window and gazed at the winter scene. The trees were barren and looked lonely. Mrs. James brought her coffee and dry toast. Amanda ate in silence.

The funeral limo picked Amanda up at 9:15, and took her to the chapel. At the front of the chapel was a large portrait of Bentley. He was sitting at his desk and had the smile that Amanda loved. Placed below the portrait was the urn containing Bentley's ashes. Beautiful flowers adorned the chapel and there were several rows of chairs for the mourners.

Amanda was greeted in a hushed tone by the mortician and led to the front. "Mrs. Rogers, everything has been taken care of per your husband's instructions."

Amanda looked at him with a questioning expression on her face.

Seeing that she was confused, he explained, "Mrs. Rogers, your husband made arrangements several years ago. He planned both of your funerals, and gave us detailed instructions on how the final rite was to be handled. For himself, he was to be cremated and he picked the urn that his remains were to be placed in. For you, he picked the casket and the burial plot."

Amanda was becoming enraged and spoke, "Sir, I can see that everything is in place, and I thank you for taking care of all the arrangements. My husband neglected to inform me that he had chosen my final resting place, but I can tell you now that I will no longer let him run my life. I will choose where and how I'm buried."

The mortician stepped back, "Mrs. Rogers, I didn't mean to upset you. I thought that it would be comforting to know that everything has been decided and that you don't have to make any decisions."

"I'm sorry that I reacted so badly. I was taken by surprise that Bentley had thought about death, and had made all of these plans without letting me know. I apologize."

"Would you like to take a seat while I fill you in about the memorial today?" He led Amanda to a seat in the front row. "First we will have a eulogy from the mayor, a city councilman and a state representative. We also have the hymns that your husband requested. Then you will make the closing eulogy."

Amanda was stunned and replied, "I will make a closing eulogy? I'm not prepared to say anything."

The Mortician reached in his pocket and brought out an envelope with her name written across the front. He handed the envelope to her, "Your husband left this with me and said to give this to you before the service." The Mortician stood and left the room to give Amanda time to read her husband's last message to her.

Amanda's hands were shaking as she took the thick pages from the envelope. The first page was a message to her. She glanced through the rest of the pages and found that they were a glowing testimony to Bentley. She shook her head in dismay, and started to read the first page:

Ms. Amanda, if you are reading this, it must mean that I have passed away before you. What a waste for this to be so because I have so much to offer the world. You in turn have never offered anything to anyone but your face and your body. I have to admit that I'm going to miss our little games and the skillful ways that I taught you to please me, though enough of memories. I have more important things for you to do. I knew that you would not be able to handle anything as important as my memorial, so I did it for you. I have arranged for my eulogy to be delivered by several of my closest and most influential friends. I even gave them detailed instructions on what to say. I wish that I could be there to see all the mourners, and to witness their show of respect for me. I have enclosed the eulogy that I want you to read. Go over it before the service, so that you don't stutter when saying it. I also added emotions, such as tears, which will give my words more meaning. Make sure that you deliver it as it is written. I have made provisions for you in my will, but you will be made aware of them at a later time. I know what a scatterbrain you are, so I won't burden you with too many details. Look over the eulogy, and say it from your heart. Don't make me have to punish you!

Yours Bentley

Amanda held the pages before her, and then began to shred them. The Mortician saw her actions and rolled his eyes. Putting on his solemn smile, he turned to welcome the first of the mourners.

The service was smaller than Amanda expected. Half the chairs in the room were empty. Bruce and Alice arrived, and took the seats directly behind Amanda. They both touched her shoulder and gave her a warm smile. She was glad that they came, even though they were not whom Bentley considered friends. The mayor, councilman, and representative sat across from Amanda, and appeared ill at ease. Some of their friends from the country club were there, and sitting in the last row was Detective Roberts. Amanda smiled at him, and he returned her smile.

The piped music was becoming annoying, and the mourners were beginning to shift in their seats. After a long wait, it was apparent that no one else would be attending. Amanda motioned to the mortician to start the service. He made a few generic comments about Bentley, and then introduced the mayor.

The mayor rose slowly making his way to the front of the chapel. Taking an envelope from his pocket, he placed his glasses on his nose and began to read. Amanda recognized the envelope as being the same as the one she had received from Bentley. The mayor read in a monotone voice, and actually dabbed at his eyes, as if the words he read were his own. There wasn't feeling in the words. The mayor quickly finished, and returned to his seat.

The two remaining speakers repeated almost the same words, and seemed relieved when they returned to their seats. The hymns that Bentley had selected were piped into the room, and the audience seemed bored and anxious for this to be done.

The Mortician offered his hand to Amanda to escort her to the front of the chapel. She refused to stand, and he leaned close to her, "Mrs. Rogers, now it's time to say some words about your husband."

Amanda looked at him with such rage that he withdrew his hand. Through clenched teeth she said, "Get up there and end this."

He was confused, "Aren't you going to say anything? It was my instructions that you would end the service with a testament to your husband."

The corners of Amanda mouth curled slightly, "You have got to be kidding. I have nothing nice to say about the man. It's best that we end this and get on with our lives."

The Mortician did as he was instructed, and led Amanda to the back of the chapel to receive condolences from the mourners. Amanda braced herself for this final ordeal, and extended her cold hand to each mourner.

Detective Roberts followed Bruce and Alice out of the chapel. Alice took Amanda's hand, and then hugged Amanda, offering her condolences. Tears were visible at the corner or Alice's eyes as she stepped aside for Bruce to embrace Amanda. Bruce offered his condolences, and added that if she needed anything to let him know. Amanda took both his hands and held them for a moment before Alice took his arm.

As they began to walk away, Amanda asked, "Are you coming to the house?"

They both looked puzzled as Alice spoke, "Are you having

something at the house today?"

Amanda spoke softly, "Mrs. James has prepared sandwiches and coffee for all the mourners. We have enough food to feed an army. Please come."

Both Bruce and Alice nodded in agreement. Alice added, "Do you need a ride?"

"No, thank you. The limo will take me back. I have to pick up Bentley's ashes first."

They looked at each other and started walking to their car. Detective Roberts was the last to offer his condolences.

Amanda took his hands warmly and smiled, "Thank you for coming. Please stop by the house for some refreshments."

The detective smiled and whispered, "I'll try."

The Mortician checked that everyone had left before he brought Amanda back to the chapel. "Mrs. Rogers, please join me in a seat."

Amanda dutifully sat clenching and unclenching her fists. She turned to the Mortician, "Okay, let's get this over with. Give me Bentley's ashes, and let's be done with all of this."

The mortician rose slowly, bewildered by her actions. Reverently, he lifted the urn and handed it to Amanda. She held it with both hands and stood to leave. "Mrs. Rogers."

Amanda turned, "Yes, is there something else?"

"Yes, there is," he said with a strong voice, "There is the matter of the bill for the services."

Amanda turned to face him, "Send the bill to our accountant."

He looked down at his feet, hating this part of the business, "The instructions that Mr. Rogers left was to collect the money from you, not from his estate."

Amanda was becoming angry. "I don't know what you mean. I have no money of my own. Bentley's estate can pay for Bentley's funeral. If Bentley's estate can't pay, keep this." She thrust the urn at the Mortician and walked out of the chapel.

Walking to the limo, Amanda felt elated. The wind was cold against her face, but it felt refreshing. She looked up at the cloudy sky, and then raised her arms and began to twirl. The driver, showing a bewildered look, waited holding the limo door open. When she had finished, she took a deep cleansing breath got in the car and went home. She felt relieved that this ordeal was over and her new life was just beginning.

Malano and the Sheriff worked heartily on the second pot of coffee. The wind was picking up, and heavy clouds embraced the mountain. Malano looked out the window. "Do you think we are going to have another one of your snowstorms?"

The Sheriff joined him at the window, "Well, I don't think I can take credit for the snowstorm, but I do think we will be having some snow before nightfall."

Malano walked to the evidence table, and picked up the sack containing the boots. He placed them carefully next to the mold.

"Roberts said that Mrs. Williams was upset about us wanting her husband's shoes. He also told me that Dr. Rogers was being investigation in a wrongful death suit. This information came from Mr. Williams. You got two sets of prints, didn't you?"

The Sheriff pulled the second set of molds and examined them. "These footprints could belong to a woman. I bet they are about a size six."

"What size do you wear Sheriff?"

"A seven or eight, depending on the shoe."

Malano chuckled.

"What is so funny about that?" she asked.

"Nothing, nothing really." He picked up the book found in Bentley's car. It had not offered any clue to the numbers on the children's pictures. Malano picked up his phone and dialed Detective Roberts.

"Roberts, how may I help you?"

"Brian, Bill. Did you go to the memorial?"

"Hey…Yes, I did. Not many people showed up. The eulogy was offered by some powerful political people."

"Did the Williams' show up?"

"They were there and some other people that looked like the country club group. Mrs. Rogers invited me to go to the wake."

"Are you going?" Malano said.

"I wasn't, but if you think I should, I will."

Malano was quiet for a moment. "Yes, go and look around. Find out Mrs. Rogers shoe size. I also want to know what size shoes Mrs. Williams wears. Ask where she was at the time of the accident."

"What?" Roberts said.

Malano cleared his throat, "I want you to find out what size shoe both women wear. Also, talk with Dr. Powell. I want to know the extent of

Mrs. Rogers' injuries and why a hysterectomy was performed in the first place. Lean on him if you have to."

"You got it, Boss. When I was at the Williams' house, her car was in the garage. It looked like she had been four wheeling. The funny thing is that Mr. Williams said that she just uses the car around town and drives his car when it snows. The mud on her car looked like the red stuff that you find in the mountains."

"You should have taken a sample of the mud from her car. Never mind. I need you to talk to the doctor and let me know what he says. Make your appearance at Mrs. Rogers, and get her shoe size. Think of some excuse to get back in the Williams' house. You said that they have a mudroom, where his dirty hunting clothes were stored. Check to see if there are some muddy boots that might belong to his wife." The detective laughed. "I'm serious Roberts." Malano hung up.

The Sheriff was looking at the address book. "Have you noticed that each of the names listed also has an e-mail address? I wonder if Dr. Rogers had an e-mail address, and if we could get his password to read his mail. I think that it is apparent that this man molested some of his patients. We saw some of his handiwork with the video camera. Do you think that he was involved with some kind of group that distributes this filth?"

"I don't feel that Dr. Rogers was the only one involved. These initials stand for names. We just have to figure out the names. The money that was listed in that one book had to be from these dealings. I don't think the doctor was that successful? I think that either the names in that book are involved with these kids or Dr. Rogers has something on them. The money could be from selling this porn or from blackmail. Either way this is going to be big when the news breaks. We have to proceed slowly on this part of the investigation. Nothing will be said to anyone about what we have found. That includes your father," he looked sternly at the Sheriff.

The Sheriff nodded, "I understand."

The Sheriff walked over to her desk, and picked up the pictures. "I have been thinking about these numbers since we found them. I have an idea that I wanted to tell you about." She laid out the pictures and began, "What if the 19 that starts all of the numbers is like the first two numbers in a year. The second two numbers could be the child's age and the last two numbers the end of the year."

Malano studied the pictures, "You know that could be it, but what do the two letters stand for?"

"That I haven't figured out yet, unless it is the child's initials, or it could be the person that took the picture," the Sheriff replied.

Malano began to shake his head in agreement, "I think you got it, but look at the pictures here in the back. They all have a 'V' after the initials."

The Sheriff thought for a moment, "A 'V' could be the Roman numeral 5, or it could stand for video."

Malano agreed, "I don't think it's the number 5. I think you have something with video. The pictures in the front might have been videos, but maybe they were for his private use, and the later ones might have been passed around to all the other sick bastards. I'm going to call Mrs. Rogers, and see if she knows if he has an e-mail and what his password is."

Malano dialed the number and Mrs. James answered, "Mrs. James, this is Detective Malano. I need to speak with Mrs. Rogers."

"Mrs. Rogers has company right now. She had a memorial for her husband this morning." Mrs. James' tone had an edge to it.

"I am aware of the memorial service this morning, but I still need to speak with Mrs. Rogers."

"Please hold and I will see if I can disturb her." The phone was laid down. Presently, Amanda picked up.

"This is Mrs. Rogers. How may I help you, detective?"

"I'm sorry for the intrusion, but I needed to know if your husband used the Internet and if he had an e-mail address?"

The line was silent and Malano thought they had been disconnected, "Mrs. Rogers?"

"Yes, detective. I'm here. I know that we have an AOL account, but I was not allowed to use it. The only reason I know that he had an account is, because I saw it on our credit card bill each month. I have no idea what his screen name is."

"Do you have a computer in the house?" questioned Malano.

"Yes, Bentley has one in his study. He would spend hours locked in there. I don't know what he was doing."

"I want you to go into the study and turn on the computer," instructed Malano.

"Right now? I have people here because of the memorial. That would be very bad manners for me to leave my guests and go into the study."

"Mrs. Rogers we are trying to investigate your husband's death. You need to be cooperative," Malano was losing his control. Taking a deep breath he continued, "Mrs. Rogers, is Detective Roberts there?"

She hesitated, "Yes, he is. I invited him at the memorial service this morning."

Holding his temper, "I need to speak with Detective Roberts. I'm going to ask Detective Roberts if he can go into the study and check your husband's computer."

Again, she hesitated, "I don't know if I should do that."

"Listen, we can make this easy or hard," Malano's patience's was spent, "You either let Detective Roberts look through your husband's study or I will come personally and confiscate everything in that house. Now are you going to let the detective into your husband's study?" Malano rubbed his neck and rolled his eyes as he looked at the Sheriff.

Detective Roberts answered the phone, "Hello! This is Detective Roberts."

"Brian, this is Bill."

"Bill what's up. Mrs. Rogers seemed really upset."

Malano cleared his throat. "She should be upset. I can't believe her. Her husband has been killed, and she seems to throw up roadblocks at every corner. The secretary didn't want anyone going through Dr. Rogers' belongings. Like any of that matters now. I've about had it with all of them."

"I haven't been able to find out her shoe size yet or Mrs. Williams, but I'm working on it. Did you need anything else?"

Malano lit a cigarette, "Is Mrs. Rogers around you?"

"She is talking with some of the people who are getting ready to leave," replied the detective.

"When they have left, I want you to have her show you the computer in the study. Call me back when you are in the study," Malano hung up before the detective could answer.

Amanda closed the door after her guests had departed, and turned to see the detective waiting. Taking a deep breath, she joined him.

"Mrs. Rogers, Detective Malano said that you are to take me to your husband's study."

Amanda's voice quivered, "Yes, he told me that if I didn't do it he would confiscate everything in the house until the investigation is over. Why does all of this have to happen? It was an accident. You people don't need to dig into our lives."

"Mrs. Rogers, we have to do what Detective Malano has asked. The quicker we give him the information he needs, the quicker he will rule the investigation an accident."

Amanda looked around at her guests. She smiled pleasantly and spoke in a lower tone, "I know that it was an accident. My husband was a well respected man, and if that is good enough for me it should be for you too,"

"Amanda, I am not the enemy. Now I need to go to the study and see the computer."

Amanda bowed her head and led him to the study. She paused for a moment, and then opened the door. Roberts sat in front of the computer and dialed Malano on his cell phone.

"Malano speaking, are you in front of the computer?"

The detective chuckled, "Hey Boss. I'm in front of the computer."

In an excited voice Malano spoke, "Do you see an icon for AOL?"

"Yes!"-replied Roberts.

"Okay, bring up AOL and tell me the master screen name?" They waited as the program loaded.

"Bill, the master screen name is "Intruder," and there are several other names. Do you want those too?" "Intruder sounds like an apt name for the good doctor. Okay, can you tell me if the password is stored, or do you have to enter it?" instructed Malano.

"It's asking for the password. Let me look around the desk. Maybe he has it written down somewhere."

The sound of opening and shutting drawers could be heard. The detective returned to the phone, "No luck, but the bottom drawer is locked."

"Get Mrs. Rogers, and ask her if she has a key." Malano turned to the Sheriff, "That woman isn't going to help."

The Sheriff nodded with a smile.

The detective returned to the phone, "She claims that she is not aware of a key," laughing he continued. "She did say that we better not damage the desk, because it is very expensive."

Malano became livid. "I'll give that woman expensive. You open that drawer. I don't care how you do it."

"Okay, you're the boss. Do you want to hold while I get this open?" questioned Roberts.

Malano was growing impatient, "Just open the damn drawer. I'll hold."

"Got it!" yelled Roberts. He laid the phone down, as he began going through the drawer.

Anxious to know what the drawer contained, Malano called to Roberts, "Well? Don't keep me in the dark."

Roberts picked up the phone. "Well there are two more video tapes and a journal with names and addresses. Get this: there is a Swiss bank name and an account number. Okay, let me try this."

Malano lit another cigarette while he waited. The Sheriff busied herself with village business and tried to listen to Malano's conversation.

"Okay, Bill I'm in. What do you need now?"

Malano took out a piece of paper to write the password, "Give me the password."

"You won't believe this. The password is porn123. Pretty sick!" replied Roberts.

"This is what I want you to do. Go ahead and close AOL. Is there anything else besides the videos and that book in the drawer?" questioned Malano.

"There is also something like a strong box. Just a minute while I take it out. Wow! There must be around $20,000 in this box. They are new bills and still have the bank wrapper around them. What do you want me to do with all of this?"

Malano thought for a moment, "I want you to bring Mrs. Rogers into the study before anything is removed. I want her to write down each item that is taken. That way she can't say that we took things that we didn't. I'll tell you right now I don't trust her. She has that victim look about her, but I don't think that she is helpless. The money is to be counted. Then I want you to sign a record of it and have her sign it. Make two copies and leave one with her. Take the second one to the property room. Make sure that everything is relogged and the paper is also logged in. I want you to take the computer also and everything that is in that locked drawer. If she gives you any problems you let me know immediately."

"Bill, did you still want me to find out her shoe size and also Mrs. Williams'?" asked Roberts.

"Yes, I want to know everything about her, and find out what she was doing on Saturday while her husband was having his accident." Malano slammed down the phone and leaned back in his chair.

The Sheriff pulled out her cigarette, and then offered fresh coffee to Malano. He accepted the coffee, but remained silent. The curiosity finally was too much, and she asked, "Well, are you going to tell me what Roberts found in the drawer?"

Malano sat up and smiled at her, "Roberts found more proof that the doctor was into porn. I also got his AOL screen name and password. Do you have a computer and an AOL disk, so that we can install it and pull up the doctor's account?"

The Sheriff pulled one of the disks from her drawer and started for the computer in the back of the room. Malano followed. The Sheriff installed the program and signed on as an existing member.

Turning to Malano she asked, "What is the doctor's screen name and password?"

Malano gave her the information and waited to be welcomed. The familiar voice welcomed them and then said, "You've got mail." The Sheriff clicked on the mailbox, and down came the listing of over a 100 pieces of mail. They looked at each other and began to read the mail. Several hours passed, as they read each e-mail.

The last piece of mail was from a woman, screen name: AWill4u. The first part of the letter was a remembrance of a past love affair. The writer was calling to mind the happy times of learning about each other and the intimacy that they shared. She spoke tenderly about the way he had instructed her in the art of lovemaking and the pleasures that she obtained when she pleased him.

The writer then became angry when she was discarded for another lover that was younger, prettier and thin. The woman spoke of Amanda with hatred and how one day she would get even with both of them. She described how his cruel words, about her weight, had ripped at her heart and made her cry. The last sentence, of the letter, stated "YOU WILL PAY FOR THE PAIN THAT YOU HAVE BROUGHT TO MY HUSBAND AND ME! WHEN YOU FEEL THE WARM SUN ON

YOUR FACE LOOK UP AND YOU WILL SEE THE FACE OF DEATH. WHEN YOU LOOK INTO THOSE EYES, YOU WILL FEEL A BURNING IN YOUR CHEST AND YOUR LIFE WILL FLOW FROM YOUR BODY."

A

Malano jumped up and grabbed his coat. Looking at the Sheriff he said, "Are you coming?"

She looked up confused, "Where are we going?"

Malano glanced back, "We are going to interview Alice Williams."

The Sheriff grabbed her coat from the rack and followed Malano to the car. Heading for the interstate, the Sheriff turned to Malano, "You think the writer of that letter is Mrs. Williams. Don't you?"

Malano kept his eyes on the road and answered, "Yes! I do think that Alice Williams wrote that letter. It all adds up now. Alice Williams must have been one of Dr. Rogers' patients. She is probably that young girl that we saw in the video. He addressed that girl as Alice and she was overweight. I need to speak with her and find out if indeed, she was a patient and where she was on Saturday. I know that she wasn't home when Bruce Williams tried to call her on Saturday after the accident. He told me during our interview that he had to leave a message on the machine. What better cover up then to have your husband be the victim's partner? If Mr. Williams hadn't insisted that he didn't shoot the arrow, we would have just ruled it an accident. Maybe that garage also contains the missing equipment"

The weather was beginning to turn colder and a light snow was starting to fall. They continued their journey to the Williams house in silence.

Bruce Williams' 4X4 was in the driveway when they arrived. When they approached the door, Malano stopped and spoke to the Sheriff, "I'm going to give you first hand experience in how to interrogate a reluctant suspect. I want you to keep Mr. Williams occupied while I go after the wife."

The Sheriff gave him a half smile and waited for the door to open. Bruce couldn't hide his surprise at the two unexpected visitors.

"Detective Malano, Sheriff Forbes, we weren't expecting you. Please come in."

Bruce looked out the door to see if anyone else was present. He showed them into the living room where a warm inviting fire was burning.

Malano spoke first, "Mr. Williams, we need to talk. Is your wife at home?" Bruce jumped to his feet as the door to the kitchen opened and out stepped Alice.

"Alice, we have quests."

Alice wiped her hands on the kitchen towel that she was holding. She extended her hand, "Hello, I'm Alice Williams."

Bruce rubbed his sweaty hands on his pants leg, and made the introductions. Alice and Bruce sat on the sofa near each other, and the Sheriff and Malano sat in the wing chairs. All could feel the tension in the room.

Malano took his notebook from his pocket, "Mrs. Williams, I have a few questions for you."

"For me?" she questioned.

Malano proceeded, "Can you tell me where you were on Saturday?"

Alice was confused. "I don't know why you need to know where I was. I had nothing to do with the accident."

Alice looked to Bruce as Malano continued, "Mrs. Williams, were you ever a patient of Dr. Rogers?"

Alice gasped, "What has that got to do with Bentley's accident? Bentley was a child psychiatrist."

Malano cleared his throat, "I'm aware that Dr. Rogers treated children. I want to know if you ever had occasion to see Dr. Rogers' professionally when you were a teenager?"

Alice stood and began to pace.

Bruce spoke up. "Detective, I would like to know what this has to do with Bentley's accident."

Malano sat back in his chair and smiled, "Mr. Williams, we know that this was not an accident. We know that the arrow used to kill Dr. Rogers was not one that was issued the morning of the shoot. We also know that you and Dr. Rogers had an altercation on New Year's Eve at the country club. During our interview, you informed us that this was to be the last shoot for you as a team. You also stated to the Sheriff that you never went near the body, but we have your boot prints that indicate you did stand next to the body."

Bruce began to stutter as he tried to find words to explain, "Maybe I went near the body. I don't remember. Everything happened so fast I couldn't recall. Even if I went near the body that doesn't mean that, I killed Bentley. Have you found my equipment? Maybe the person that shot Bentley picked up my equipment when I went for help. I told you that I heard an arrow go by my ear. The Sheriff found evidence that someone was standing behind me. She even found cigarette butts. What about all of that?"

The Sheriff remained silent.

Malano watched as Alice continued to pace, "Mrs. Williams, would you like to join us?"

Alice was visibly upset and reluctantly returned to her seat next to Bruce.

"Mrs. Williams, I will ask you again if you were a patient of Dr. Rogers."

Alice began to weep and Bruce tried to comfort her.

Malano continued with the questioning, "Mrs. Williams, I need an answer to my question."

Alice dabbed at her eyes and spoke in a soft voice, "Yes, I was a patient of Dr. Rogers." Bruce looked at her with surprise as she continued, "I was 15 when I started the sessions. I was having a hard time in school because of my weight, and I was depressed. My parents were worried, and thought that maybe talking with a doctor would help."

Bruce removed his arm from Alice's shoulder and stared hard at her, "Alice, why didn't you ever tell me?"

Alice moved away from him, "Because it happened long before I knew you."

Malano and the Sheriff looked at each other and nodded at the couple's exchange.

Bruce was very upset, "I can't believe that you never told me about you and Bentley."

Alice replied in anger, "There was not a me and Bentley. I was 15 and that time had nothing to do with you. Anything that was between me and Bentley was over when he met Amanda."

Fearing that she had said too much, she sat back on the sofa and was silent.

Bruce stared at her in disbelief.

Malano waited to see if any more information was going to be revealed then asked, "Mrs. Williams, where were you on Saturday?"

Alice thought for a moment before she spoke, "I was out shopping for our holiday dinner."

"Was anyone with you?" he continued.

Alice shifted in her chair, "No, I dropped my kids off at my sisters in the morning."

"When did you drop your kids off at your sisters? Can you tell me where you went, and did you meet anyone on your shopping trip?"

Alice stood and began to pace, "I dropped the kids off around eight. I just had odds and ends to pick up for our dinner, and I don't remember seeing anyone that I knew."

Malano persisted, "Picking up odds and ends took you all day? What time did you get home?"

Alice rubbed her head. "I don't know what time I got home. The weather was bad, and I know I wanted to be home before the snow started and before Bruce got home."

Malano shocked her with his next question, "Mrs. Williams what size shoe do you wear?"

Taken aback by this question Alice stared at him, "What?"

Malano repeated, "What size shoe do you wear?"

"I wear a size six, if it's any of your business."

Malano was not put off by her show of anger. "I would like to see the shoes that you were wearing on Saturday."

Clinching her fist, she raged, "Maybe I don't want to show the shoes that I was wearing. Maybe I don't want to answer any more of your questions. I think that you need to leave my house now!"

Malano smiled, "Mrs. Williams, don't make this difficult. Just let me see the shoes."

Alice sat on the sofa and crossed her arms. "I have nothing more to say to you, detective."

Malano rubbed his chin and looked at Bruce, "Mr. Williams do you know what shoes your wife was wearing on Saturday?"

Bruce nodded.

"Can you get them for me?"

Bruce looked at Alice, but she lowered her eyes. Rising from the sofa, he indicated that the shoes were located in another room.

Malano joined him. They walked through the kitchen to the garage.

"Mr. Williams, do you use an internet service?"

Bruce stopped and faced Malano, "Yes, we do. We use America Online. Why do you ask?"

"Do each of you have your own screen names?" Malano questioned.

"My son has his own screen name, but he is not allowed to be online unless one of us is sitting with him. Alice and I each have our own names."

Malano smiled at him and they continued to the garage.

"What is your screen name?" Bruce blushed, "I go by big bad John. My parents nicked named me Big John when I was little. I used to love the song Big Bad John."

Malano chuckled, "That's good. Do you know your wife's screen name?"

Bruce replied, "Sure, her screen name is AWill4u. I don't know how she came up with that."

Malano just smiled.

Entering the garage, Malano saw Alice's car, "Who drives that car?"

Bruce looked over his shoulder, "That's Alice's car."

He opened the door to the mudroom and turned on the light. He pointed at the muddy shoes as Malano entered the room,

"Could you get me a bag for these shoes? I need to take them with me."

Bruce went to the kitchen and returned with a plastic bag. He hesitated before handing Malano the bag, "Detective, can you tell me what is happening here? My wife had nothing to do with any of this. Why are you bringing up things from long ago?"

"Mr. Williams, as I told you before this wasn't an accident. There were two sets of footprints at the scene, and I want to compare these shoes with the second set. Do you have the keys to your wife's car?"

"I'll have to get the keys from the kitchen."

Malano waited by the car until Bruce returned. Taking the keys from Bruce, he unlocked the front door and sat in the seat. He looked at the floor mats: there were clumps of dried mud. The mud was the same red clay that was on the boots. Getting out of the car, he proceeded to the trunk.

Alice and the Sheriff appeared at the door, and Alice spoke, "What do you think you are doing?"

Malano looked up as he unlocked the trunk, but didn't answer. There in the trunk was the missing hunting equipment. Malano motioned for the Sheriff to approach. Bruce looked in and gasped, and then turned to look at Alice. She remained in the doorway with a look of bewilderment on her face.

"What is it Bruce," she screamed.

Malano handed the bagged boots to the Sheriff and brought out the equipment with the arrow.

Alice's voice was quivering, "What is that? I don't know how that got into my trunk. Bruce is that your equipment?"

Bruce nodded, but didn't speak. Alice fell to the floor in tears.

Malano gave instructions to the Sheriff. She gathered the boots and the equipment and proceeded to the car. Malano walked to Alice and helped her to her feet. "Mrs. Williams we need to talk."

Alice continued to sob, "I don't know how that got into my car."

Malano pulled out one of the chairs at the kitchen table and indicated for Alice to sit and he took the chair opposite her. "Mrs. Williams, were you molested by Dr. Rogers?"

Alice hung her head and refused to speak.

"Mrs. Williams, we have a tape of a young girl named Alice that was found in Dr. Rogers's office. Were you that young girl on the tape?"

Alice remained mute. The Sheriff returned and Malano cautioned her to remain silent.

"Mrs. Williams, I will find out if you are the girl on the tape. I would like to hear your side of this or if you want to remain silent we can just take you to the station and book you on a count of murder."

At the sound of this, Alice began to cry harder and she held out her hands to Bruce. Looking up into his face she said, "Bruce, I didn't tell you about Bentley, because I was ashamed about what he had done to me. I was young and I thought that he loved me. I was flattered that a handsome man like him would even want a fat pig like me to touch him. I didn't know what he was doing was wrong. I thought he loved me. He promised that if I learned how to please him that I would be his wife. I lost weight and did everything that he told me. Everything was going to be beautiful. He told me what to wear and how to act. I felt like I was somebody. He loved me. Then Amanda came into the picture. He would taunt me with her. She was so beautiful and thin. I felt terrible and started to eat. This made Bentley angry and he told me that I was no longer welcome to come see him. I begged him, but he refused to see me again. Bentley told me that I needed to get on with my life.

He also warned me that if I ever spoke of what we had done that I would be labeled a whore and no other man would ever want me. He had videotapes of me begging him to touch me and he promised to show them to everyone if I told. When I met you, I finally found out what real love was and I feared that Bentley would tell you. You thought I was a nice girl. How would you have felt if you knew that Bentley had been with me? I was 18 when we met starting my first year in college. You were already set up in your career and an important man in the community. Bentley told me that if your family ever knew what kind of girl I was they would never let you marry me. You had all those women in love with you. I was afraid that you would leave me too so I didn't say anything."

Bruce hugged her and wiped her eyes.

Malano interrupted, "Mrs. Williams, how did your husband's equipment get into the trunk of your car?"

Alice looked at him. "I have no idea how it got there. I didn't put it there. You have to believe me, detective."

Malano continued, "Mrs. Williams, did you send an e-mail to Dr. Rogers on Saturday?"

Alice looked confused. "I don't know what you are talking about."

"We know that your screen name is AWill4u. That screen name sent a threatening e-mail to Dr. Rogers on Saturday morning. The e-mail contained a death threat. Are you telling me that you didn't send it?"

Alice slapped the table, "I haven't been online in a month. What is happening here? What are you trying to do to me?"

Malano tried to calm her, "Mrs. Williams, where were you on Saturday? How did your car and your boots get so muddy?"

Alice began to weep softly, "I was at the cemetery. I went to visit my grandmother's grave. I go there often just to talk with her. She is the only one who knew what Bentley did to me."

Malano's look was stern as he spoke, "Because of these new

developments I'm going to have to ask you not to leave the city." Both Bruce and Alice stared at him.

Alice was shaking as she asked, "Are you putting me under arrest?"

Malano stood to leave, "At this time, I'm not putting you under arrest, but I'm telling you not to leave the city. You need to make yourself available for further questions."

As they drove back to Farmingdale, the Sheriff turned to Malano and asked, "Do you think that Mrs. Williams killed Dr. Rogers?"

Taking a deep breath, he spoke, "All the evidence is pointing to her. She had the motive. Sounds like the doctor has been making her life hell for sometime. If her shoes match the footprints by the body that means that she was at the scene. The equipment was in her car. All of these things are adding up."

"She looked shocked when you removed the equipment from the trunk of her car. Don't you think that she would have gotten rid of the equipment before it was found?"

Malano chuckled, "You are just a rookie, and it is showing. I have been doing this for a long time and nothing surprises me anymore. If, and I say that is a big IF, she did it, she probably never thought that an investigation would go this far. She probably thought it would be written off as an accident. The first thing that you will learn is that everybody thinks that they will never be caught. What you have to remember, as a cop is that there is never the perfect murder. There is always something that wasn't covered, and it's your job to find that clue."

The Sheriff settled back and went over everything that they had discovered.

The snow was coming down harder as they neared the turnoff for Farmingdale.

Malano turned to the Sheriff, "You have been very quiet. What have you been thinking about?"

She stretched, "I was thinking of everything that we have learned about the doctor. Last Saturday, I felt bad that the accident had happened. Getting to know the history of this man I have to reevaluate my feelings towards him. One part of me says that everyone has a good side, but my other part is trying to find a good part to this man and can't seem to find any reason for his existence."

"No matter how evil the man was he deserves justice. The person that did this took the law into their hands and that is wrong. It is our job to find that person, give the information to the DA and let justice take its course. It is not our job to judge, no matter how much we want to," instructed Malano.

The Sheriff smiled. The clock on the dash read 7:00.

"I can't believe that it is already this time. Your father is going to think that I'm a slave driver," he chuckled.

As they were getting out of the car, his phone rang, "Malano, what's up?"

"Bill, this is Brian. I just finished talking with Dr. Powell, and you will never guess what he told me."

"Okay, I'm waiting," Malano said impatiently.

"Well, first of all he didn't want to talk, but when I leaned on him he spilled his guts. He said that he was present at the New Year's Eve party, and witnessed Mr. Williams pushing the doctor in the pool. He said that after the accident most of the people left and he didn't know where the Rogers had gone. He said that he received a call from the Dr. Rogers at about five in the morning saying that he needed to get to the hospital that the doctor's wife had had an accident. When Powell arrived at the hospital, he found Mrs. Rogers beaten and stabbed several times. The knife sliced both of her ovaries, but surgery could have saved them. He asked Rogers why he hadn't taken the time to bring his wife to that hospital when St. Francis was nearer to his home. Dr. Rogers told him that he needed a large favor. Rogers requested a hysterectomy be performed on his wife and he wanted the records to show that the surgery was the result of the assault.

I asked him why he would do this and endanger his medical license. He said that a couple of years ago he had been in an accident. Alcohol was involved and he was driving. Rogers had contacts in the police department and they fixed the report and he became indebted to Rogers for life."

"Good work. Now I want you to look into traffic accidents that occurred two years ago, and see if there is any record of the accident. If there is, I want to know who the investigating officer was. I bet you ten bucks that if there is an accident report; Reed has his name on it.

Call me when you find out. Did you get Mrs. Rogers' shoe size?"

"Yes, Boss. She wears a size seven. You know Bill it is seven o'clock, and tomorrow is Thanksgiving. Do you think I could look up the report on Friday?" Roberts waited for Malano's reply.

"Well, I guess you can call it a day. You did a good job on getting that information from Dr. Powell and Mrs. Rogers' shoe size. There is one last thing. Did you get the computer and money over to the properties?"

"Yes, I did just as you told me. Mrs. Rogers signed both copies, and I made sure that property logged everything in the books including the receipt."

"By the way, how much money was in that drawer?" questioned Malano.

"There was $35,000.00 in that drawer. Mrs. Rogers was shocked when she saw all that money. I don't think she has any idea how much her husband was worth, or where he kept all of his money. She was asking how she would find out how much money his estate is worth. I told her that I'm sure her husband had a will, and she will need to get in touch with their lawyer. I also told her that she should talk to their accountant. Maybe he would know about her financial situation. I didn't know what more to tell her. I feel sorry for her."

Malano rubbed his chin and thought for a moment, "Brian, I want you to stay objective about this woman. I need you to take a step back and look at this woman as a potential suspect in a murder. Don't get wrapped up in her past life. I can't emphasize this point enough. You have to be objective, or you will overlook clues that could solve this case."

There was silence on the line. "Okay, Bill. I know what you are saying. I have let her get next to me, but I will correct that now. One thing I forgot to tell you is I went into the garage, and her car had mud on the tires and on the inside of the car. It's like the mud that Mr. Williams had on his boots that I picked up. You know the red clay type mud. I asked her when the last time that she drove it was and she said that she was running errands on Saturday. Also, by the door were the boots that she had worn on Saturday, and they had mud on them. I asked her where all the mud came from, and she said that she had no idea. I haven't noticed that red mud around here.

Well Bill, if you don't have anything else for me I think I will head home. Happy Thanksgiving and tell the Sheriff Happy Holidays."

"Happy Holidays? Wait one minute did you bag the shoes? Did you collect a sample of the mud on her car? What the hell are you thinking man? I need for you to do your job and quit thinking about poor Mrs. Rogers," Malano roared.

The line was silent.

The Sheriff was at the evidence table comparing Alice Williams' boot to the cast. It was not a fit.

Malano joined her, "Is it a match?"

"Sorry, the treads on the bottom of the shoes are different. See here, Bill?" she said.

Malano looked at her quizzically, "That's the first time you've ever called me Bill."

The Sheriff blushed, "Well, since we will be eating dinner together, I thought I would call you something besides detective. I also have to introduce you to the rest of our company."

"Who is going to be at the dinner tomorrow?" asked Malano.

"There will be my grandfather, my father, Franklin and Laverne, and Doc Amos. I was going to invite Seth Peters, but I haven't had the chance and he has been in a sour mood," the Sheriff told him.

"Sounds like it will be a full house. I'm not used to being with a family for the holidays. I do call my parents on Thanksgiving morning."

The Sheriff smiled, "Well, I guess a phone call is better than nothing. If we are done for the day, I think I will head home to start the preparations for our dinner. We are eating at one sharp. I have appetizers, so you can come early or when you are ready. I can send my dad to pick you up."

Malano grinned, "This town isn't that big. I think I can find your house. Just write down the address for me. Do you need me to bring anything, like beer or booze? What kind of liquor does your dad like?"

Picking up her coat, she turned and said, "My dad likes scotch and we have everything. You just need to show up and enjoy yourself."

Malano grabbed his coat, and they both started for the door.

At his car, Malano yelled, "See you tomorrow."

The Sheriff smiled and waved.

11

SAMANTHA WAS UP AT 5:00 AM on Thanksgiving morning. The first item of business was to get the turkey washed and stuffed. She had stayed up late with her father preparing the stuffing and getting the house decorated and the dinner table set. Everything was perfect.

She lit the oven and took the huge bird to the sink to wash. She looked out the window to find the streetlight barely visible because of heavy fog. Checking the clock and marking time, she put the bird in the oven. She loved the smell of roasting turkey.

The thought also brought to mind Thanksgiving with her mother. When a youngster, she would wake up early, enjoying quiet time in bed and listening to her mother singing in the kitchen. The smell of the cooking turkey filled the house with a savory aroma. Deciding eventually to get out of bed, she would run downstairs to find her mom at the stove mixing something delicious with Christmas carols ringing softly throughout the house through the stereo. After the huge dinner was finished, there was the football game, and the evening would end with the three of them sitting around the TV and watching "It's a Wonderful Life," the classic with Jimmy Stewart and

Donna Reed. Samantha closed her eyes in a moment of silent prayer for her mother.

Wiping tear from her eyes, she turned on the Christmas music and retired to the living room. Her father had laid a fire the night before, so all she had to do was put a match to it.

Curling up in the easy chair, she pulled a blanket around her, closed her eyes and thought about past memories of Thanksgiving time. This had become her tradition, and she cherished the quiet moment to be with her mother yet again.

The sound of her father descending the staircase brought her back to the present. Jumping up from her chair, she met him on his way to the kitchen, "Good morning, Daddy."

He hugged her, "Good morning, my Little Bear. How are you this fine day? Did you get the bird in okay?"

"Yes, Daddy. Everything's under control."

Norm looked at her with love in his eyes. He knew that she had been thinking about her mother. That was the only time that she would address him as Daddy.

"What time are all of these people supposed to show up?" Norm said in a snippy voice.

"Now, Daddy, you promised to be nice. We eat at one sharp. That'll give you time to eat and then watch your football game. Please try and be gracious."

"Bear, you know I'm always gracious," he chuckled, "Do I finally get to meet this big city detective that has kept you late all week?"

Samantha blushed, "Yes, daddy, but you better not give him any trouble. Promise me."

Norm held up three fingers, and then crossed his heart.

She hugged him, "Daddy, I love you."

"Ditto for me, baby girl. Now that we have all the mushy stuff out of the way, can I have some coffee?" They sat at the kitchen table watching the mountain where the sun was trying to peek her face above the clouds. The snow was gently falling and the wind was calm.

Malano sat up in bed and glanced at the clock. The clock showed 8:00. Easing back on the pillow, he shut his eyes and tried to clear his mind. The case had filled his dreams with images of children calling out for help. They were crying and a dark shadow kept poking them with a stick and laughing at their pleas. His head felt heavy and it ached. He rubbed his temples and tried to erase the images. Lying there for several minutes, he decided to give it up and get dressed. He walked down the hall to the community bathroom, showered, shaved and dressed. The smell of breakfast coming from down stairs aroused his appetite, and he decided a light breakfast wouldn't ruin his appetite for the dinner that Samantha was making. Making a mental note to call his parents before he set off to the Sheriff's house, he ventured downstairs to get something to eat.

Belle had an assortment of breakfast delights to choose from. Malano took a plate and made his choice of a cinnamon roll and a large cup of coffee. He sat at the end of the dining table.

Several families were eating their breakfast and talking excitedly about dinner with their families. Malano looked on this scene, and an empty feeling began to ache in his chest. Just as he was about to leave the table, Belle came over and wished him a good morning and Happy Thanksgiving.

"Good morning," he responded.

Belle beamed at him, "Are you going to be eating with us or are you going to the Sheriff's house."

Malano shifted in his seat and blushed, "I'm having dinner with the Sheriff and her family."

Belle patted his hand, "That's good. I hate to have anyone alone during the holidays. Well, if you are still hungry when you get home, there will be leftovers in the fridge. Make yourself a sandwich, and there will be eggnog to wash it down. You have a great day. Are you going over early? I know that Norm will have the football game on and Samantha always has loads of goodies to snack on until dinner."

Malano stood and spoke softly, "I have to place a call to my parents before I go over. Thank you for the wonderful breakfast."

He was feeling uncomfortable and wanted to get away. Belle saw that she had made him feel uneasy, so she excused herself wishing him a Happy Thanksgiving and to tell Samantha and her family happy holidays.

Malano dialed his parents, and waited for his Mother to pick up the phone.

"Happy Thanksgiving."

"Hey mom, Happy Thanksgiving."

"Son, I'm so happy that you called. Wait a minute while I get your father."

"Mom, how are you?"

"I'm fine son, but I miss you. Do you have a girlfriend yet?"

"Sylvia, don't hound the boy. Happy Thanksgiving, son."

"Hey, Dad, how are you?"

"Well we have been playing a lot of golf, but now that the holidays are here your mother wants snow. Can you believe it? It's a beautiful 70 degrees, the sun is shining, and I'm wearing shorts, and your Mother wants snow."

"Dad, I can still hear mom saying that the real Santa is only found in Macy's. Every holiday you and I went through mom missing snow and Macy's. Maybe you should come for a visit here. I have snow."

"Son, this is mom."

"Yes, mom I know," he chuckled. "Do you really want us to visit you for the Christmas holidays? Oh Sal that would be so wonderful to be in the city and with my baby boy." Sal hesitated, and Malano knew that he was going to cause a fight between his parents.

"Mom, you need to think about it. Dad, I'm sorry I shouldn't have just dropped it on you like this. I just wanted to wish you a Happy Thanksgiving."

"Son," it was his Mother, "Are you working today or are you going to spend the day with friends?" "Well mom, I'm on a case right now, but I am having dinner with the Sheriff and her family. So don't worry about me, okay."

"Bill did you say that the Sheriff was a she?"

Malano knew that she would pick up on that slip, "Yes, mom. The Sheriff is a woman. The case that I'm working on is in a little village called Farmingdale. It's in the mountains, and it is so beautiful here. I just looked out the window and the snow is coming down. When I drove through the village, I thought of you. It looks like some of those cards you used to show me when I was little."

"You mean the Christmas cards by Currier and Ives."

"Yeah those are the cards. I would love you to see this place. It's like time has not touched it."

"That sounds wonderful son. Now about the Sheriff. Is she a nice lady? Is she pretty? Do you like her?"

Sal interrupted, "Sylvia you are overwhelming the boy. When he wants to tell you he will."

Malano chuckled at his parents. "You two are too much. Its okay, dad. I know how to handle mom. I have been doing it for a long time."

Sylvia began to cry, "I just don't like you to be alone. I love you son."

"I know you do, mom. Don't cry. I called to make you happy, not to upset you."

Sal interjected, "Your Mother cries about everything. She will be fine when you get married and present her with a bunch of grandchildren."

Malano laughed, "Well mom, I'm looking. Just haven't found a woman like my mom."

Sal laughed and said, "Hey, Boy. I got the best woman in the world and you will have to keep looking."

Malano could picture his parents hugging, and he missed them.

"Mom, dad I have to get ready to go to dinner. I just wanted to let you know that I love you and Happy Thanksgiving."

"Happy Thanksgiving, son. We miss you. We love you."

Malano hung up with a smile on his face.

Samantha was running from here to there making sure that everything was cooking right. The house was filled with the aroma of Thanksgiving. She had made a list of to-dos for her dad. Looking around for her father, she spotted him through the window shoveling the walk. Putting down the turkey platter, she started for the door.

Taking a deep breath, she opened the door, "Father, will you please come here."

Norm slowly turned with a smile on his face, "Yes, dear."

He reluctantly came to the door. Holding up his finger to silence her he spoke, "Bear, I'm sorry. I forgot that I'm not supposed to be doing this. You were making me so crazy with all the running around. I couldn't breathe in there. You are going to pass out before your first guest arrives. You are the one that wanted all these people over and now you are acting like a BEAR."

Samantha smiled, "I'm sorry dad. I know I'm driving you crazy, but I'm just so nervous and want everything to be so perfect."

"Bear, it will all be fine. We have everything done. Everything is ready to be placed on the table at one. The bird will come out of the oven at 12:30, I will carve him, and he will be delicious. Relax a little. I think you need a stiff drink. When is the detective supposed to show up? The game starts in about 20 minutes, and you know I don't like to hold serious conversations while the game is on."

"Dad, come inside. I wanted to talk to you about the detective."

Norm frowned, "What are you going to tell me?" "Dad, I don't want you questioning him about the case."

"Bear, I was a cop and I know the procedure. Tell me now if anything else is off limits."

Samantha bristled, "Dad, let's not get upset. I just don't want you interrogating the man. I know that this is the first man I have ever asked to Thanksgiving Dinner, and I don't want you to make a big deal about it."

Norm smiled, "Oh so we are to think of him as a man coming to dinner instead of a detective coming to dinner."

Samantha gave her dad a push, "Dad, I'm serious. You behave yourself and please try an engage Franklin and Laverne in conversation. I don't want you and grandpa to argue about the football game or about anything."

Norm took off his coat. "Well you better talk to your grandpa about the arguing. He starts most of our battles."

Samantha started for the kitchen, "I intend to talk to grandpa. I want you both to be on your best behavior."

Norm looked out the window, "Well, can I at least be the one to answer the door, because your young man is coming up the walk."

Samantha's heart skipped a beat and she started to stutter.

Norm squeezed her hand, "Take a deep breath, Bear. You are beautiful. The dinner is going to be delicious and the house looks great. Did you buy some more beer, because me and the neighbor finished off what you had in the fridge?"

Samantha looked ashen as Norm let out one of his deep laughs, "Just kidding, baby." The bell rang and they both started for the door.

Malano was nervous as he waited for the door to open. He wiped his hands on his pants, and berated himself for being so nervous. The door opened, and there stood Samantha and her father. Samantha smiled brightly and warmly greeted him. Norm extended his hand and welcomed him to their home.

"Come on in. It's freezing out there," Norm greeted him. Malano entered the warm home, and felt the love contained within. Samantha took his coat, and Norm led the way to the living room where a warm fire was burning and the football game was in the first quarter. Bill was offered refreshments, and was making his selections when the doorbell rang announcing another member to the Thanksgiving feast. Samantha's grandfather was introduced to Malano. The old gentleman had a strong grip and a warm smile.

"Glad to meet you, sir," Malano said.

The old man chuckled, "I'm no longer on the bench, so you can call me Mike."

Malano looked confused.

"I see my granddaughter neglected to tell you that I was a judge of this great village. Samantha's great grandfather was also a judge. My son here broke with tradition and became a cop. Norm tells me that you are an important detective in the city and that you are heading the investigation of the accident that happened at the shoot."

Malano was embarrassed, "Well sir, I mean Mike. I don't know if I would say that I'm important, but I am lead on the investigation."

Samantha joined the men and scolded her grandfather, "Grandpa I told you no business today."

All the men laughed and the doorbell once again rang. This time the guests were Franklin and Laverne. The couple was smiling broadly, as Samantha welcomed them and took their coats. The assembled guests welcomed them, and Norm introduced the couple to Malano.

The doorbell rang once again and Samantha asked her father to greet their last guest. Soon Doc Amos joined everyone. Samantha stood back, with a smile on her face, and watched her guests enjoy themselves. She thought to herself that she was glad that she had invited everyone. Malano approached her and asked, "Why are you just standing here with that big smile?"

"I'm just happy that everyone seems to be enjoying themselves. I need to baste the turkey, so I will be back."

Before she left Malano touched her arm, "Can I help you with anything?"

Samantha grinned, "If you would like you can take the turkey out of the oven. He is a big bird, and with the stuffing in him he weighs a ton."

They both laughed as they went to the kitchen.

As Malano was taking the bird from the oven he said, "I want to thank you for inviting me. I normally work today, but this is very nice. Your dad and grandpa are great guys."

Samantha leaned close to him. "You are very welcome. I'm glad that you could join us. It is usually just dad, grandpa, and I at dinner. This year, I decided that I wanted to share some of the love with others."

Malano looked into her eyes. "Well I'm glad that you decided to share this year."

Samantha was feeling giddy and didn't know how to respond to his closeness when Laverne entered the kitchen. The couple looked embarrassed and moved apart.

Laverne also felt embarrassed, "I'm sorry for interrupting. I just wanted to know if you needed any help."

Samantha took her arm and led her back to the living room. "I have everything under control, but thank you for the offer. You just need to relax and enjoy yourself."

As they left the kitchen, Samantha looked over her shoulder at Malano and grinned.

Samantha began to set the dishes of food out. "Dad, I need you to carve the turkey."

Norm replied, "Sure, baby. Right after this play."

Samantha brought out the hot rolls and again called to her father, "Dad, the turkey is ready to be carved."

"Okay, Bear. I'll be right there. I just need to watch this replay."

Samantha stood at the doorway and tapped her foot.

Malano jumped up and volunteered to carve the turkey.

"Are you sure you know what you are doing?" she laughed. Malano played indignant, "I'm an important detective from the city. I can do anything."

Norm smiled to himself as the couple retired to the kitchen.

At one, Samantha announced that dinner was served, and the group made their way to the table and sat in their assigned seats. The candles were lit, the crystal sparkled, and the food smelled delicious. Norm filled each guests' glass with wine, and then bowed his head as he said a prayer.

Sitting down, Norm announced, "Let's eat this bird."

Everyone applauded and began to pass the food. When everyone's plate was filled, Norm tapped his wineglass with his fork, "Before we partake of this feast I would like to thank all of you for coming and sharing our feast. We have a tradition in our home that before we eat we take a moment to reflect on what we are thankful for today. I will start. This Thanksgiving Day I'm thankful for my father, my lovely daughter and good friends. Okay, dad you are next."

Mike reached for Norm's hand and squeezed it, "I'm thankful for my son and granddaughter. My health is good and I pray that my granddaughter will find someone who will make her happy and bring me great grandchildren."

Samantha blushed as she looked at Malano.

Franklin was next, "I'm thankful for my wife and the company at this table."

Laverne hung her head for a moment, "I'm thankful for each of you, especially my husband."

Doc Amos sat back and smiled at each person at the table, "I am thankful for each day that I live. I have a good life, good health and very good friends. I thank God for each day that I can share with you."

Samantha took a moment to get her emotions under control, "I'm thankful for my family. I'm thankful for old friends and new friends. I'm very thankful for everyone coming today and that I didn't burn the dinner." Everyone laughed.

Malano was the last to speak, "I called my parents in California this morning, and I realized how much love I come from. I'm thankful that my roots have grown from that love. I'm thankful to be with this family and their friends. I'm also thankful that Samantha didn't burn the dinner." Everyone laughed, wineglasses clinked, and everyone began to eat.

When the meal was finished, Samantha and Laverne began to clear the table. Samantha started to protest, but Laverne waved her aside. Malano picked up his plate and started for the kitchen.

Samantha showed him where the dishwasher was, and he began to load it. With their help, the kitchen was quickly cleaned, and Samantha put on a pot of coffee to go with the pies.

As the three entered the living room, Norm was putting another log on the fire, "You are just in time for the third quarter. Cowboys are up by three. You do like football don't you, boy?"

Malano sat on the couch next to Samantha, "Yes sir, but I'm a Bronco fan."

Norm stood and looked at him, "A Bronco fan, well I would never have thought that. Where did you go to college?"

"I went to UCLA. Go Bruins."

Norm chuckled, "Did you play any football?"

"Not football, but I did play a little baseball."

"College ball?" Norm asked.

"Yes, I played college ball. I was a pitcher."

Samantha looked at him in surprise, "I didn't know that you were a ballplayer."

Malano smiled at her, "Well, when I meet someone I usually don't say that I was a college pitcher. It usually doesn't come up in conversation, especially in my business."

Norm returned to his chair and turned to Malano, "I bet you didn't know that Samantha played college ball. She played fast pitch softball, first and third base."

Malano looked at her and she blushed.

Doc Amos joined in, "That girl was always running around with bruised shins and fat lips. I bandaged up skinned knees and elbows many a time."

Mike chuckled, "Her Christmas list would be for softball equipment. For her sixteenth birthday I bought her a batting cage." Everyone laughed.

Samantha was blushing, "Okay, let's just change the subject. We are all intelligent people and I know we can find something more interesting to discuss."

Norm looked lovingly at his daughter, "Bear, you are the most interesting subject that I think about each day. I miss the days when I would come home and she would be leaving with hair in a ponytail, ball cap on and cleats thrown over her shoulder on her way to the ball field. I can tell you honestly, Bill that she is the best third baseman that

I have ever seen. Her senior year, she hit two inside the park grand slams. The best ballplayer that school ever saw."

Samantha went to her dad and put her arms around him, "I love you daddy."

"I love you too, Bear." Everyone in the room was touched by this tender moment.

Samantha wanted to lighten the mood, so she announced that coffee was ready and pie was being served. Everyone had pie and coffee and watched the game. The afternoon continued with friendly conversation and the football game.

Mike was the first to announce that he needed to get home so he could take his medication and sleep off some of the food that he had consumed. The snow had been falling all day, so Norm volunteered to drive him home. Doc Amos also excused himself and left with Norm.

Malano put some more wood on the fire, which indicated to Samantha that he was not ready to leave. Franklin and Laverne seemed to be enjoying themselves and remained in their seats. Samantha asked them if they would like something more to eat, and they declined. Malano asked if he might make himself a turkey sandwich and she showed him to the kitchen.

As they were making their way to the kitchen, Franklin asked Samantha if she could speak with them. Malano took the hint that they wanted to speak to her alone, so he continued to the kitchen.

Samantha sat on the sofa, and waited for Franklin to speak. She could see that he was uncomfortable, so she tried to ease it by starting, "I hope you enjoyed yourselves today. Did you have something that you wanted to talk about?"

Franklin rubbed his hands together and looked at Laverne. Laverne remained mute and wouldn't look at them. In a soft voice he began, "Sheriff, this is very hard to say, but I think it needs to be said. We are aware that the hunting accident on Saturday is under investigation and eventually the whole truth is going to be found out. Most of the people here refer to us as just Franklin and Laverne and never use our last name." Samantha looked confused and he continued, "Our last name is Rogers."

Malano entered the room eating a turkey sandwich, "Am I interrupting something? I can eat this in the kitchen if you need to be alone."

Franklin looked at him, "No, you probably need to hear this too, detective."

Malano sat on the couch and Franklin continued, "The victim of the accident on Saturday was our son." Laverne began to weep and Franklin hugged her shoulders. Malano looked at Samantha with a confused look and she tried to fill him in on what Franklin had just said.

Malano put his sandwich down and leaned forward, "What exactly are you telling me? I know that you stated that you are Dr. Rogers's parents, but why was this such a secret?"

Franklin rubbed his hands on his pants, "Bentley didn't ever want to see us again, and he warned us that we were not to let anyone at the shoot know that we were related."

Malano shook his head. "Your son didn't want anyone to know that you were his parents?"

The couple shook their heads in agreement. Malano stood in front of the fire and looked at the flames. The couple held hands and waited for the detective to speak.

Malano slowly turned toward the couple, "Okay, why have you waited so long to give this information to us?"

Franklin spoke, "Because we didn't have any information about the accident. The only information that we have is that we were his parents, and that he turned his back on us after his high school graduation."

Malano joined Samantha on the couch and looked at both of these people, "When did you know that your son competed in this shoot?"

"It was reported in our local newspaper. That was before we moved here. Laverne and I talked at great length, after seeing that article, and then we saw the advertisement for mill workers needed at the Anderson Mill. We decided that if we moved here that we might get to see our son at least once a year. We knew that he didn't want to be near us, but we thought after all of these years that maybe his feelings towards us had changed. Laverne and I love our son. We don't know what we did to him as a child that made him hate us so much."

Franklin broke down and cried. This time Laverne comforted him. The room was silent. Samantha went to the couple and tried to comfort them.

Laverne looked at her with a tear-stained face, "I'm sorry to have ruined your beautiful Thanksgiving."

"Don't worry about that," Samantha softly spoke.

Malano spoke directly to Franklin, "Why are you telling us this information at this time?"

Franklin dried his tears, "Because we knew with this investigation that eventually this information would come out. We thought that maybe we could help in some way."

Malano cleared his throat, "Mr. Rogers, are you aware of the net worth of your son?"

Franklin, Laverne and Samantha were shocked by this question, and they glared at him.

"I'm not trying to upset you, but when the accident happened, you didn't step forward. There have been a lot of articles in the paper about how influential, respected and wealthy he was. Now that he is dead and buried, you come forward and claim to be the long lost parents. In fact it is believed that the two of you are dead a long time past."

Franklin became angry and answered, "Sir, I resent the implication that we are telling you this information in hopes of getting some of my son's money. We just thought that maybe we could help with the investigation."

Malano shook his head, "What information, besides that you are the victims parents can you offer? Did you speak to your son on that morning? What was your relationship like since you moved here? Did you see anything that would help solve this case?"

The couple held hands and said nothing. Franklin stood and helped Laverne to her feet, "I think we need to leave now. Thank you for inviting us we had a really good time. I'm sorry that we ruined the end of the day."

The couple headed for the door and Samantha got their coats. When they opened the door, the snow and wind greeted them. Franklin looked at Laverne and told her to wait inside while he warmed the car. Laverne stood at the door and waited. Samantha wanted to embrace this sad woman and to try and ease her pain. Franklin beeped the horn to signal that the car was warm. Laverne hugged Samantha and once again thanked her for the day.

Samantha watched until she had reached the car safely and then she turned on Malano. "I can't believe you. That was so hateful."

Malano stood, "I was doing my job."

Samantha stormed into the kitchen and Malano followed. "What are you so upset about? That I asked them if they were in it for the money. That's it! You are upset that I asked them about wanting money from their son's estate."

Samantha replied, "Yes! That was a terrible thing to ask. They told you how hateful their son was to them."

Malano touched her arm. "Samantha, how do we know what they told us was true. How do we know that he was really their son? You have to look at this in a pure light without any emotions. Forget about their appearance, and look at the facts. The doctor was very rich, and here is this poor couple that is barely getting by. If indeed they are his parents, they might feel that he owes them something. Maybe not him personally, but his estate. When people die, rats come out of the woodwork in hopes of getting part of the estate. It happens every day."

Samantha was still angry, but she was beginning to understand. Malano smiled at her and he touched her chin. Slowly she smiled back at him.

"Let's make some coffee to have with some pie," he said.

Samantha laughed, "Are you still hungry?" Malano shrugged, "Hey I'm a growing boy."

They were sitting on the couch eating pie and drinking coffee when Norm returned. "The roads are getting really bad," Norm said.

"Did you get grandpa home okay?"

"Yes, he was really tired, but I think he had a wonderful time. Did Franklin and Laverne get off okay?"

Samantha neared her father, "Yes, they did. I was going to call and make sure that they got home. Did you want some coffee and pie? The coffee is fresh."

"No, I think I'm going to retire and leave the downstairs to you young people. I'm just going to say goodnight to Bill. Love you, baby. The day was great. I'm glad that you invited everyone."

Samantha smiled at her father and hugged his neck, "Dad, we haven't watched "It's a Wonderful Life" yet. Don't you want to watch it with us?"

"No, Bear. I'm a little tired, so you two enjoy it."

Samantha squeezed his hand as she went to the kitchen to call Franklin and Laverne.

The phone rang several times before there was a weak, "Hello?"

"Laverne this is the Sheriff. I just wanted to make sure that you got home okay."

"Thank you, Sheriff. Yes, we are fine. The roads are getting pretty bad. Thank you again for the wonderful day. We both had a great time."

"Laverne, if you need anything, just call. Thank you for coming today." Samantha hung up and joined Malano and her dad in the living room.

"Hey guys," she greeted, "I hate to break this up, but with the storm getting worse. I think that I should make my rounds and make sure that the village is okay."

Both men looked at her in surprise.

Norm spoke first, "Bear, the roads are terrible out there. Isn't the deputy on duty today? Let him make the rounds."

"Dad, this village is my responsibility, and I'm going to do it. You go on to bed and I will be back later."

Malano walked to the hall closet and got his jacket.

Samantha looked at him. "You don't have to go. It won't take very long and then we can watch our movie."

"I'm going with you. What am I supposed to just sit here by myself while you are out being responsible?" he laughed.

"Well, I guess I could use some company. I don't know how much help a California boy is going to be in the snow." They both laughed as they left the house.

The snow was heavy and visibility was nil. The Sheriff stopped the car in front of a row of stores and started to get out.

Malano questioned her, "What are you doing?"

Samantha smiled at him, "I'm going to check that the doors are locked and look in the windows to make sure that everything is okay."

"You do this every night?"

"Sure do. I know you are a big detective, and this is something that is alien to you. Our motto is "Protect and Serve," she laughed.

Malano jumped out of the car and started checking doors and looking in windows. He was checking the last shop on the block when a snowball hit him. He turned to see Samantha balling up snow for another attack. He quickly grabbed some snow and started for her.

Samantha continued her assault, "You forget that I played softball."

Malano launched his attack, "You forget that I was a pitcher."

The battle continued until they were both so cold that their feet and hands ached.

Malano was the first to concede, "I give up. I'm freezing. I'm a California boy. I'm not used to this kind of cold."

Samantha doubled over in laughter. "I win! I win! Let's go home, city boy, and watch the movie."

Malano left around one in the morning.

Samantha walked slowly up the stairs with a wide smile on her face. The day had been perfect, except for the bombshell that Franklin and Laverne had dropped.

"I have to learn to be more objective about everything. To be a good cop you must detach yourself from the world. I'm too trusting. I must remember what Bill told Detective Roberts about not letting anyone involved in the case gets too close. When your judgment is clouded with emotion, clues can be overlooked. Why did Franklin and Laverne wait until the investigation had gone this far before telling us of their connection to Dr. Rogers? Franklin participated in the shoot this year. That could be a very important clue. I have to tell Bill."

She looked at the clock. It was past 2 AM. "I guess it can wait until morning."

Malano stared up at the ceiling. His mind was reliving the best Thanksgiving Day he had ever had. Rolling over on his side he told himself, "You need to sleep."

Sitting up, he rubbed his feet. They were ice cold. He got up and looked through his bag for some socks. He placed the extra blanket, which Belle had left for him on top of the comforter, and snuggled back in bed. Still, sleep eluded him. Thinking about the case, Franklin and Laverne came to mind.

"I wonder why they admitted to being Dr. Rogers's parents. It didn't help the case. In fact, it probably will add two more suspects to the list. I need to question them tomorrow. I will have Samantha show me to their place. Listen, city boy, you have to be professional tomorrow. The holiday is over, and you have an important case to solve. Be objective. Don't let the Sheriff influence the way you do your job. After this case is solved, then we can see if there is something between us."

Closing his eyes, he felt sleep numbing his brain. "Thank you, God, for a wonderful day," he whispered as he fell into a restful sleep.

12

IT STOPPED SNOWING EARLY FRIDAY morning. Malano awoke early, envisioning Samantha. She had such a sweet smile, and he loved the easy way she handled people. She made everyone feel they had her undivided attention. This was definitely someone he wanted to get to know better and have as a part of his life. Throwing back the bed covers, he sat up, scratched his head, jumped out of bed and stretched.

He grabbed his robe and headed for the community bathroom down the hall, showered, shaved and dressed. Then he made his way downstairs and grabbed a cup of coffee and Danish.

Glancing through the newspaper as he ate his breakfast, he once again realized just how small this little community was. Farmingdale wasn't big enough for its own paper, so the news he was reading was already a day late. Traditionally, the mayor and his staff would serve Thanksgiving dinner at one of the homeless shelters on Wednesday. The front page showed pictures of the mayor serving dinners, sitting, and talking with the homeless. Yeah, right. Standing next to the mayor was the state representative. Malano thought about what Detective Roberts had said that both of these men had offered up a eulogy at Dr. Rogers' memorial. In both of the address books, that Dr. Rogers had hidden away, were initial that could fit these men. This could be the clue that had been evading him. Everything was falling into place.

He grabbed his coat, and started for the door. Belle was entering the dining room as he was leaving, "Good morning, Belle. Sorry to eat and run." Malano gave her a salute, and out the door, he went.

Samantha leaped down the stairs. Entering the kitchen, she kissed her dad and grabbed a cup of coffee. Norm was cooking eggs, and asked if she wanted some?

"Sorry, dad, no time. I have a million things to do, and I only have time for coffee and a piece of toast."

Norm looked at his daughter. "You look beautiful this morning, Bear."

"Well thank you, dad. Are you saying that I'm not usually beautiful?"

Norm laughed, "You know what I mean, girl."

"I do, dad. I have to get to the station. I will call you later if I'm going to be really late. Love you dad."

"Love you too, baby. Let me know if that city boy wants to come to dinner. I was going to make SOS with that left over turkey."

"I'll ask him and let you know."

Norm smiled and shook his head. He knew that his little Bear had met the man that she was going to spend the rest of her life with.

Malano was waiting in the parking lot when she pulled in. He smiled warmly as they both exited their cars.

"Good morning, detective. I trust you slept well."

"Yes Sheriff I did sleep well, and you?"

"Wonderful," was her reply.

They set their things down, and the Sheriff went to make coffee. Malano was looking at the address books when she neared his desk.

"Detective, there is something that I wanted to let you know. I didn't think about until I was in bed, so I thought I would let you sleep. Franklin participated in the shoot this year. I know that he has participated in the past. I'm not sure how many years he has competed, but we could look it up in the records. He sometimes helps

Seth with the arrows if my deputy is busy. That means that he has had access to the shed."

Malano sat back and lit his first cigarette of the day. "That is very interesting. Did you have a change of heart since last night?"

"What do you mean by a change of heart?" Malano sat up, "Last night, you were all over me for questioning the Rogers. This morning, you are telling me information that could make him a suspect."

"After you left last night, I did some thinking about what you had said about being objective. I want to be a good cop. I just need to learn to put my feelings aside and look at things objectively."

Malano smiled, "I wish more cops would listen to that advice. I think what we need to do is talk with Mr. Peters. Do you know if he is in his office?"

"I'll have to check on Seth."

"Before you do that, I want you to look at something." Malano brought out both of the address books. One book had dollar amounts then initials, and the second book had names and addresses.

"Where is the book with the kid's pictures?" questioned Malano.

The Sheriff went to the evidence table and returned with the pictures.

Malano scanned both books and then pointed, "Look at this. The number under this child's picture matches the number in this book and the initials after are MJ. What if the MJ stands for Mayor Johnson or Mathew Johnson, the mayor's full name? In this other book it shows $10,000MJ."

"Are you saying that the mayor had something to do with this child and gave the doctor $10,000?" asked the Sheriff.

"I don't know what I'm saying, but it is some kind of explanation. Look, this one shows this child's number matches with this one and the initials are SR. In the newspaper this morning, it showed a picture of the mayor and state representative serving the homeless Thanksgiving dinner. The state representative's name is Steven Russell. The dollar amount in this book shows $15,000SR. Steven Russell also was present at the doctor's memorial and gave one of the eulogies. We need to get Seth Peter's records from past hunts up to this last one, and see if either of these men participated in the shoot."

The Sheriff checked her watch. "He should be in by now. Let me tell him that we need his records."

She returned shortly with a puzzled look on her face, "He's not in yet. That's strange he is always here by eight. We will hear him when he comes in, and I will talk to him then."

Malano continued to go through the books and started writing down dollar amounts on a sheet of paper. Malano's cell phone rang and he picked it up, "Malano."

"Malano, this is the captain. I wanted to know how the investigation is going."

"Hey, captain. Well, the investigation has changed from an accident to a murder investigation."

The captain hesitated, "How did you come to that conclusion?"

Malano thought before speaking, "We found the missing equipment. They were in the trunk of Mrs. Williams' car. Mr. Williams' arrow from the shoot was with his equipment. We also retrieved the arrow from Doctor Rogers and it was from a prior shoot. I have a detailed report of our findings and there are also some business dealings that we have uncovered that you need to see. I have e-mailed the report to you with an attached file. Right now I'm not ready to arrest anyone, because it's seems like our list of suspect keeps growing."

"When will you be back in the office?" the captain questioned.

"I'll be in on Monday," answered Malano.

"Well have a good weekend. How was your Thanksgiving?"

Without any hesitation Malano said, "It was wonderful."

The captain chuckled, "Well I need to meet the person that made your Thanksgiving so wonderful. Before you go Bill, make sure that nothing is leaked to the press. I want to see everything about this case first thing Monday morning."

Malano blushed and hung up.

The Sheriff returned from Seth Peter's office with a concerned look on her face.

Malano turned to her and inquired, "What's wrong?"

The Sheriff looked at her watch and back toward Seth's office, "It's almost ten, and Seth is still not here. I'm kind of worried about him. I think I will call his home and make sure that he is okay."

Dialing the number from memory, she waited for him to pick up. After the tenth ring, she hung up, grabbed her jacket, and started for the door.

Malano called out to her, "Where are you going?"

With concern in her voice she said, "Seth's. I think something might be wrong."

Malano grabbed his coat. "I'll go with you." When they arrived at Seth's house, his car was parked in the driveway covered with snow.

"Looking at his car, he hasn't been out yet this morning. Maybe he decided to take vacation until Monday," smiled Malano. The Sheriff went to the front door and rang the bell. There was no answer, so she knocked. Still there was no answer. They tried looking through the window, but the drapes were drawn tight.

"Something is wrong. I feel it," she said.

Malano went to the front door and knocked loudly. Not receiving an answer, he tried the knob and it opened. He looked at her to get her approval before he entered.

There was no movement, so they called out, "Seth! Seth!" "Is anybody home?" Still there was silence. The Sheriff started for the back room, which was Seth's bedroom.

Opening the door slowly she called, "Seth, Seth. This is Samantha are you okay?" There lying on top of the blankets was Seth. She felt for a pulse, and confirmed that he was dead. The Sheriff left the room quickly and called Doc Amos. Malano joined her in the kitchen. She was visibly upset, so he rubbed her shoulders.

Malano whispered in her ear, "Are you okay?"

She shrugged, and then turned to him. "I haven't seen anyone dead since my mother died when I was 22. In the past week, I have seen two dead bodies. I thought I handled myself very well with Dr. Rogers, but Seth is an old friend. I have known him all my life. The thing that really hurts is that I was going to invite him for Thanksgiving dinner and I didn't. He was all alone when this happened. I feel so bad."

Malano pulled her close and hugged her, "I know it's hard, but you are doing fine. Hang tough." She nodded and buried her face in his chest.

Presently, there was a knock at the door. Malano answered the door and found Doc Amos on the step.

"Hey, detective. I didn't know that you were here. Samantha called and said that I needed to get over here. Is Seth sick?"

Malano stepped aside as the doctor entered. "Well Doc, it appears that Mr. Peters is dead."

The doctor stared at him in disbelief and started for the bedroom. The Sheriff joined them. She waited at the bedroom door.

Doc Amos checked the body, and then slowly turned to Malano, "I think we need to call the medical examiner to take the body. I'm not equipped to do an autopsy. I don't have the means to determine the time or the cause of death. Would you like to make that call, detective?"

Malano nodded his head, and went to the kitchen to make the call. Presently, he returned and informed them that it would be about an hour before the medical examiner could be there to pick up the body. Doc Amos took a sheet and covered the body, and then left the room. As Malano was leaving, a note on the nightstand caught his eye. Malano ushered Doc Amos and the Sheriff out the room, and then suggested that the Sheriff make some coffee while they waited. After they had left Malano picked up the note. It read:

To Whom It May Concern:

I am leaving this note so everyone will understand my frame of mind at the time of my death. I have done things in my life of which I'm not proud. First of all I deserted my family. I had a wife and a daughter. One day, I left for work and never returned. I turned my back on the two of them. My wife died. I learned that my daughter married and had a daughter. My daughter and her husband were killed in an auto accident. My granddaughter was placed in foster care. I followed her progress throughout her life, but would not make my presence known. I knew that she needed me but I was not man enough to be there for her. When she was older, she was taken to a doctor for help. I felt that he would do good things for her. She married that doctor, and I felt that she was going to be fine, but I was wrong. I learned that the doctor was abusing her and I did nothing. I learned that the doctor had molested her when she was a child. I remained silent.

I have recently become aware that this man attacked my granddaughter on New Year's Eve and hurt her badly. She will never be able to have children. I was given this information by a reliable source that promised to do justice to the doctor if I let them have access to the arrows used in the shoot. This I did, because I felt that this was the only way that justice would be served on the doctor for all the wrongs that he did to my granddaughter and all the other children that he and his friends molested.

I want to confess to my part in the murder of the doctor. I don't want anyone to pay for what I have done. I was not man enough to take care of my wife and child and never came forward to help my granddaughter. I can't live with the way my life has turned out. I have quilt for everything that I haven't done. I know that what I have done will become public and I can't face the granddaughter that I rejected.

I have taken my own life, and I pray that God will forgive me for all of my faults.

Seth Peters

Malano folded the paper and walked to the kitchen. The Sheriff and Doc Amos were talking softly when he entered. Malano handed the note to the Sheriff and she began to read.

Laying the note on the table, she spoke to no one in particular, "I can't believe this."

Doc Amos looked at her and asked, "What is it Samantha?" She handed him the note and he began to read.

Malano was getting a cup of coffee when the Sheriff joined him. "So this was a suicide. I just can't believe he was a part of this accident, murder whatever it is. This means that he is Mrs. Rogers' grandfather. The note doesn't say who he let have access to the arrows."

Doc Amos had finished the note, hung his head, and cried. The Sheriff hugged him and tried to give words of comfort.

Shaking his head, he spoke softly, "I thought that we were friends. Why didn't he tell me how he was hurting? I wouldn't have judged him. We were supposed to be friends. Friends are supposed to help each other. I wouldn't have judged him."

The Sheriff rubbed his shoulders and gave him words of support.

Malano took the seat across from Doc Amos. "Doc, I know that this is hard, but we need to find the person that was giving Mr. Peters this information. Did you know that he had a family or about his granddaughter?"

Doc Amos just shook his head and said nothing. The three drank their coffee, while the silence hung heavily in the room.

Finally, Doc Amos started to speak, "Seth and I have been friends for longer than I care to remember. This was the first year that we didn't share Thanksgiving dinner together. I thought that he would be there."

The Sheriff hung her head as Doc continued, "Thinking about it, he did tell me once that he had a family, but never explained what happened to them. I thought that maybe they had been killed in a car accident or some other kind of tragedy. He would get upset when I brought up the subject, so eventually I stopped bringing it up. I know that the last several years he talked about grandchildren. Since he didn't have a family, I just thought that he was dreaming about the way we wished our lives could be. We would sometimes play games about being married and having children and grandchildren. After doing this we would laugh and say if we had only found the right woman and were 30 years younger."

Doc chuckled, "Every 10 years, we would play this game, and of course we would wish that we were 10 years younger each year."

This brought tears to his eyes and he paused for a moment, "I knew that something had been bothering him. He came to me and told me that he was having trouble sleeping, and asked if I could give him something. That was back around the first of the year. He never said anything after that, so I thought that everything was fine."

Doc looked at Malano, "Was there a prescription bottle on his night stand?"

"Not that I saw, but let me go look." Presently, Malano returned with a bottle, "I found this empty bottle on the vanity in his bathroom. Your name is on it as the physician."

Doc hung his head. "I only prescribed enough for one month. If he used it to end his life, he must not have taken them when he first asked. That means that I helped him to end his life."

The Sheriff held his hand. "You didn't know Doc. This is not your fault. Seth made the decision to end his life."

There was a knock at the door. Malano excused himself to answer the door. It was the boys from the medical examiner. He showed them where the body was and asked, "Is the medical examiner coming?"

"He was right behind us."

There was another knock and Malano welcomed the examiner,

"Hey Jeff."

Jeff extended his hand, "Hey Bill, what do we have here?"

Malano led him to the bedroom as he spoke, "Looks like a suicide. There was a note and an empty bottle of sleeping pills in the bathroom. I have bagged both, so you can take them back with you."

The Sheriff and Doc joined Malano at the door to the bedroom. They watched as pictures were taken and Seth's hands were bagged. The medical examiner took out the body bag, and Malano ushered the Sheriff and Doc to the living room, "You don't want to witness them bagging the body. I think that is the hardest part for loved ones to witness."

The Sheriff sat with Doc on the sofa and spoke softly to him. The gurney carrying the body of Seth Peters was wheeled past them and out the door. The examiner came to both of them and expressed his condolences.

Malano handed him the bagged note and bottle.

"I should have the results next week. Will you be in your office, Bill?"

Malano walked him to the door, "Yes, I will be in my office on Monday. See you next week."

"Sure thing, Bill."

Malano returned to Doc, "This is very important, and I want you to think hard. Did you ever see Mr. Peters talking to anyone that he normally didn't talk to? Was there anyone, maybe a stranger to you, whom he was talking to? I want you to take your time, because you are upset right now. I'll drive you home now if you feel like you can't drive."

Doc put on his coat and grabbed his bag. "No, I'm fine. I think I will go home and lay down for a while. I will let you know if I remember anything."

The Sheriff hugged him and walked him to his car. Malano returned to the bedroom and looked around for something that he might have missed. The Sheriff watched him from the doorway. Malano searched every corner of the room, including the dresser drawers and the nightstand. Opening the closet, he perused every article of clothing and checked each pair of shoes. Having found nothing, he proceeded to the bathroom, and went through the medicine cabinet. Confident that there was nothing to be found, he turned and saw the Sheriff staring at him.

He went to her and put his arms around her, "I know that this is hard, but we need to focus to make sure that this was really a suicide. We need to find out who was giving him this information and who decided that the doctor needed to be killed. I don't think that he was killed because of what he did to Mr. Peter's granddaughter, but what he had on someone. Someone got tired of being controlled by this man. We need to lock up this house, and I want to talk with Franklin. We also need to get the records from Mr. Peter's office."

Returning to the office, the Sheriff proceeded to Seth's office. Inside everything was organized, and she had no trouble in locating the list of hunters for this year's shoot.

Malano was on the phone with Franklin when she returned. "Okay sir, I will see you in about 30 minutes. Yes, I'm at the Sheriff's station." As he hung up the phone, the Sheriff handed him the ledger. The second name on the list was Franklin Rogers.

"Okay, he does have some explaining to do. He told us that his son didn't want to see him, but he didn't tell us that he participated in the same shoot as his son. This would give him the opportunity to commit the murder."

The Sheriff lit a cigarette and spoke her thoughts out loud, "If Franklin did kill his son, and how did he put Mr. Williams' equipment in the trunk of Mrs. Williams' car? How would Franklin have known about his son's business dealings? The information that Seth talks about seems to come from someone with police connections. Didn't you have some questions for one of the officers about his accident report?"

Malano answered, "Officer Reed. Let's check if he ever participated in past shoots. Also check to see if there is an entry for the mayor and the state representative."

The Sheriff returned with several large ledgers, "Seth combined several shoots in these ledgers." They each took a ledger, and started to search for Reed or anyone that was connected with this case. The search proved fruitless.

Franklin arrived 30 minutes later. Malano stood and shook his hand, "Mr. Rogers, it has come to my attention that you were a participant in the shoot."

Franklin took a chair, "Yes, sir. I participated in the shoot each year since we moved here."

Malano lit a cigarette and looked straight at Franklin, "Last night when you were telling us about your relationship with the doctor, why didn't you tell us that you saw him each year at the shoot?"

Franklin looked down at his hands, "I thought that the Sheriff knew."

Malano picked up a piece of paper acting like he was reading, "Mr. Rogers, were you friends with Seth Peters?"

Franklin was caught by surprise, "I knew Seth, but I don't think you would say that we were friends."

Malano continued, "Did you help Mr. Peters with the shoot?"

Franklin took his time, "I don't know exactly what you mean. I sometimes helped him carry the arrows to Cora's. I only did that if the deputy was busy."

"Did you help him take the arrows for this shoot?" questioned Malano.

"No, the deputy helped him."

"Do you have a key to the storage shed, Mr. Rogers?"

Franklin looked straight at the detective, "Why would I have the key to the storage shed?"

Malano dismissed his question and continued, "Mr. Rogers were you aware that Mr. Peters was the grandfather to your son's wife?"

A shocked looked crossed his face and he nodded that he didn't know.

"Was Mr. Peters aware that you were Doctor Rogers' father?"

Franklin was becoming nervous and wiped his hands on his pants, "The Sheriff and you are the only ones that know that I was Bentley's father."

"Do you know if your son ever told anyone such as his hunting partner that you were his father?"

Franklin looked at the Sheriff and requested something to drink. She returned with a glass of water and asked if he would like a cup of coffee. He nodded in agreement.

While they were waiting for the Sheriff to return, Malano again asked, "Do you know if your son ever told anyone about you being related to him?"

Franklin crossed and uncrossed his legs before he spoke. "I don't know what my son told his friends. He made it clear to Laverne and I that he didn't want anyone to know that we were related. I never spoke to him at the shoots. He and his partner hunted on one side of the mountain and I went on the other."

"Who was your partner, Mr. Rogers?"

Franklin hung his head. "I hunted alone. It is not required that you have a partner. There are some of us that like to hunt alone."

Malano leaned back in his chair, "Is there anything that you would like to tell me?"

Franklin shifted in his chair, "No, I have told you everything."

"Well, I would like to thank you for coming in," Malano dismissed him saying nothing further.

Franklin hesitated to stand. Then he rose and started for the door.

"Good Day, Sheriff."

The Sheriff waved, "Have a good day, Franklin."

As he opened the door, Malano asked, "Mr. Rogers are you a good shot?"

Franklin turned and spoke, "I'm a great shot." He left the station without another word.

Malano and the Sheriff looked at each other after Franklin left. Malano's cell phone rang, "Malano."

"Bill, this is Brian."

"Hey Brian! What's up?"

"Well, I have been doing some investigating."

"Okay and what have you come up with?"

"Well, I talked with Reed's supervisor and was told that a couple of years ago the officer was divorced and was having money problems. At one point, there was garnishment for back child support. Shortly after this, the money problems seemed to disappear and Officer Reed showed up with a brand new sport car. When asked how this happened, he told them that a rich uncle had died and left him a large inheritance. Since that time he has bought a large condo, wears only designer labels and vacations twice a year in Europe. I also checked if he was on duty Saturday. He was not listed on the roster, but he was the one that went to Mrs. Rogers' house and brought her back to the morgue to identify her husband's body. I think we need to speak with him. I asked if anyone knew where he was going for the holidays and no one was sure. I think I will run by his house and see if he is at home."

Malano spoke, "When is he due back?"

"He is on call starting Sunday, and he has day shift on Monday. When will you be back?"

"I will be in the office on Monday. What time is Reed on duty?"

"He is scheduled for duty at 7 AM. Do you want me present when you question him? In addition, I got a call at home on Thanksgiving from Mrs. Rogers. She was very upset with the way you had talked to her. She also told me that she found something in her husband's study that I might want to see. I'm going over there when we are through."

Malano voice had an edge when he spoke, "Let me know what she has discovered. I don't care how upset she is with me."

"Okay Bill, I will let you know what I find. Did those boots that we got from the Williams' fit the prints?"

"Mr. Williams boots fit one set of prints, but the treads on the smaller don't match Mrs. Williams. I want the boots you saw at the Rogers house brought in. Didn't you say that there was mud on Mrs. Rogers's shoes and in her car that matched the mud from here?"

"I don't know if they matched. I didn't pick up her shoes or any of the mud from her car."

"Come on, Brian. Use your head. That could prove that she was at the scene. I want the shoes that you saw, and I want a mud sample taken from the interior and from the tires of her car."

"I'm sorry Bill. I guess that I just wasn't thinking. I'll take care of that when I'm at her house."

"Okay, let me know what you find."

Malano turned to the Sheriff, "What needs to be done now is to box up all the evidence, so I can take it back with me."

The Sheriff looked surprised, "I thought that you would be leaving on Sunday?"

Malano rubbed his chin, "There really isn't anything more to be done here, but I do need to put everything together for the DA. I also need to go through the evidence that Roberts has collected."

The Sheriff began to gather the evidence and box it. Malano took her hand, "Hey, I'm not leaving until tomorrow. Let's have dinner tonight."

"Oh, I almost forgot my dad wanted to know if you wanted to come over for leftovers tonight. You don't have to. We can go out."

Malano smiled, "You know, I think I would rather go to your house and have some of your great leftovers. I eat restaurant food all the time. It's a great treat to eat home cooking, and you made the best turkey that I have ever tasted. Don't tell my mom."

The Sheriff returned his smile, "I won't tell your mom, but I do need to call dad and let him know that we both will be there. I also need to let him know about Seth."

"You call your dad and I will get everything together." Malano grinned.

As Malano drove them to her house, she took out a piece of paper and looked at him, "We need to write down everything that we have learned about this case."

"I agree," said Malano, "First we know that the doctor was involved in some kind of shady business. We also know that Franklin and Laverne are his parents and that Seth Peters is the grandfather to Mrs. Rogers. We know that someone was giving Seth information about what the doctor was doing and what he did to his granddaughter. Seth also gave someone access to the equipment shed and they took an arrow that was used in the crime. We also know that Mr. and Mrs. Williams didn't have a good relationship with the doctor and that he molested Mrs. Williams as a young girl. We also know that he molested and abused Mrs. Rogers. The doctor also used damaging information about people, which he used to control them. One of those people was Dr. Powell, and he used a police report to control him, which means that he had access to an officer."

"Now let's list what we need to find out," said the Sheriff.

"The killer!" piped Malano.

The Sheriff gave him a sideways look, "Well, talk about stating the obvious, "she laughed, "Seriously, Bill, we need to find out who was giving the information to Seth, and who asked him for access to the equipment shed. Who picked up Mr. Williams' equipment and put it into Mrs. Williams' car?"

Malano pulled into the driveway and turned off the car. The Sheriff reached for the door handle and he touched her hand. Turning to him, he leaned towards her and kissed her lightly.

"I have been wanting to do that all day," he smiled.

The Sheriff blushed and touched his cheek with her hand, "I was hoping you would." They got out of the car and started for the front door hand in hand.

The front door swung open as they neared the house, and Norm greeted them warmly.

"Hey Norm. Thank you for inviting me to your home again."

Norm shook Malano's hand and patted him on the back as they entered, "Good to see you, Bill. Thanks for coming. I thought that by inviting you to dinner my daughter would get to come home early."

They all laughed, "I guess that I'm a slave driver. I have been called that before."

Closing the door Norm asked, "Bill would you like a beer."

"That would be great. Thank you, sir."

Norm returned with the beer and they all sat in the living room.

Norm asked, "Now what is this about Seth?"

Samantha started, "Well we had some ledgers that we needed to look at that were in Seth's office. He didn't come in, so I called. There was no answer, so I felt that something might be wrong, so we went over there and found him. He left a note to the effect that he had taken his life. It was so sad, dad. I'm worried about Doc Amos. He gave Seth the sleeping pills that he overdosed on."

Norm sat back and was silent for the moment. "Did he explain why he felt that he couldn't go on?"

Malano fielded this question, "Mr. Peters explained in his note that he had abandoned his family. His wife died, and then his daughter and her husband were killed in a car accident. They left a daughter who turns out to be the wife of Dr. Rogers. Mr. Peters felt guilty that he was not strong enough to step forward and take the child. Mr. Peters was then given information about the doctor and was asked for access to the equipment shed so that an arrow for the shoot could be taken. That person then used that arrow to kill the doctor. Mr. Peters was afraid that this information was going to become public, and he couldn't face his granddaughter."

Norm looked to Malano, "Did Seth say who this person was or did he give you any kind of clue as to who this might be?"

"No sir, he just confessed to his part in the crime."

Norm stared into the fire. "It's hard to believe that Seth would do that. I know that he was a private man, but I never thought that he had a family."

"Well dad, we have some more information that was told to us last night when you drove grandpa home. Franklin and Laverne are the parents of the doctor that was killed."

Norm looked at her with surprise, "They told you that?"

"Yes, after you, grandpa and Doc Amos left, they told Bill and me."

"I need another beer. Would you like another one, Bill?"

"I'll get it, sir. Are they in the fridge?"

"You're the detective. You find them," Norm chuckled.

The rest to the evening was passed in pleasant conversation. Around ten, Norm made his good nights and retired upstairs. Malano put another log on the fire, and returned to the couch sitting next to Samantha. They smiled at each other, and Samantha spoke first, "I hate to see you go. I wanted to thank you for letting me participate in the investigation. I have learned so much from you in just a week."

Malano pretended to blush, "Well thank you, ma'am."

Samantha playfully punched him.

He became serious. "You have a real knack for police work. You have handled a lot of information and you kept it to yourself. I thank you for that. The first thing in police work is to learn to listen and to see. Remember criminals are stupid and cops are lucky. Most cases will solve themselves if you listen and see the clues without bias."

Samantha leaned close and they kissed.

"Excuse me!" said Norm. The couple jumped apart.

Norm entered the room, "I didn't mean to interrupt, but I just thought about something."

"What's that, daddy?" Norm sat across from them, "I was thinking about Seth and I remembered a time that I saw Seth and a policeman talking. It was at that new steakhouse. I had gone into the city and I stopped by for lunch. Seth and this policeman were having a discussion in one of the back booths. I saw them and they both stopped talking and looked uncomfortable being seen together. I didn't mean to interrupt, so I said hello and moved on to my table."

Malano questioned, "Did Mr. Peters introduce you to the officer?"

"No, he just greeted me and looked uncomfortable, so I moved on."

"How did you know that the other gentleman was a police officer?"

"He was in uniform and I also noticed his cruiser in the parking lot.

In fact, that is what made me decide to stop for lunch. Everyone knows that cops know the best places to eat," Norm laughed.

"Norm, was the officer wearing his name tag?"

"Not that I remember. Shortly after I sat down, they both left. I don't know if any of this matters, but I thought that you should know."

"Thank you. That is very important information."

"Well, I'm going to go back to bed now. You two can resume what you were doing."

They laughed as Norm retired. Samantha turned to Malano. "It looks like Officer Reed could be the one that gave Seth the information."

"If the officer was Reed, and that has not been verified, I can't wait to talk to him on Monday."

13

MALANO LEFT EARLY SATURDAY MORNING, bidding Belle a big thanks for her hospitality and good wishes for the coming holidays.

The drive home was lonely. He wouldn't be seeing Samantha today, but the separation would be good for both of them. He would be able to sort out his feelings for her. First, he had to clear his mind to be able to concentrate on this case. There were so many people involved, but the primary suspects remained the same. Malano felt in his bones that Reed was a dirty cop. Somehow, Doctor Rogers had bought him off, and he needed to find out to what extent this might be true.

Malano's cell rang, "Malano, speak to me, guy!"

"Hey, Bill, this is Brian. Wanted to let you know what Mrs. Rogers found in her husband's study."

"Why didn't you call me earlier?" Malano questioned.

"Well, she was very upset at the findings. Then when I asked her about the dirty boots, she couldn't find them. We looked all over, but couldn't find them. Strange, no?"

"What about the mud sample from the car?"

Roberts chuckled, "Mrs. Rogers had the car detailed on Friday. That right there tells you something."

Malano was livid, "Tell me what you found."

"A secret room behind the bookcase in the study. There were all kinds of editing and video equipment. There were racks and racks of pornographic videos ranging from child porn to snuff films. The film that was in the VCR was labeled Amanda and it showed the New Year's Eve attack. The bastard filmed the whole thing! I also found hidden cameras in the bedroom and bathroom. The man was a real sicko."

Malano paused, "Do you believe that she knew nothing of the hidden room or the cameras in the bedroom and bathroom?"

Without hesitation, Roberts answered, "I don't think she was aware of them. When we viewed the tape, she appeared to be in shock and trembling. She couldn't have faked it, not what we saw."

"I just don't buy it," said Malano, "She was molested as a young girl by this man. She was aware there was another child named Alice that he was doing, but she never said anything. Did this man manipulate her to that extent? It's just a bit too convenient for her. She was a victim and now she wants us to know how depraved her husband was and how innocent she is. It feels like overkill to me. What was her explanation about the missing shoes? She can't blame that on her husband."

"When I asked her about the shoes, she said she didn't know what had happened to them. I asked if the housekeeper might have cleaned them and put them away. She had no explanation. She had given the housekeeper the weekend off to be with her family for Thanksgiving," explained Roberts.

"Did you ask her why she had the car detailed? I mean it has been snowing for the last couple of days. Why did she pick now to have it cleaned? Was there any mud samples left in the garage?"

Roberts was silent for a moment, "She has been so upset. I didn't want to bother her with any further questions. I'm sorry Bill."

"I'm almost at the city limits. Where are you right now?" asked Malano.

"I was on my way home, Bill."

"Well turn around and get back to the Rogers house. I also want you to get some uniforms to the house to pick up the evidence that you found in that room. I also want Brandon from the visual department to meet us there. I should be there in about 20 minutes," instructed Malano.

"Got you, Boss. We'll be waiting for you. You know, Mrs. Rogers is not going to like this."

"Brian, this is a murder investigation. Ask me if I care what the lady likes," Malano ended the call.

Thinking to himself, Malano went over these new developments, "Ms. Amanda keeps discovering new info to prove what a scumbag her husband was, but is unable to give us the muddy shoes that she wore on the day of the murder. She claims that she was doing errands at the time of the shooting, but there is mud all over her car. I need to find what errands were being done that day, and when she returned home."

Scratching his head, "I wonder if the lady knows how to handle a bow and arrow?"

When he pulled in front of the Rogers estate, the gates were open and Detective Roberts' car was in the driveway. Malano exited the car and looked around the grounds before proceeding to the front door. He could feel eyes on him.

Roberts opened the door, "Hey Bill, come on in."

Malano frowned, "Making yourself at home here, Brian?"

Roberts looked sheepish and stood back to let Malano enter.

"Where is Mrs. Rogers?" Malano barked. "She is waiting in the living room. She is still very upset about the new findings."

Malano stopped and looked Roberts in the eye, "You need to put some distances between yourself and Mrs. Rogers. I think I told you this before, but I haven't seen any of your usual professionalism. I don't want you in the room when I talk to Mrs. Rogers. Wait here for the uniforms to arrive." Roberts hung his head and nodded his agreement.

Malano entered the living room to find Mrs. Rogers curled on the couch.

"Mrs. Rogers! I'm Detective Malano, and I have some questions for you."

Amanda lifted her head and spoke in a soft voice, "Where is Detective Roberts?"

Malano didn't wait for an invite to sit. Taking the seat across from her he answered, "Detective Roberts is busy. You need to speak to me now."

Amanda visibly trembled and looked away.

"Mrs. Rogers, we have determined that this was not an accident, but that someone murdered your husband." Amanda gasped, but refused to look at him.

"It has also been learned that your husband not only sexually abused you, but he also physically abused you. It appears to me that your husband has been sexually abusing you since you were a child. Am I correct on this point, Mrs. Rogers?"

Amanda's voice sounded weakly, "Yes."

Malano continued, "We also know that you were aware that your husband was the intruder that attacked you in the early hours of New Year's Day. That attack resulted in you being unable to have children. Is this also correct?"

Amanda nodded in agreement.

"Detective Roberts informed me that you found a hidden room in your husband's study."

Amanda again nodded.

"Detective Roberts also found video cameras concealed in your bedroom and bathroom. Did you know about these cameras?"

Amanda sat up and looked Malano in the eye, "No! Detective, I was not aware of the concealed cameras." The anger in her eyes flashed then disappeared.

"Mrs. Rogers, you were aware that your husband was molesting other children that he had as patients."

Amanda stormed at him, "I was the only one that he loved. I was the one that he groomed to be his wife. What does it matter to me what he did with his patients. I'm the one that is important in his life. I'm the one that went through the beatings and the humiliations that Bentley doled out. I'm the one who was forced to stand by his side and watch as Bentley ruined people's lives, and smile all the time. My life has been a living hell, and now you come in here and accuse me of knowing and not doing anything to stop my husband."

She chuckled and then stopped. "You didn't know my husband, Detective Malano.

This outburst appeared to leave her exhausted. She curled back up, on the couch, and covered her face.

Malano was not put off by her display, "Mrs. Rogers where were you on the day of the shoot?"

Amanda gave him a pitiful look, "Bentley left me a "to do" list and I was running all over town getting it accomplished."

Malano shifted in his chair, "What time did you finish your errands?"

"I got home early. Then I had to leave again, because I had forgot to pick up Bentley's tux."

Malano reiterated his question, "What time did you get home?"

"I don't remember. I went to the seamstress, the florist, had lunch. I remember I had a terrible headache that day. I arrived home and was taking out my gown when I remembered Bentley's tux. I got back in the car, went to the cleaners, and then returned home. I recall that I was happily surprised that I beat Bentley home."

Malano moved closer to her, "So normally Dr. Rogers would have been home early in the day?"

Amanda thought for a moment, "If it was a good shoot, and he and Bruce won, he would get home late, but if the shoot went badly he would be home early. Since he wasn't home yet, I figured that he had won the event this year, and was out celebrating with his friends."

"Did Mr. Williams participate in the celebration when they won the shoot?"

Amanda sat up, "No! Poor Bruce didn't care for the shoot, but he was too sweet to tell Bentley. As soon as they had bagged their prey and the winner was announced, he would leave."

"Were you and Mr. Williams close?" Malano continued.

"Bruce is a sweetheart. He put up with Bentley's abuse for so many years. I often told him that he needed to give Bentley some of the abuse back that he handed out to everyone else. Bruce really made Bentley upset at the New Year's Eve party when he pushed him in the pool. It was the best comeuppance that Bentley ever received. He was totally embarrassed in front of all his high-powered friends. After that embarrassment Bentley had to take his anger out on someone and I was that someone." She hung her head and began to cry.

Giving her a few moments to collect herself, Malano continued, "Mrs. Rogers, do you remember being interviewed at the hospital after the attack?"

Amanda dried her eyes, "Yes, an Officer Reed took my statement. I didn't tell him that it was Bentley that had hurt me, because he wouldn't believe me. He had been to our house on several occasions because Bentley had hurt me, but nothing was ever done. Bentley told me on many occasions that no one would believe me if I told them. Everyone loved him, or that is what he thought. Bentley had something on everyone, so he could do exactly what he wanted and no one would do anything to him. I was trapped and he knew it."

"Mrs. Rogers, did it seem to you that Office Reed and your husband were friends?" Malano questioned.

Amanda spoke, "You would have to have known Bentley. He could charm anyone, but he was not a friend to anyone. Bentley played parts. I don't think anyone really knew Bentley, just what he wanted you to know. He was always in control, and issued orders that were not to be questioned. Bentley charmed people until he got something on them. Then the charm would disappear and the control freak took over."

Malano sat back in his chair, "Mrs. Rogers, did your husband ever invite you to the Turkey Shoot?"

Amanda smiled to herself and then spoke, "I wanted to do things that would make Bentley smile. He had the most beautiful smile. No matter how much he hurt me I loved to see his smile. I would forgive anything if he would just smile for me. He loved the shoot. He spent hours with his equipment making sure that the shafts weren't bent and the tips were razor sharp. I thought that it would be a wonderful surprise if I would learn the sport of archery and maybe I could be his partner since Bruce hated it so much. Bentley entered a contest and I secretly entered too. I had spent months practicing and I was pretty good. Anyway, I also entered the contest. I was pitted against women and him against the men. I took the women's division and the last part of the contest was for the top woman to go against the top man. To Bentley's and my surprise, we were going to go against each other. Bentley was not pleasantly surprised, as I had hoped.

He was so angry, and it must have affected his aim. I took the contest. Everyone was kidding Bentley and asking him if I gave him lessons. You heard the phrase, "If looks could kill." Well that is the way he looked at me," she began to cry; "I don't want to remember what he did to me."

Malano stood, "Thank you for your help, Mrs. Rogers. We are going to be taking the video equipment that was found in your husband's den and the cameras from your room and bathroom. Before I go, were you able to find the boots that you were wearing on Saturday?"

"No!" Amanda spoke softly.

"Is your car still in the garage?"

"Yes!" was her reply.

"Have you driven it since that Saturday?"

Amanda looked up, "No! I haven't gone anywhere since I heard about Bentley. I only went to the memorial and I had a limo pick me up. I did have it detailed. It was very muddy and Bentley doesn't like anything dirty."

"Thank you, Mrs. Rogers. We'll be talking again." Malano walked out the door, and Amanda stared at his back.

Malano entered the den, and proceeded to the hidden room. It was alive with activity. Detective Roberts was instructing an officer on labeling the evidence and making an inventory of everything that was being removed.

Malano came up to Roberts and asked, "Has Brandon arrived?"

Roberts was startled, and turned with a jump, "Hey, Bill. Brandon is over there."

Malano spoke softly to Brandon, and then both men left the room and proceeded upstairs. Entering the bedroom, Brandon began to examine the walls for the hidden cameras. Four camera lenses were located in the bedroom and three in the bathroom. The equipment and recording device was found on a shelf in Bentley's closet.

Shaking his head Brandon spoke, "This was quite a set up. This equipment must have cost a fortune. The man has every angle covered, even if you happened to be sitting on the john. The rooms have also been wired for audio, so he could listen to whatever is being said. There is a timer on the equipment, and it can be operated by remote control. The master control for everything is in the den, so he didn't have to be here to start the cameras. There are motion detectors, so if the person happens to wander out of camera range, the other cameras would adjust to capture the shot. That's not all, Bill. There are cameras in every room, but they are not as elaborate as in this room. Talk about Big Brother watching. The man that designed this system was a real a genius. There was no privacy."

Malano glanced around the room. "I need you to do a schematic of everything that you find. Where are the cameras and microphones located? I need all the rooms done in detail. I don't care how long it takes. If you need some help to get everything detailed, you will get all the help you need. Let me know when you get the report done. You have my cell phone number?"

"I have your number. This is going to take a while."

"That's fine. I want the job done right, but time is very important here."

"I understand, Bill. I will do my best," Brandon smiled.

Malano returned to the den and motioned for Roberts, "Brian, I have Brandon working on the video cameras, and he knows what I need done. I want you to remain here until all the videos have been logged and the equipment loaded. Make sure that the inventory is correct. Then when it is logged in properties, you compare their log with what you have. This is very important. I'm going to run by Reed's townhouse and see if he has returned from vacation. Then I will be at my office. This has to be logged into properties today. When you are finished, bring the inventory list to my office. I will be waiting there for you." Malano gave him a friendly punch as he left the room.

Malano started for the front door when he remembered that he wanted to check the garage. Entering the kitchen, he marveled at the orderliness of the room. Walking past the sink, he wiped his hand over the faucet, and again was surprised that there was not even a water spot visible anywhere. Opening some of the drawers, he noticed that everything was labeled, and that the drawers were labeled.

He thought to himself, "Everyone has a junk drawer that is a mess." To his surprise, the next drawer he opened was labeled junk drawer, and each piece of junk was in its labeled place. Malano smiled to himself.

The car was clean. Checking for any signs of mud, Malano found bits that were lodge in the treads. There was no evidence left on the floor. It looked like it had been mopped. Opening the driver's door, he found bits of mud on both the brake pad and the gas pedal. Taking another plastic bag, he took scrapings from each of the pedals. Labeling each bag, he returned to the house.

Heading for the front door, he noticed that Mrs. Rogers and Detective Roberts were in a hushed conversation. He stood for a short time watching them. Roberts looked up to see Malano, and quickly stepped back from Mrs. Rogers. Confused by Roberts' retreat, Mrs. Rogers looked in Malano's direction, and then quickly turned her head. Roberts started towards Malano, but Malano waved him off and continued towards the door.

As he got into his car, Malano was confused by the unprofessional behavior that Roberts was displaying. He had never had to reprimand him before about his behavior on a case. An uneasy feeling was descending on him, and he didn't like the feeling. Once again, he felt eyes on him. He looked at the living room window just as the drapes moved. Putting the car in gear, he roared the engine and left. The back of his neck began to burn, and he rubbed it to ease the tension.

Pulling his notebook from his pocket, he turned to Reed's address. Driving slowly down Reed's street, he looked for the correct condo. Locating it, he pulled into the driveway. Rubbing his neck, he exited the car and started for the front door. The drapes were closed tightly on all the windows, so nothing could be viewed from the outside.

Malano recalled the conversation that he had with Roberts. Roberts had stated that Reed was to be on call on Sunday and return to duty on Monday morning. Being on call meant that you were to be available if needed. That would mean that Reed should be returning from his vacation today. One of the neighbors was watching, so Malano decided to introduce himself.

"Good afternoon, ma'am. My name is Detective Malano."

The lady took his hand with some reservation. "I don't mean to be rude, but may I see your badge?"

Malano reached in his pocket and showed her his badge. The lady breathed a sigh of relief.

"You can't be too careful these days." Malano smiled, "You did the right thing, ma'am. I was wondering if you could help me with some information."

The lady took a step back. "I don't like to get involved. I have to live here and I don't want any trouble."

"I understand," Malano smiled, "I just need to know if you have seen Officer Reed lately? I know that he went on vacation for Thanksgiving, and I was wondering if you have seen him today."

The lady looked confused, "I don't get involved and I don't snoop, but I think you're wrong about Officer Reed going on vacation. I saw him go into his house on Sunday, and haven't seen him leave. I know when he leaves because his car's lights reflect on my window. You know these new cars lights automatically come on when you start your car. That is how I know when he comes and goes."

"Ma'am, could he have taken a cab to the airport?"

The lady thought a moment then said, "I'm all alone here, except for my dog. I'm not a snoop, but I very interested in what is going on around me. I have very good hearing, and I would have heard if a taxi had come for Brett, I mean Officer Reed. I have been concerned about him, and I even went to his door a couple of times, but there has not been an answer. I was bringing him some pie for Thanksgiving, but he didn't answer the door. I even called the police department on Sunday evening because I was concerned."

Malano rubbed his chin, "What made you so concerned on Sunday?"

"Well, I got up late on Sunday, at least late for me." She smiled then continued, "I had coffee and a cigarette before I ventured out for the Sunday paper. I usually pick up my paper while waiting for the coffee to brew. Anyway, I went out around 9:30 to get the paper, and I thought I heard Brett's car running in the garage. There was a lot of snow, but it is very dangerous to run the car with the garage door shut. I came back in and waited to see the reflection of his lights, but they never appeared. I waited until the afternoon then went and knocked on his door, but there was no answer. The car was no longer running, so I thought that maybe I had been mistaken. That evening I called the police and told them. They sent a car and the officer knocked at the door then left. I haven't seen anyone or any movement until I saw you drive up."

Malano asked, "Was there another detective around. He was probably in plain clothes like me."

"There has been no one."

Malano thanked the lady, and returned to Reed's front door. Banging on the front door this time, Malano thought, "This is loud enough to wake the dead." The uneasy feeling returned. Getting no response, he pulled a file from his pocket and began to work on the door. After a couple of turns, the door popped open.

Malano poked his head in and called "Officer Reed." There was no response, so he entered and began to look around. There was a strange odor permeating the house. He walked back to the bedrooms and found everything in place. Smiling to himself, "Officer Reed had expensive taste." He continued his walk through the house noticing that luggage had been placed in the spare bedroom, but it was not packed. Opening the fridge, he found it was almost empty, except for a couple of beers and some out dated milk. The unidentified odor was stronger in this room. Off the kitchen, a door led to the garage. Malano cautiously approached.

Opening the door slowly, he could see the outline of a car. Reaching in the garage, he felt for the light and switched it on. As the light illuminated the area, the smell assaulted his nose and he knew without going farther that Officer Reed was dead. Pulling a handkerchief from his pocket, he covered his nose and walked in. There sitting in his red sport car was Officer Reed. Malano checked the ignition and saw that it was on, but the car had stopped, because it had run out of gas. He looked around on the front seat for a note, but there wasn't one. Malano returned to the kitchen and called the medical examiner.

Jeff answered on the second ring, "ME! You stab 'em and we'll slab 'em. Jeff speaking."

"Hey, Jeff. This is Malano I have another one for you."

Jeff chuckled, "Detective, you are keeping us busy. I don't have to worry about job security with you around. Okay, where do you need me?" Malano gave him the address, and then sat at the kitchen table to wait.

As he waited, he took out his notepad and turned to the list of suspects. Going down the line, he came to Officer Reed and crossed out his name. The uneasy feeling again descended on him, as he wrote Detective Roberts on the list of suspects.

"Something is not right. Everything has been pointing to Reed and Mrs. Rogers. Now I have to take Reed out of the picture. Do I put Roberts in his place? Reed was involved with the doctor, but maybe not to the point of killing him. Who would benefit from Reed's death?"

Just then, the idea came to him to fax the picture of Reed and Roberts to Samantha, and she could show them to her father. Malano dialed her number and waited for her to answer.

"Sheriff's Office, Sheriff Forbes. How may I help you?"

"You just did, baby. I have been missing you all day. What are you doing at the office on a Saturday?"

Samantha laughed, "I was hoping that you would call. I missed you. The office seems so empty. I think my deputy wishes you were here too. I have been biting off his head all day. We have been going through Seth Peter's office. Did you just call to hear my sweet voice?"

"Well that was very high on my list." He chuckled.

"Liar," called Samantha, "What did you really call me about?"

"Well, there have been some new developments in the case. Right now, I'm waiting for the ME to come collect the body of Officer Reed."

Samantha gasped, "Was it murder or suicide?"

Malano rubbed his chin, "Looks like another suicide. I found him in the garage. He was sitting in his fancy sports car with the door closed and the motor running."

"Did he leave a note?" questioned Samantha.

"Not that I have been able to find. Let me tell you what I want to do. I have to wait here until the ME arrives. Then I'm going to the office. I want to fax a picture of Reed and Detective Roberts to you to show to your dad."

He waited for her response, but the line was silent. "Samantha, are you there?"

"Yes! I'm sorry. I don't understand why you want me to show these pictures to my dad."

"Samantha, your dad saw an officer talking with Seth Peters. We assumed that he was talking to Reed, but it could have been someone that was just wearing a police uniform."

"Wait a minute. Detective Roberts doesn't wear a uniform, and what has happened to make you suspect him?"

Malano heard the ME at the door and hurriedly told Samantha that he would be calling her back from his office.

Malano opened the door, and greeted Jeff warmly. "Hey, Jeff. Long time no see. Are you the only one working down at the tombs?"

They both laughed. Then Jeff answered, "Well they thought that it would be kind of quiet, so they left a few of us top examiners in charge. I will have to put your name on the list for possible business. The bodies seem to follow you."

"Well Jeff, this one is one of our own, so I want it prioritized. The body is in the garage. I need you to put a rush on the tox and the time of death. It looks like a suicide, but I need the whole house dusted for fingerprints. You know the routine. Priority, and mums the word."

"You got it, Bill. I hope you are on your way home now, so that we won't be called out again."

"Sorry, Jeff. I'm on my way to my office. If you come across anything unusual, please give me a call there or on my cell." Malano started for the door as Jeff made his way to the garage.

As Malano stepped from Reed's house, he spotted the neighbor watching.

As he walked in her direction, she began to cry, "I knew that something had happened to Brett. He was such a good boy. Was it the fumes from his car?"

Malano took her hands, "Yes, ma'am. It appears that he committed suicide."

The lady wiped her tears, "That just doesn't seem possible. He was always smiling, and would take the time to talk to me. Most young people don't have time for the old people, but he would always ask me about my dog and how my flowers were doing. He even told me that he was going to be putting in a big flower garden and wanted my expert advice on what flowers to plant. Such a nice boy."

Malano placed an arm around her and led her back to her house. "You get in out of the cold. You were a great help to me, and I appreciate it. You take care, and if you remember anything give me a call." He handed her one of his cards. She smiled and went into her house.

Malano pulled into his space, turned off his car and sat. His neck burned, and now he could feel the pressure of a headache forming behind his eyes. An uneasy feeling persisted, and a wave of nausea churned in his stomach. He thought to himself, "I haven't eaten since Belle's breakfast. Boy, do I miss that sleepy little village of Farmingdale with that magical mountain protecting it."

He exited his car and started for his office. He stopped by the records department, and requested the pictures that he was going to fax to Samantha. There weren't any pictures of Detective Roberts except in uniform. Malano smiled and told the clerk that that was fine. When he reached his office, a pile of paper work greeted him. He groaned at the sight. Pushing the files to one side, he dialed Samantha's number and waited.

"Sheriff's Office, Sheriff Forbes."

"Hey, Sheriff Forbes, what are you doing tonight?"

Samantha's voice took on a lilt, "I'm waiting on a crazy detective to fax me some pictures. What are you doing?"

"In case you didn't recognize my voice, I'm the crazy detective that you are waiting for."

"You sure are," Samantha replied.

"Okay, Sam, this is what I want you to do. I'm going to fax the two pictures to you now. The second picture is Detective Roberts, but it is an old picture, so he is in uniform. Don't identify the pictures to your dad. Let me know if either of the officers is the man that he saw talking with Mr. Peters. Okay? Are you ready?"

"Yes! I'm ready."

Malano sent the pictures and waited for Samantha's reply. In the background, he could hear her talking to someone then the phone was dropped.

"Sorry about that, Bill. This is Norm. How you doing, son?"

"Very fine sir, and you?"

"Well let me tell you that Samantha is living up to her nickname. She has been a BEAR today. When are you coming back?"

Malano chuckled, "As soon as I get this case wrapped up. I need you to take a look at the pictures that I just sent Samantha."

The line was silent as Norm studied each picture.

Finally, Samantha picked up the receiver, "Bill? Dad picked the picture of Detective Roberts as the man talking with Seth."

"Is he sure?" questioned Malano. "He says that he is positive. He remembers the cleft in the man's chin. What does all of this mean?"

Malano pounded the desk. "It looks like things are beginning to fall into place. I have to go. I'll call you later." Malano stopped himself before he said, "Love you. Tell your dad to take it easy and you quit being a BEAR or I'll have to come up there and adjust your attitude." Samantha smiled into the phone,

"I'll be good, but I'll be waiting for your call and your visit. If you need any help just give me a call."

"Miss you," Malano said, as he hung up the phone.

Malano was arranging his notes on the case, and for a moment was not aware of Roberts standing at the door. The sound of his voice startled Malano, and he looked up.

"Hey! Bill. I have the inventory list that you requested."

Malano wouldn't look at him, but instructed him to put the list on the side desk. Roberts did as he was instructed, and returned to Malano's desk.

Slowly Malano looked up, "Is they're anything else?"

Roberts was feeling uncomfortable and didn't know how to begin, "Bill, I heard about Reed. That's too bad that we didn't get to speak with him."

Malano didn't raise his head, but continued to sort the evidence. "I wanted to explain what you saw at Amanda's this afternoon."

Malano put down the papers and looked at Roberts, "Okay, I'm waiting."

Roberts took the nearest seat, but just looked at his hands.

Malano reiterated, "I'm waiting!"

"Amanda was very upset about the things that she told you, and wanted to make sure that you hadn't misunderstood her."

Malano picked up a pen and began tapping it on the desk, "So now you are on a first name basis with one of our suspects. Well what did Amanda think that I would misunderstand?"

Roberts rubbed his hands on his pants, "Well about her feelings for her husband. She is tired and stressed, and didn't want you to think that she didn't love her husband."

"So noted, detective. Is there anything else?" Roberts could feel the coldness in Malano's voice.

"Is there anything else that I can help you with?" stammered Roberts.

Malano gave him a cold look, "No!"

Roberts stood to leave, and then stopped at the door, "Did Reed leave a suicide note?"

Once again Malano looked up, "Who told you that it was a suicide?"

Roberts blushed, "No one. I just assumed."

Malano returned to his paperwork, watching from the corner of his eye Roberts' departure. Malano stood and shut his office door.

Then he grabbed the phone, "Murph! This is Detective Malano. I need someone tailed, I need to be kept informed everywhere this person goes, and it must be kept between just us. Do you have anyone that can do that and keep his mouth shut?"

"I have just the person. Well it's a woman. Is that okay?" replied Murph.

"I don't care what the sex is, as long as they can tail without being noticed and keep their mouth shut."

"Do you want me to send her up to your office now?" asked Murph.

"No! I'm coming down. I will need an office to give her some instructions."

"You got it, detective."

Malano left his office rubbing his neck. He was careful to make sure that Roberts was not in his office as he made his way downstairs. He could see Murph sitting at the big desk. Murph was a big man, tipping the scales at over 300 pounds. His voice boomed throughout the station, and when he laughed, the walls seemed to vibrate. Murph spotted Malano, and motioned for him to enter the door to his left. Malano slowly opened the door and found a little snip of a woman sitting at a large desk. Almost knocking over her chair, she stood and extended her hand.

Malano extended his hand and smiled, "Don't be nervous. I'm Detective Malano."

In a shaky voice she spoke, "I'm Officer Jen Anderson." Her handshake was firm, but her hands were ice cold.

Malano motioned for her to sit, and he took the chair opposite her. "Jen, Murph recommended you for a job that I need done. How long have you been on the force?"

"I have been on the force for one year, sir. I come from a long line of cops. Just let me know what you want me to do."

Malano smiled, "Okay, Jen. I need a Detective Roberts followed. Do you know him?"

"I have seen him walk through the station, but I have never met the detective."

"Do you have any problem informing on a fellow cop?" Malano probed.

"I have no reason to question your orders, sir. If you want the detective followed, then you must have your reasons. It's not my place to question you."

"Great! Now I think that he has just left the building. Murph will give you the license's plate number of his car. It's a blue Caprice. I need to be informed where the detective goes. If by chance, he goes to the Rogers estate I need to be called immediately. Is that clear? No one is to know what you are doing, especially Roberts."

"I understand, sir, and I will file a full report with you or let you know if the detective goes to the home of the Rogers." She stood and extended her hand. Malano stood, shook her extended hand and watched her leave.

Malano's stomach was starting to burn, so he stopped at Murph's desk. "Hey, Murph. Do you have any food stashed behind that big desk?"

Murph smiled, "You know me, detective. I didn't get this way by missing meals." He patted his stomach and reach into his desk. "Are you in the mood for a hot meatball sandwich?"

The smell made Malano's mouth water. "You are the man, Murph." He took the sandwich and returned to his office. The smell was intoxicating, but when he swallowed the first bite, his stomach refused. Putting the sandwich aside, he walked around his desk to the coffeepot and filled his cup. His thoughts drifted back to Samantha and the wonderful Thanksgiving Day that he shared with her. He thought to himself, "I'm going to have to make a visit to that girl. Maybe she isn't as wonderful as I remember." He laughed out loud.

Returning to his desk, Malano picked up the inventory list. As he glanced over the items, the number of videos seemed to be less than what he had estimated when he was there earlier. Calling the properties room, he inquired how many videos had been turned in on the Rogers case.

"Detective, our records show we inventoried 150 videos, five racks, one editing machine, one VCR,"

Malano interrupted the officer, "Did you place the videos on the racks that were brought in?"

"No, sir. Detective Roberts said that the videos were to remain in the boxes that they were brought in."

"Well I'm Detective Malano, and I'm senior on this investigation, and I'm instructing you to place the videos on the shelves. Let me know when that is done."

"Will do, detective." The connection was severed.

Malano rubbed his temples. It was hard to grasp what Roberts was up to. "Did he think that I wouldn't check on the count? Does this woman have him so confused that he is risking his job and his family for her?"

Malano looked around his office as if waiting for someone to answer. Leaning back in his chair, he closed his eyes and pondered the evidence. When did Roberts become involved with Mrs. Rogers? Norm said that he saw Roberts with Seth Peter's back after the first of the year. He was the one that was giving Seth the information about the doctor and Mrs. Rogers. He was also off the Saturday of the murder. Malano sat up in his chair, "That's right; I had to leave a message on his phone."

Malano pounded the desk just as the phone rang. "Malano," he spoke into the receiver.

"Detective, this is Officer Anderson. I just wanted to let you know that Detective Roberts stopped for some take out and."

Malano cut her off, "Officer I don't need to know every detail. I want to be informed if he goes to the Rogers estate."

"Sir, if you will let me finish I was going to tell you that Detective Roberts got take out and went to the Rogers estate. He has been inside for about 10 minutes."

"Great work, officer. Stay there, and if the detective leaves call me on my cell phone. I will be there shortly."

Malano pulled up to the gate and was surprised to find it open. He motioned for Officer Anderson to follow him. Malano instructed her to stay alert. Malano rang the doorbell, and then stepped out of the range of the peephole. No one answered. This time he kept his finger on the doorbell and remained out of view. In the distance, he could hear someone's approach on the marble entryway. The door was flung open, and Malano stepped into view. Roberts stepped back in astonishment and began to straighten his clothes. Amanda was half way down the stairs when she spotted him. She was dressed in a revealing back teddy.

Malano closed the door behind him, "Mrs. Rogers, don't be shy. Come join our party."

Amanda began to stutter and back up the stairs. "I wouldn't try and run, ma'am. We just need to talk. If you are not comfortable here, we can go to the station. You might want to slip into something a little warmer. The police station is kind of drafty."

Roberts hung his head and followed Malano into the living room. He sat on the sofa and watched as Malano circled the room. Standing behind Roberts, he slapped both hands on the cushion of the chair.

"Why Roberts? Is she that good of a lay that you would risk your career and not to mention your family?"

Roberts remained silent.

His silence enraged Malano, "You better talk now, because I swear your ass is going to rot in jail. I don't care how long it takes me to get to the truth, I will. Do you think that little tart upstairs is going to take the blame by herself?" Malano laughed.

Roberts began to cry, "You don't understand, Bill. Dr. Rogers was the devil incarnate. He deserved to die after what he did to those children and especially to Amanda. I don't regret that I helped her cover it up. I have known Amanda for two years, and I have witnessed how his violence towards her has escalated. He would have killed her, and Reed would have covered it up for him. I knew about Reed for some time. He was always showing off and bragging about his friendship with the good doctor. He was the one that told me about Seth Peters being Amanda's grandfather. The old man knew that the doctor was married to his granddaughter. I guess he was feeling guilty and wanted to get to know Amanda. The doctor used this information against both Seth and Amanda. The man was a demon."

Amanda entered the room in a roar, flinging her arms and shouting obscenities at Roberts, "You low-life coward. You promised that you would never tell. You are no better than that scum I was married to. All men are cowards and deserve to die. Just like that sniveling little man that tried to tell me, he was my grandfather. That dirty little coward didn't want the world to know the truth. Where was he when I needed him? I made him swallow those pills. He wanted to go to the police and tell them what had happened. I'm not going to jail, because he didn't have the balls to protect me. I enjoyed sitting and watching him take his last breath. He knew that I loathed him. I let him read the note telling the world that he was worthless. I think he agreed with everything that I wrote. It was kind of touching that I gave him a kiss before he died."

Malano looked at Roberts, "Bill, I didn't know that she had done any of this. We agreed that the doctor had to be stopped for her sake. No one else was supposed to get hurt."

Malano spoke, "Mrs. Rogers, I'm going to have to take you down to headquarters."

Amanda stopped and stared at him, "I'm not going anywhere. Who do you think you are? I have dealt with stronger men than you. No one will ever tell me what to do again."

Amanda's eyes were wide as she pulled the gun from under her shirt. "Like I said before detective, I'm not going with you or any man."

Malano tried to move closer.

Amanda screamed, "If you move without my permission, I will put a hole right through this man's head." Malano stopped as she pointed the gun at Roberts.

Malano spoke softly, "Mrs. Rogers I just want to help. Detective Roberts just wants to help. Now put the gun down and we can talk."

Amanda began to laugh, "You are going to help me? I needed your help before, but not now. Where were you when I was 12 and the great doctor was molesting me? Where were you when I was getting beaten? You are both probably Bentley's friends. I don't trust any of you men in blue. I thought Officer Reed was going to help me. That was a joke. Sometimes I think he did feel bad when he saw what Bentley had done to me, but not enough to help me. The money that my husband gave him helped wipe away those thoughts. I took great pleasure in watching Officer Reed die. He had helped Bentley cover up the abuse. He didn't know what I was going to do when we were at the morgue. When he was driving me home, he tried to apologize for his part. I think he was afraid that I would tell. I thought about leaving a note to let the world know what he had done, but there wasn't time. He was leaving. He tried to tell me that it was just for the holidays, but I didn't believe him. It was quite fitting him to beg me for his life. I had to laugh after all the times I begged him to help me."

Malano moved closer, "Mrs. Rogers, how did you do it? I mean he died in his garage with his car running?"

Amanda smiled as she outlined Roberts' head with the gun, "That detective is a little trick I learned from my husband. It's a drug that they use for surgery. It paralyzes the body. One shot of Succinylcholine, and he couldn't move. I just had to stand there and watch. Of course, I had a gas mask on. I really enjoyed seeing the fear in his eyes. I know how Bentley must have felt. The power of life and death can be exciting."

Malano moved closer, "I would stop right there, if I were you detective. I won't hesitate to shoot."

"Mrs. Rogers there is no need to hurt anyone else. Let's just sit down and talk. I know that I can help you."

Amanda spun towards him, "Don't give me that you can help bullshit. All my life people kept telling me that they wanted to help. Bentley always told me you have to help yourself. Oh, by the way, Mrs. Miller won't be showing up for work anymore. I took care of her last Monday. That stupid old woman wanted me to stop you from checking into Bentley's life. She knew what he did to all those kids and she was still loyal to him. I made her suffer for her part. She was just as evil as Bentley was. She loved him. I put that old woman in the ground. She can meet Bentley in hell for all I care. Yes, I killed all of them, but I did it out of love. Bentley always told me that you could do anything you want to another person as long as you love them. Their pain makes you strong."

Amanda's eyes were wild as she lunged towards Roberts. "You are such a fucking loser."

Malano jumped for her hand with the gun. There was a struggle for the gun, and then there was a shot. Everything was moving in slow motion. Roberts slumped forward as the blood gushed from his wound. The officer waiting outside came rushing in.

Malano yelled, "Call for an ambulance. Officer down."

Malano cuffed Amanda and threw her on the couch. Grabbing a towel, he tried to stop the bleeding. In a weak voice Roberts spoke,

"Bill, I didn't know about all of this. She just wanted me to cover up what she did to her husband. Please don't tell my wife and kids."

Malano tried to quiet him. "You need to save your strength. You are going to be fine."

Roberts squeezed his hand as he took his final breath. In the distance, the siren could be heard, but it was too late for Roberts.

Amanda became calm and childlike, "What are you doing? I haven't done anything wrong."

Malano glanced around the room at the conspicuous splendor. Shaking his head over some people having it all, he turned out the lights and left the estate.

14

MALANO SMILED AS HE TOOK the ramp to the interstate. The mileage marker showed Farmingdale was 52 miles away. In less than an hour, he would be with Samantha. It had only been eight days since he saw her, but so much had happened. Amanda Rogers had been charged with the murders of her husband, Seth Peters and Brett Reed. Mrs. Miller had not been found, but a full investigation had been launched to find her whereabouts. Mrs. Rogers would opt for an insanity plea, and probably get off. Detective Roberts died while on duty and was given a hero's funeral. His wife and children would receive his benefits. Bruce and Alice Williams were going to be fine. They would receive counseling and planned an extended family trip.

Franklin and Laverne were heirs to a multimillion-dollar estate, courtesy of their son. The exact amount of the inheritance was not known because of the Swiss bank accounts and the not insignificant detail of Uncle Sam waiting in the chow line. The plan for the money was to set up a ranch for abused children. The mountains were made for so daunting a task, beautiful and magic in the ever presence. Maybe it could help to mend some of the children their son had hurt. They never thought about leaving the area. This was paradise to them.

The mayor, state representative and several other influential people waited uneasily for the FBI to knock on their door. The FBI took Dr. Rogers' computers, medical records and tapes.

As for Bill Malano, a new year was fast approaching, and change comes with any new year.

"I want a family," Malano spoke out loud, "I want to get to know Samantha Forbes, and see if we are really soul mates. I want love."

Taking the off ramp to Farmingdale, Malano thought of his parents and the love they shared with each other for almost 40 years. When he asked his dad about marriage and loving the same woman for so many years his dad took him aside and said, "Son, Charley Pride said it all in his song, 'Kiss An Angel Good Mornin', and love her like the devil when you get back home.' "

Malano began to grin as he approached Samantha's house. She and her father were in the front yard throwing snowballs at the neighborhood kids. When she saw Malano's car approach, a smile brightened her face, still beaming as Malano got out of the car.

She motioned for him to join in. "Come on, city boy! You're just in time to help us beat the red coats."

Malano smiled and happily joined in; all the while thanking God, he was home, at last.

Printed in the United States
45174LVS00005B/140

9 781413 796094